GW00360301

Kyle Demore and the Timekeeper's Key

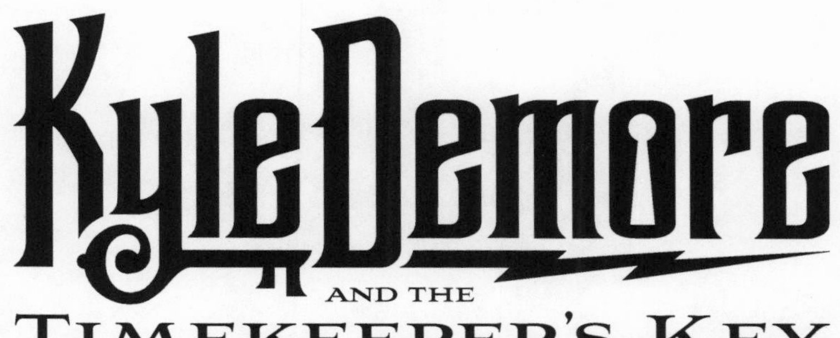

Kyle Demore and the Timekeeper's Key

BOOK ONE

Dani
Hope you enjoy!

SAMUEL J. VEGA

Kyle Demore and the Timekeeper's Key
Copyright © 2013 by Samuel J. Vega
All rights reserved.

ISBN 978-0-9911773-1-8

No part of this book may be reproduced by any means, graphic, electronic, or mechanical, including photocopying, recording, taping, or by any information storage retrieval system without express written permission of the author. The only exception is by a reviewer, who may quote short excerpts in a review.

Permission can be obtained through www.samueljvega.com

This is a work of fiction. Names, characters, places, and incidents either are the product of the author's imagination or are used fictitiously. Any resemblance to actual persons, living or dead, events, or locales is entirely coincidental.

Cover Illustration by Fernanda Suarez
Cover Design and Page Layout by David Richards

To Isaac and Paul,
for being exactly the kind of brothers
I would have always wanted

Contents

ONE
Kyle Demore • 1

TWO
Dream • 14

THREE
Endera the Unlocked Realm • 22

FOUR
The Door to Another Realm • 38

FIVE
Soul Gate Academy • 50

SIX
The Reader • 68

SEVEN
The Newest Tyro • 89

EIGHT
The Masters • 118

NINE
Proculus the Storm • 136

TEN
The Tortoise Coin • 154

ELEVEN
Key of Throne Arms • 169

CONTENTS

TWELVE
Lightning • 181

THIRTEEN
The Contract • 201

FOURTEEN
X Marks the Spot • 213

FIFTEEN
Dilu Village • 225

SIXTEEN
The Forger's Cavern • 245

SEVENTEEN
Out of Options • 271

EIGHTEEN
The Timekeeper's Key • 279

NINETEEN
The Four Keys • 299

TWENTY
The Basilisk • 324

TWENTY-ONE
Healing • 334

TWENTY-TWO
The Visitor • 350

Kyle Demore and the Timekeeper's Key

CHAPTER ONE
KYLE DEMORE

Less than a mile from a small-town high school and middle school stood a vibrant blue three-story house with a sophisticated hand-painted sign in the front yard that read *The Grayling Home for Children.* Mr. and Mrs. Shadoclaw had built the home years ago in order to help young men and women who were considered too old by many parents looking to adopt a child.

They were an older couple who never had any children of their own. Throughout Grayling, the two were known for running a strict but loving home. To the foster children, they were known as Nana and Paps.

Nana was a thickset, dark-skinned woman with large beady eyes and though she was big, she could not be considered plump. Paps was short, muscular and clean-shaven with tidy dark brown hair. The years had added inches to his waist, but Nana always teased that she could do with loving a few extra pounds. The children were grateful for their generosity, love, and stability, entrustments that they never took for granted. Abiding by all the rules was required or a child risked being sent to another home. To this date, Mr. and Mrs. Shadoclaw were proud to say that none of the teens had ever been sent away.

On one chilly Friday morning, Mr. and Mrs. Shadoclaw's house slowly started to stir as five of their six teenage boys reluctantly awoke to the sun shining through their large third floor windows. The long, simple room consisted of six beds, three on each side, facing the wall with a door at each end. One of the doors led to a large bathroom that the boys shared. The other led to the staircase that went down to the other floors.

In the corner, the sixth boy, a thirteen year-old with a thin face and naturally wavy black hair, continued snoring peacefully through the morning noises of his roommates. His shirtless body was only half covered by the blanket in which he slept. His pale and skinny frame looked fragile as glass. Normally, when he wasn't sleeping, his hair would partially cover his crimson-orange eyes. The only possession he cared about hung from his neck: an ancient-looking key encased in rust. Not a single one of the other boys paid any attention to the heavy sleeper.

The staircase door flew open. "Oh Kyyyyyyle," sang Nana. The large woman, dressed in sweat pants and a stained shirt, stood with her hand on her hips. She styled her hair in a bun and wore no makeup, making her appear all the more motherly. "Wake up, honey. It's time for school." This was a regular ritual.

"Ugh," he snuffled into his pillow. "No, thanks. I'm cool, Nana."

"I'm cool, Nana?" repeated the woman. "Boy, you better get up before I throw you out into the *cool* snow." The boy knew the threat was not genuine since all he did was roll over. However, she was not at all defeated. "Oh, I see. I suppose you don't want to go skiing with the rest of us tomorrow?"

Everyone in the room stopped what they were doing.

Kyle sprung up in to a sitting position. "There's no way we can afford it."

"We couldn't afford it," she said truthfully, "but last night while all of you were sleeping, a nice man visited and made a large donation."

"Really?" Kyle's eyes were now wide open. A large smile spread across his face as he remembered his first snowboard trip last year, which had made his love for the sport instant.

"Would I lie to you, Kyle?"

He knew she wouldn't.

"I guess I can deal with Mr. Lindshell one more day, but I don't ski, I snowboard!"

"Get ready quick or I'll have you stay home while we're tearing up the slopes," teased Nana. "You hear that boys? We're all going snowboarding tomorrow. Paps'll have breakfast in fifteen, so get ready."

The boys excitedly resumed their morning routines. On the second floor, where there were identical sleeping quarters for five teenage girls, the commotion was even louder. Mr. and Mrs. Shadoclaw were fond of skiing. In a way, it was how the two foster parents had met years ago. If funds would allow it, they tried to take the kids to the slopes each year. Trips like this were rare, so the announcement gave everyone good reason to be delighted.

When Kyle and the other boys came down for breakfast, the girls were already chatting and eating food. Because of Kyle's normal sleeping habits, this was his least favorite time of the day. Sleeping late outweighed breakfast in his opinion, but he did enjoy watching Paps at work in the kitchen when he could get to breakfast early enough. Nobody other than Nana dared to wake the young man if they had the choice. Most of the others, although all of them were older, feared Kyle in one way or another. It wasn't because he was particularly scary—not at all actually—but Kyle Demore was strange.

Red had been living at the Grayling Children's Home for over two years. He was a tall seventeen year-old who liked to wear overalls. He wasn't a bad kid but he didn't like how Kyle seemed to live in his own world. In a way, it was jealousy, but what irked him most was Kyle had not acknowledged him. Red thought that his seniority deserved an amount of respect that the newcomer wasn't giving. Kyle had arrived from an adoption gone wrong only a couple months earlier when Red hatched a plan to take Kyle's only valued possession away. He planned to return it, but only when Kyle had learned to show him some respect. Stealing was, of course, against the rules, but Red thought it necessary to prove his point. What point, exactly? When he thought about it afterwards, he wasn't sure either.

The theft had gone much easier than Red anticipated. One night, he had snuck up to Kyle's bed and removed the key from his neck while he was fast asleep. Like a ninja, Red tiptoed back to his bed to hide the key and fall back to sleep. When morning came, Kyle woke up a little earlier than all the other boys and went directly to Red's bed. He woke Red, which startled him and caused most of the other boys to wake up. Without hesitation, Kyle asked Red for his key as if he had simply lent it to him.

"Don't know what you're talkin' bout." Red was a little

intimidated by Kyle's knowledge of his plan; however, he had too much confidence in his own age and cleverness to care.

"Hmmm, are you sure?" Kyle stared into Red's eyes.

"Y—yeah man." He was flustered by the gaze he was receiving. "Why would I want your stupid key?" Some of the others had known Red's plan and whispers of how it was possible that Kyle could have found out were already circulating.

"Oh, I see my ba.... whoa!" Kyle tripped onto Red's shoes, which sat nicely at the end of his bed. "Oh, look here. I must have dropped the key in your shoe somehow."

"What the? How could you've..." How could Kyle have known that he had placed the stolen key in his left shoe?

"Ah, don't worry 'bout it," said Kyle in an unfamiliarly cold voice. He edged closer to Red to whisper something in his ear. No one other than Red heard what he said, but Red looked flabbergasted. It didn't take long for Kyle to finish. When he did, everyone in the room watched Kyle casually return to his bed, place the key back around his neck, and quickly fall back to sleep.

The others eventually asked Red what Kyle had said to him, but he always replied the same way, "Nothing man, nothing. Just don't mess with him anymore, okay? He's all right."

They asked him again, of course, but every time they did, a shiver ran down his spine and Kyle's stinging whisper rang in his memory. *Your mom, she said:* 'I love you, Red. I know I won't be around anymore, honey, but I know you'll always make me proud.' *You're a good guy Red, don't let her down.* Red had never spoken a word of his last moments with his mother to anyone, so he had no idea how Kyle had known his mother's dying words. It had been enough for Red to decide that Kyle was not a kid to mess with. The young newcomer had earned his respect.

After some time, some of the boys asked Kyle how he had known about the key. Kyle replied confusedly, unsure of what they were talking about. Although Kyle was telling the truth, the others wanted nothing to do with someone who wouldn't share their secrets. When Kyle thought about it hard, he could only remember having a dull dream about Red—*definitely not a dream worth remembering*, he thought. However, this was normal for Kyle. Sometimes weird things like this happened to people and sometimes, especially weird things happened to him. Being ostracized for something he couldn't explain had been normal to him since his earliest memories. He couldn't even remember how many times he had been adopted, only to be taken back to the adoption home to wait again. After this 'incident,' everyone, other than a select few, had decided he was definitely a mysterious boy that should be left alone.

This suited Kyle just fine.

After breakfast, a school bus rolled in front of the blue house's short cement driveway. The eleven orphans, now full and excited, suited up against the cold before filing out the door and into the vehicle that would take them to Grayling's junior high and high school. Kyle was, as always, the last to get on, but this never bothered the bus driver. She was a petite, skinny, old woman who looked as if she barely had her eyes open. Kyle always thought it was odd for her to be driving with eyes that were nearly closed, but he liked the old woman. She was always happy to patiently wait for him.

Once on the bus, Kyle walked to the seat with the only person at the foster home, apart from Nana and Paps, who did not think he was unbearably weird. She waited for him every morning with a striking smile. Her long red hair sat on her right shoulder as she brushed it casually, trying to work out a knot. Kyle waited until her gem blue eyes invited him to sit.

"Morning, Garnet," he said as he sat. Shyness usually kept him from talking much, but he was in an unusually brave mood because he would be snowboarding soon.

"Good morning Kyle," said Garnet Nemos in a soft and soothing voice. "Excited about snowboarding?"

"Yeah, I can't wait."

"Me either, but you know what? I've never been snowboarding. I hear you're pretty good, though."

"Well, I've only done it once." He scratched his head making his wavy hair untidy. "But maybe I could give you some lessons."

"That'd be great! But Kyle, you're scratching your head again." She giggled. As always, she pointed out this habit of his and Kyle couldn't help but look pleased every time she caught him. Before anything else could be said, they arrived at school. The smile Kyle had had all morning faded as he exited the bus and remembered his least favorite person...Mr. Lindshell.

Mr. Lindshell was undeniably the most boring, strict, and uptight math teacher the eighth grade had ever seen. His rules in class, and perhaps everywhere else, were followed religiously and he loathed anything out of the ordinary. Step out of line once and you were certain to receive a detention. It was thought that his roar was loud enough to compete with a lion's. He was a short, heavy man in his fifties that waddled like a duck when he walked. What little brown hair remained on his head was overshadowed by the hair coming from his ears and nose. For the eighth grade class of Grayling Junior High, he was absolutely the worst teacher of all time.

Even though today was the school's last day before winter break, Mr. Lindshell arrived early to school like he did every day. To him, winter break was nothing special, so lessons needed to continue as normal. He was prepared to hand out detentions to any student who acted too excited about the holidays.

Halfheartedly, Kyle arrived in Mr. Lindshell's bare and undecorated classroom. Mr. Lindshell did not normally acknowledge his existence until the morning bell rang, but Kyle sat down in his seat in the back with careful silence. It wouldn't be unusual for Mr. Lindshell to find a reason to hand him a detention.

When the bell rang, Mr. Lindshell's class began immediately. Kyle instantly grew bored. He simply could not focus on Mr. Lindshell's lecture on basic algebra. He began doodling on his notebook without realizing it. The upcoming trip was all he could think of. Daydreams of snowfall flocked his mind. He could almost feel himself gliding down a mountain full of snow. As he thought this, his eyelids grew heavier. A warm blissful sensation was building in his chest, and Mr. Lindshell's words became more sluggish as he drifted off into a dream.

Kyle awoke standing in the middle of a wide field. Trees were the only things that could be seen off in the distance as snow gently fell. Weather conditions worsened as the wind roared louder and snow fell harder, clouding his visibility. The flurry fell faster than Kyle had ever seen, but what was more miraculous was that he was not cold. He tried to move but realized he could not. He stood there for a long time, watching the snow fall in all directions. The wind tickled his skin, sounds were distinctively separate, and each snowflake was visible. His senses were inhuman, much sharper than they had ever been.

Though the snow fascinated him, he felt the need to bring out his key. The old key radiated with comforting warmth, and began glowing silver. His body moved inherently, making him feel like a controlled robot. Kyle bent down and thrust the key into the ground. The key stopped as if it were entering a key hole. Suddenly, across the field, men screamed at him. He assumed they were men, but their features were hidden beneath their lengthy hunter-green hooded cloaks. Kyle had an eerie feeling that he had seen them in the past. He noticed swords and spears at their sides as they edged closer.

Their yells, drowned by the thrashing wind, were incomprehensible. Instinctively, Kyle turned the key. Gold lights shot out from it, forming a square perimeter around the field with himself in the center. Just before the men could reach the boundary, Kyle and the snow disappeared.

It was the last thing he remembered.

"DEMORE," roared Mr. Lindshell at the top of his lungs. "What on earth have you done?"

Kyle woke with a scare on the top of a snow hill that was inside his school's gymnasium. There were other piles of snow throughout the gym, melting into puddles of water. Freezing, Kyle lay on the snow, bewildered at what was happening.

"DEMORE," bellowed Mr. Lindshell again. "Get down here NOW!"

Still confused, Kyle slid down the hill and made a sad attempt to stand. His legs buckled when he realized every muscle in his body was screaming to lie back down. He nearly collapsed from how exhausted he felt. "What's going on?" he asked.

"What's going on?" repeated Mr. Lindshell. "That's exactly what you are going to tell me. Gone all day and now here you are with snow all over the gymnasium. I don't know how you did it boy, but you are in for it!"

"Gone all day? What are you talking about? I was just in your class."

"Do not play dumb with me, Demore! It's nearly two o'clock and we have been looking for you since you pulled your little disappearing act in my classroom."

Kyle looked at Mr. Lindshell, expecting the teacher to tell him this was some sort of trick. Moments earlier, he had been in Mr. Lindshell's classroom listening to a boring explanation of math equations. Now he was in a snowy gym with wet clothes. "Is this some kind of joke?"

"Joke? If you consider getting expelled a joke, then maybe, yes."

"Expelled?" Being expelled would mean he would be kicked out of the foster home.

"Yes," said Mr. Lindshell in triumph. "You picked a bad day to pull a prank like this. The blizzard caused us to close the school early. You're the last student here. Mr. Corsell and I have not been able to leave due to your 'missing' status."

"Blizzard?" asked Kyle. Without thinking and against his body's wishes, he rushed out of the gym to find the nearest window as fast as his exhausted body would let him. Mr. Lindshell's yells followed him down the hall to an upstairs classroom. The blizzard was intense. Visibility was horrible, inches of snow had already fallen, and in the distance, the town snow plows were working hard but losing the fight against nature. The snow was overpowering, almost unnatural.

It was then that he saw the football field.

From the window, it was obvious there was more snow there than anywhere else. The bleachers that stood on each side of the field were half covered in snow. Snow was piled ten feet high down the middle. How could so much snow have fallen in that one place? Had it been under different circumstances, Kyle would have been much more excited about all the snow. However, his dream was still fresh in his mind.

Mr. Lindshell waddled into the room, gasping for breath. Kyle patiently waited for him to talk. "Boy," huffed the heavy man, "you… are... coming...with…me."

He led Kyle down to the principal's office on the first floor near the middle of the building. Mr. Corsell, the principal, was more or less exactly like Mr. Lindshell. They looked identical except for the principal's white hair and large hooked nose. Kyle had often wondered if the two men were related. On their way to the office, they passed the front glass doors. Inches of snow were already packed against the entrance. They would need to get home soon.

Kyle had visited the principal's office many times before, but he never noticed the extraordinary door that led to his room. When Mr. Lindshell opened the door, Kyle noticed a silver key sticking in the office door. It struck Kyle as odd, but he did not question it. Slowly, the two entered the high-ceilinged office. A crystal chandelier hung from the middle of the ceiling, complimenting the polar bear fur carpet that covered the white school tile floor. The entire back wall was covered with books from floor to ceiling. Extraordinary and mysterious looking bows, shields and swords decorated the walls. As they edged closer to a large wooden desk in the middle of the massive room, Kyle finally realized something was wrong.

This was not his principal's office.

Behind the desk, there was a massive rotating sofa chair that faced away from Kyle. He could only see the back of a blonde man's head.

"Kyle Demore!" boomed a deep voice. "Do you like what I've done with the principal's office?"

Exhaustion spread through Kyle. He could barely stand and thought he was hallucinating. He kept silent.

"Boy," bellowed Mr. Lindshell. "You will speak when spoken to."

Kyle swayed back and forth.

"Don't worry about that idiot," said the deep voice. "He can't hear or see anything that's in front of him. It is the fate of those without keys."

"Keys? What are you talking about?"

"All will be explained soon." The room, along with the blonde man, evaporated. The room began looking more familiar. The principal's office was simple again. An old metal desk covered in papers sat in the middle of the room. Plain white walls held old awards that the principal had won in his younger years. Kyle knew he was finally in the principal's real office. Relieved, but still thoroughly confused, he sat in front of the desk, listening to his principal and teacher trying to figure out what to do with him.

"Lindshell," said Mr. Corsell calmly. "How do you expect me to believe that a thirteen year-old boy could have gotten that much snow in the gym?"

"I don't know how he did it," answered Mr. Lindshell. "But I am telling you, I know he's got something to do with it. Gone all day and then I find him lying in the snow that is destroying our gym!"

"Hmm... DEMORE," snapped Mr. Corsell. "Did you or did you not pile snow into our school gym?"

Kyle tried to refuse but found he could not. Then, he alone heard the deep voice come out of nowhere. *Say yes, Kyle. Say you did it and you're sorry.*

"Yes," said Kyle, though immediately wishing he hadn't. "I did it, and I'm sorry." His lips moved by themselves.

"Ah ha!" exclaimed Mr. Lindshell. "There you have it. A confession. I told you, Corsell. He admitted it. Now he has to be expelled."

"Well boy, sorry isn't gonna do it. I didn't think I could possibly place the blame on you for this, but since I have a confession, you are hereby expelled from Grayling Junior High. I imagine there is damage to the school gym which you will also be held accountable for. Due to the weather, we can figure that out later. I would call the police right now, but I am sure, with this weather, they have more pressing things to deal with than vandalism. Consider yourself lucky for the time being."

"Shall I call his guardians?" asked Mr. Lindshell with a large mocking smile.

"Yes," said the principal. "Tell them to get here quick too, he looks like he'll keel over soon. Probably from shoveling all that damn snow. I don't know what you were thinking, Demore."

Kyle felt more fatigued by the second, but understood that he was being expelled. "Expelled?" he blurted out. "They'll kick me..." He trailed off at the end of his sentence, fading into sleep.

CHAPTER TWO

DREAM

Frantically, Nana unlocked the door to let her husband, who carried Kyle, into the house. Worried at the sight of an unconscious Kyle, she looked to her husband for a reason.

"He's just sleeping." Paps placed Kyle down on the couch in their living room. The other kids were trying their best to stay out of sight and listen in on the conversation. Nana and Paps paid them no mind. "See, all that worrying and he was just causing trouble at school."

"Can they really expel him?" asked Nana. "How can they blame a thirteen year-old for that?"

"He's almost fourteen," said Paps with a smirk. "He's been making sly little remarks on what he'd like for his birthday dinner."

"I know that, Ethan!" snapped Nana, shooting her husband a look of fury. "This is serious. Thirteen or fourteen; what's the difference? How could they say he did it?"

"He admitted it," said Paps simply. "They told me when I got to the school. Right before he passed out, Kyle told them he put the snow there. And I got to admit, he was soaked like he'd been playing with snow all day. It's a good thing you had me take some extra clothes because I had to change him there or he would have frozen to death. They had no choice but to expel him, Anna."

"But that means..." Nana was unable to finish her sentence and on the verge of tears. Kicking Kyle out of the house would affect her immensely. Although she loved all of the children in her home, she couldn't deny that she had grown strongly attached to Kyle.

"What it means is that we will have to talk to Kyle first, okay? He'll be hungry when he wakes up. I'll go make him some food. Maybe an early birthday meal is in order. A couple days hardly makes a difference anyhow. Think he'll notice?"

"Ethan..." She grabbed his arm tenderly. "We can't just send him away. He belongs here, with us."

"I know, Anna, I know, but we knew that someday this might happen. That man last night…It can't be just some coincidence."

"You're right." Nana gazed at him, taking in her husband's warm wisdom and his ability to stay calm in situations where she would normally lose her sanity. "You're right."

"Don't worry, that man will return. Now let the boy rest. We have to get ready for dinner."

"Okay." Nana took one final look toward Kyle. "Everyone, come on out now. Let's get ready for dinner."

The teenagers came out of their hiding places with pink faces, halfheartedly moving to help with chores before dinner. Some of the boys and girls were sent to clean their rooms and complete house chores while others went outside to shovel the sidewalk and driveway. The snow still fell harder than ever, while Kyle dreamed an extraordinarily *real* dream.

Kyle awoke naked except for his boxers and the key that always hung around his neck. It was dark and he could not see where he was, but he knew the ground he laid on was dirt that was close to the same texture of sand, but not quite. The coolness of the ground made his skin tingle. Out of nowhere, the sun climbed unnaturally fast, lighting up the sky and warming him like a hot drink. With the daylight, there were cheers and shouts around him, so loud that his ribcage vibrated. He rose and looked at his surroundings.

He was surprised to find himself in the middle of a large open arena. All around him people dressed in tunics and togas cheered in stands that circled where he stood. The massive arena was similar to the Roman Coliseum he had studied in history class. He noticed a short man with blonde hair who wore a wintery blue toga. The man stood up near the front of the crowd in a box seat. It was clear this was a man of high importance because the crowd settled down when the man raised his arms. Kyle stood there confused and scared, but he could not shake the feeling of excitement swelling within his chest.

Before he had more time to think, the short man shouted loudly, "Begin the fight!"

Kyle felt a short double-edged sword form out of nothing in his hand. The key hanging from his necklace began radiating heat through his body, and he felt himself grow calm. To Kyle's left, a gate opened and a man charged wildly toward him to attack with a sickle as his weapon. Kyle wasn't sure how, but he instinctively brought his blade up and defended the blow. He was thrown back from the force, yet he was still standing. The man went berserk, slicing at

Kyle. For some unknown reason, Kyle was able to block every move. Dust filled the air as they two of them danced around the arena. Sweat began to form heavily on their brows and dripped down their faces. When the chance arose, Kyle retreated out of range. Both Kyle and his opponent breathed heavily while the crowd cheered madly, evidently enjoying the fight.

The two fighters circled each other. Finally having a moment to think, Kyle studied his opponent. The man was older than Kyle but not by much. His muscular body was tanned from many days in the sun, and he wore only shorts. His black hair was cut short and his face was still, blank, showing no trace of emotion. What Kyle found most disturbing were his opponent's eyes, which were completely white. It made Kyle wonder if the man was even conscious. On top of that, Kyle now noticed that the sickle was not his only weapon. A curved sword was also strapped to his back, smacking against his skin every time he moved. The saber looked as though it would need little help in splitting Kyle in two.

"I don't want to fight you!" pleaded Kyle. "Please, let's stop."

The man responded by spitting on the ground before taking his sickle and throwing it sideways at Kyle. As the weapon flew directly at him, Kyle kicked off the ground, jumping high over the whirling sickle. It stuck into the wall behind Kyle just as he landed. He wondered how it was possible to have jumped that high but having a deadly weapon hurled at you might make such a thing possible.

There was no time to think. The white-eyed man took out his sword. In that moment, Kyle realized he would have to fight back.

He charged with all his might, hoping to surprise the man, but instead was met with equal force. Their swords crashed against each other with loud clangs, but they were barely heard over the thunder of the crowd. Shocked by his own skill with the sword, Kyle let go of his fears, losing himself, and somehow actually enjoying the fight. It was as though he had been training to do this all his life.

The white-eyed man's attacks grew weaker and Kyle knew he had a chance to end the fight. Like earlier, he kicked off the ground hard, taking a leap into the air which caught his adversary off guard. Before the man could defend, Kyle jabbed his blade deep into the man's neck. Blood poured out of the wound like a fountain. The man dropped his sword as he fell to his death with a heavy thud. Kyle landed on top of him but then stumbled off of his body in astonishment. For one wild moment, the crowd's explosive roars were blocked out.

He had just killed a man.

"What is going on?" he muttered to himself in disbelief. His senses were coming back and the noise in the arena was deafening. He stared at the man who now laid still. *I didn't mean to kill him.* Dizziness made the world spin and his stomach want to tear away from his body. He took deep breaths in an attempt to calm himself, but he was having difficulty as the sickening smells of sweat, dirt, and blood filled his nostrils. *I didn't mean to kill him.* The crowd grew silent, forcing him to finally take his eyes off the bleeding body. The man in the box seat was now standing.

The short, blonde man now wore a red ball cap on his head and was dressed in a white tuxedo with a long sword on his side. At that exact moment, intense sunshine reflected off the short man's weapon as if it were a mirror, blinding Kyle. When Kyle looked for the man again, he was gone.

"Hello, Kyle," said a voice from behind. Kyle whipped around to see the man standing inches from him. He jumped back, holding his sword defensively. Up close, the man's age was more defined, perhaps forty, and he was indeed short, hardly an inch taller than Kyle. Despite his size, Kyle knew the man was not someone to mess with. "Ah, no need to be unfriendly. I am only here to say you passed." The man spoke with grace like there was an air of royalty to his voice.

"I passed?" Kyle repeated as he lowered his sword gradually. "I don't understand." Kyle slammed his hand against his forehead and tears began to form. Confusion, frustration, and the fact that he had killed a man strained his young mind. "Who are you?"

"Ah, of course, how rude of me. I am Alexun the Path Guard."

"The Path Guard? What are you talking about?"

"Well, there is no need for me to explain," said Alexun. "You passed and that is all you need to know. Do not worry about the man, you didn't really kill him. Umm, let's see—think of this place as a simulation; ah, no a dream would be better. Yes, a dream."

"This…was all a dream? But it feels so…"

"Real?" added the Path Guard. "Ah, I assure you it is only real in some ways. No need to worry, but please allow me to send you on your way."

"That doesn't make any sense." He was relieved, yet defiant at the idea that he had not in fact killed anyone. The body lay in front of him clear as day. "How can something be real in some ways? It's either real or it isn't. And what do you mean, 'send me on my way?'"

"I imagine that some of your questions will soon be answered, but not by I," responded Alexun. "Now, we have talked long enough. The crowd grows bored, be gone."

"No." said Kyle. "W—"

Before he could finish, Alexun pulled out a French rapier that looked as if it had been fused with a key. The silver blade had teeth and grooves similar to that of a house key and it was thin as a finger, but it still looked sharp enough to poke holes through steel. The sword sported a majestic silver hand guard that looked as beautiful as it did useful. The Path Guard pointed the key rapier directly at Kyle and unexpectedly dashed at him. Kyle raised his sword and swung at him in defense, but his parry was swatted away with ease. The Path Guard was much more skilled than Kyle's previous opponent. Just when he thought he was about to die, Alexun turned his sword around and gently hit Kyle's key with the sword hilt's pommel. The key began to shine with blinding violet light. Then, he was melting into the wind like loose sand. He witnessed, in horror, as his legs became dust and, faded out of existence. In a sad attempt to stop it, he swung his sword again, but his arm broke off and disappeared also.

"Farewell, young one." Alexun scratched his chin, looking amused. "Not many could have raised their sword up in time to defend and no one so young has ever been close. Intriguing." He turned around, sighing as he began walking away. "I must be getting old. May we meet again someday, Kyle."

Kyle tried to scream, but before he knew it, the world around him was gone.

"Kyle." The voice was familiar, sweet as honey and a warm fire. "Kyle, wake up."

He opened his eyes to the familiar living room he had grown to love. He was back in the Grayling Home for Children. Sitting next to him on the couch was a pretty girl with long auburn hair. *Garnet. She's always paying attention to me for some reason.*

"Hey, Garnet," he said, barely audible. "What's today?"

"You're awake!" I was worried, but today is still Friday."

"Friday still, huh? I guess it just feels like I've been away for days. Weird dreams, ya know? Well, I think they were dreams."

"Yeah, a dream," she agreed. "I know exactly what you're talking about. Well, looks like my time is up. I'm glad you woke up. I'll see you later, Kyle Demore."

They stared at each other as though frozen in time. It threw Kyle off guard to be receiving such an intense gaze from Garnet. It was almost like she had just experienced the same dream as he but knew more about it than he did.

"Wait. What do you mean see you lat—"

Before he could finish, Garnet kissed him fully on the lips. When she pulled away, Kyle tried to say something, but his voice failed him. He noticed the tears falling down her cheeks. He wanted to console her somehow, but she vanished in the blink of an eye. For a while, he continued to lay on the couch, attempting to work out what had just happened. *Another dream.*

His stomach growled loud enough to rival a bear. He felt like a car that had run out of gas; never had he felt hunger like this. Just as he rose to find food, he heard a knock at the door.

CHAPTER THREE

ENDERA THE UNLOCKED REALM

"Can someone get the door?" yelled Nana from the kitchen, not realizing that Kyle was the only one nearby.

"I'm on it," Kyle said weakly as he edged toward the door.

"Kyle!" cried Nana. She was so surprised to hear his voice that she dropped an empty pan. "I'll get the door, you sit back down." Perhaps it was because Kyle was moving so sluggishly, but he thought Nana moved faster than he had ever seen. In seconds, she was in the living room, shuffling him back to the couch, then opening the door.

"Good evening, Mrs. Shadoclaw." The deep voice was strangely familiar to Kyle. "I am sorry to come so late, but as you can see, the weather has slowed me down tonight."

"Oh," said Nana, genuinely surprised. "What a surprise to see you again so soon, Mr. Proculus. Please, come in."

A tall man that Kyle had never seen before walked into the living room. He wore a puffy black coat and khaki pants. He had a wicked scar down his right cheek and long blonde hair that was speckled with melting snow. His blue eyes glowed through his stylish glasses and although he was a stranger, Kyle felt as if he knew him.

"Please," he said politely as he entered, "call me Proculus."

"And you can call me Anna," she said. "We are about to eat dinner, Proculus. I hope you can join us." She shot him a look that sent a silent message, daring him to say no.

"I would love to."

"Good. Please let me take that coat for you and we can find you a seat in the dining room. Kyle, how are you feelin'?"

"I'm fine." Kyle tried hard to ignore the man who had arrived. This proved hard due to his size. "What's for dinner?"

"Oh, Paps made your favorite, so get to the dining room, we're about to eat."

"Umm, Nana," said Kyle timidly, "About what happened today—I don't know what—"

Nana rushed over to hug Kyle and he felt his face turn a deep scarlet. "Don't worry about that now," she whispered. "You, Paps, and I will sit down and talk about it later."

Nana took Proculus's coat and briskly walked back to the kitchen to finish helping Paps prepare for dinner, leaving the guest and Kyle alone in the living room. Kyle looked at the man in amazement. The man towered over him and had arms like tree trunks. Had it not been for the man's bulging muscles, the coat would not have looked so puffy. Proculus's forest green sweater looked a size too small. *What does he do to get muscles like that?*

Kyle realized he had been staring at the stranger and noticed Proculus was also studying him.

"I'm a teacher," supplied Proculus as if he was reading Kyle's mind. "At a school far away from here."

At the word 'teacher,' Kyle remembered the ordeal in the principal's office. Chills crept under his skin like an ice cube had just slid down his back. He knew Proculus was no ordinary man. Even more strangely, a smile crept across the large man's face as he made his way pass Kyle into the dining room. *That voice. Who are you?* He would have to wait for answers.

Most of the other teens had already seated themselves at the dinner table when Kyle walked in behind Proculus. He instantly noticed that the table was full of many of his favorite foods: steamed rice, breaded fish, chicken glazed in honey, an array of seasoned vegetables. He was pleased when Paps and Nana gave them permission to eat. The group piled food onto their plates and began their feast.

For a small time, whispers circulated about the guest. The boys, intimidated by his powerful build and scar, debated whether he was a professional wrestler or boxer. The girls, awed by his good looks, giggled as they wondered if he was single or married. As the guest's impressiveness faded, the teen chatter resumed to its normal loud gossip about school, friends, and the upcoming trip. Proculus and the foster parents ate quickly and quietly, only exchanging small pleasantries here and there. Kyle, who was too busy eating more food than he could ever remember, said very little to anyone. Dinner sped by swiftly. With a full and warm belly, Kyle regained some of his energy.

Near the end of dinner, he noticed that Garnet was missing. He wondered where she could be, but was too embarrassed to inquire for her whereabouts. The memory of her lips on his still felt hot. He felt his face turning red just thinking about it.

When the other teens finished their meals, Nana and Paps

excused them to get ready for bed. Only Kyle was asked to stay behind with Proculus, Paps, and Nana. His foster siblings stomped upstairs with looks of disappointment. They wanted to know what would become of Kyle as much as he did. Kyle had been expecting a talk, but he still felt uneasy as he sat there. The chilling tension in the air was thick as custard while they waited silently for the last footsteps of Kyle's foster siblings to die down.

"Kyle?" asked Paps. "Do you have any idea who this is?"

"No."

"He's your uncle."

Kyle gaped at Paps lost for words. He didn't believe it.

"Proculus is also looking to adopt you," Nana added somewhat sadly.

"He is?" asked Kyle in a small, thin voice. His experiences with adoption had not gone well. He was happy living with Nana and Paps.

"So he says," said Paps. "We haven't confirmed it yet. Please feel free to jump in, Proculus. Adoption was the purpose of your visit last night, wasn't it?" The big man crossed his arms in his chair and frowned.

"I see no reason to continue misleading you," he said unexpectedly. "I am not, strictly speaking, looking to adopt Kyle. Nor am I his uncle."

Paps sat statue-like, clearly unsurprised. Nana shifted uncomfortably in her chair. Kyle felt as if he would be caught in some kind of tug of war soon. He waited silently.

"I figured as much," said Paps calmly. "Who are you, truly?"

"My name is Proculus. I did not lie about that. I have come from...Endera."

Nana let out a sharp gasp of horror. The wood of Paps' chair screeched on the floor as he backed up to stand. Proculus threw his hands up in surrender. Kyle was totally confused. He had never heard of Endera. It sounded like a foreign country, far away from Grayling. However, he knew from the strain in his foster parents' faces that it was something more. "Peace, Shadow. Let's not make more of this than we have to." *Shadow*?

Paps' eyes widened when Proculus had called him 'Shadow.' He balled up his fist and sat back down.

"So you know who we are?" asked Paps.

"I suspected," said Proculus. "You confirmed it for me. You should have picked a better last name. Shadoclaw practically gives you away." Paps gritted his teeth.

"We thought if we didn't use our keys we'd be fine," said Nana. *Keys?* Kyle's hand found its way to the key wrapped around his neck. Without thinking, he gripped it tightly.

"That is still true, Annabelle the Claw," said Proculus. "You're still safe." *Claw?*

"Then why are you here?" snapped Paps.

"For Kyle," he answered simply. "I mean to take him with me."

Take me? Kyle felt his heart beating in his throat. He swallowed uncomfortably, still lost for words. *I won't go. I'll never go.*

"No, I won't let you."

Kyle nearly leaped with joy. Of course Paps and Nana wouldn't let this stranger take him.

Proculus sighed. "I don't mean to take him by force."

"There will be no other way to take him," growled Paps.

Proculus rubbed his chin thoughtfully. His scar guided his thumb up and down his cheek in a way that made Kyle shiver and grow more nervous with every moment. Nothing they said made any sense to him. He looked back and forth from Paps to Proculus. Paps looked like he would pounce over the table. Kyle hoped he wouldn't. Proculus was nearly twice his size.

"Your threats won't work with me, Shadow."

"My tolerance is thinning, Proculus. Just who the hell do you think you are?" A vein on Pap's forehead looked ready to burst. Nana, on the other hand, looked like she was about to faint. The color had drained from her face.

The warm, usually pleasant room became icy and silent, except for the wind whistling against the dining room window as the blizzard continued outside.

"Stop it, Ethan," said Nana weakly. Paps opened his mouth to argue, but saw the state of his wife and thought better of it. Nana turned to Proculus. "Are you the one known as Proculus the Storm?"

Proculus smiled as if remembering a fond memory. "I have not been called that for some time. They call me Proculus the Master now."

Storm? Master? What are they talking about?

Paps's shoulders fell after that, as if he had been defeated in a fight he was sure he would win. Nana looked more nervous and it made Kyle feel helpless. Proculus sighed deeply.

"Please relax," Proculus said sincerely. "I am not here to cause trouble. I think Kyle deserves the truth. You two must have known who he was for some time now. Some might call it fate that he had the chance to be raised by two Enderians like him. Perhaps it would be best to start off by telling Kyle exactly who the two of you are?"

It wasn't a demand, but a request. Somehow this made Kyle feel less tense, even a little excited, as if he was finally going to find an answer he had always been looking for. *Who am I?* Paps and Nana looked at each other with uncertain eyes, but Kyle knew they were considering what Proculus had said. Proculus sat silently, waiting for the situation to unfold.

"He's right. We should tell Kyle." Nana nodded to Paps with resignation. The foster father simply shrugged. Kyle looked to Nana with eager eyes. "I suppose we all must sound crazy to you," she said with a forced smile.

"A little bit. You guys are talking like you're from a different planet."

"That's the general idea," said Nana. "My real name is Annabelle the Claw and Paps is Ethan the Shadow. We are from another realm called Endera. If Proculus is here, it's clear that you are also from our old realm."

"I don't understand," said Kyle. "If you're from another realm, then why are you in this one?" Kyle looked to Nana to answer, but she cringed as if troubled by the question.

"Due to certain circumstances," said Paps, "we were forced to escape."

"What could make you have to change realms?"

"We were thieves," Paps grumbled. "Well-known thieves who had stolen a few too many times and angered all the wrong people. We fled for our lives."

"Thieves?" The very word left a sour taste in his mouth. "You two, yeah right." Since he had known Paps and Nana, they were always well-spoken against stealing.

"It's true," said Nana, though Kyle still shot her a skeptical stare. "Would we lie to you, Kyle?"

She asked it in the same voice she always used when he questioned her about something. At that moment, he knew she wasn't lying; he knew this was all true.

"You were thieves?" Kyle felt like his mouth was full of sand instead of words. Nana let out a noise that sounded like something between a sob and a yelp.

"We were," admitted Paps. His voice had aged twenty years. "It is our deepest shame, but it is true. We came here about ten years ago, after we stole a rare book. We tried our hardest to escape, but we were chased then cornered. In one last attempt to get away, we opened a door to a different realm. It is an extremely dangerous thing to do. Most who have attempted to change realms have died.

"Somehow, we survived and made it here. Upon our arrival we knew there was nothing left for us in Endera. That realm only knew us as thieves and, though we knew it was no less than we deserved, we were tired of that life. We took the chance to do things over. We changed who we were. We wanted to do some good for a change. We became parents to kids that reminded us of ourselves and we wanted to make sure they wouldn't make the same mistakes as us."

"But how?" Kyle tried to logically piece the situation together. "What do you mean, you opened a door to another realm? How is that possible? Even if there was another realm, you can't just travel between them. That doesn't make sense."

"Keys." Proculus finally broke his silence with the answer.

"Keys?" repeated Kyle. "Keys can't do that."

"We Enderians," said Proculus, "are also known as key sages or key champions. From birth, we have the gift to wield keys and all their powers."

"Powers? Keys don't have powers."

Proculus reached into his pocket to retrieve a navy blue key that looked like an ordinary house key. As if an invisible door was directly in front of him, he jabbed the key into thin air and released it. Kyle watched in silence and, to his amazement, the key floated above the table. Then, Proculus took hold of the key again and turned it.

It first appeared as if nothing had happened, but Proculus placed his free hand near the floating key. The air had become distorted like a haze of heat above a summer road. Proculus's hand disappeared into the haze, which almost caused Kyle to jump out of his chair. Proculus pulled out his hand, only something followed it out of the nothingness. He held a shining double-edged sword with a wooden hilt. Without a word, he carefully handed it to Kyle.

Words would not come to Kyle as he stared at the blade. Half of him expected the weapon to disappear as if he was imagining it all, but the weight of it in his hand silenced his doubts.

Paps and Nana looked unsurprised, yet they were nervous.

"Don't worry," said Proculus to the foster parents. "It was undetectable." He grabbed the key, which still floated in the air, turned it and put it back into his pocket.

"Undetectable?" said Kyle.

"The use of keys is highly regulated in this realm." Nana's eyes glittered with tears. "To hide, we can never use the power of keys again. If we did, it is likely they would find us and send us back to our realm where we would be sentenced to death for our crimes. Proculus made his ability undetectable so it wouldn't give us away."

"Sentenced… to death?" He could not believe that Nana and Paps could have ever done anything to warrant such a harsh punishment.

"The problem now lies," said Proculus, "with you. You have inadvertently started awakening your powers with keys. If you stay here, the Keyways will eventually find you, which would mean that they would find your foster parents."

Kyle didn't know who the Keyways were, but it didn't matter. He already had a solution.

"I just won't use the key! I'll get rid of it and then it won't be a problem anymore." He looked to Nana and Paps, expecting them to smile and tell them that this idea would work. They shook their heads.

"Kyle," said Proculus, "do you remember the silver key when you were walking into Mr. Corsell's office?"

Kyle's eyes opened wide, now knowing for a certainty that the man who had been talking to Kyle in the office was Proculus. He pictured the silver key before nodding.

"That key was activated by your power. It summoned me to the school. You will have this effect on any key that comes near you; it is impossible to avoid. It's not something you will be able to control without proper training. Your life has been filled with these kinds of things happening even without your knowledge. Nevertheless, I am sure that you *have* noticed by now that some people have treated you oddly for no reason. They blame you for things you can't quite explain, yet you feel responsible for them. You have been involuntarily using your power. It will only get worse if you don't train it."

Kyle swallowed hard. He realized, without a doubt, it was true. All his life, there were times when he'd wake up with people treating him differently than they had the day before, as though he knew one of their darkest secrets. Other times he'd wake up to find himself holding a keepsake of someone's that had been locked in a safe. Just hours ago, he had woken up on a pile of snow in the school gym, encompassed by a raging snowstorm that seemed so unnatural.

Somehow he did always feel guilty, as if he knew deep down that he made these things happen.

"But—I—can't just leave." He struggled to contain tears. He could not accept that he would have to leave, or even that he was Enderian, despite the mounting evidence. It still felt impossible. "How do you know it's me? Are you sure it's not some other kid you're looking for? There are two whole realms full of people. Maybe you mixed me up with another one?"

"There are four realms, actually," said Proculus.

"What? There're four?" he stammered.

"Yes. There is Endera, Librium, Anulis and Unara."

"Then how can you be sure I'm even the right kid?"

Proculus sighed deeply. "I know because I knew your mother. A long time ago, she asked me to come find you when the time was right."

"My mother?" The subject of his parents was not something he liked to talk about. "So she wanted to get rid of me so badly, she sent me to another realm? She has nothing to do with me now, so why should I care what my mother wanted for me? How do you even know I'm her kid?"

"Your hair and your stubbornness are remarkably similar," Proculus said with a grin. Then he became serious again. "I am not sure how or why she brought you here, Kyle. Years ago, when I last saw her, she begged me to retrieve you. I gave her my word that I would, so it is my duty to take you back with me."

"I don't care about that. I'm not going."

"It's natural that you may hold resentment, but you must understand that you place yourself and this home at risk if you do not come with me. That danger goes double for Anna and Ethan here. As I said earlier, they will be caught if you stay here."

A weight fell heavily on his shoulders. Putting everyone in danger was certainly not something he wanted to do. He thought his head might explode. His foster parents had always been good to him. It would be a poor way to repay them if he stayed and was responsible for sending them to their deaths. Paps and Nana sat silently. Kyle knew they were letting him make his own decision. He was thankful for their patience and he realized that he loved them the way a child should love their parents. It was in that same moment that he made his choice.

"Fine." He felt like his mouth was moving on its own. "I'll go to Endera."

Nana grabbed her husband's hand on the table and squeezed it tightly.

"I'm glad to hear it," said Proculus.

"Proculus," said Paps suddenly. He sounded more like his usual self. "Do you plan to take him to the academy?"

"Yes."

"Is there a chance he'll suffer for having been under the care of The Shadow and Claw thieves?

"None," Proculus said without missing a beat.

"You swear it?"

"I swear it."

Ethan gave Proculus a piercing gaze, looking for hints of deception. He sighed with relief when he found none, yet his face still looked as sad as Nana's.

"Will Kyle," asked Nana, "ever be able to come back?" Proculus gave Nana a sympathetic look.

"I will come back, Nana." Kyle declared it before Proculus could speak. "I promise. I will come back."

Proculus turned his attention to the young man and shot him an amused look, seemingly full of fond memories. Then he beamed and laughed heartily.

"Well, there you have it, Mr. and Mrs. Shadoclaw. This young man says he will return and I believe that you should trust him to do so." Proculus then spoke to Kyle. "Are you sure you want to come?"

"No," said Kyle. "But I don't really have a choice, do I?"

"There is always a choice."

Kyle thought on that for a moment. "I don't want to cause trouble for Nana and Paps. I'm going." When he looked back to the couple who were the closest beings he'd ever had as parents, there was a glimpse of pride mixed in with sorrow in both their eyes.

"Excellent! Then perhaps we should be off, the sooner the better."

"Now?"

"I'm afraid we can't wait."

Nana's glossy eyes gave way to tears that began pouring down her cheeks as she sobbed. Paps blinked rapidly while staring at the ceiling with something crossed between a frown and a grimace.

"You know," said Kyle, "since I can remember, I have been jumping from home to home. People adopted me and then decided that they couldn't handle having a kid like me. It hurt for a long time." He felt a burning in his eyes that strengthened beneath the gazes of his foster parents. Unsure of whether it was embarrassment or sadness, he tried his best to look at the ceiling. "I came here, and this was the one place I felt like I belonged. It was the first time in my life…" he choked back tears. "…it was the first time I felt that someone cared about me. It was the first time I felt like I had… parents. I want you to know how grateful I am for you two. Even though we haven't been together very long, I want you to know that I'll always see you two as my parents." Kyle felt his throat grow tight and he tried hard to swallow, but it was impossible. He scratched his head and felt some tears fall down his cheeks. "I'm really gonna miss you both."

Trying hard not to look at them, Kyle walked around the table to hug them tight and true. He realized what he was giving up when Nana cried into his shoulder and Paps patted his back. Leaving them hurt, but it was the same pain as running a race. It was a good, satisfying feeling that could never be taken from him. After a few moments, Kyle let go and wiped his tears away with his forearm. Proculus had been kind enough to become extremely interested in the sword he had made appear with his key.

"Should I get my stuff?" Kyle asked. Proculus set the sword down.

"There's no need," he answered. "The key around your neck is all you'll need."

Kyle nodded. "I still have a lot of questions."

"I would be surprised if you didn't. First we must leave and then I will do my best to answer them all on our journey. One final thing. I have a request of Ethan and Anna."

"Is it the book?" asked Paps.

"You're a sharp man, Shadow. If it's not too much trouble, I was hoping you could return it to the academy."

"They stole the book from you?" Kyle asked incredulously.

"They stole it from the academy of which I am now a master of, so in a way, yes."

"No words will ever be enough to tell you how sorry we are." Nana stood up and wiped her puffy eyes. "I'll go get the book. It'll be just a moment." She left the room, leaving the three others in the room.

"Please don't think too ill of us, Kyle."

"You two are completely different now. I don't care about what you did then. That is not the Nana and Paps I know so don't worry about it, okay?"

Paps stood up and ruffled Kyle's hair gently as he turned to Proculus. "I hope you can forgive us for what we did."

Proculus stood up, shaking his head before answering. "There is nothing to forgive. It is good to know that Kyle had you two to care for him for some time. Had you not stolen the book, that may have never happened. Now how about we wait at the door? We really must get going."

They moved to the living room. Kyle readied himself to go out into the cold by putting on his coat and shoes. As he finished, Nana walked in with a heavy-looking book that had a tattered black leather binding. It was dusty and by far the oldest looking thing Kyle had ever seen. "Why is that ancient thing so important?" he asked.

Nana gave the book to a laughing Proculus, who pressed his key to the cover and turned it, making the old thing vanish. "Thank you. When the time is right, I will tell you. It is good to see that you kept it safe all these years. We should be off. I'll wait outside for you, Kyle. Please say your goodbyes. Ethan. Annabelle." With a nod, he let himself out, leaving Kyle alone with Nana and Paps. Nana sobbed again as she spoke.

"You take care of yourself, honey. Make sure you get enough to eat. Train hard at the academy and listen to Proculus. He's a good man. Make lots of friends and a few really good ones that you can trust—I know girls will come at you in groups, but make sure you choose only one. I love you, Kyle. Never forget that we both love you. Make sure you never forget that. Oh, I'm sorry; I'm rambling." Tears streamed down her face. Kyle was about to respond, but Paps spoke, instead.

"Never forget the advice of a nagging mother, Kyle. We love you like a son. If you ever question all else, never question that."

"I won't forget. I'll make you proud and I'll come back." Kyle hugged them one last time before grabbing the door handle, but then he paused. "I love you both."

"Go on." Nana gave him a light pat on the back. The wind whistled into the house when Kyle opened the door. "Remember you always have a home here. Goodbye, honey."

Kyle rubbed his head leaving them with a smile as he shut the door.

CHAPTER FOUR

THE DOOR TO ANOTHER REALM

The wind blasted snow into Kyle's face as he stepped outside to join Proculus. He hugged himself to keep warm and wondered if he was still dreaming. Everything still felt so unreal. Proculus, with his muscular figure now beneath his puffy coat, waited at the foot of the porch, steps ready to leave. The weather had become so cold that by time he reached Proculus, his feelings of sorrow were replaced by his focus to stay warm. Still, he couldn't help but wonder where exactly they were going.

"Follow me," said Proculus. "We have a bit of a walk ahead of us."

Kyle followed silently. The two of them trekked through snow that was up to their knees, moving further and further away from the foster home. Kyle looked back to say a last farewell to his home, but he could barely see the house through the flurries. He realized that Proculus was leading them to Grayling Junior High.

He wanted to ask why they were heading toward his school, but the cold weaved into his skin so deeply that he had no desire to waste energy on anything other than keeping warm. He had made this walk many times. On days that he had slept in too late, Nana made him walk to school, but sometimes Paps made an excuse to go out so that he could give Kyle a quick ride on the way. Nana would laugh and call him a softie. The memories made him grin.

Upon arriving at the school, he caught a glimpse of the heap of snow covering what used to be the football field. The icy bleachers were now almost completely covered. A sense of guilt poured over him. Proculus finally turned around when they reached the school's front door.

"It's locked," he said without so much as a tug on the door.

"Are we going to break in?" *They can't expel me twice.*

"No need to break in. How about you unlock the door? I think you and your key can handle it."

Kyle didn't know how he could expect such a thing from him already, but he was eager to get inside. "I guess," he said uncertainly. "I guess I can try." He reluctantly fished out his key from around his neck. He shivered as he held the key in his hand. He wished nothing more than to be inside the school, away from the cold. As if the key had read his thoughts, it guided his hand to the lock of the double glass doors. It was obvious that Kyle's key would not fit into the keyhole, but he tried anyways. Rather than hitting the metal, his key melted into the metal as easy as a hand enters water.

"Well, unlock it before we freeze to death." Proculus smiled at him warmly, but Kyle looked at the man, puzzled as ever. It was nerve racking, but he turned his key counter clock-wise. A strange tingle spread through his arm and the door opened with a loud click.

He thought it strange how natural it was for him to use this power. How had he not noticed it? Kyle removed his key, looking at it with awe as they walked in. Proculus slammed the door, causing it to echo down the hallways.

It was distinctly warmer in the school and Kyle was grateful for it. "Why exactly," he asked as he placed his key back around his neck, "are we here?"

Proculus did not answer. Instead, he began walking down the hallway. He walked with long strides, forcing Kyle to walk faster than normal to keep up. Kyle knew by memory that they were working their way to the principal's office. When they arrived, Proculus sat down at Mr. Corsell's desk and signaled Kyle to sit where he had been seated just hours ago.

"We are here," he said with a smile, "because this is where the Path Guard has allowed us to enter into the Unlocked Realm."

"Alexun?"

"So you've met?" he laughed. "If I had known that, we could have stayed in the warmth of your foster parent's home a bit longer."

"Oh," Kyle felt a little annoyed. He could have used a few moments more with his foster parents. Still, if they had extra time, he hoped that Proculus would be able to explain the questions regarding today that still clouded his mind. "I thought meeting Alexun was just a dream. Wasn't it?"

"Well," Proculus said, scratching his chin, "I can see you have a lot on your mind. Tell me about this dream and anything else that might be troubling you. After you're finished, I will do my best to explain everything."

Kyle was happy to obey. He spoke rapidly as he told Proculus about everything that had happened recently. Proculus listened attentively and reverently. The young man recounted his daydream in class about the snow and the men with weapons, the principal's room changing magically, the fight in the coliseum and his meeting with Alexun the Path Guard, and finally, he embarrassed himself by telling Proculus about his kiss with Garnet. He scratched his head as he waited patiently for a response.

"Small wonder you're confused. Let's start from the beginning. There is no way for me to be completely certain, since I was not there, but from what you have told me I believe I have some suitable explanations. This morning, during your class, you said you were daydreaming of snow. I believe this accidently activated your key's power and you shifted to a place where there was a lot of snow."

"Shifted?"

"Yes. It is what we call when we vanish and then reappear somewhere else. It is the main way we travel in Endera. Normally, it only works when you open a ShiftDoor. Being able to shift without a door is rare, but not unheard of. According to your dream, you arrived at this snowy place. I believe that you then unconsciously decided to bring snow back with you. The second time you shifted, you opened a giant door, which brought the snow back along with you. Most of it landed on the field with seats around it. It also seems to have caused this blizzard."

"So I did all this?"

"You did. To open such a big door is an impressive feat for someone so young, but that is neither here nor there."

Kyle didn't like the idea that a blizzard like this was considered impressive. He worried that it may put people in danger, which left a horrible feeling in his gut.

Proculus continued, "The men in cloaks with weapons—I think

it is safe to say that these men were from the organization called the Keyways. The Keyways are a special force from Librium that oversees the use of keys in the four realms. Your ShiftDoor is what must have drawn them out. When they tried to stop you, you were too quick for them. I am unsure as to why they did not follow you, though. It seems luck was on our side for that." Proculus laughed heartily.

"After you returned with the snow, you were extremely fatigued. Normally, only powerful key wielders can open up such big doors without completely exhausting themselves. The strength of your ShiftDoor was enough to notify me that you were ready. I have been waiting in this realm for nearly a month. A three hour walk from here, there is a nice cabin I found in my short time exploring this realm. It is deep into the woods on the side of a mountain. Very secluded, but animals roam freely enough so I never went hungry. Regardless, when your power was awakened, I manipulated your mind. The changes you saw in this office were only a trick to your inner eyes. You saw what I wanted you to see; meaning you saw yourself sitting with me inside the cabin in which I have been living.

"I unlocked your mind, taking control as you sat here awaiting punishment. That is how I made you confess for the snow. Although I am not sure why the two men seemed so angry with you for the little damage you caused. In Endera, my students at the academy frequently cause damage that is much more severe. There has never been an expulsion for something so trivial."

"Are you saying," Kyle asked hesitantly, "that you can unlock people's minds and control them?" He felt vulnerable just thinking about it. *Is there anything these keys can't do?* If students were likely to cause damage with their powers, Kyle wondered how safe he would be. He was amazed as much as he was overwhelmed and frightened.

"It is a difficult thing to do, but yes. There really is no limit to the power of keys," he said seriously. "You will be learning these things in much greater detail soon enough. Now, as for your fight in the arena, that is quite interesting. Alexun does not do things without good reason. If he had you fight, he must be very interested in you and your future. It is quite an honor."

"Honor? I thought I killed a man!"

"He did seem a bit harsh. When we met, he threatened to throw me into his arena as a prisoner. Obviously, he chose not to. He normally only imprisons those who mean to travel between realms illegally. These people become his prisoners and are forced to fight in his 'Eternal Arena.' I am guessing he wanted to see if you were worthy enough to travel to Endera. You proved that you were. I doubt that the man you beat in the arena is dead. The Path Guard revealed to me that the arena is eternal because his criminals are forced to fight, die, revive, and fight again for an eternity. Or until Alexun feels otherwise."

"That's…horrible."

"Horrible?" asked Proculus. "How so?" The man looked at Kyle with a peculiar expression.

"Nobody deserves that kind of punishment. It's cruel."

"The people he keeps there are usually trying to avoid capture for the punishment of crimes they have committed in their realms. They believe if they can get to the next realm, they can escape to live a new life. These people are mostly murderers, thieves, torturers, or worse. They deserve punishment. Would you have murderers reign free in any realm they like?"

"No."

"Then I fail to see why you think the punishment is horrible."

"People can change! Look at Nana and Paps! They are great people. They don't deserve to be fighting and dying in some arena forever!" Kyle thought that Proculus would get angry with him, but the big man waited patiently for him to calm down.

"Your foster parents," Proculus started, "are an exception. Many of these criminals have had plenty of chances. They take lives or ruin them then they flee. Try not to feel sympathetic for them. This kind of thinking could prove costly. It's possible that the one you fought has been dead a long time."

The idea that he fought a dead man sent chills down Kyle's spine, but he still had a defiant look in his eyes. "I still think it's wrong," he muttered.

"Tell me," said Proculus. "If I returned to your home to kill your foster parents, what would you think of me? Would you like me to be free of punishment on the promise that I would change my ways?" There was coldness in Proculus's eyes that hadn't been there a second ago. For just a moment, Kyle thought the man was serious.

His heart came to a stop. He realized that for the first time in his life, he felt true fear. It was as if he was staring at a mountain he knew he would die climbing. His mind scrambled for words that would not come.

"I do not mean to frighten you, Kyle," Proculus let out a deep sigh. "You think as many young and good children think. You see the good in the world. Consider this my first lesson to you. There are people out there who would do harm to others in order to do harm to you. Keeping criminals imprisoned in Librium is already a kindness too great. Do not let your kindness cloud your mind when it comes to punishing those who truly deserve it."

Kyle had no argument to offer Proculus, and he knew it was

pointless to try. Still, he couldn't bring himself to agree.

"You are still young," said Proculus conclusively. "You'll find your own answer soon enough. I just hope it's not too late." There was no more to say on the matter. Proculus waited quiet as a ghost and Kyle knew it was for him to break the silence.

"So I am worthy to travel to Endera, then?" he asked in an attempt to steer the conversation elsewhere.

"It would appear so." Proculus answered with a smile.

Kyle relaxed at this and found the atmosphere had lightened considerably.

"You have been given permission by The Path Guard himself to travel back with me to our realm. Alexun is the lord of all paths to realms. His territory is part of Librium, and he is just short of being considered a god. Only a mad man would attempt to attack him."

Kyle shifted uncomfortably in his seat as he remembered his encounter with the Path Guard. He had swung his sword at him.

"So, let me get this straight." Proculus leaned back in his chair, drumming his fingers together. "After your fight in the arena, you awoke in your house? And you say you had an encounter with a girl there?"

"Yes."

"What exactly happened again?"

"Well." Kyle scratched his head. "She kissed me and then disappeared."

"I see. This is most interesting. Definitely the most interesting experience you have had today. You said her name was Garnet, right?"

"Yeah, do you know what it means?"

"I think so." Proculus chuckled. "It would appear that you genuinely had a dream. And by that ruby red blush on your face, it was a good one. If there is one thing that I know to be true, it is that no matter what realm you are in, there will always be men who dream of women."

Kyle sat embarrassed, but before long he remembered that he had not been able to say goodbye to Garnet. She had been at the foster home longer than Kyle, but she was happy to be his friend from the moment he had arrived. He would miss her along with Nana and Paps. It saddened him as he wondered if she would remember him.

Not for the first time, Proculus seemed to read his mind. "Perhaps, when you return to this realm, it would be wise to visit her."

Kyle nodded. He then witnessed a small black hole no larger than a penny form on the wall behind Proculus, as if someone had punctured it with their finger. At first, he thought it was just a trick his eyes were playing on him, but the hole grew larger until it shaped itself into a keyhole the size of a wine bottle.

"Something's on the wall!" Kyle pointed behind Proculus. "It looks like a keyhole."

"Oh." Proculus rotated his chair around. "It would appear so. Looks like it's nearly time. I just need to verify my identity. And if you were wondering, this keyhole is specially sent by the Path Guard to ensure that only those who he has given permission to travel between realms are allowed to pass through. It requires a special key given to me by Alexun, along with my blood." Proculus pulled out a large pale yellow wooden key from a drawer in the desk. Kyle wanted to ask how it had gotten there, but decided against it. Its bow was a wide oval with a jade stone fit snugly inside it.

"Blood?" Kyle asked looking worried.

"Yes, just a little." Proculus picked up a small letter opener that had been sitting on the desk. "This will do the trick." Proculus pricked his index finger and some blood emerged from his skin. He smeared his blood on the wooden key so that a streak of blood now stained both sides. "Now, then."

Proculus stood from his seat and inserted the key into the keyhole. As he turned it, the key began vibrating with so much force that it shook the floor. Kyle thought the wall might fall apart, until the shaking ended. The key then burst into flames, nearly making him shout in surprise. It turned to ashes unnaturally fast, floating gracefully like gray snow and landing in a small pile next to Proculus's feet. The man frowned at the keyhole as it dissolved from the wall.

"Umm...is that bad?" asked Kyle.

"Hmm, I am not sure. I suppose we will find out soon enough. The Path Guard mentioned that it may take a few minutes for the door to appear." Proculus stared at the wall curiously, rubbing his chin as if the wall was the most fascinating thing to have ever been conjured.

Kyle ruffled his hair impatiently. "Proculus, I have another question."

Proculus's eyes did not leave the wall, but he responded. "Yes?"

"I was wondering...you said you knew my mother. Where is she now, and why did she leave me in another realm?

"You might be angry with me for saying this," replied Proculus, "but that is better left for another day."

"Why?" he asked in disappointment. "Why not now?"

"I told you earlier that I did not know how or why she left you here. I have guesses, but nothing more than that. I would like to have more answers myself rather than confusing you further. I will reveal everything I know someday, but until then, I ask that you do not press this subject. I hope you can understand." There was nothing for Kyle to understand. He knew Proculus would not tell him now. Yet, he still wanted to know at least a little.

"Is she dead now?"

"I do not believe she is," answered Proculus. "I wish I could give you more than that, but I cannot."

"That's okay. Sounds complicated, anyhow."

In the blink of an eye, there was now a great forget-me-not blue door in the middle of the wall. It towered over Proculus, nearly touching the office ceiling. It was plain except for a perfectly round gold doorknob that reminded Kyle of a billiard ball. Blinding white light seeped through the cracks that bordered where the door met the wall. Simple as it all was, there was still such impressiveness to the sight that Kyle instantly knew it was the door to another realm.

"It is time," said Proculus. "Are you ready?" He turned to face Kyle.

"Y—yeah, I'm ready." Kyle rose from his seat. He was nervous, but when he thought of Nana, Paps, and Garnet, it made him feel braver.

"Good. Now then, open the door."

"Shouldn't you?"

"Trust me, Kyle. Open the door and walk through. I'll be right behind you." Proculus beamed at him happily and in that instance, Kyle knew he could trust the key sage. The comment earlier about killing Nana and Paps had just been a lesson he wanted to teach Kyle, and nothing more. There were few people Kyle had ever trusted, but he knew Proculus was now one of them. It was a good feeling.

Kyle let out a deep breath as he placed his hand on the door, knowing it led to a world completely unknown to him. With a nervous gulp, he turned the golden doorknob. It clicked softly. Warm light poured into the office as he gently pushed the door open. Forgetting his worries, he walked forward to Endera, the Unlocked Realm.

CHAPTER FIVE

SOUL GATE ACADEMY

Kyle felt weightless as a warm breeze hit his skin. They were flying through the sky much too fast to see anything other than shapeless blurs. Next to him, Proculus moved at the same speed with his eyes closed. Kyle noticed that Proculus began disintegrating, and he was doing the same. He panicked for just a moment, but they had stopped. He and Proculus now stood in front of a white door poised in the middle of complete darkness. Kyle scanned the area to see if there was anything other than the door, but there was not. Baffled, he looked at Proculus, only to see him nod toward the exit. They walked through.

Kyle gasped as they stepped out. He now stood still on a cliff's edge of a mountain side, higher in the sky than he had ever been. He was not scared, just awestruck. He could see the new realm's countryside with an impressive view. The sunlight reflected off the widest river he had ever seen, curving away from the mountain to his right. Smaller rivers broke off and spread across wide plains. Scattered villages stood apart from each other, connected by dirt roads. Vast fields were abundant in the landscape, as well. Farthest away in the distance, there was a grand castle with a commanding view of the entire area. Any other time, Kyle would have wondered who could live in such a place, but everything was so beyond anything he had ever seen in his short life that he could hardly believe it was real.

"Beautiful, isn't it?" Proculus smiled.

When Kyle finally tore his eyes from the view, he saw the door had disappeared. He also noticed that Proculus was now dressed differently, wearing a shirt and pants that were clean white. Proculus was in the process of buttoning a heavy-looking ivory white vest over his shirt, which reminded Kyle of a bullet proof vest. On his left vest pocket was an emblem that consisted of two majestic keys crossing each other like an "X" and the letters *S.G.A.* On the back of it was a large foreign symbol painted in black and blue. Proculus threw Kyle some clothes, answering his question before he could even ask it. "The symbol means Storm. As I mentioned earlier, it is my eternal title. You'll learn more about that later. For now, you'll want to change into this before you sweat to death."

Kyle had to admit that he was sweating underneath his coat. He hadn't expected such an extreme change in weather. He took off his coat and changed.

"This is one of my favorite places. I love the view."

"This is Endera?" asked Kyle as he pulled on his blue vest with the same emblem over his black shirt. His pants matched his vest. Proculus waited until he was fully dressed to speak.

"Yes, welcome to The Unlocked Realm. We are in the Eastern Kingdom called Dusk, my homeland." He said it cheerfully. "The uniform suits you well."

"Why are we wearing uniforms? Is there a reason mine is different than yours?"

"That uniform is what you will wear from now on," said Proculus seriously. "You are now a tyro of Soul Gate Academy. I wear the uniform of a Master; all teachers are referred to as Masters. From this point on you will refer to me as Master Proculus or Master only. Understood?" Kyle eyed him carefully to see if he was joking, but he was not.

"Yes…Master," said Kyle oddly. "What is a tyro?"

"A tyro is what we call all our students at Soul Gate Academy."

"And what exactly is Soul Gate Academy?"

"You will see soon enough!" said Proculus happily. "It is your new home, after all."

Satisfied enough by the answer, Kyle turned his attention to his surroundings. The mountain side bloomed beautifully. Thick green bushes and trees gave off a sweet scent. There was a field of grass decorated with colorful flowers and Kyle heard the sound of small streams that trickled nearby. It was still hard to grasp that they were on a mountain.

"Is it far from here?" Kyle asked, seeing that there was nothing that looked as if it had been touched by people for miles. "Why didn't we just shift directly there?"

"Arragin Mountain is one of the closest places we can shift to SoGA. SoGA is what we call the academy for short," answered Proculus. "The academy's land is protected by a lock that does not allow anyone to open a ShiftDoor directly onto it. It is a short walk from here."

"We're walking?"

"Yes."

Kyle sighed. He wanted to see what Soul Gate Academy looked like and walking seemed too boring for his impatience. His excitement was overwhelming. Now that he truly realized this was where he belonged, his real home, he was anxious to prove that he could be a proper Enderian—though he wasn't exactly sure what that entailed.

Proculus took out his key. Like he had done at the foster home, he jabbed the key into the air in front of him, turned it then pulled out two swords. The first was a big two-handed broad sword. "This one's mine, and this one's for you." He handed Kyle a much smaller, one-handed blade. It was light and more suited for Kyle's small frame, yet something felt off about it. He turned it in his hand, unsure whether he should be holding a weapon. Still, it made him feel empowered, as if he was the hero of a fantasy novel.

"Are you sure that I need a sword? I don't exactly know how to use one."

"You are to be on guard at all times. You would be surprised at what you are capable of when you are attacked."

"Is that likely?" Kyle gripped his new weapon tighter.

"It is possible," laughed Proculus. "But don't worry, you are with me and we are headed toward one of the safest places in all of Endera. Well, strictly speaking, it is safe." He muttered the last part more to himself than to Kyle.

"What do you mean, 'strictly speaking?'" asked Kyle.

"We should get going," Proculus ignored his question. "No use in staying here. It would be best for us to arrive at SoGA by nightfall. Since you are new, I am allowing it to slide, but, again, remember you are to address me as Master."

"Yes, Master," Kyle ruffled his hair. Calling someone master felt strange.

"Good, now as I said, be on guard." Proculus set off at a brisk pace with Kyle following a few paces behind. Kyle turned to look at the view one last time, watching the castle disappear as they walked further away from the cliff's edge. He turned back to following his master, who was also looking back. "Place might be worth fighting for, no?"

Kyle nodded, although he wasn't quite sure what Proculus meant.

They marched without speaking down a mountain trail surrounded by trees on both sides. Kyle felt odd carrying a weapon and thought he looked like a joke in comparison to Proculus, who looked quite deadly with his sword. Thinking that his master wouldn't notice, he practiced thrusting and swinging the blade while walking behind.

However, Proculus heard the whooshes of Kyle's sword as it cut up the wind. The master found himself smiling as he wondered how the young man could adjust so effortlessly. It was odd for a child to be this casual and accepting, wasn't it? *Only your child*, he thought to himself as he scratched his chin.

After sometime, Kyle began to feel tired. He had long stopped swinging the sword, but walking was becoming more difficult. He still hadn't rested properly from all that happened today, making him certain that his energy was close to being completely depleted. He looked forward to resting, but his tiredness left him when he heard a sound behind them. The hair on his neck stood instinctively, sending a chill went down his spine.

Something was wrong.

"Master," he whispered softly.

"Quiet," Proculus said coolly. "Get ready." Kyle wasn't sure what he meant until a moment later.

Four figures emerged in front of them. Before Proculus and Kyle could react, three others lined up behind them. The group spread out, surrounding the two. Kyle noticed five boys and two girls, not much older than he; a couple of them even looked younger. Each of the newcomers held at least one weapon. They were dressed exactly like Kyle, but Kyle didn't exactly feel relieved with the way they held their weapons.

"I wonder if you can prove to me that you are, in fact, Master Proculus?" called out the largest and oldest looking in the group. He had short brown hair and a distinctive aquiline nose. He was holding an odd spear that reminded Kyle of a screw. It looked deadly.

"How should I prove it?" asked Proculus. The master rolled his shoulders, readying for a fight. Seeming happy to give him one, the group closed in brandishing their weapons.

"We don't want any trouble," said Kyle weakly. The last thing he wanted to do was fight for his life against seven well-armed teenagers. "Master Proculus, can't you just prove…?"

All of them laughed and maybe he imagined it, but Kyle thought he heard his master give a soft chuckle, too. Kyle's uncertainties were hushed when the one with the spear spoke again.

"We don't want any trouble," he said mockingly over their laughs while he pointed his spear at Kyle. "Annie, James, get the kid. Everyone else, formation three on the big guy."

Kyle automatically readied his weapon. His master smiled from ear to ear as he raised his sword. It was an impressive and terrifying sight. Kyle thought that a group of twenty well-trained men would hesitate before engaging him but there was no hesitation with these kids. They looked more like they had found toys that they had long lost. The seven moved in, causing him to separate from Proculus. Without hesitation, the five sent flurries of attacks against Proculus.

"Worry about yourself!" yelled Proculus as if the matter were trivial. "I can handle these five." He was in no way exaggerating. Expertly and gracefully, the brawny man dodged and deflected all attacks. The five teenagers, with their slashes and stabs, were swatted away as easy as flies. That wasn't for lack of trying, though. Each of the fighters wore fierce looks on their faces full of concentration and determination. Proculus jumped high into the air over the attackers to avoid a stab at his leg. When he landed, the relentless attacks from the teenagers continued. The gap between him and Kyle became wider as the young man prepared to defend against his own attackers.

The two named Annie and James seemed much more hesitant to make the first move against Kyle, but they also looked younger than the rest. They circled him like owls studying their prey, readying to swoop in for the kill. Kyle couldn't help but dread that he probably knew much less than the two when it came to sword fighting.

Annie had short dark hair, ebony skin, and a thin, wiry build. James looked like her twin brother. Their grins looked sinister as they twisted the blades in their hands. With the simple motion, each of their swords split into two.

"Great," muttered Kyle. "Four swords against one." He glanced over at Proculus and noticed how much he seemed to be enjoying the fight. Fearlessly, the man showed no openings to the five who restlessly attacked him. He brought his attention back to the twins. *Better off fighting these two than those five, I suppose.*

Without warning, Annie launched at him. Kyle instinctively

ducked then jumped aside. James took advantage of the dodge and went in for a blow. Kyle luckily defended it with his own sword, backing away from both of them. He worked out that part of their technique used back-to-back attacks. They edged in closer, allowing him no more time to think.

The young girl charged, attacking with her left sword then with her right; she rapidly repeated the sequence over and over. Kyle moved back to block each blow while trying to keep his eyes on her brother. Suddenly, James seemed to vanish, moving toward his left side. Annie focused her attacks toward his right. It was impossible to defend both sides at once, unless...

Instinct kicked in as adrenaline sped through his veins, switching his fear to excitement. With a forceful step toward Annie, he defended one of her blows with all his might. It threw her off balance, granting him an opportunity to uppercut her other sword hand with his left fist. This caused that sword to be thrown into the air. He moved his hand swiftly, catching the sword. It left his side open, enabling Annie to deliver a powerful kick to his ribs. He could already feel the pain of a bruise forming. When Annie recovered, she and James sliced at him from both sides.

Kyle blocked with both blades, halting the fight just for a second. Now armed with two swords, he felt better about his odds, especially because the twins looked agitated. They attacked again, leaving him little time to think. He blocked the three swords as the pair pressed him backwards. Each time the swords clashed, a clang rang through the air. Annie focused on trying to stab him while James tried his best to hack off one of his arms. James fell into a pattern of attacking high then low, but Annie's attacks were random at best. It was good teamwork and Kyle knew he was lucky to have survived this long.

After some time, his arms grew tired, his breathing was heavy and his aching, burning muscles were begging him to end the fight.

It was a small consolation to hear the twins winded as he was while they continued to drive him back. Unable to see behind him, Kyle tripped over a small log. The two took advantage of the fall by going in for the kill before he even hit the ground. They thrust their swords down while Kyle brought up his for a counter. The blades slid off each other, all stopping just an inch from each other's neck. For a moment, two swords stopped just inches from Kyle's neck, while his swords hovered closely to theirs.

"ENOUGH!" yelled a familiar voice. "A draw. It's a draw. You three can stop now."

Immediately, Annie and James withdrew their swords. Kyle hesitated, but after a moment he lowered his swords and sat up. He searched the eyes of his opponents for treachery, but found nothing. The two smiled awkwardly as though unsure of what they should do. Kyle was perplexed as they walked over to the other five who were now resting in the shade of a tree. Looking around for the familiar voice, he saw Proculus casually walking toward him.

"What's going on?" Kyle tried to bite back his anger as his master smiled warmly. "Why has everyone stopped fighting?"

"They have all stopped on my orders." He grinned as though it were obvious.

"Your orders?"

"Yes, my orders."

"Then why did they attack us to start with?"

"Also my orders," he said, laughing. "Think of it as your entry exam to becoming a tyro. I am pleased to announce that you have passed."

"Passed?" Kyle muttered furiously. "Why is everyone trying to kill me when they test me today?"

"You were never in any real trouble," said Proculus while helping Kyle to his feet. "These seven are your fellow tyros at the Soul Gate Academy and they had orders to go easy on you. You will be training in classes with some of them very soon. It is common and encouraged for students to challenge the masters to a fight. I asked them to bring Annie and James to test you since it is also common for students to duel each other. However, while you're at the academy there is no need to worry about serious injury. The blades of these weapons have all been locked by the Grandmaster himself."

"The blades have been…locked?"

"Try to cut yourself with the sword."

Kyle gawked at Proculus, but saw that his master was serious. He placed its edge to his skin, but a force that felt like hardened air surrounded the weapon. No matter how hard he pressed it to his skin, it would not cut. "It will still give you a mighty bruise, but you won't die," added Proculus.

"That's nice to know," said Kyle bitterly. "I hope my master will be kind enough to give me a heads up next time." Proculus ignored him. He grabbed Kyle's elbow unceremoniously, dragging him over to where the seven other tyro waited.

"You two sure have improved," said one of the older boys to the twins. "You're gonna be able take on a master soon enough." The twins smiled, trying not to look too pleased.

"Everyone," said Proculus, displaying Kyle, "this is SoGA's newest student, Kyle."

Everyone stood up, looking much friendlier to Kyle now that they weren't trying to kill him. They did give him inquisitive looks as though he was made from a different stock. Kyle suspected that they knew he was from another realm. He scratched his head, suddenly really nervous.

"Could I have my sword back?" asked Annie, stepping forward from the group. Her voice was timid, making Kyle feel guilty as he handed her the sword. He found it hard to believe that she had just been fighting with him. As she put away her swords, she asked him another question. "What's your full name?"

The group nodded in agreement, as if this was an important piece of information.

"Kyle De—more," stuttered Kyle.

"Kyle the More?" said Annie uncertainly. She obviously thought it was an odd full name. "The More?"

"No, D-e-more"

"Oh," said Annie. "Kyle D-e More. That is an odd name."

Proculus laughed warmly. "Kyle is from a realm where they do not have titles as we do. He has yet to earn a proper title so for now he will be known as Kyle the Tyro just as all you started. Understood?" They all whispered like teenagers, obviously thinking this was the weirdest thing they'd heard in a while, before Proculus demanded, "Understood?"

"Yes, Master," they replied in unison.

"Now, introduce yourselves."

Annie spoke first. "I am Annie the Second Blade. Nice to meet you."

The one with the spear and aquiline nose stepped forward. "I am Nero the Cyclone," he said with a nod.

"My name is Sabina the Mender," said a pale girl with curly mahogany hair.

"Name's Rufus the Dice," said a tall boy with a thick British accent.

"Malcolm the Ripple," said a lanky boy holding two whips.

"James the First Blade," said Annie's twin brother with an awkward smirk.

"I'm Kane the Ace," said a boy with spiky black hair as he sheathed his two daggers. He looked about the same age as Kyle, although he was a bit taller.

"Nice to meet you all," said Kyle. "I guess I'm Kyle the Tyro then." He scratched his head in embarrassment. Unsure of what else to say, he looked to Proculus.

"I must say," said the master, "I am impressed at how well you did. You were able to notice them before they came out of hiding. And it didn't look like James and Annie were holding back at all." He glanced at James and Annie, who simply shrugged as their eyes altered back and forth from Proculus to the ground.

Kyle exhaled deeply to relax himself. He was unsure of what to say, so he tried to change the subject. "Are we close to the school?"

"Just around the bend and you should see it from there."

"Master Proculus," said Nero, "may we head back now?"

"Yes, of course. Let's all get going"

"Wait!" It was Kane the Ace who spoke. "With your permission Master, I was hoping it would be okay to challenge Kyle to a duel."

"Now?" asked Proculus looking intrigued more than anything. Kane nodded. Proculus then turned to Kyle with raised eyebrows. "What do you say, Kyle?"

Kyle was unsure as to why Kane could possibly want to challenge him to a duel. Though Proculus had just mentioned that students often fought each other, he didn't expect to be experiencing it again so soon. He wondered if Ace was trying to make a fool out of him, but he didn't get that vibe. It felt more like simple curiosity. As he thought about what to do, he wanted nothing more than to say no, but part of him was also curious. He didn't want to be looked at as weak or soft. Of course, fighting someone who was bigger and looked to be much more experienced might accomplish that regardless. In the end, having everyone's eyes on him made him feel obligated.

"Sure," he finally said, instantly regretting it. The others moved away to give them room for the fight muttering with interest.

"Excellent," said Master Proculus as he joined the other students. "Weapons only. On my signal."

Kyle moved to face his opponent, who was now removing his daggers from his sheath. Kyle turned his sword in his hand and again exhaled deeply, trying to relax. With the long drag of breath that escaped him, his reservations became replaced by anticipation. As he concentrated on Kane, the world around them blended into a blur. Nothing had ever seemed so exciting to Kyle as this; to fight with his own power, relying on no one else. It helped knowing that he wouldn't really be killed now, but it wasn't just that. This felt exhilarating. It reverberated through him like it was his purpose. He almost smirked, but thought better of it.

"Begin!" yelled Proculus.

Without hesitation, they charged at each other. Kyle knew his sword had a longer reach than the Ace's daggers so he took the first swing, aiming for Kane's side. It was a powerful swing, but Kane had no problem using both daggers to defend against it. Kane then slid the daggers along Kyle's blade and rushed toward him to close the small gap between them. Kyle knew he was in trouble if he let his opponent get too close. He pushed off Kane's daggers with the sword, using the momentum to scramble away. Kane read the move and pursued.

Kane followed with accurate, powerful jabs aimed at Kyle's chest, shoulders, arms, and legs. It took all of Kyle's effort to defend against them, but it was hardly enough. Each blow was enough to make him feel as though he were deflecting bullets. The attack forced Kyle's back into a tree, causing him to panic and swing down haphazardly at Kane. It surprised Kane, forcing him to jump back to avoid the blade—just barely. Kyle was breathing hard now. The Ace, on the other hand, looked as though the fight hadn't started yet.

Suddenly, Kane threw his right dagger at Kyle. As his eyes focused on the flying blade, he knew it was a mistake. The dagger missed, but Kane used the distraction to disappear from his view. Kyle let his instincts take over, causing him to take a gamble and swing wildly to his left. When the sword smashed into the ground, causing dirt to fly into the air, he knew he had guessed wrong.

It was too late.

Kane wielded his dagger so fast, it sounded like it was slicing into the wind. It hit Kyle's shoulder with such a force that it knocked him to the ground to skid a few feet. The sting of the injury made his breathing even heavier, making it hard to stand. He expected the Ace to continue with his attack, but when his eyes found his opponent, Kane was walking over to him casually. The fight was over.

"Another excellent fight, Kyle," said Proculus happily. "But the win goes to Kane."

The single blow to his shoulder had been enough to win. Kyle almost wanted to argue the decision. It hardly felt fair that one hit ended the fight; however, the bruise on his shoulder reminded him that if the weapons hadn't been locked, the fight would have surely been over with bloodier results. A shiver ran down his spine, silencing any argument he might have offered.

"Good fight," said Kane as he reached him. He extended a hand.

"Thanks," said Kyle, shaking his hand. "Sorry I didn't put up much of a fight."

"You're kidding, right?" Kane chopped the air with his hand. "If I had gone to your left, you would have had me."

"It was just a guess." Kyle shrugged and chuckled. "A wrong guess."

"Most fights are guesses hidden under the guise of skill," joked Proculus. "Next time, guess better. Come now. We should be on our way."

Proculus led the group down the trail in the same direction that they had been heading before their encounter. The students chattered along the way, recounting their stories of the battle with their master and the duel that had just taken place. Kyle lingered behind the group with Kane the Ace.

"I hope there're no hard feelings about the duel," said Kane. He looked guilty. "Didn't mean to put you on the spot or anything. I guess I was just curious."

"Because I'm from another realm?"

"So you really are from another realm?"

"Yeah."

"What realm?"

"I don't know; we called it Earth." He remembered that Proculus had named four realms, but had never mentioned which one was Earth. He would have to figure that out later.

"Is it much different than here?" Kane asked. Kyle thought

about this for a little bit. Things didn't really seem all that different, but then again…

"Not as many swords," he said. "No magic keys either."

"No keys?" Kane asked, surprised.

"There are keys," Kyle explained. "But they can't open doors to other realms or make you teleport or anything."

"I see." The information looked like it intrigued Kane greatly. "Can you pull things out of nowhere like Master Proculus?"

"No," answered Kane. "But I'm pretty good at unlocking minds. I can read people's thoughts pretty well."

"You can read people's minds?"

"In a way." Kane went pink yet looked rather pleased. "It's no big deal, though."

"That's amazing." Kyle tried to say his next words with nonchalance, but in truth, it was a fear that been swelling in him like a balloon since he'd left his old realm. "I wouldn't be surprised if I am the worst student at SoGA. I've never used keys before. Well, not on purpose. And sword fighting is new to me, too."

"You won't be the worst. Your sword fighting is already pretty advance. It's better than half the academy already. Trust me, I should know."

Kyle seriously doubted it, but he appreciated Kane saying so. "Thanks."

Kyle then froze with surprise as they came around the bend.

"Is that Soul Gate Academy?"

"The one and only," Kane looked down the path with great fondness.

Standing behind high walls, in the brilliance of a setting sun, was a massive castle with twin towers at its side that reached for the sky. In the background was an ice blue ocean bringing in a pleasant sea breeze.

The entrance gate led to two rows of tall wooden statues of people carved to perfection. One wood carved man carried a great golden oak sword over his head. Another was of a woman with a bow and arrow. At least twenty of the sculptures lined up to the castle. Each looked taller and more magnificent than the last. Kyle even thought he saw one that looked like its hands were on fire.

Hedge bushes trimmed into shapes like triangles, keys, and other shapes and symbols foreign to Kyle were plentiful on the landscape. To the left of the castle was a luscious garden filled with ripe fruits and vegetables. There were also many trees that he had never seen before, some with blood red leaves, others with indigo leaves shaped like hands, and a single tall spiraling pine tree that looked like it was spinning. Thick emerald grass filled up the rest of the many acres enclosed within the walls and ocean. What interested him most were the people spread out across the Soul Gate Academy grounds, speckling the land with blue and black.

"We're going to be left behind." Kane beckoned Kyle to follow the rest of the group. "I wouldn't be surprised if Master Proculus locks the gate on us."

"Really?"

"Nah. Not really. Well maybe."

The two of them hurried to catch up.

By the time they reached the front gates, Proculus was taking out a key the size of Kyle's head. The massive key shined in a greenish-silver as his master drove it into a giant keyhole in the center of the gate. He turned it, causing a loud click to split the gate in two. As some of the group pushed the doors open, Kyle's eyesight became blurry. The world was spinning around him. With alarm, he reached for Proculus.

"Master Proculus," he said. "I…I'm real…ly slee—" He fell back, unable to complete his sentence.

"I think he fell asleep," said Kane the Ace loudly. He and the other students erupted into laughter.

It brought a smirk to Proculus's lips. He had wondered if Kyle would be able to make it to Soul Gate Academy. The young man had gone through a lot in one day, and it was hardly surprising to see him so worn out. After a quick check to make sure Kyle was in no danger, the master gestured for his students to continue on before he scooped up the young sleeper. The seven dispersed, some headed toward the castle, some helped close the gate, and others joined fellow tyros who were plentiful on the SoGA grounds. Some students, who were walking by, stopped in their tracks to glance at Master Proculus carrying Soul Gate Academy's newest tyro. A few greeted the Master, inquiring who was being carried into the academy, while others kept their curiosity silent. One girl even yelled, "Master Proculus, you should go easier on newbie tyros!" Those who heard her snickered.

"Welcome to Soul Gate Academy," he said to the sleeping boy who could not hear him.

CHAPTER SIX

THE READER

Kyle awoke in a large room as the afternoon sun shined in through the window standing high in the middle of a cloudy sky. He sat up to look around. The room had one window and many beds, but he was the room's only occupant. He imagined this must be some sort of hospital, as it was very clean and very white. However, he wondered why the academy needed so many beds for its hospital room. Suddenly, someone—something—walked into the room. Kyle nearly leaped off his bed. It was as if someone had mixed an owl with a small man. The white feathers covering his body dragged on the tile floors like a feathery lab coat. The small owl man had spiked neon orange colored feathers sticking out of his head as if someone had shown him how to use hair gel. He walked toward Kyle casually, hands in his feathery lab coat pockets. He had no neck and in the middle of his face was a large flat yellow beak that moved when he spoke. Eerily, he spoke in a voice that was just as human as Kyle's.

"Ah, he is awake," he called back to the room he had just come from. He spoke in a sophisticated yet slow voice. He turned to Kyle, looking jolly and bizarre mixed in one. "Had quite the sleep, didn't you?"

Kyle stiffened, unable to speak, unsure of whether to be scared or laugh.

"What is the matter with you? Never seen a Tytodwarf?"

Kyle shook his head.

"Ah, I see. How odd. Master Proculus did tell me you would be a bit odd. Ah, I suppose we are all a bit odd, are we not?" When all Kyle could do was blink rapidly, still having trouble registering what was in front of him, the owl man went on in a hushed voice, "Between you and I, I like being odd." He brought up his hand which was, of course, five long feathers which functioned exactly like human hands. He half blocked his face as if he was telling a secret to Kyle. "I mean, check out my cool hair."

At this, Kyle let out an awkward laugh.

"Odin," said a female voice outside the room, "how's he doin'?" A lady dressed exactly like Proculus, except she wore a long skirt rather than pants, walked in holding a clipboard. She was older than Proculus, and had a single gray streak in her brown hair that was tied tightly into a neat bun. She wore rectangular spectacles loosely on the tip of her nose.

"Ah, well, let's ask him," said Odin. "How are you doing?"

"I'm okay."

"Ah, he is okay, Master Yvette."

"Yeah, I heard him ya' old pigeon," said Yvette the Master.

"Ah, I believe you meant 'old owl,'" said Odin merrily. Kyle chuckled softly.

"I know what I meant, now get outta here and do something useful. I'll be taking this one down to the Reader if he's feelin' up to it."

"Ah, but of course. I bid you farewell, young Kyle the Tyro." The Tytodwarf walked out much like the way he walked in, with his feathery hands in his feathery pockets.

"Now let's see," said Yvette, looking at her clipboard. "You are Kyle the Tyro, correct?" Kyle nodded. She scribbled on her clipboard. Noticing his puzzled looked she answered a question before he even asked it. "Just doin' some of the necessary paperwork. Remember paperwork is very, very important. Wish I could get that point across to the Grandmaster, but ya don't need to worry 'bout that. Ah, let's see here. Master Proculus brought ya in three days ago."

"Three days ago?" blurted out Kyle.

"Yup, three days ago. I was told that it was your first time usin' keys, so really three days is nothing. First time I used my keys I was knocked out for a week. My mum thought I'd been locked into a coma. When I woke up she kept thanking the Gatekeepers for granting her a miracle." She shook her head, reminiscing on old memories as if they had taste. "Sweet ole mum, she believed the Gatekeepers made the sky rain and the flowers grow, whereas my Pops, he gave credit to some magical munchkins living in the depths of the earth. According to him, they'd come out every night to plan out the day. Crazy old coots, my parents." Laughing, she gave Kyle a kind smile.

Kyle smiled back clumsily, hardly understanding what she was talking about. Deciding to ignore it, he asked, "Where am I?"

"This is the Academy's Nursing Department and I am Master Yvette. Master Olivia and I are the Medical Masters. We rotate between running the Department and teaching class. I've been in charge of watchin' after ya, since Master Proculus dropped ya off."

"Oh." Kyle couldn't believe that he had spent the first three days in a new realm sleeping. He had slept through his birthday, not that it mattered much to him. He had never liked celebrating it. Still, it felt odd waking up to be fourteen. "Thank you for taking care of me, Master Yvette."

"Oh, jeez hun, don't mention it. Now, as I was saying. I am supposed to take ya right to the Reader, but first I'd like to ask you some questions.

"Questions?"

"Nothing too personal," said Master Yvette. "I just need to know your age and whether or not ya've been sick lately. We don't want anyone dying from some other world disease now, do we?

"Er, yes—I mean no. I don't want anyone to die." Kyle cleared his throat, feeling stupid as Yvette just smiled waiting for him to continue. "I'm thir—I mean fourteen and I haven't been sick in a long time."

"No coughs, sneezes, fevers, or random pains?"

Kyle shook his head.

"Excellent." Master Yvette wrote a few things down on her clipboard. "One last thing. When is your birthday?"

"December twenty-second."

"December?" repeated Yvette. "What does the Gatekeeper have to do with this? You sure you're feeling okay?"

"It was yesterday." Kyle had little clue as to what she meant about the Gatekeeper.

"Oh, then you meant Juniper twenty-second." Yvette finished scribbling on her clipboard. "Happy Birthday." *Juniper?*

"Thank you." Kyle scratched his head, feeling odd.

"I imagine you're a bit hungry, aren't ya?" Yvette's tone had changed. She sounded kinder, more motherly. It reminded Kyle strongly of Nana. "We can worry about getting ya to the Reader after ya get some food in ya."

"I am hungry," admitted Kyle as a small growl escaped his stomach. "But what is the Reader?"

"She's just the person who will tell ya what key abilities you're able to do. Every tyro goes through this so don't worry too much. Now, how 'bout that food."

Discovering which key abilities he'd be able to perform was as nerve-racking as it was thrilling. Proculus's ability to take swords out of the air was so beyond anything he could have imagined. Would he be able to do the same? What else could keys do? He was eager to find out, but another growl from his stomach momentarily pushed thoughts about the Reader from his mind.

Yvette took out a key, turning it in front of her. Kyle watched her intently as she reached into space next to the floating key to pull out a plate with a large warm roll and grilled chicken seasoned with garlic and parsley. His mouth watered as the air filled with the savory food's smell.

"There ya are," she said. "Eat up, then get dressed. When ya finish, we'll get goin'."

Kyle gulped down the delicious food then dressed into the clean uniform at the end of his bed. Feeling revitalized, he left the room to find Master Yvette writing intently at an organized desk stacked with papers in the next room over. He didn't want to interrupt her, so he waited quietly. A moment later, Odin walked in from the hallway, delightedly clicking his beak.

"Ah, Master," said Odin, ignoring Kyle. "I have informed Master

Proculus that Kyle has awoken. He said he will be there to meet him at the Reader's room."

"Good," said Yvette without looking up. "If ya want, go check on Kyle again. He's probably close to being done by now."

"Ah, yes of course." Without skipping a beat, he turned to Kyle. "Hello again, young man. Have you come to this room in hopes of checking out my hair? Ah, well you may look, but please do not touch." Kyle couldn't help but grin; the Tytodwarf was the most bizarre thing he had ever met.

"Wha," said Yvette, looking up. She was surprised to see Kyle standing in the doorway. "Sorry, I didn't notice ya, you're quiet on your feet, ya know that? Didn't even hear you get outta the bed. Next time just hit me on the head er something."

"I didn't want to bother you," muttered Kyle. "Thank you for the meal, Master."

"Not a problem, kiddo. Well if you're done, the Reader will be wantin' to see ya. Let's not keep her waitin'." She stood up, signaling Kyle to follow her, which he did.

"Bye," Kyle said awkwardly to the strange creature.

"Ah, goodbye," he replied dramatically. "Should you ever want to have hair like mine, please come visit me."

"No one wants hair like yours, ya old bat," said Yvette.

"Ah, I believe you meant 'old owl!'"

Kyle wasn't sure what he had expected to see in the castle, but as they walked down the hallway he was surprised to find an elevator. Master Yvette pushed the single button outside the sliding doors which caused them to open. They stepped in and Kyle was letdown at the normality of it. His disappointment vanished when he saw four rows of keys stuck inside keyholes instead of numbered buttons to each floor. To the right of each key was a different label. A few read "Dining Hall," "Grandmaster's Office," and "Nursing Department." There was only one keyhole that did not have a key in it already. It was labeled, "Reader."

"Why isn't a key inside it already?" asked Kyle.

"This floor is normally off-limits," answered Yvette. "Visiting for a reading is the exception, of course." She pulled out a small pink key, placing it into the empty keyhole. She gave the key a full turn before returning it to her pocket. In an instant, the elevator doors opened up into a small corridor that smelled strongly of lavender. Master Yvette moved into the different hallway without missing a beat. Kyle, on the other hand, was left in awe by the abruptness.

"Something wrong?" Yvette asked when she noticed he hadn't followed her. "Are ya sure you're feeling well?"

"Yeah—thanks, I'm fine," said Kyle. "How did the elevator just open up into a new place without moving?"

"It's a modified application of ShiftDoors. I don't imagine ya understand any of that, but basically it's like instant transportation. Same principle you and Proculus used to get to Endera."

"I thought Master Proculus said you couldn't open ShiftDoors within the academy's boundaries."

"That's true, but this method is different. The elevator itself is mixed with the specially modified keys, creating an exception that applies only within the elevator. Ya might have to wait till ya get to class 'till this makes much sense. Are elevators that interesting to ya?"

"Not really. It's just the elevators only moved up or down to change floors in my realm."

"Sounds boring," she said blatantly. "Well, come on, I don't want to stay here all day."

Kyle followed her down the short corridor which opened up into a small room. The familiar laugh of Master Proculus became louder as they came closer. For the first time since he'd woken up, he felt reassured that this whole experience wasn't a lengthy dream of his overactive imagination. The last thing he wanted was to wake up only to be back in Mr. Lindshell's classroom.

The room ahead was brightly lit and round, furnished with a handsome seat in the middle and large fireplace full of purple fire. The ceilings curved toward the center like a dome. Large windows, taking up most of the wall, were decorated with ancient-looking symbols that had been carved into the glass itself. Outside the windows, Kyle saw clouds close enough to touch with his hands. He had never been afraid of heights, but the surprise of being so high gave him a uneasy feeling that made him look down to the floor, which was fluffy and pink. Yvette stopped him just before they entered.

"Take off your shoes," she said. "Readers tend to be finicky about their carpet."

"Umm, yes Master." Kyle removed his shoes, placing them next to what he guessed were Proculus's large shoes.

"Reader, the young tyro has just arrived," said Proculus as he gave a slight bow. "It is an honor to meet you and I hope you pardon me for not coming by sooner."

"Think nothing of it, Master Proculus," said the soft voice of a young lady.

"Kyle," said Proculus. "Come here and introduce yourself to the Reader."

"Yes, Master," said Kyle. Unsure of what to expect, he walked briskly over to sit next to Master Proculus. Yvette followed, greeting Proculus before turning to the Reader. To Kyle's surprise, a girl sat in the large comfy chair with her legs crossed. Except for her overshadowed eyes and mouth, her face was completely covered by a simple white mask. She wore a white hooded robe covered in magenta colored symbols that decorated the robe like vines around a tree. By the sound of her voice, Kyle guessed she couldn't be much older than him, but since the robe hid all her features, he couldn't be certain. Next to the Reader sat a small glossy wooden case that gleamed in the sunlight. Kyle was unsure if he should say anything. Luckily, Master Yvette spoke for him.

"Hello, Reader," said Master Yvette. "This one's name is Kyle the Tyro." Kyle waved toward her with a rigid motion.

"The one from the other realm?" She eyed Kyle curiously. Master Yvette nodded. "I see. Kyle, do you know why you are here?"

"To find out my key abilities?"

"Yes," she said before further elaborating. "It's traditional for readers, such as myself, to place the students in four to five classes that match their abilities best, not including weaponry and history. You can of course choose what classes to take, but with each added class you must prove you can use that key ability. It is extremely difficult. This reading allows us to see your natural affinities. Classes you most certainly will be able to do. Does that make sense?"

"So," said Kyle, piecing together what she had just told him, "you're giving me my schedule?"

"Yes, that is the gist of it." She giggled, making Kyle smirk in return. "To do this, I will unlock the deepest part of your mind. Your mind has areas which are vastly uncharted, but that does not mean it is incomprehensible. Within its depths lie answers to who you were, who you are, who you want to be, and who you will become. Readers have the power to find this sacred information, which is normally unknown or yet to be discovered. In doing this, I will be able to assign the appropriate classes which you will take, along with weaponry and history, for no more than seven classes. If all goes well, the key abilities I find you to be proficient in will lead to maximum growth here at Soul Gate Academy. I hope that makes things clear?"

"Yeah, I think so." He shifted nervously. It all sounded somewhat invasive to Kyle, but he didn't think he should raise objections before he was even given his class schedule.

"Good," she said. "Now, we should just wait for—"

As if on cue, a thin old man with salt and pepper hair stood at the doorway trying to look impressive. "Good afternoon," he said in a theatric voice. He pointed his wooden cane at the sky much like a baseball player does when calling a homerun. Like the masters, he wore white pants and shirt, but his vest was a bright gold. His nose was crooked and his five o'clock shadow looked like it was minutes away from turning into a beard. "The Soul Gate Academy Grandmaster has arrived!" He was much beyond anything Kyle had expected, but he had to admit that this old man carried himself with a certain whimsy impressiveness that proved he was in charge.

"Grandmaster Dante," said the Reader as she, Proculus, and Yvette stood from their seats. Kyle gawped as he stood with them. "Nice of you to join us."

"Oho, thanks for having me," said the Grandmaster as he eyed Kyle. Kyle looked at the floor, unsure what to do in the presence of the Grandmaster. "What do we have here? The boy from another realm? Are you destined to be the new shining star of SoGA? What say you, young man?"

Kyle felt like sinking into his chair to disappear forever. Keys still felt like such a mystery to him that he was certain he wouldn't be the shining star of SoGA any time soon. He certainly hoped that it wasn't expected of him.

"Grandmaster," said Proculus, grinning profusely, "shall I get you a chair?"

"No need, no need." Grandmaster Dante casually walked to where the four of them stood. As he did, he twisted his cane, which made a chair as comfy looking as the Reader's rapidly sprout from the floor like a tree. As he sat down, he motioned to the others to do the same. "Now that we're all comfortable, let's do some introductions. This one doesn't even know who I am. But you first young man, please tell me who are you?"

"Umm," said Kyle feebly. "I'm—"

"Speak up," said the Grandmaster. "I want to hear some power behind your voice."

"My name is Kyle Demore." He paused. "Sorry, I mean Kyle the Tyro."

"Excellent! Kyle the Tyro, I like it! Addressing yourself with your title will become second nature soon enough," said the Grandmaster enthusiastically. "You will address me as Grandmaster Dante, but as for my title, I have many. Dante the Magnificent or Dante the Awesome are two of my more popular ones. The ladies like to call me Dante the Handso—"

"Grandmaster," interrupted Yvette with a stern look, "don't start off with tellin' tall tales. The poor boy just got here."

"Oho!" Dante exclaimed. "This is what it's like to have the wife at work." He winked at Kyle.

"You two are married?" Kyle asked before he could stop himself. "I'm sorry, I didn't—"

"We are," sighed Master Yvette. "Grandmaster Dante does

like to tell the truth occasionally." The Grandmaster smiled widely, signaling Kyle with a childish thumb up. "Stop it, ya old fool. Get serious." Although Yvette tried to have a strict tone, she let a chuckle escape her. Kyle was reminded of when Nana and Paps would tease each other.

"Right," said the Grandmaster. "No need to be nervous, Kyle. We're just here to make sure everything goes well. We won't be part of the process. Whenever you're ready, Reader?"

"Yes, of course," she said. Kyle wasn't sure, but he thought she seemed a little nervous. She stood up, grabbed the little case, and walked over to stand directly in front of Kyle. "Master Proculus could you hold this for me—thank you. Now let's see, this will be my first reading so please bear with me."

"That's okay," said Kyle while scratching his head. "This is my first reading, too." He wasn't sure, but he thought he saw that Reader's lips form into a smile underneath her mask.

"You'll have to stop scratching your head," she said. Kyle stopped immediately. She opened the case that Proculus held. There were five simple silver keys inside. She grabbed the middle one then turned to Kyle. "Now, you will have to stay still as I do this. When I became a reader, they had me undergo a reading, so I know what you'll experience. You might feel a slight tingle, but it's completely painless, I promise." After Kyle nodded, she stated, "Here we go."

The Reader positioned the key precisely to the center of Kyle's forehead. It stayed stuck as if it were glued. She repeated the process with the other four keys, fixing them on four other spots on his head. After all five keys were placed, he did in fact feel a slight tingle.

He expected her to begin turning the keys, but instead she rolled the sleeves of her robe back to reveal to long slender arms that were also covered in the same mysterious writing that was on the robe. Kyle eyed her carefully as she ran her right index finger in a straight line down her left forearm. As her finger slid closer to her hand, the tattooed symbols began to glow pink. She alternated arms, repeating the movement on her other arm so when she finished, both her arms glowed. The Reader then positioned one of her hands close enough to his lips that he could have leaned forward to kiss it. It made him feel warm around the neck.

"For me to properly read you, I need you to bite my hand," said the Reader.

"What?"

"You have to bite me," she repeated. "It is part of the process. A reader must connect to the book and the book must connect to the reader."

"What does that have to do with me biting you?"

"If you bite me, my pain will be directly linked to you. To put it simply, it is the easiest way for us to connect. There are other more… intimate methods, but it wouldn't be appropriate."

Kyle was sure his face went red with embarrassment. He had gone along with everything that had been expected of him so far, but he couldn't bite someone. He certainly couldn't bite a girl who was simply trying to do her job. It just seemed so barbaric and wrong.

"Can't I just pinch you or something?" he asked, hoping for a loophole.

"It has to be deeper than that," she said. "When you bite, it must break skin and draw blood." This made things final for Kyle.

"I'm not going to bite you," he said firmly.

"You found us quite a stubborn Tyro didn't you, Master Proculus?" said Dante sounding delighted. "Just like you if I remember correctly?"

"You must do as she asks, Kyle," said Master Proculus, kindly ignoring the Grandmaster's jibe. "We all had to do this when we were younger."

"You all bit her?" His eyebrows crashed into his hairline. "Are you all vampires or something?"

"Oho, vampires?" Dante guffawed hard. "As in Dracula the Vampire? I'm surprised you know such an old legend." He laughed again. This puzzled Kyle, but he didn't want to be sidetracked. "Of course we didn't bite her. We experienced this discomfort with other readers from our time."

"There has to be another way," Kyle frowned, trying to think some way out of this ritual.

"There is always a choice, I suppose," said Dante. "What do you think, Reader?"

"I can reverse the position, but Kyle will have to be the one to be bitten and it might be—uncomfortable."

"We'll do that," Kyle let out a breath of relief. "I'd much rather be bitten than—well—the other way."

Her eyes narrowed beneath the mask, delivering to Kyle a piercing look that felt oddly familiar yet completely new. He returned the stare without hesitation, hoping to demonstrate his unmoving position on the matter.

"Fine," she said suddenly. "You must do exactly as I say, then." She explained to him what he needed to do, which he immediately agreed to.

When the Reader gave him the nod to proceed, Kyle brought his right hand up to his mouth, turning it enough so that he could bite the section underneath his pinky finger. He bit down hard, but it wasn't nearly enough. It needed to break skin. He bit again with more force, causing a pain to shoot up his arm, but this time warm salty blood spilled into his mouth.

As the blood slithered down his arm, he gave his hand to the Reader. She immediately took it, lifted her mask enough only to expose her mouth, and bit down on it hard. He expected the same pain to shoot up his arm again, but this was different. His whole arm went numb. Still, he wanted to rip his arm away from her mouth but he could not. It was as though a giant weight had been pressed down on him. He tried to cry out for help, but couldn't make a sound.

That was when things really got weird.

The whole room began to dissolve into grains of sand, which swirled into a whirlpool of colors. When the strange storm suddenly stopped, he was deep in the middle of a forest, breathing hard. Menacing growls came from behind, making him sprint the opposite direction with all his might. Shooting a look over his shoulders, he saw a pack of grey wolves chasing him with ravenous hunger in their eyes, but before they could reach him, the scene began to dissolve again. The forest and the wolves blended into a mixture of grey and green.

As the second swirl slowed, the scene changed again. A man was resting up against a tree, eating an apple and humming a foreign tune. The stranger finished his meal, tossing its core toward Kyle. As it rolled toward him, the tree came to life, lowering a branch full of fresh supple apples, offering the man another. Autumn leaves rained down in a heavy torrent before swirling around him like a colorful tornado.

Kyle blinked, finding himself in another place completely. He was walking along a shoreline with the chilly ocean splashing against his feet. In the distance, a little girl with black hair skipped toward him. He felt happier than he ever had in his life—but she disintegrated into the wind. He wanted to chase after her, but a wall of water crashed down, walloping him with the force of a bus.

He was dragged into the depths of the sea. Falling into the darkness, he held his breath. He gasped, expecting water to fill his lungs, but bitter air filled them instead. The water had disappeared, but the darkness had stayed with him. It felt cruel, like he'd never feel happiness again. When all hope was lost, he heard the panicked voice of a woman whisper, "Kyle, are you there? Kyle?"

The room came back as suddenly as it had disappeared. He blinked rapidly, unsure of what had just happened. The Reader's blood red lips were still connected to his hand. She released him, wiping the blood with her forearm before placing her mask back on properly.

"What just happened?" Never had he felt fear like this. It was cold, brutal, and terribly real. He wished he had just bitten her.

"I don't know." Her eyes shook beneath the mask. The vision had left an impression on her also. "Perhaps things to come. Perhaps things that have already come to be. When one normally bites the reader, the process of diving into the mind is omitted. When it is reversed, we both get a peek into something which is not fully understood. It would be wise for you to forget what you saw. People have gone mad trying to figure out what is impossible to decipher."

"I'll try to keep that in mind." It didn't come out of him with confidence. The woman's whisper still rang through his mind, echoing like thunder in a valley. He tried to get his mind off it by asking, "Did it work?"

"It did. I can read you now."

"Great." He let sarcasm rule the words. He hadn't exactly enjoyed the first part.

"Right. Here we go."

She turned the key on his right temple. After a second, he heard a soft click, and she pulled the key away from his head. As she did this, symbols made out of glowing yellow light followed the key out of his head. It was all illegible to Kyle, who tried to keep still but wanted to leap from his chair when he saw light being dragged from his head. He wished they'd warned him about these types of occurrences. The Reader, who had clearly been expecting this, read the symbols before they disappeared.

"Hmm, the first is Amplifications." She handed the key to Proculus, who placed it back into the case. Master Yvette scribbled onto her clipboard while the Reader continued to pull out the others. "The second is AuraBending—third is PsyBending—fourth is MicroDimensions, to which Proculus whispered, "Excellent," and the fifth is…"

She slid the fifth key away from the middle of his forehead, and the yellow light looked different. It shook as if it were having a hard time staying in one spot. It began zapping and wiggling like live electricity.

"The fifth is Synchroneity."

As she said this, the light couldn't contain itself. It shot into the air, an electric, zigzagging snake, making a loud clap like thunder. The Reader fell back with a stifled scream, landing on the floor. "Oh dear, that was unexpected."

The light left a hazy imprint in the air. For some reason, yellow lightning shooting from his head had not fazed Kyle; in truth, it seemed quite natural to him. *Synchroneity, I think I might like that one.* The laughter escaping from the three masters suggested that they found the whole matter comical rather than surprising.

"Sorry," Kyle said as he ruffled up his hair. He hadn't meant to shoot lightning from his head, but it still seemed right to apologize.

"It's okay." The Reader brushed herself off as she stood up. Her hood fell, exposing beautiful long red hair that fell over her white mask. She hurriedly placed it back over her head, shoving her hair back into the hood. "It's not your fault, but you're scratching your head again."

Kyle didn't know if it was because of the way she said "you're scratching your head again," or her distinct red hair, but he instantly knew the identity of the Reader hidden behind the mask.

"Garnet?" It felt like ages since he had spoken her name. "Garnet, is that you?"

"Garnet?" repeated the Reader. "Garnet?" Then all of a sudden, she fell to her knees, throwing her head back as she let out a heart-stabbing scream. Scarlet light beamed from her eyes and mouth, even cracking through the white mask. Malicious heat emitted from the Reader like a volcano about to erupt.

It all happened so fast, Kyle was nearly burned by the emanating heat. Fortunately, Master Proculus was quick to act. He grabbed Kyle and yanked him back to safety while Grandmaster Dante turned his cane, causing the floor to encase the Reader inside a protective box. Having jumped to safety also, Yvette stood with key in hand, ready to help.

Kyle watched in horror as the Reader screamed like she was being tormented. He tried to run forward to do something, anything to help, but Proculus kept him firmly in place. "Wait," Proculus ordered.

The screaming stopped and so did Kyle's heart. *Is she..?* Another turn of the Grandmaster's cane and the carpet set itself back in place, though it was now burned to a black crisp. Smoke trailed away from the Reader as she collapsed to the floor with a soft thud, unconscious. The mask shattered like glass on impact, finally revealing that Kyle was correct.

The Reader was his friend, Garnet Nemos.

"Garnet!" Kyle screamed, trying to break away from Proculus. "Please, I have to help her!"

Proculus's grip remained true but Yvette leaped into action, moving closer to the fallen Reader. Beneath the tattered, torn, and singed remains of her robe, Garnet was breathing violently. Burn marks the size of bottle caps riddled her body. Her arms were no longer glowing with pink symbols, but bloodied as if they'd been sent through a shredder. Other cuts and gashes made it look like she had been attacked by a lion. The blood from them was already soaking into the carpet. Yvette lost no time in closing up wounds with each turn of her key.

The Grandmaster had also leaped into action, turning and sliding his cane in such rapid motions that it looked like one fluid movement. Suddenly, the elevator that had been down the hall crashed into the room.

"Yvette, I'll move her in," said Dante. "Let's get her to the nursing department."

With a nod, Yvette backed away from her patient. The carpet underneath Garnet lifted her up to waist level before moving her carefully into the elevator as though she were lying on a conveyor belt. Yvette and Dante followed in haste and the doors shut behind them.

Kyle doubled his efforts to get away from Proculus. "Let me go," he growled. "We need to follow them."

"We will," Proculus grabbed him by the shoulders. "But first you need to settle down."

"We have to help her! That's Garnet. She's my friend. Let me go!"

"How do you expect to help her?" bellowed Proculus. "Master Yvette will do all she can and you will not interfere, or I swear to the Gatekeepers, I'll lock you up until the full moons."

Kyle's head sunk in shame. He knew he'd gone too far. Garnet was beyond any help he could offer. He would have to trust Master Yvette and the Grandmaster to aid her back to health.

"Sorry," Kyle mumbled. "I didn't mean to—"

"You must learn to control yourself, Kyle," Proculus cut in. "Now will you be able to do that?"

"Yes," Kyle answered at once.

"Good. Follow me."

Proculus finally released him and they hurried to the elevator that was still in the middle of the room. Proculus turned the key to the Nursing Department and they arrived there instantly. Kyle nearly ran down the hallway to the long room where he'd woken up earlier. Dante and Yvette were calmly using their keys in valiant efforts to heal Garnet, who was laying in one of the many beds.

He slowed down as he neared the bed. Garnet looked notably better but was still unconscious. He tried to make sense of what had happened. *All I did was say her name.* He thought he'd never see Garnet again, but here she was in front of him. Unconscious, but still the Garnet he knew. Something was different about her, though. Now that he looked closely, he could see that she was almost as tall as him. Her face looked more mature, her body more womanly. He didn't understand. It had only been a few days since he had last seen her. How could she have changed so much?

"Garnet?" he whispered, "Is that really you?"

As though she was reacting to his question, blinding white light began to surround her. Kyle thought Dante and Yvette were the cause of this, but by their stunned looks and cautious steps back, he knew they were just as surprised as him. The light began condensing into her body like it was being sucked in by a vacuum. Garnet's bed shook as the light became smaller and smaller. With one final surge, it vanished. All was still.

For the second time, Kyle's heart stopped.

No one prevented him this time as he moved closer to his motionless friend. He expected her chest to be rhythmically rising and falling, but there was nothing. His throat felt like it was being squeezed shut. He tried to swallow but couldn't.

"Kyle." Yvette reached out for him but Dante stopped her.

"Wait," Dante told her.

Kyle made it to her bedside, feeling like the blood had frozen in his veins. He reached out to touch her; to make sure, when suddenly Garnet gasped in search of breath as though she were returning to the surface after a deep dive into the ocean. Her eyelids opened, but only the white of her eyes showed. Before Kyle could react, she grabbed his left hand, drawing it to her mouth. Knowing what she was about to do, he tried to pull away. It was too late. She bit down with impressive power, breaking his skin to erupt in blood.

"Ah!" yelled Kyle in pain. She released him.

A moment later, the gem blue of Garnet's eyes returned.

"Kyle?" she said dazedly. "Kyle!"

CHAPTER SEVEN

THE NEWEST TYRO

"This has to be some kind of record," said Grandmaster Dante quietly.

"I believe so," agreed Proculus.

"I've never heard of the reader's name causing such a violent reaction."

"The fact that she was a new reader must have something to do with it."

"That seems to be the logical explanation. I wonder if…"

Proculus and Dante continued talking as they left the room. Garnet had healed abnormally fast, which concerned Master Yvette rather than relieved her. She was in the process of her second complete examination, pressing her key on various points across Garnet's body and stopping occasionally to scribble comments on her clipboard. Kyle watched with overwhelming curiosity. He had visited doctors various times throughout his life, but this was different. There were no other tools involved except for her key. Each turn and slide of the key had a purpose that was totally lost to Kyle, but he knew that every part of it made perfect sense to the master.

It all confirmed to him that his friend from Grayling had indeed undergone notable changes. Certain curves, which had not been so profound, were one of the particular things he noticed. Suddenly aware that his curiosity might be seen as intrusive, his face began to burn like a lantern. He tore his eyes away to stare at the floor, grateful Garnet was too busy being examined to notice.

"All the damage seems to be gone," Yvette frowned as she looked over her notes. "Are ya sure you're feelin' alright?"

"I feel perfectly fine," said Garnet.

"I still want ya to rest," Master Yvette planted her hands on her hips firmly. "With the damage ya had earlier, ya should be in bed for a week."

"I really am okay. I promise."

"We'll keep ya under watch for a while just to make sure. Need anything else then?"

"Kyle's hands are still—"

"I knew I was forgetting something." Yvette turned to Kyle. He had been quietly sitting next to them. "I imagine ya'd try to keep a sword in the chest quiet if ya could."

"I didn't think it was a big deal," His hands did hurt, but he didn't mind waiting. "Garnet needed to be looked at first."

"Yes, yes," she moved over to Kyle. "You men are always so considerate. Let me see 'em."

Kyle lifted his hands, which were caked with dry blood. Yvette pressed her key against his hands so timidly that he barely felt it. With a couple turns, the bite wounds were completely gone. She cleaned up the dry blood with another turn. He squeezed his hand in disbelief. It looked and felt as good as new.

"Excellent." Yvette was evidently pleased with her work. She turned back to Garnet. "Now once we figure out what we're gonna do with ya, we'll go from there. For now, ya stay in that bed."

"What *is* going to happen to me?" asked Garnet miserably.

"I'm not sure hun, but if I know my husband, he's in the other room figuring that out as we speak. He might not look it on the outside, but Dante knows what he's doing."

"I don't want to trouble all of you."

"Oh hush. Ya served Soul Gate Academy. No matter for how short a time, ya served us. We help those who help us. Simple as that."

"But—"

"I won't hear another word about it. Relax and talk with Kyle here. I'm sure ya both have some catching up to do." Without another word, she left to join Proculus and Dante in the other room.

"Thank you," Garnet whispered. She looked like she was going to cry but then thought better of it. After closing her eyes, she took a deep breath. With its release, she controlled her tears.

"I'd ask if you were really okay, but I know you're not," said Kyle. It wasn't meant to be funny, yet Garnet burst out in laughter. It felt immensely good to hear the sound. Kyle relaxed at once.

"You're different," said Garnet. "Has this realm changed you so much already?"

"Me?" Kyle raised his eyebrows in disbelief. "You're one to talk. I mean look at you. You're completely different from a few days ago."

"That's because it hasn't been a few days for me, Kyle."

"What do you mean?"

She sighed, looking unsure of herself. "It's been two years."

"Two years? Garnet, that's not possible."

"It is possible. You'll learn this soon enough, but there are infinite amounts of dimensions, Kyle. Some are used to store weapons, others are the housing world for summons; the uses go on, unlimited. Why would all of them have to run time the same way? These dimensions are part of no realm, part of no world, part of no nation. The Readers control many of them, one of which was created by someone known as the Timekeeper. Time runs quicker in that place. It's all a mess of knotted thread in my mind now, but I was in there for two years training to become what I am now: a failure."

"You're not a failure."

"Oh? Then what am I?"

"You're Garnet."

"That's cheesy."

"Maybe," said Kyle, unembarrassed. "I still don't really get it."

"How else can I explain it to you?"

"Why does hearing your name take away your powers?"

She chuckled. "You know so little, Kyle Demore."

"Then explain it to me." Kyle put a bite into his words.

"Don't get mad. I didn't mean it like that." She moved in her bed, her mind busy at work. "You see, it's not about hearing my name." She let out a long sigh. "I think it's best if I start at the beginning. The day you disappeared in Mr. Lindshell's class, a reader came to visit me. I was the only one to notice you vanish into nothing. It freaked me out. I tried to scream for help, but then everything just froze in place. It scared me enough to make me think the world was going to end. A Reader appeared before asking me to go with him to the Reader's First Dimension. I said yes right away. I'm still not sure why I went or why they chose me.

"When I arrived, I was greeted almost like royalty. It was like I was returning home after a very long absence." She began running her hands through her hair. Her fingers looked like blades running through a sheet of fierce red silk. "I was given the introduction into what I would become: a reader for the realm of keys. It's not something I can really explain. Even if I was still a reader, the words wouldn't come to me. All I can tell you is that it was purpose, destiny, fate; whatever you want to call it. I couldn't say no. It came at a price, though. I had to give up every part of who I was and who I would become.

"I gave them one condition, which surprised them, but they agreed to it easily enough. I wanted to say goodbye to you. Maybe that's what screwed everything up. You, and everyone else, were supposed to forget me. That should have wiped Garnet Nemos from existence. After I…said goodbye…"

Both of them diverted their eyes from each other as though it would lessen the embarrassment of the memory. After a moment, she continued, "…I was immediately put to my training. Over time, I forgot who you were, I forgot who I was. It was part of the progression. I learned the secrets of the realm, the old and new, the beginning and the end. When I finished, I was a reader as good as any other. All memories of my former self were locked away deep in my mind. I would have remembered eventually, but only after a long time.

"So you see, hearing my name isn't the problem. If that were the case, anyone could just yell names at random and guess the names of readers with enough time. You remembered me. You remembered who I was. I still meant something to you, Kyle. It shattered the lock my training had spent two years setting up. Memories returned to me, others left me, forcing my reader abilities to diminish."

"So all of that is gone?" asked Kyle, feeling guiltier by the second.

"It's not all gone," she answered. "There are still remnants lingering. I remember the recent things, like performing your reading. I still remember the old stuff from when we lived in another realm. It's the in-between that's a mess. They're like memories from someone else's perspective. They keep coming and going. I'm not exactly sure what it means."

"You probably hate me now, huh?"

"How can I? It's not like you knew any better. Anyone would have done the same."

"Still, if I could take it back I would. I really am sorry."

Garnet looked more hurt than touched by this. "You want to be rid of me so soon?"

"That's not what I—"

"It doesn't matter. It's done and there's nothing we can do about it."

Kyle wanted to say more but was temporarily lost for words. It was the sort of situation where nothing he could say would rectify his wrongdoings, no matter how accidental they were. "So you're fifteen now?"

"Yep," she answered, looking happy to talk about something else. "Older than you. How does it feel?"

"Weird." Kyle grinned. "But you've always acted like you were older than me. Plus it's only a year."

Her gem blue eyes found Kyle's, and he was pleased to see a smile in them. There was no doubt that things would be different between them, but they were still friends. That was something worth cherishing.

"So what's going to happen now?" asked Kyle.

"I really don't know. This is all such a mess." She rubbed her temples, looking strained.

"As to that, I believe I have come up with a suitable solution." Grandmaster Dante walked into the room looking quite pleased. "Really quite a simple solution if you think about it. I thought we could think of something with more flair, but alas we'll—"

"Get on with it," said Yvette, trailing behind him. Proculus was close behind her. "Don't make a fuss out of it."

"Oho, of course, dear." He glanced at his wife with a playful smile before facing Garnet. "It is my understanding that it is quite impossible for you to return to being a reader. We will contact the Reader's Headquarters to make certain, but I know some of the old laws. The readers won't allow you to return to their ways. Do you agree with this assumption?"

"Yes." Garnet nodded. "I'm certain you're right."

"Then I would like to propose that you stay here as a tyro. You meant to serve this academy as a reader, so I think you would be more than qualified to serve here as a student. The decision is entirely up to you."

"Stay here as a student?"

"I think Garnet the Tyro sounds splendid, doesn't it Kyle?"

"Yeah," said Kyle, who was happy at the idea of Garnet staying.

"I—you," Garnet stuttered. "Are you sure?"

"Entirely."

"I'd be honored, Grandmaster." Garnet gave a respectful half bow to accept.

"Excellent!" Dante clapped his hands together. "It would seem there is much to be done, then. Yvette feels strongly that you should remain in bed, so I will heed her advice. You are to remain here until she says otherwise. Kyle, on the other hand, has some other obligations. He has yet to see all of Soul Gate Academy properly and seeing as class is going to start, I think it's important he learn his way around."

"I think I should stay here, Grandmaster," said Kyle.

"I thought you would say as much," said Dante, smiling. "However, I believe there will be a need for privacy. Yvette mentioned her needs to examine Garnet a little more closely."

"Oh," said Kyle. "Umm—but—"

"It's okay, Kyle," said Garnet. "You should go check the school out. You're still the newest person here. You'll get lost if you don't figure this place out."

"I just—"

"Kyle," she said a little more forcefully, "I'm fine. Go, okay?"

He knew there was no use in arguing. She did look well and he had to admit that he was dying to see the rest of the school. "All right. I guess I'll go look around."

"Excellent," Dante said again. "There's one thing I'd like to add though. We think that it might be better keep the fact that Garnet was a reader a secret." He looked at Kyle.

"Um, why?" asked Kyle. "Is it bad?"

"Not at all," answered Dante. "In truth, it's the opposite. People are especially interested in the minds of readers. Best to keep this quiet and save ourselves from unwanted trouble."

"Is someone going to try and dissect her brain or something?" said Kyle half-jokingly.

"Kidnapping is the more likely scenario," Dante drummed his

fingers over the top of his cane. "Not very likely, but possible. We can avoid that problem all together by never telling anyone she was a reader. Understood?"

"I don't want to be a burden," Garnet seemed to sink into her bed. "It's a good idea, but I don't want to put any pressure on all of you."

"Nonsense," said Dante. "We're all quite capable, Garnet. I'm sure now that Kyle understands the situation, he will be more than willing to comply."

"I won't say a thing to anyone," said Kyle.

"There you have it."

Garnet didn't look overly pleased, but she knew there was little else to say on the matter. It was for her wellbeing, after all. She muttered, "thank you."

"We should be off, then," said Dante. "I leave Garnet to you, Master Yvette."

Yvette rolled her eyes in a lighthearted way.

"One last thing," said Proculus, turning to Kyle. "Is this the girl you mentioned from your dream?"

Kyle's felt his face redden as he shot the master a look that begged him to say no more. Proculus guffawed with all the dignity of a bear.

Garnet's face also became a lovely shade of pink.

Dante, Proculus, and Kyle left the Nursing Department, making their way to the elevator.

"Will she be okay?" Kyle asked Dante.

"She'll be fine, young man. Master Yvette is one of the best Enderians to ever hold a key. Her eternal title is Yvette the Harmony and she has personally brought me back from the dead once or twice.

She's not too bad on the eyes, either," he added.

"I believe the count is at three, Grandmaster."

"Ah, well. What's life if you don't put it on the line sometimes, huh?"

Both men laughed.

"Okay," said Kyle unsure if they were joking or not.

"I think Kross should be waiting for us at the Entrance by now," said Dante.

"More than likely," Proculus agreed. "He's not one for being late."

"Kross?"

"A fellow tyro," said Dante. "A second year we asked to show you around."

"You're not going to?"

"That had been the plan," Dante opened the elevator, "but certain circumstances have called our attention elsewhere. Kross is more than qualified to show you around."

They entered the elevator and Proculus turned the key labeled "Entrance" as the doors slid shut behind them. When it opened a second later, they walked into a magnificent lobby. A crystal chandelier hung high above. Couches and tables were spread throughout the room. Students filled the seats, lounging and buzzing with gossip. Many of them greeted the Grandmaster and Master Proculus, while others kept their distance, looking more interested in Kyle. Mutters of "other realm" began circulating the room. Kyle did his best to look nonchalant, but he felt overly stiff.

They walked toward a great circular fountain in the middle of the large lobby. In the pool's center was an enormous triangular prism that had been engraved to look like three stone doors which stood back to back. Rather than gushing water like a normal fountain, water emerged from in between the three stone doors, splitting into three floating rivers that swirled, zigzagged, and waved through the air before falling gently into the pool. Kyle had to stop himself from reaching out to touch the floating water. Once he looked past the water, he noticed that each of the doors had a large symbol etched into them. The first door had a man with no head, and the second had a large infinity sign. They walked around to the other side, where he saw that the last door had a key very much like the one Kyle wore around his neck.

Standing in front of the fountain was a young man with buzzed short black hair. His head looked overly round because of it. He had his arms crossed which made him looked extremely calm or bored; it was hard to tell which. He was taller than Kyle but they wore the same uniform which made Kyle feel less intimidated as they walked up to him.

"Oho," said Dante. "Did we keep you waiting long, Kross?"

"Not at all, Grandmaster. I only just arrived. I hope you are well."

"Excellent, thank you."

"And you, Master Proculus?" added the student Kyle now knew as Kross.

"Excellent, as well. How was your break?"

"Slow, Master." He uncrossed his arms, paying no attention to Kyle. "My parents were busy with their work and since I am of little use to them when it comes to Medications, I spent most of my time training." Kyle noticed the slight sullenness in his voice.

"A son's only use to his parents is to be a son," the Grandmaster said wisely. "Remember that when you think you are of little use to them." Kross seemed to digest these words, saying nothing in response. Dante continued, "It is good to hear you have been keeping up with your training. Master Proculus has told me you are advancing well in weaponry."

"Master Proculus is too kind," said Kross with a humble bow, though he looked pleased all the same.

"Not at all," said Proculus. "Grandmaster, we should get them acquainted and ready to leave. We must depart soon if we want to make it before nightfall."

"You're leaving the school?" Kyle blurted. He saw Kross's look of surprise and thought to add," Master?"

"Only for a short time," Dante answered for Proculus. "But you're right, Master Proculus. Kross, this is Kyle the Tyro, our newest tyro." Kyle almost wanted to protest this, since technically he'd been made a tyro before Garnet, but it seemed like a petty complaint. "Kyle, this is Kross the Monk, a second year here." Monk seemed a very fitting name for the young man.

"Hi," said Kyle awkwardly.

"Hello," said Kross stiffly. Kyle was getting the feeling that Kross didn't like him. Neither masters appeared to notice.

"Well, then," said Dante. "We'll leave it to you, Kross." With nothing else to say, the Grandmaster turned to leave, giving Kyle only a nod as he departed. Proculus smiled warmly, patting him on the shoulder before following Dante.

It was an abrupt farewell, making Kyle feel deserted, and increasing his nervousness. He watched them go before facing Kross, who looked like he was sizing him up.

"Grade F," Kross brought out a small notebook, scribbled a note and shoved it back in his pocket. "That's a pretty low first impression if you ask me."

"What?" said Kyle. "Grade F?"

"Your current level of ability." Kross sniffed in disdain.

Kyle was annoyed already. He'd been graded before and wasn't exactly pleased to hear a fellow student 'grade' him lowly.

"I heard you show some promise with the sword. I suppose we'll have to wait and see if you can do anything with that."

"Do you normally grade people before you know them?"

"Yes," said Kross simply. "We should get going. Are you ready?"

"Right," said Kyle with a shallow sigh. "Lead the way."

"I should mention students are not supposed to use the elevator except for emergencies," Kross said as they began moving away from the fountain. "If a master catches you using the elevators out of laziness, the student is required to challenge the master to a duel."

"Aren't we supposed to duel the masters?"

Kross looked at Kyle with a peculiar frown. "It's good to challenge the masters sometimes, but it is probably not wise to do it too often."

"Why is that?" They were at the foot of one of the two immense staircases leading up to the other floors. It was really too bad that they couldn't use the elevator.

"It's embarrassing," Kross answered. They began ascending the steps. "I imagine it hurts, too."

"You've never challenged a master?"

"Not alone." He gave Kyle a puzzled look. "Is dueling your masters a more common event in your old realm?"

"Um, not exactly," said Kyle. "We don't have the same type of curriculum. There is no dueling. Just tests and stuff."

"I see." He looked intrigued but did not inquire further.

They walked around the castle for an hour. The Monk showed

the new tyro where he would be taking his classes. Many of the rooms had desks in them but they were pushed to the side, looking scarcely used. Other rooms were larger than cathedrals, stretching on for what seemed like miles. A few looked like the inside of martial arts practice halls with mat-covered floors and walls.

Located on the second floor was the Dining Hall. There were long tables with benches inside, with enough room to sit at least seven hundred people. A small mezzanine was located within the hall itself, but it was strictly for Masters. A small balcony protruded off that area, making it the perfect place for addressing the students while they ate. The castle had looked big from the outside, but now that Kyle had walked around inside, it felt larger. There were a total of four floors, not including the basement level, which was off limits to everyone except masters and eternal title students.

"I keep hearing eternal title, but what exactly does it mean?" Kyle asked Kross. He was more curious about what was in the basement, but Kross had made it clear that he did not know.

"Eternal titles are exactly what they sound like," Kross told him as they walked back to the main entrance lobby. "It is a permanent title that you will hold for the rest of your life. Master Proculus's eternal title is Proculus the Storm. We call him Master out of respect, but he is still the Storm. Titles like mine and yours will definitely change while you train here, probably more than once. To receive your eternal title, three masters have to recommend your title to the Grandmaster, which he approves or disapproves after you duel him." Kyle felt almost like Kross was reading out of a textbook with how serious his explanations were.

"Students can duel the Grandmaster?"

"Only for an eternal title. The Grandmaster is a grade A-plus

plus. If I were you, I wouldn't worry about fighting him any time soon."

"You even grade the Grandmaster," Kyle muttered. "Makes me wonder what you grade yourself?"

"Grade B-minus," said Kross without missing a beat. "Not nearly as good as I should be." He added this more to himself than to Kyle. Kyle thought 'grade B-minus' sounded pretty high, but Kross didn't sound arrogant about it. It sounded like disappointment more than anything.

"What's the Grandmaster's eternal title?" Kyle asked to change the topic.

"Dante the Keybane."

"Cool name. How long does it take to become strong enough to challenge him?"

"Normally about four years," said Kross. "However, that is only enough to challenge him for your eternal title. It will take a lifetime to be good enough to give him a worthy fight." Kross talked about Dante with genuine admiration and respect, which surprised Kyle. Of the people he'd met so far in Endera, Kross seemed like someone who would be annoyed with Grandmaster Dante's eccentric behavior.

"He's that strong?"

"Probably stronger." They entered the lobby where students still lingered filling the room with an awkward buzz of whispers. As they walked by, the noise became less hushed. Kyle guessed that the absence of Master Proculus and Grandmaster Dante was the reason for this. He was grateful that Kross ignored them and he tried to do the same. *Guess it's something I'll have to get use to.*

"When does class start?" Kyle realized it was something he should have asked long ago.

"Tomorrow," answered Kross.

Kyle's insides deflated like a balloon. He would have liked a little more time to get use to everything, or at the very least, explore the place with Garnet. However, he knew that it was only by chance that she was around in the first place. He would have been alone had he not remembered her name. The idea made him feel thankful she was now going to be a student with him, though he simultaneously felt guilty. In a way, it felt like he had ruined her life. It was a happy distraction when Kross talked again. "That is all there is to the castle. The only things to show you now are the grounds and your room."

"My room?"

"Of course," said Kross. "Everyone is assigned a room and a roommate. Where did you think you'd be sleeping?"

The answer to that honestly hadn't occurred to him. The prospect of meeting his roommate caught him off guard. It didn't bother him to be sharing a room. He had done that his entire life, but what would his roommate be like?

Kross pushed a great oak door open, leading them to the front yard. There were lots of tyros sitting under trees, out for a jog, or just enjoying the day. Nearly all of them were dressed in blue and black, though some of them were dressed differently, in what Kyle presumed was casual attire. Kross led the way, explaining the sights as they explored the vast grounds.

"These wood sculptures are replicas of Soul Gate Academy's Grandmasters." Kross explained it as they walked down the lane surrounded by wooden sculptures.

"Is this one Grandmaster Dante?" Kyle pointed in disbelief. The sculpture's hands were on fire. How it didn't make the entire thing burn to ashes was beyond him.

"It is," said Kross, not elaborating. "Come on. There is plenty more to see."

Kyle tore his eyes away from the wooden statues with some difficulty. Each of them, although twice the size of their Grandmaster counterpart, were chiseled to such realness that Kyle thought they looked alive.

Everything he had seen on the landscape from afar two days ago looked even more spectacular up close. Lined up against the castle walls, hedges were trimmed into a variety of different shapes ranging from symbols to animals. Shrubs, trees, and flower beds littered the grounds in a wide variety of magnificent colors like periwinkle, canary yellow, and maroon. They decorated the outside with all the radiance of summer.

However, not everything looked so vibrant. There were large patches of land that looked dead and disturbed, as though frequently trampled on by horses. Noticing Kyle's curious face, Kross explained that those were the areas where most of the weapons training took place. When they neared the beach, a cool salty breeze hit them. Kyle expected to see students littered on the beach as they were everywhere else, but no one was present except for a few couples walking along the shore holding hands. They seemed to be keeping a cautious distance from the water. It was a warm day making it odd for a beach to be so ignored when there were so many young people around.

"Is it a rule not to go into the ocean?" Kyle asked.

"Strictly speaking, no," said Kross. "But unless you'd like to freeze to death, you should stay out of the water. It is called the Cold Ocean for a reason."

This made Kyle more curious than anything. *How cold could*

the water be? He had never been much of a strong swimmer so he wouldn't have liked being on the beach very much anyways, but it still intrigued him.

"Anything within the castle walls and the Cold Ocean shore is free game for us tyros, so you will have plenty of time to explore it on your own in case you didn't see enough today." Kross guided them back to the castle. "Keep in mind, we're not allowed to venture outside the walls unless given permission and we're also not allowed into the girl's dorm, which is the South Tower. The boy's dorm is the North Tower, which is where we're going now."

They walked to the tower left of the castle. The tower stood ten stories higher than the main building of the academy and was just as wide. As they neared the North Tower, they noticed a large crowd of students gathering. Kyle wanted to find the cause of the excitement so he quickened his pace. To his surprise, Kross did the same.

"What is that gorilla doing now?" Kross muttered, rolling his eyes.

"Wha—"

Kyle's question was cut off when the crowd suddenly began cheering, and two figures shot up quicker than shadows up the tower's wall. As easily as spiders, two tyros were climbing up the wall higher and higher.

"What are they doing?" Kyle was astonished yet thoroughly impressed.

"Climbing obviously." There was a tired annoyance that had not been in his voice earlier.

"Yes, but why?"

"Because that's what Kevin likes to do."

"Kevin?"

"My roommate, Kevin the Stone." Kross sighed. "He is the one on the right."

Kyle looked at the right figure climbing toward the top of the tower. He was already too high to make out any distinct features other than his long glossy black hair.

"Kevin is from a large mining town called Garsoa. They say that if you grow up there, you learn to climb before you learn to walk. I'm guessing that he challenged one of the other guys from Garsoa to a climbing race."

"Is he good?" asked Kyle.

"He's the best," answered Kross. For the first time since Kyle had met him, Kross smiled in an amused kind of way.

"What's his grade?" asked Kyle half-jokingly.

"For climbing, he's grade A-plus. Altogether, he's grade B. He's one of the best at SoGA and he's only a second year like me."

"You're grade B-minus. Does that mean you're one of the best, too?"

Kross shrugged. The crowd cheered loudly as Kevin the Stone scaled the tower's side like a cat up a tree. His opponent was some distance behind him, moving speedily to close the gap. They climbed with inhuman speed, already nearing the top. With one giant lunge Kevin grabbed onto the final ledge, lifting himself over with little difficulty. The crowd—Kyle now noticed that most of them were girls—burst into wild cheers.

Kevin the Stone stood on top of the tower, posing victoriously. The other climber was now reaching the top, though he looked quite defeated in comparison. With little warning, Kevin jumped off the tower. Kyle gasped as his insides froze in horror, though he was alone in reacting. The cheers did not change to screams; the atmosphere was still lively; Kross still looked amused.

Kyle couldn't just stand there as a fellow tyro fell to his death. He jumped into action, running as fast as he could through the crowd, much to their displeasure. He positioned himself directly under where Kevin was just about to crash land, when an iron grip pulled him out of the way.

"Are you crazy!" spat Kross as the Stone crashed into the ground, shaking the earth. Kyle looked in horror at the cloud of dust that had shot up. Kevin had died, he was certain of it.

Then, from the middle of the dust, there was a loud, "Ahhh." It sounded oddly childlike, though Kyle didn't think anything of it. He was just relieved to hear that the Stone had survived. He expected the crowd to rush forward to help Kevin, but everyone was temporarily sidetracked.

"What was that kid doing?"

"I think he was trying to catch Kevin."

"Catch him? Is he insane?"

"Who is he, anyway?"

"Monk, who is that kid?"

There were mutters in agreement, all excitedly demanding an answer from Kross. Releasing Kyle from his grip, he said, "This is Kyle the Tyro: the boy from the other realm."

The crowd burst into wild whispers, making Kyle's face burn in shame. He had just been trying to save someone from falling to their death. His body had reacted on its own. Now that he thought about it, trying to catch someone from such a height was positively stupid.

A second later, another figure crashed into the ground with heavy force. The other climber had jumped off, as well. Kyle now realized that this was normal behavior.

"Ah," said Kevin again. He walked out of the dust cloud toward Kyle and Kross. He looked much different than Kyle had imagined. For one thing, Kevin the Stone was completely uninjured from his fall. He towered over Kross with impressive muscles, making it hard to believe that he was only a second year. His face was almost girly, though. Good-looking, childish, and innocent. It was easy to see why so many girls were in the crowd. An odd clipboard with a key fused to the top of it hung around his collar like a necklace. Kevin smiled profusely, looking at Kyle with fascination as he took giant steps to reach him.

"Umm," said Kyle. "Sorry." It was the only thing he could think to say.

"Ah," Kevin said again. He reached out and squeezed Kyle's cheek with surprising gentleness, finishing with a genial pat on Kyle's head. He looked to Kross and again said, "Ah."

Kyle was confused.

"He wants me to introduce you two," said Kross to Kyle. "This is Kevin the Stone, Kyle. You might have noticed that he hasn't said much. Kevin was born deaf. He can't speak, but as you know, he can make a few sounds and grunts. Those are mainly to just get your attention. He wants you to introduce yourself."

Kyle still did not entirely understanding what was going on. The crowd's eyes were watching them, which made the whole situation even more awkward. "Er…I don't know sign language."

"Just speak," said Kross. "Kevin has had his eyes modified so that he sees words form in the air in front of the speaker as the person is speaking. It's a unique key ability: a mixture of AlterDimensions, Modifications, and Amplifications of the eyes. Complex as it is, the result is simple enough. Well for him."

Kyle did notice that Kevin's eyes were different. They were lemon yellow with black slits making them look eerily like cat eyes.

"Hi, my name is Kyle the Tyro. I'm from another realm." When Kyle was finished, Kevin grabbed the clipboard around his neck and began scribbling on it with his key.

The clipboard came to life with a robotic voice that sounded like a computer talking program, "Hello, Kyle. I am known as Kevin the Stone. I hope we can be friends." Kyle nodded, unsure of what else to say. He was amazed by this technology and he was equally amazed by Kevin. He'd never met anyone like him before.

Kross silently mouthed a message to Kevin who, with his unique eyes, was the only one who could understand. Kevin left Kyle with a smile before moving back to the center of the crowd.

"Ah!" yelled Kevin. Most of the tyros shifted their attention to him. There were some who eyes still lingered on Kyle, staring with keen if not disturbing interest. Kyle squirmed. He had never been one for making great first impressions.

"Let's go," said Kross, beckoning him to the tower entrance. As Kyle followed him into the boy's dormitory, he continued, "You might want to try and keep a lower profile."

The dormitory did not have the magnificence of the rest of the castle but was certainly nicer than any place he had ever called home. It reminded him of the lobby of a hotel. Forest green carpet and some lounging chairs decorated the round bottom floor. Opposite of the entrance was a grand set of stairs spiraling to the top of the tower and the only other floor.

"Umm, we're all on the top level?" Kyle asked uncertainly.

"Yes," answered Kross. "Though not technically. Our doors are all located on the top floor, which then take us to our rooms. The rooms themselves are located within the walls of the tower. You probably noticed that this bottom floor looks much smaller width-wise than it did from the outside. We're just in a hollowed out center, while the rooms stack themselves all the way to the top."

The explanation impressed Kyle, but he was still unsure how any of it actually worked. "Key abilities are involved in everything, huh?"

"Of course," answered Kross. And so they started their long ascent.

"So what were you saying about keeping a low profile?" Kyle asked.

Kross didn't answer him at first. His mind was deep in thought. "Not that I feel the same," he started, "but some people are openly against your admission to the school. They number few, but their barks are loud."

"Because I'm from another realm?" He hadn't considered this possibility. It was unfair. It wasn't his fault he had been raised in another realm. As his legs began to burn from the climb, his mind filled with bitter thoughts against his parents.

"It is a silly argument, Kyle. They believe that allowing someone from another realm is some form of blasphemy. All the while, many tyros are from lands all over Endera, brought here by masters or eternal-titled tyros. Soul Gate Academy is the most diverse academy in the entire realm."

"But you still think I should keep a low profile?"

"I only say that as a suggestion to keep you from attracting unwanted trouble. If I can deter it before it ever reaches you, I will."

Kyle looked at Kross with a new sense of respect. Kross had gone through the nuisance of showing Kyle around, which meant, in a way, he was siding himself with the new tyro from another realm. It was a statement; one Kyle appreciated immeasurably.

"Thanks." Kyle ruffled up his hair.

"Become strong and you won't have to thank me." It wasn't said to demean Kyle, but like a fact of the world. The message was clear: the strong control their destiny.

"I will," said Kyle, his eyes burning with determination. "I will."

Kross nodded in recognition but said no more as they continued their climb. Kyle would have liked to talk some more but was grateful for the silence. It took a considerable amount of resolve to keep up with Kross, who took the steps with much practiced ease. Nearing the top, Kyle was out of breath and his legs were screaming at him in agony.

"Hmm," said Kross as they walked onto the top floor. "Maybe I was too quick to grade you." Kyle dropped himself on to the floor, laying on his back gasping for breath. "Maybe not."

The top floor was similar to the bottom floor, but it was twice the size. Instead of walls encircling them, numbered doors were lined up side to side. Opposite of the stair entrance, there were two double doors with the word *BATHROOM* engraved over them. Kross walked over to where Kyle lay, looking at him with the pity an older brother might show his younger.

"You will get use to it sooner or later." He offered a hand. "Just think of the stairs as part of your training."

"Yeah, I think training is gonna kill me."

"Of course not," said Kross, very seriously. "No one has died at SoGA for several years."

Kyle gulped. He had just been joking.

"Your room number is one-eighty-eighty. Should be right over here."

As Kross led Kyle closer to the room, Kyle's weariness turned to anxiety. Behind that door would be his new roommate. He never had many friends and his old roommates had scarcely liked being alone in the same room with him. Kyle hoped it would be different in this realm.

You should be able to open the door with your key," said Kross as they reached the door. "Go ahead and give it a try."

Kyle took out his key and slipped it into the keyhole underneath the doorknob. He stopped right before turning it.

"Do you know who my roommate is?" he asked Kross.

"Yes, of course. From what I hear, so do you."

"What? I don't know anyone."

"Just open the door." Kross rolled his eyes. "You'll see soon enough."

With one final deep breath, Kyle turned the key. There was a soft click and he pushed the door open. The room was lit with evening sunlight. Lazily laying on his bed was a young man who Kyle recognized: Kane the Ace, the one who had challenged him to a duel. It seemed odd for them to now be roommates, but Kyle felt relieved. Though they had fought on their first encounter, Kyle couldn't help but like the spiky-haired young man.

"'Bout time you guys show up." Kane rose and walked over to greet them. "I was getting bored."

"We ran into a delay," said Kross. "Kevin is showing off again. Climbing the tower."

Kane laughed. "The king gorilla is already at it. Thought I heard a bunch of noise. Did he win?"

"Naturally," said Kross.

Kyle was surprised to see the two on such friendly terms. They seemed like opposites.

"Well, whatever." Kane turned. "How's it going, Kyle? I'd introduce myself, but I hope you still remember me."

"I'm good. Kane the Ace, right?"

"The one and only, but just call me Kane," he replied. "My title is a drag. Kross show you around the place?"

"Yeah."

Kane brought up his hand to cover his mouth as though he were telling a secret, though he failed to keep his voice down. "Did he show you the secret entrance into the girl's dorm?"

"There's a secret entrance?"

"Oh, so you interested in that kind of thing?" Kane nudged him. Kyle's face began to grow hot.

"There is no such entrance," said Kross.

"Says you. With talk like that I might keep you out of the loop when I do find it, Kross."

"If you say so. I know you'll tell Kevin though and he's probably the worst person to keep a secret."

"Ah forgot about that big bear. Doesn't matter now, I suppose. Let's get you acquainted with your new room, Kyle. You sticking around, Kross?"

"I'm afraid not. It was nice to meet you, Kyle. Remember what I said earlier. If you have any questions, just ask when you see me." Kross left the room, closing the door behind him.

"So how'd he grade you?" asked Kane immediately.

"F," said Kyle hesitantly.

"What? I told him about your fighting, you should have least gotten a grade D. I wouldn't worry about it, though. He's just some weirdo with a grading complex or something."

"What grade are you?"

"He's got me at a C-plus, which is a disgrace. I'm an A-plus if I ever saw one." He laughed and Kyle joined in.

Kane showed him around the room, which was simple. Two four-poster beds sat in opposite corners. Each of them had their own drawer and desk beside their bed. There was a large shared closet for shoes and jackets. Kyle had never felt so right in a room before. This was a place to call his. It reminded him of the cozy home he'd had with Nana and Paps, which made him love it more than any room he'd ever been in.

"Everything you need should be in your drawer," Kane said as he finished showing him the room. "If you need anything else, just let me know. Did Kross show you where all your classes will be?"

"Everything except for Synchroneity."

Kane raised an eyebrow. "Synchroneity? Impressive! What element?"

"Element?"

"Don't you know what Synchroneity is?"

"I don't really know what anything is," Kyle plopped himself on his bed, feeling like he could melt into its soft sheets.

"Oh. Well, you see…Synchroneity, as I understand it, is the key ability to lock one of the elements to your body: fire, water, earth, air, or lightning. That's why I asked you what element."

"Oh." Kyle thought of his reading. "Then it's lightning, I think. It's not impressive. I'm sure there are a bunch of people with the same ability."

"Not at all." Kane tapped his temple. "It's a rare and powerful ability. You have to be the first person in at least a decade."

"Really? Does that mean I won't be taught?"

"I dunno," said Kane. "The Grandmaster is an expert with Synchroneity fire. Maybe he'll teach you."

"The Grandmaster?" said Kyle. "He wouldn't teach me, would he?"

Kane shrugged. "I guess you'll find out sooner or later. You'll have your hands full with the classes you already have, I'm sure. Training here is no easy thing. What else did the reader pull out of your head, anyways?"

Kyle told him. Kane spent a few minutes trying but failing to explain what those classes entailed. Kyle figured he would just have to wait 'till he was there to find out.

The rest of the evening consisted of Kane bombarding Kyle with questions about the realm from which he came. The Ace, who found Kyle just as interesting as Kyle found him, wanted to know all about the different names for the months, as all of the Enderian months were named after trees, as well as cars, computers, television, and his school.

It was between all this that Kane brought out his secret stash of sweets, which were unlike anything Kyle had ever seen before. There were things called Candy Cones, Key Poppers, Bubble Songs, Chocolate Knights, and many others. Kyle's favorite was Kookie Melters, a pack of cookies called that came in the shape of keys. You could place the cookie key into a keyhole that came on the package and turn it, then the key would make the dipping block turn all warm and gooey. There were many different flavors: chocolate, vanilla, butterscotch, blueberry jam and several others that he didn't get to try.

The hours passed, making the two of them full and sleepy, but they stayed up late into the night. Kyle couldn't remember the last time he'd had such fun. The two of them got along very well, laughing as Kyle waddled like a duck when he did an impression of Mr. Lindshell. And although he wanted to know all he could about this realm, he decided it could wait. After all, this would be his life now. What was the rush? Kane had quickly become his friend, which was something new and enjoyable to Kyle. Even Kross the Monk and Kevin the Stone seemed like they were willing to befriend him. For once in his life, he finally felt like he fit in.

CHAPTER EIGHT

THE MASTERS

The next day, Kyle woke with a shake from Kane, who was fully dressed and in uniform. "You sleep like a drunk," he said, grinning. "Get ready quick or we'll miss breakfast."

Kyle rose from bed with squinted eyes and readied himself. He asked what he needed to take to class, which confused his roommate enough to make him ask, "What more would you need than your key?"

When they arrived to the Dining Hall, it was full of students waiting for the first breakfast of the semester. The loud conversations of tyros meshed together, echoing into the hallway. Kane led Kyle to a table where Kross the Monk and Kevin the Stone greeted them. It seemed that Ace, Stone, and Monk were a group, and Kyle had unceremoniously become a part of it. It felt surreal, though he was distracted from this new phenomenon of spontaneous friendship because of his search for his one familiar friend. At every sight of red hair, Kyle turned his head in search of Garnet but she was nowhere to be seen. He guessed that she was still in the Nursing Department with Master Yvette.

As they sat down, Grandmaster Dante struck a homerun pose on the second balcony to which many students snickered at as they settled down. "Good morning, tyros of Soul Gate Academy," he shouted. "Welcome, welcome. Oho, look at this full house! Another year begins. Let us start it with a good meal, a hall full of friends, and the hunger to learn. I expect you all to work hard, listen to your masters, and aim to be next rising star of SoGA! Now no more talking from me. Let's eat!" He struck his cane hard to the floor and turned it. Suddenly, the tables flipped. Some students screamed or, like Kyle, fell out of their seats. Most of the older students erupted in laughter.

"Every year," said Kane the Ace as he gave Kyle a hand, "he tries to scare us tyros by making the food come out in some crazy way." The Stone smiled as he helped a girl back up to her seat while Kross tried to not look annoyed.

"Oho," laughed Dante. "Laughter is the *key* to success! Enjoy the meal."

When Kyle sat back down, the newly flipped tables had plates, silverware, and dishes full of food. He followed the others' lead and started piling food onto his plate. He ate his fill of bacon, eggs, pancakes, and some type of pudding that wasn't quite vanilla nor was it quite butterscotch. In the end, he decided it had a bland taste, but he liked it anyways. *Food is not too different here*, he thought happily.

During the meal, Kyle felt curious to ask a few question, "Are you three all pretty good friends then?"

Kevin, who could not respond without writing on his clipboard, continued to shovel food into his mouth, allowing the other two to answer.

"We are friends," said Kross. "But we're also team members."

"Team members?"

"I knew I forgot to mention something last night," said Kane. "You had me laughing too hard with that impression of Mr. Lintsell." Kyle didn't bother to correct him that it was Mr. Lindshell. "We're all put on mission squads in SoGA. It's mainly to learn how to work with other people, but we also partake in missions, mock games, or duels with masters. That's how we first met, remember? I wasn't part of that team, but I asked to tag along since they assigned you as my roommate."

"I see," said Kyle. "Will I get to be on a team too?"

"Yes, or you will be added to an existing team," answered Kross. "It depends."

"On what?"

"A bunch of things," said Kane. "But I think the masters all look to put us in groups they know we'll get along with."

"Do you think I can get added to your team?" Kyle asked wishfully. He was hoping that Garnet could join the team as well, though he didn't want to mention her yet.

"We do not make the decision," said Kross. "Though I hope you can get to at least grade C-minus before they add you to a team. You've got work to do."

Kyle's expression fell, but then a big hand patted him on the shoulder. Kevin the Stone looked at him, exposing his big white teeth in a wide smile. He began writing on his notepad and it spoke as he did so, "Do not worry, Kyle. You will be strong in no time."

Kyle grinned. "Thanks."

"I almost forgot," Kross dug into his pockets. "Master Proculus asked me to give you this." He handed Kyle a small piece of paper.

"What is it?" inquired Kane.

"Just his schedule," answered the Monk.

"What do you have first?" Kevin asked with his clipboard.

"It says I have AuraBending first." He was too full to eat another bite so he read off the rest of his list. "Then I have Amplifications, followed by PsyBending and History. Just weapons skill level one and double MicroDimensions tomorrow."

"That doesn't sound too bad," said Kane. "It's lame we don't have any classes with you. If you get good enough though, you can always jump to the advance classes with us. We're all in advance Amplifications. Kevin has advance AuraBending. Kross and I both have PsyBending, but we're in the advance class for that one too. And none of us have MicroDimensions."

Kevin nodded while munching on a full strip of bacon. "But you'll be in weapons skill level two in no time. You might even make it to level three before long. We're in level five though so that might take you a bit."

"It won't be easy," said Kross. "You must train hard if you want to reach us."

Kyle doubted that he would be able to catch up. He didn't know much about this realm yet, but it seemed like the Ace, Monk, and Stone were extremely talented for second years.

During the rest of breakfast, the three boys reassured Kyle that he would, in fact, be fine. They explained to him that at SoGA, classes operated different than what he was used to. Rather than moving into higher classes after every year, students advanced only when they were good enough for the superior level of each class. The three explained that the levels of classes were called starters, advanced, and champion. The only exceptions to this were weaponry and history. Like the other classes, weaponry depended on each individual's skill level; however, since there were so many students and everyone had to take weaponry, that subject had seven skill levels. History was the only subject where the level of difficulty was determined by how many years a student had attended. It was required for four years, so first years all took it together, and then second years, and so forth. After the explanations, Kyle believed he understood things well enough.

Grandmaster Dante stood on the balcony again, scanning the room to see if everyone had finished eating. He twisted his cane again, making all the food vanish.

"How does he do that?" asked Kyle. "I mean, doesn't he have to have a key?"

"His cane is his key," answered Kross. "The older tyros all say that it's a Kota, but I don't believe it."

"A Kota?"

"It means Key of Throne Arm," explained Kane. "Or Kota for short. Or KeyArm too, I guess. Some people say they're phony legendary blades that are basically weapons that were fused with keys. Master Oisin, he's the old relic that teaches history, he says they're definitely real. Kross doesn't believe it, though."

"I hope they do not exist." Kross stared intently at Dante's cane. "Weapons like that would be too powerful, wouldn't they? I think the Grandmaster made a groove in his old cane and locked in his key somehow. To me, that is more likely than a Kota."

"It matters little," said Kevin with his clipboard. "You can decide whether you believe in Kotas or not soon enough. Master Oisin loves to talk about them."

Kyle thought the idea of a Kota seemed extraordinary. He tried to picture himself with his own Kota, but was distracted when Grandmaster Dante cleared his throat loudly. All the masters stood behind him on the balcony. He noticed Master Yvette, looking annoyed as she saw her husband strike the homerun pose once again. Master Proculus smiled with amusement. The other masters were unknown to Kyle, but they all looked equally impressive, dressed in their white master uniforms. He wondered which masters would be teaching his classes.

"I hope you enjoyed your meals, tyros," the Grandmaster announced. "Rather than getting into the rules that nobody wants to hear, I would like to start off the semester with a challenge. Listen carefully now." The students all became completely silent. "Anyone who is able to beat their masters to their classroom will be allowed to skip the first week of class!" Many of the older students stood up immediately, while Kyle looked around, confused. "Oho, young ones stepping up to the challenge, I love it! Let's see it then, ready—GO!" Kyle couldn't believe it but all the masters except for a very old man vanished in the blink of an eye. The old one vanished a moment later.

"Don't let Master Oisin's looks fool you," Kane stood up and stretched. "That geezer likes to challenge himself more than the rest."

"Should we have tried to beat them to class?" asked Kyle.

Kross gave Kyle a peculiar glance. "The challenges are mostly for the tyros who are getting close to having eternal titles,"

The Stone stood up, patting his stomach. "Ah," he said. Most of the students were now leaving the Dining Hall and making their way to class. Kyle stood up anxiously. He knew the way, but he was nervous to go on his own. "Ah," said Kevin again. He beckoned Kyle to follow him.

"I think he means to show you to class," said Kross. "And he's being too lazy to write it down."

"Oh, okay," Kyle relaxed. "Thanks, Kevin."

Kevin led Kyle to the third floor, and the classroom at the end of the hall. At the doorway, Kevin again said, "Ah." He patted Kyle on the back before leaving for his own class.

"Thanks again," Kyle mumbled before entering the classroom.

The classroom was spacious, empty except for desks and chairs, which were horribly dented and stacked against the wall. The tyros, none of whom Kyle recognized, sat on the floor looking to the front of the classroom where a pretty woman with light brown, shoulder-length hair stood waiting. Her eyes were demanding but kind. Kyle joined the other students on the floor, sitting near no one.

"Ahem," she said as the last of the students filed in. "I am known as Helen the Fortress. For those of you who are new, welcome. For those of you who aren't, welcome back." She scanned the room. "Good. Now…"

Master Helen stopped mid-sentence as another tyro walked in. Garnet, dressed in the tyro uniform, apologized for being late. Master Helen waved her off almost instantly.

"It is not a problem," she said. "Please sit down." Garnet's ears went pink as she sat next to Kyle. "Right, let's get right to it. Tonya the Runner and Neodo the Violet, please come to the front of the class."

"Hey," Kyle whispered to Garnet. "Master Yvette let you out already?"

She answered him in a hushed voice. "She didn't want to at first. I feel fine though, and if I'm going to be a student, I have to go to class." Kyle didn't think it was a big deal for her to miss a few classes, but there would be no complaints from him. It was nice to have someone he knew in class with him.

"You sure you feel all right?" he asked.

"Never been better."

Kyle wondered if she was telling the truth but thought it best to keep quiet for now

A short, petite girl and a boy with very frizzy purple hair were now standing in the front of class waiting for instruction. Master Helen looked them both from top to bottom before starting. "AuraBending can be used in a variety of different ways. Simply put, with this key ability, you are unlocking the mind, giving it the power to bend your aura to use as you see fit. Every living thing that can think has an aura which acts as an extension of the mind. Mastery of AuraBending can protect you against enemy attacks or even be used to attack. These two tyros will demonstrate this. Tonya, I'd like you to attack Neodo with a strong amplified kick and Neodo, defend with your aura any way you'd like."

They both nodded and backed away from each other. Tonya the Runner took her key out of her skirt pocket, pointing it at her calves and turning it. She dashed at Neodo with frightening speed. Meanwhile, Neodo stabbed his key into the ground. He turned the key to create a circle of symbols that rapidly scribbled onto the floor around him. When Tonya reached him, she kicked at him with all her might, but was stopped by an invisible force.

"Good," praised Master Helen. "You two may sit. Neodo's guard was simple, but effective. He surrounded himself with his aura and it acted like a shield. Can anybody tell me what color his aura was?"

A stout girl to Kyle's left raised her hand and answered, "It was violet." Kyle hadn't seen anything.

"That's right," said Helen. "Most of you were probably able to see the symbols, but were unable to see his aura. The symbols that formed around him marked where his aura extended. These symbols are purely a side effect of using your aura. Just like aura, they vary from person to person, so I wouldn't try to decipher what they mean. It's ancient script. You'd have to be a reader to understand it." Kyle glanced at Garnet, who returned a quick amused grin.

Master Helen continued, "Learning how to see aura will be your first lesson. This requires a great deal of focus and determination, which is needed for all key abilities, so you better get it down quickly. To be able to see aura, place your key on one of your temples, turn the key counterclockwise and then slide it to the bottom of your ear. This motion must be precise. Those of you with long hair might find it useful to tuck it back. Any questions?" The class looked eager to try it, but Kyle was lost as how to actually do it so he raised his hand.

"Yes, Kyle?"

"I don't really understand how to do it." A couple of scoffs and snickers sounded off behind him, but he ignored them. Garnet turned to shoot the teasers a disgusted glare.

"Were my instructions unclear?"

"It's not that," he said, ruffling up his hair. "I just don't know what I'm looking for."

"What's your favorite color?"

"Crimson orange."

"Our auras tend to take after our personalities, our likes, our strongest emotions. Imagine yourself shrouded in crimson orange smoke, when you are unlocking your mind's eye. That's the best advice I can give you."

"Can't you just tell me what the actual color of my aura is?"

"I could," said Master Helen, "but it's best to learn on your own. Think of it as painting a picture of yourself. Other people will always have their own way of viewing you, but the way you view yourself is most important. That clear things up any?"

"I think so."

"Excellent. Then get started, everyone. Those who know how to see aura are forbidden from helping those who can't. If you are in this category, you must work on further extending your aura further from your body. Aura is like a muscle; it must be worked if you want it to get stronger. If anyone needs any assistance, let me know."

The class, Kyle and Garnet among them, stood up, eager to give it a try.

"Crimson orange?" asked Garnet. "That's a pretty specific, favorite color."

"Yeah." Kyle slid his key down to his ear. Nothing happened. "What's yours?"

"Crimson orange," she teased as she turned the key on her temple.

"Oh very funny." He smiled. "Really, what is it?"

"When you learn how to see aura, you'll see it," she said. She frowned when her attempt to see aura failed. "This is harder than it looks though."

"It might be easier if both of you stopped talking," said Master Helen, who was standing behind them.

They apologized and began concentrating on the task. Their efforts were to no avail. Kyle and Garnet, along with most of the other tyros, had failed to see their aura by the end of class. Master Helen, however, smiled delightedly at the results. When she dismissed them, she waved them all off pleasantly, leaving Kyle feeling puzzled.

When they stepped into the hallway, he was surprised to see Kevin the Stone walking toward them.

"Ah," he said. He looked at Garnet with intrigue. Garnet, who had never met him before, met his curious stare with a suspicious one.

"Hey, Kevin," said Kyle. "What are you doing here?"

Kevin started writing on his clipboard fervently. "Just thought I would show you to your next class. Who might this beautiful friend of yours be? A girlfriend already?"

Garnet looked more confused than embarrassed.

"This is Garnet," said Kyle, his ears and face now hot. "She's a friend—" Kevin suddenly stepped forward and gave a gentle squeeze to Garnet's cheek. Kyle almost laughed by how bewildered Garnet looked. "Garnet, this is Kevin the Stone. He can't speak since he is unable to hear sound, but his eyes pick up our words as we speak them. The clipboard is his way of speech. Did I explain that right, Kevin?"

"Yes, excellently," said Kevin's notepad. "We shall be late to class if we do not hurry." Kyle was getting use to Kevin's way of speech, but it still felt odd to be spoken to so formally. "Pleased to meet you, Garnet."

"Y-you too, Kevin."

Kevin marched through the hallway with the jolly expression of a child with a new toy. He led them first to Garnet's BioDimensions classroom, where Kyle uttered a quick goodbye. Kevin then took him to Amplifications before leaving for his own class.

Amplifications was taught by a man named Logan the Supersonic. His classroom was much longer than most rooms and had a floor which resembled the rubbery material used to make outdoor tracks. After a short time, it became obvious why. The curriculum of

Amplifications included a lot of running.

Master Logan spoke with a slow, broken-up rhythm. He had copper-brown dreadlocks that hung down his face, extending over his sunglasses and down to his very square jaw.

"Ya know. Amplifications. Is about. Running. No, it's about. Using the keys. To use your energy. To enhance your body. To make your running. Explode! Like. This." Master Logan pointed his key at each of his calves and turned it twice. He then threw his key at the other end of the long classroom. It clinked off the far wall loud enough for everyone to hear, but then Master Logan disappeared for just a second. When he reappeared, his key was twirling around his fingers. "I ran there. And back. In the blink. Of an eye."

Everyone in the class, including Kyle, was anxious to try it. Their instruction consisted of a large of amount of running in short spurts, but Kyle ran at a tortoise's pace compared to his teacher. Tired and sweating, he expected his clothing to be a nuisance as the class progressed. However, he was also pleased to find that their uniforms were much more flexible than they looked, and remained quite dry. A nice second year named Josie the Merry explained to him that the clothes were specially crafted to do so. They had been locked by professional StitchLockers, who'd used the powers of their keys to enhance and modify the clothes. This amazed Kyle, but did little to help him with his task. When class was finished, he felt discouraged. He hadn't had much success with his first two classes. But again, his master looked very pleased when they were dismissed.

Kevin was there to meet him after class yet again. This time Garnet trailed after him, looking amused to be associated with the big childlike young man. The three of them went to the Dining Hall, where Kross and Kane were sitting at a table waiting for them. After a brief introduction, Garnet joined them for lunch. Kyle nearly let it slip that she had been the Reader, but a swift kick to his shin under the table reminded him of his promise.

"You two seem like you know each other pretty well," said Kane with a raised eyebrow.

"We got to know each other while we were sitting in the Nursing Department," Garnet lied. "Not much to do there other than talk."

"And you're just friends?" he inquired further.

"Yes," said Kyle. "We barely know each other."

"Okay." Kane did not look entirely convinced.

"D-plus," said Kross suddenly. "I think you'll move up fast, though."

"What?" Garnet gave him an awkward half-laugh.

"My grade for you."

"You have me at Grade F," said Kyle in disbelief. "How is she higher than me?"

"She just is," said Kross with a rather emotionless face. "Garnet has a certain… authority about her."

That made Garnet shift uncomfortably. "I'm confused."

"Quit with your grading, you weirdo," said Kane. "Don't mind him, Garnet. He has some sort of complex."

"It's not a complex," retorted Kross. "I just happen to think it's important to hear where your abilities stand in the eyes of others."

"Your eyes maybe," muttered Kane.

"Ah," added Kevin. He smacked both Kross and Kane on the backs as though to remind them of something. "Ah."

"Ah, yourself," said Kane as he tried to rub the pain from his back. The Monk sighed, saying nothing. "You should learn to use those big bear paws of yours more gently."

"I don't mind being graded," said Garnet, looking relieved now that she understood Kross's meaning. "I'm guessing A is that highest grade?"

"A-plus-plus actually," Kross answered.

"No sweat." Garnet smiled. "You'll have to grade me that high in no time at all."

Kyle relaxed, happy to see Garnet take the grade with good humor. Though he was annoyed that she had been graded better, he understood why. Her presence was a mixture of beauty and intimidation, as though pieces of her reader powers lingered around her. Having known her before her remarkable change, it took some getting used to.

"Well, it's better than Kyle," Kane joked. "And better than me! He started me out an F-minus. I started out as lowest of the low and look at us now, best friends."

Kane erupted in laughter, which turned out to be contagious. From that moment on, the five of them got along as though they'd been friends forever. It was simple, easy, and fun. Even Kross had a smirk across his face by the end of lunch. And for the first time in Kyle's young life, he had a group of friends.

Kevin offered to chauffeur Kyle to class again, but upon learning that Garnet was also in PsyBending, he turned the Stone down. The two of them walked to class, sitting down at a desk for the first time that day as another interesting master strolled into the room.

"I am Master Ellwood," said the tall and lanky man. Square glasses fit tightly to his large nose. He wore a white lab coat over his master's uniform, making him look more like a scientist than a teacher. "In this class, we will learn to dive into the mind. The mind, mind you…" he chuckled. "…is a powerful thing. It can send telepathic brain waves to other brains, it can reveal memories, it can manipulate reality, and, most importantly, your mind allows you to think. Without your mind, you would be an empty shell. You would all do well to remember this, because PsyBending is just as much offensive as it is defensive. You must never underestimate the power of the mind." He searched the room for his most confused looking student: Kyle. "How about a demonstration? Kyle the Tyro, come here."

The master studied him with a gaze full of intrigue as Kyle nervously walked to the front of the class to sit on a chair. He suspected that Ellwood was extremely interested in the fact that he was from another realm. After promising that he wouldn't reveal anything too embarrassing, Ellwood placed his key on Kyle's right temple. As the key turned, the chilling metal immediately sapped energy from Kyle, but then stopped abruptly.

"Kyle Demore," said Ellwood. "You're name in the other realm is Kyle Demore, correct?" This information ignited whispers around the room, though Kyle was not impressed. He was sure that all of the masters knew who he was and where he was from.

"Yes, Master," answered Kyle.

"You enjoy something called snowboarding? Is that right?" Master Ellwood looked into Kyle's eyes as to verify this, and Kyle nodded. *Impressive.* "And your favorite food is rice, though you wouldn't say no to garlic bread, either?" Garnet and a few others giggled.

"That's true, Master," admitted Kyle. Smiling warmly, Master Ellwood directed Kyle to return to his seat.

"There you have it," he said. "So if all of you want to win

Kyle over, get him some rice or garlic bread." The class laughed. "PsyBending, to explain it simply, is to unlock the mind internally to read the mind, cause dreams, temporary insanity; that kind of thing. It is quite a useful ability. Now, to the point of our first lesson. As you all saw me do with Kyle, I want you to partner up and attempt to read the mind of your partner." Some of the class looked worried, but Master Ellwood calmed their concerns instantly. "You will just be trying to find out which hand has a coin in it. One person in each pair will hide a coin in one of their hands, while the other will attempt to read their mind to find out which hand it is in. Simple enough, I think."

Kyle partnered up with Garnet. He tried to read her mind with all his might, but he was completely unsuccessful. Garnet, on the other hand, proved that she was very good at PsyBending. After reading Kyle's mind correctly every time, he suspected that her reader abilities were giving her an edge making him vaguely jealous.

Kyle left class feeling utterly defeated. He was convinced that Master Proculus had surely picked up the wrong kid because he had to be the worst tyro in all of Soul Gate Academy. Garnet tried cheering him up as they walked to history class, which they also had together. As they entered and sat down, he tried looking on the bright side of things. *Three classes with Garnet, that's not too bad.* Kyle looked around the class to find Annie the Second Blade and James the First Blade waving at him enthusiastically. *And people who actually seem pleased to see me.* Though uncertainly at first, he waved back with a smile.

Master Oisin, who taught history, looked old and fragile. He reminded Kyle of Albert Einstein, with wiry gray hair and a bushy mustache. He paced the front of the room with his hands behind his curved back.

"Oisin the Detective is my eternal title," he said energetically. "Remember it well. All of you here are new tyros. Many of you probably believe that history is the least important subject you have here at Soul Gate Academy; however, ask any of the other masters and they will all tell you that history is the *most* important. Can any of you tell me why?" Master Oisin called on James, who had raised his hand along with a few others.

"To learn from our mistakes," answered James.

"Ah, yes of course, that is important, isn't it? Learning from our mistakes. It is what we humans know we should do, yet history shows that we are destined to repeat our mistakes. Any other reasons as to why history is so important?"

A few others raised their hands, Oisin called on a girl with long brown hair and thin eyebrows.

"Because history shows how we developed throughout time."

"True," said Oisin, "but no. Anybody else."

"To predict what will happen in the future."

"Another splendid *answer*, but not the one I am looking for." He walked through the aisle between desks and hummed a tune foreign to Kyle. "Can the boy from the other realm possibly tell me?"

Whispers circulated. Kyle sighed. He wished some of the masters would stop singling him out. "May-be," he stuttered, "for answers?"

"Yes!" Oisin shouted excitedly. "Yes, indeed, that is the ticket. For answers! Brilliant, simply brilliant. The reason history is so important is because it holds answers!" He cleared his throat. "Ah history, it is an infinite pile of answers. We here at Soul Gate Academy strive to find these answers. That is our purpose. We train your young minds and then you are sent off into the world in search of answers, answers that our ancestors left hidden or scattered or half destroyed. To find these answers, strength and knowledge of the key is vital. You would do well to remember this; in fact, you should engrave it into your being…"

Master Oisin lectured more about answers and how important they were for the rest of class. Although Kyle found it repetitive, he also found it quite informative. Soul Gate Academy took a deep interest in the world's history. This was secondary to training students the proper use of keys and weapons, but Master Oisin made it clear that it was no less important. Kyle had never particularly had any interest in history, nor the uncovering of facts long lost and forgotten, but Master Oisin made it sound like a life full of mystery and adventure.

"Remember, your keys are important to unlocking the answers," he said with finality. "Do not take your training lightly or you risk your life itself." On this note, he ended class.

Garnet and Kyle walked outside the castle, finally finished with their first day's classes. He fell to the ground, stretching out under a tree, while Garnet sat down next to him. Today had been frustrating, yet the day had not been wasted. It left Kyle with a determination to train hard and become a tyro worth mentioning.

"Quite a bit different," said Kyle with a yawn. "Not exactly what we're used to, huh?"

"Yeah, I know." Garnet drew a long breath then exhaled. "But we can't go back now."

"True," said Kyle with a wide smirk. "But who'd want to?"

CHAPTER NINE

PROCULUS THE STORM

The next day, Kyle, much to his own surprise, woke up earlier than Kane. Weaponry skill level one was his first class of the day, and he was excited. In truth, he knew he was still a novice, but he had at least displayed some amount of natural born ability when he had a weapon in his hand. As the Ace readied his daggers, Kyle suddenly realized he did not own his own sword. Kane informed him that he would be receiving one. The two of them rushed down to the Dining Hall to meet Garnet, Kross, and Kevin for a quick breakfast. It was nerve-racking to see the hallway now half full of students with weapons. One of them was Kevin the Stone, wearing a fierce-looking, double-bladed axe on his back. The weapon was a stark opposite of Kevin's child-like persona.

"Why didn't you bring your weapon, Kross?" Kyle asked.

"People who can use MicroDimensions or BioDimensions do not need to carry their weapons. At class, I will summon my weapon to me. You will learn the skill soon enough since you're learning MicroDimensions."

"What's your weapon?"

"It's called a Shaolin spade." Kyle wasn't sure what a Shaolin spade was, so he imagined Kross swinging around a sharpened shovel.

Weaponry classes were held out on the grounds so when they finished with breakfast, Kross led Kyle and Garnet outside, toward a group of younger students who were waiting for a master's instruction. Garnet and Kyle joined the small crowd, while Kross, Kane, and Kevin went to find the skill level five group. It was such a nice morning that Kyle took notice of the sun's vibrant shine through the sky's clouds. Above the castle, he observed a cloud that seemed oddly solid. He stared at it, trying to determine what it was, when a blurry silhouette flew from it and became larger and larger. The thing crashed only thirty paces from where they stood with a loud smash that shook the ground, causing a large plume of dust to form.

Kyle, who was beginning to see that it was a waste of energy to be surprised anymore, ran to see what had fallen from the sky. The other students stepped back in fear. As the dust cleared, a man in a master uniform became visible.

"Damn, Proculus," he coughed. "Never knows how to hold back."

A second figure flew down, landing next to Kyle with a soft thud.

"Sorry, Master Julius," said Proculus, shirtless and covered in sweat. "You know how I get with morning training. Good morning, Kyle." He patted Kyle on the back.

"Where did you come from, Master?" asked Kyle.

"Oh," said Proculus, "I just jumped down from the master's training facility. It is technically the sixth floor of the castle. You see that cloud there?" He pointed at the cloud that Kyle had just been staring at. "That's it floating up there. Strictly masters and eternal titles only."

"A floating facility?"

"Yes, technically that's what it is."

"How do you get up there?"

"A special elevator from the Grandmaster's office." Proculus helped up Master Julius, who looked hesitant to be standing just yet, but otherwise completely unharmed. "We can jump up and down if we like though, it's not too high."

Kyle looked at the cloud with envy, wishing he could visit.

"Next time," said Master Julius as he regained his composure, "if you're going to use full force, I'd like to know."

"Just thought I would try and surprise you," laughed Proculus. "We would have been late to weapons training if I hadn't. You have level ones this term, right? If Kyle is here, that means this is them. Excuse me while I go find the level fives." With a casual wave, Master Proculus walked away.

Master Julius brushed himself off. He looked at Kyle almost furiously, but then let out a shallow sigh. He was a larger man than Proculus and had overly long arms. On the side of his face were thick brown mutton chop sideburns that trailed up to his thick, disheveled hair.

"Everyone, come closer," said Julius in an annoyed voice. "I am known as Julius the Chops." Some of the tyros laughed, to which he responded with another look that was clearly furious, before letting out yet another sigh. "Not for the reason you might think." He stroked his mutton chops absentmindedly. Then, he took out a flaming red key and stuck it into the air in front of him. After he turned it, he stuck his hands into the space next to the key, causing them to disappear. When his hands reappeared, they each held two butcher cleavers. He began juggling the blades as if it were as easy as breathing. The class gasped. "Chops."

"At SoGA, we aim to make everyone an expert with their given weapon," he said. "Since you are all in weapons skill level one, I am going to assume that most of you have no idea what weapon you will be best with. Luckily, it's very easy to determine. Line up here and we'll get started." He stopped juggling the cleavers and lined the tyros up near his floating key. Kyle was first.

"I want you to put both your hands in the space next to my key. Then grab the weapon that flies into your hands and pull it out. Understand?"

"Yes, Master." Kyle placed his hands into the space and saw them disappear. At first, he felt nothing, but suddenly a hilt smacked into his palms. He pulled it out and a lengthy weapon followed. It was the longest sword he had ever seen. The blade itself was close to four feet long, curved like a Japanese katana, but slightly wider. The hilt added nearly another two feet in length. Kyle felt awkward with the lengthy sword, but it felt strangely comfortable at the same time.

"A Nodachi," said Master Julius. "You seem a bit small for it, but the Weapons Select has never been wrong."

"The Weapons Select?"

"It is the name of my BioDimensions specialty. I don't have time to tell you about it now. Move out of the way. Next." Again, he looked furious, but then heaved a deep sigh. Kyle did not understand Master Julius in the slightest. It was like the man was trying to scare him but then decided it would be too much trouble. Kyle took his sword and happily moved away.

Garnet was next to follow Kyle's example. Her hands disappeared only for a moment before pulling out a double-edged spear with an azure metal handle. After her, a boy on his way to growing a particularly flat afro pulled out a sickle and chain. The class waited patiently until the others had picked their weapons, which ranged from swords to maces. The last boy pulled out a flail and said, "Cool!"

"Looks like that's everyone," Master Julius looked over the group. "Now I am going to put you into groups and then one at a time each group will attack me."

"Attack you?" said a girl holding a pair of long kitchen knives. "What if we hurt you?"

"That," sighed Master Julius, "is impossible. I want everyone to try to cut themselves with their weapons." Kyle who had already learned this shortly after arriving to Endera, watched as his class tried to cut themselves with their weapons, only to see their weapon bounce off harmlessly. "See, it is impossible. The Grandmaster has locked all weapons that come anywhere near the academy. The weapons will still act like a blunt weapon, but damage is kept to a bare minimum. A bruise or bloody nose is the most you could ever get…probably. Now like I said, groups—you here, and you few over there—there, that should do it."

"Umm, Master Julius," said Kyle, feeling left out. "You didn't place me in a group."

"You," groaned the Master, "are to fight me alone. Master Proculus recommended it. I'll take you on last. Everyone except for group one, sit. Group one, over here. Get ready to attack me. I can't help you unless you show me what you know already!"

Garnet's group, which consisted of her and three others, was first. She looked quite confident compared to the rest of her group, who seemed unsure on how to hold their new weapons. They edged toward Julius slowly. Garnet, however, did not partake in the attack. She stood by idly as the other three thrust and swept their weapons, hoping to hit Master Julius, who seemed perfectly fine ignoring Garnet's absence from the attack.

Kyle was baffled by her behavior. It was unlike Garnet to disobey a teacher's order. He wasn't alone in noticing her noncompliance. Noisy gossip sprang around him like wildfire as the fight reached its close. It had hardly been a fight. The master's skill was so beyond the students, he'd done little more than dodge their weak attacks while juggling his cleavers carelessly. The fight finished and talk of Garnet died to hushed whispers.

Finished with the others, Julius turned to Garnet with a curious look in his eyes. "Garnet the Tyro, did you not understand my instruction?"

"I understood it, Master Julius," she said. "And I mean no disrespect, but I would like the chance to fight you on my own. I don't think I can show you my skill with others around me."

Whispers buzzed louder behind Kyle, annoying him, but he focused on listening to the conversation between the master and his friend.

"Fine," said Julius, "but first give me a lap around the castle. A master's instructions are not to be ignored. If you're not back before I finish with the other groups, you'll have to wait 'till next class to get your chance."

Garnet took off at once, her spear bouncing at her side as she sprinted away. It was not a short run. She would have to hustle to make it in time.

"Right, then. Next group, let's go."

Kyle smiled as Garnet's red hair danced behind her. He had no idea why she wanted to fight the master alone, but he knew she'd make it around in time.

The rest of the groups followed, but, like the first group, they were no match for Julius. Garnet made it back as the last group before Kyle was in the middle of their fight. A plump young man with a long broadsword brought his blade down hard, forcing the master to stop juggling his cleavers for a moment. Julius pushed the broadsword away with ease, but it was the first time the class saw the master smile. As Garnet sat back down next to Kyle, he expected to find her out of breath, but she looked more energetic than anything.

"Care to tell me why you're doing this?" Kyle asked.

"No real reason." Garnet shrugged. "I just think if you can do it, so can I." Kyle smiled, knowing that there was more to it than that, but he let it go. All of her reader training hadn't disappeared, so it was possible that she was already quite skilled.

"If you say so," said Kyle. "I'm not real sure why Master Proculus suggested me to fight alone in the first place, though."

"Probably because you're a natural. Kane said you were really good too."

"They're probably just being nice," said Kyle modestly, though he was quite pleased.

Just then, the last group ended their fight. Kyle stood up, readying himself to fight, but Master Julius shook his head. "Garnet will be first."

Kyle plopped himself back to the ground.

"Attack me when you're ready." Julius commanded.

Garnet stood up, giving Kyle an apologetic look as she moved away. He wasn't mad, but watching everyone else in their fights had made him eager.

Garnet gripped her spear firmly, exhaling deeply. The temperature could have dropped ten degrees as the class waited for the young lady to attack. Then all of sudden, she lunged forward, thrusting her spear so fast, Kyle could barely see the tip. Master Julius was forced to stop juggling to block the strike. Garnet continued with her attack. Each thrust was faster than the last, aiming for different parts of Master Julius: his head, his foot, his shoulder, his chest. Master Julius never failed to block them, but he did little else beyond that. Kyle could barely believe his eyes. Garnet was moving with such precision, grace, and power that he could hardly believe it was the same girl he'd just been sitting next to.

After ducking under Garnet's spear, Master Julius countered with a powerful uppercut from one of his cleavers. The force lifted Garnet into the air but she managed to hold onto her weapon. With her footing lost, Master Julius took advantage and charged. Garnet tried to readjust in time, but the master was too fast. The point of one of Julius's cleavers was pointed at Garnet's neck.

"That's enough." He lowered his weapon. "You're quite skilled."

"Thank you, Master." Garnet bowed. "I've had previous training."

"That you have."Julius began juggling his cleavers again. "I suppose I've got to move you up. I think you'll do well in level six." Applause broke out from the class and Kyle joined in. Level seven was the highest, so jumping up to level six was an amazing feat. Kyle might have been jealous had he not been so eager to test out his own skill. He nearly jumped from his spot on the ground as Garnet moved away to sit with the rest of the class. The apprehensive whispers from earlier had turned into the excited chatter of fans, now all too happy to be seated near a wonderful tyro like Garnet.

"Ready?" asked Master Julius. Kyle nodded, relaxing with a slow exhale. The pressure to do well had doubled after Garnet's fight. "Then begin!"

He rushed in with a wide sweep from his blade, causing Julius to step back. Anticipating this, Kyle decided to change the attack into a stab forward. Master Julius stopped juggling to deflect the sword to his left, but Kyle followed the momentum into a fast rotation, bringing the blade around for another slash to his master's right. Julius leaped backwards, just missing the range of Kyle's sword.

A sense of bliss came over Kyle. He was having fun, losing himself in something that somehow felt so—natural. He felt himself smile like a madman. And though it was not deliberate, it didn't go unnoticed. The class muttered uncomfortably, but it didn't matter. Kyle was so lost in his fight that an elephant's trumpeting wouldn't have affected him. He charged in with a downward slice, following it with another a stab.

To avoid it, Julius leaped into the air and began juggling again. While floating in the sky, he grabbed two of his cleavers and threw them at Kyle, who swatted them away with his sword. Master Julius followed, coming down like a meteorite. Kyle dodged to his right just in time. A thin cloud of dust surrounded Master Julius as he picked up his weapons. Without really thinking, Kyle decided to mimic the master. He jumped, floating for just a moment before descending with a powerful slash. The master held his ground, defending against the sword with all four cleavers. The blades met with such force that Julius sank into the ground, making it look like he was standing in an impact crater. Julius pushed back Kyle's sword so hard that when Kyle landed back on the ground, he skidded back a few feet. When he stopped, he charged at his master once again.

"STOP," shouted Julius. Kyle tripped as he halted, falling to the ground in an undignified manner. Julius frowned, though he looked pleased at the same time. "Damn Proculus. He was right. You have incredible reflexes and instincts, and you learn as you fight. However, you're incredibly impatient and your footwork is weak. What should I do with you?"

"Master?" said Kyle as he stood up. He was unsure if he was being praised or not. Master Julius was hard to read.

"I'm moving you up to weapons skill level five," he said. There was no applause as there had been with Garnet. Instead, there was a chilling silence flavored with buzzing whispers of fear and unease.

"What was with them?" Kyle asked Garnet when they left class for lunch.

Garnet hesitated before answering, "They're scared of you."

"What? Why? You moved up to a higher level and they just cheered you on."

"Yes," said Garnet. "But during your fight with Master Julius, you were smiling...kind of evilly. I know you weren't doing it on purpose or anything. People see what they want to see since they know you're from another realm."

"I was smiling…evilly?" Kyle couldn't believe the injustice.

"It wasn't really evil." Garnet didn't appear to be able to look him in the eyes. "Just ignore it, okay?"

"Easy for you to say," muttered Kyle.

"Hey, it's not my fault," snapped Garnet. "If I could do something about it, I would."

"I know. Sorry, okay? I'm just—"

"It's fine," said Garnet graciously. "Just try to remember than I'm on your side."

When they arrived to the Dining Hall, Kane, Kross, and Kevin were helping themselves to lunch, eager to hear about their time in weaponry level one. Kyle had no idea how, but it seemed some rumors had already made it to their ears. Kyle wasn't in the mood to talk about what had happened, so he let Garnet tell them.

"Level five?" Kane practically choked on his sandwich. "How can you be in level five already? Is it because of that sword?" He pointed at Kyle's Nodachi sword, which leaned against the wall. "Has anyone ever jumped four classes like that, Kross?"

"Garnet jumped to level six," said Kyle. Garnet had purposely forgotten to mention her own accomplishments.

"What?" Kane spat water this time. "You shot past us?

"Ah," cut in Kevin. He began scribbling down on his notepad and it said, "You two must be extremely skilled. How long have each of you trained?"

"I've been training for two years," said Garnet.

"That is impressive for only two years," said Kevin's notepad. "How about you, Kyle?"

"Uh," said Kyle ruffling up his hair. "I never had any training."

"Natural talent?" said Kane in disbelief. "You'll rule the school by next year. Kross quit rubbing that chin and say something!"

"Hmm," hummed Kross. He was deep in thought.

"What?" steamed Kane. "Our newest friends skip that many levels in weaponry and all you say is *hmm?* Jeez."

Kyle wasn't sure how he felt about being moved up in weaponry. The gossip and whispers about him were already enough. He had a feeling that being put into a higher weapons skill group might ostracize him more. Still, he couldn't deny feeling content to have some talent in at least one area.

"Kyle you're at grade D now, and Garnet…I think grade C would be appropriate," said Kross. "Both of you moved up much quicker than I could have predicted."

"You and your grading complex," Kane shook his head. "Say something more useful."

"You're too loud." Kross rolled his eyes in a humored sort of way.

Before Kane could retort, a tall, broad-shouldered tyro walked over. He had a pointy chin that made his face look like an inverted triangle. His hair was dark chocolate and so straightly combed to the right that it stuck pointedly over his ear.

"Oi you," he said, looking at Kyle. Kyle looked behind him, confused and unsure if the big stranger was talking to him. "Yes, you—I'm here to tell ya that ye aren't ta be gettin' a big head now, ya filthy outsider. Not many trust ye. Mind yerself." He marched away proudly as if he had just laid down an important law.

"You mind yourself!" yelled Kane. "Don't worry about that idiot, Kyle."

"Who was he?" Kyle tried not to look abashed, but he was scarlet to his ears.

"A fool named Flurry," snarled Kane.

"His name is Owen the Flurry," Kross filled in. "Remember when I said some people were against your entry into SoGA?"

"So he's one of them?" mumbled Kyle. "Owen the Flurry, huh?"

"Don't worry about him, Kyle," Garnet yawned. "Not worth your time."

"Ah," started Kevin before using his notepad. "I agree with Garnet. Forget him and concentrate on your training." He stood up, looking carefree as ever.

As they all left the Dining Hall, Kyle felt envious of his friends. He wished his origins were a secret like Garnet's, or more accepted like the other three. Self pity fell over him like a chilly waterfall as his friends all left for their classes. It was like everyone was watching his every move. He had always wondered what it would be like to be popular, but this isn't what he had in mind.

He arrived to the third floor classroom with his long blade, hoping it was allowed. Other tyros were walking around the academy with their weapons so he assumed that it was, but he still felt like he was breaking some rule by carrying a weapon. The room was another with its desks and chairs piled against the wall. Kyle recognized no one in the class, but most of the students sat with their weapons across their laps. When he tried to sit near a group of fellow classmates, they moved away like he was infected. He was used to this kind of treatment, so he shrugged and kept to himself, only wishing that he could turn off his ears at the same time.

"They say he was raised by monsters," he overheard someone say. At this, Kyle laughed loudly. Since he could remember, people had called him 'weirdo' or 'stupid' or 'oddball,' but no one had ever said anything about monsters. The idea was utterly ridiculous to him and so for once, rather than staying completely silent, he laughed, much to the displeasure of those around him. Master Proculus walked in the room with his eyebrows raised, but said nothing regarding Kyle.

"We will be having class outside," he said. "It is too nice outside for us to be in here. Make sure to bring your weapons."

The class followed Master Proculus outside and as directed, they sat underneath a large tree with butterscotch colored leaves that shook carelessly in the soft summer breeze. Since Kyle was first under the tree, he helped himself to leaning against it while the rest kept their distance.

"I am known as Proculus the Storm. In this class, I will be teaching you all I can about MicroDimensions. It is a particularly useful key ability. To understand why, it would be best to define what it is. Does anybody know exactly what MicroDimensions is?"

A boy with yarn like auburn hair answered. "It's the use of another dimension," he said in a squeaky voice.

"That it is, Luke. As you all know, there are four known realms in our universe. Each of the realms shares dimensional planes that we are able to unlock with our keys. Although there are only four known realms, there is no known number of dimensions, meaning that they're likely infinite. MicroDimensions and BioDimensions make use of these limitless dimensions. Can anyone tell me the difference between these two branches of key use?

"Well it is simple, really. MicroDimensions has use only with inanimate objects such as weapons, armor, books, and things of that nature, while BioDimensions may summon forth living creatures or plants, although most times it is required for a contract to be made with the creature aiding you. Luckily, these summons tend to be quite agreeable and will accept most offers.

"Never mind that, though. We are here to learn about MicroDimensions. This ability allows you to unlock a storage-type dimension that is personally tailored for use by the person who opened the door to that dimension. However, the size of the dimensional space available varies depending on the focus and energy of the person in mind. Our goal today will be to open a large enough dimensional space for you to put your weapons in. This will allow for convenient storage that can follow you everywhere, even into other realms. As each of you train and get stronger, so will the dimension. Now, let us delay no further and get right to it. Everyone take out your keys."

"Master," squeaked Luke. "Excuse me for saying this, but MicroDimensions doesn't exactly sound...very useful. I mean, I can carry my own weapon." He lifted a small sword which wobbled in his hand. Kyle thought Proculus might burst into anger; instead he smiled.

"I seem to always have a tyro who questions whether or not MicroDimensions is useful. My word is normally never enough, but I personally must vouch for it and say that it is an extremely powerful key abil—"

At that moment, Kyle noticed what looked like a black blur shooting fast at his master. His body seemed to react on its own. Grabbing his sword, he kicked off the tree and intersected the blur, hitting it to the side. He soon discovered, along with everyone else, that he'd successfully redirected a javelin that had been thrown at Master Proculus. The thrower showed up a moment later, looking furious. Kyle readied his weapon.

"What are you doing, stupid boy?" The owner of the javelin picked up his weapon. He was older and had light brown eyes which matched his coffee-colored skin. "You dare interfere with my challenge to Master Proculus?" A couple other tyros showed up behind him, giving Kyle grim looks as well.

"Calm yourself, Jabbar the Cannon." Proculus placed a hand on Kyle's shoulder. "Kyle is not used to this realm or the way the academy works; he did not know that attacking a master is to challenge them. Regardless, we both know that I would have caught the javelin a moment later. Nevertheless, thank you, Kyle."

Kyle lowered his sword.

"The boy from another realm stopped my javelin?" spat Jabbar. "Quite lucky, aren't you? I have a mind to send you back to—"

"Watch your tongue, Jabbar."

"Forgive me, Master."

"You wish to challenge me?" Master Proculus rubbed his chin.

Jabbar took a knee to the ground and bowed with deep respect. "I do, Master."

"Very well," said Proculus. He turned to address the class. "This is a perfect opportunity to show the power of the MicroDimensions ability. Pay close attention and you will learn why I am named the Storm. Everyone stand back."

The class moved a good distance away, talking lively. None were as excited as Kyle, who could hardly believe that he was about to witness his master in a duel. He tried not to blink as Master Proculus and Jabbar pointed their keys at each other. Although faint, Kyle heard Proculus say one last thing to Jabbar. "Make sure your javelins stay away from the class."

As the keys were turned, Proculus and Jabbar distorted the air around themselves, making it almost look like liquid. The air bent and scrunched up like a transparent curtain had been draped around them. Kyle did a double take to make sure his eyes weren't playing tricks on him.

Proculus reached into two different areas of the distorted air. As his hands disappeared, the air rippled like water. He pulled out two heavy broadswords from his MicroDimension.

Jabbar would wait no more. He drew his right arm back and hurled his first javelin at Master Proculus. Without skipping a beat, Jabbar shoved his hands into his distorted space to pull out five more javelins with each hand, rapidly launching all of them like his arms were cannons. Nevertheless, Proculus knocked all the javelins to the ground with a few swats of his swords before charging Jabbar with his two blades at his side.

Jabbar jumped into the air, pulling out javelins and shooting them at the master fiercely, but without any success. When he landed, he pulled out two more javelins before again jumping, higher this time. Proculus followed. They exchanged blows almost too fast for Kyle's eyes, hanging in the air as though gravity had been turned off. With a hard swing, Jabbar pushed Proculus higher into the sky while forcing himself back to the ground. Proculus took the chance to throw his blades at Jabbar. They spun like windmills during a hurricane, but the Cannon blocked them easily with his javelins.

Like an eagle with its wings spread, Proculus grabbed onto the distorted air of his dimensions. He began pulling weapons out of his dimension with such speed that it looked like he had six arms. Spears, swords, axes, and daggers mercilessly rained over Jabbar. The Cannon blocked as many as he could, but it was too much. His left arm took a hard hit, knocking out the javelin from that hand. With only one javelin remaining, he concentrated on blocking a never ending storm of swords with only his right arm. He never noticed the master falling from the sky like hawk coming in for the kill.

When Master Proculus reached him, Jabbar's eyes widened, but it was far too late. The master drilled his right fist into the tyro's face, sending him flying back. He rolled on the ground for ten paces before stopping. On his knees, he made a sad attempt to get up, but fell down onto his face, unconscious. The fight was over.

"He is nowhere near ready," said Proculus as he pointed at the two friends who had accompanied Jabbar to his challenge. "You two grab his key and then take Jabbar to the Nursing Department. You have my permission to use the elevator." They grabbed Jabbar's key, which had fallen, and picked up their unconscious friend to carry him to the castle. Meanwhile, Kyle and the rest of the class cheered for their victorious master. All the weapons still littered the ground as if a battle involving two armies had just taken place.

"That, my young tyros, is one way to use the MicroDimensions ability," said Proculus with a wide smile. "I think I have proved that it is useful, haven't I Luke?"

"That was awesome," admitted Luke. "Sorry I said it wasn't earlier."

"Not a problem. It all depends on how you—Kyle, what are you doing?"

The entire class turned to look at Kyle, who was standing away from the group attempting to stab his rusty ancient key into the air. He got it to float and turned it, but nothing happened. It was only after that he answered his Master.

"I am trying," he said feeling almost annoyed, "to become Kyle the Storm." Proculus guffawed as the rest of the class separated to follow Kyle's example.

CHAPTER TEN

THE TORTOISE COIN

Kyle could hardly believe that Juniper had turned into Elm and Elm had turned into Hawthorn. This was partly because it was still odd to him how the months in Endera were named after trees from his realm, but the point was that time had flown by under the summer sun. As Hawthorn was quickly approaching Hickory, he felt more at home at Soul Gate Academy than he had anywhere else. He still missed Nana and Paps every now and then, but for the first time in his life, he had good friends whom were happy to have him around.

But life with his friends was not all he'd thought it would be.

His friends were talented tyros, which made him feel unaccomplished, to say the least. This was especially true about Garnet, who was not only growing in popularity due to her skill with the key and spear, but because of her beauty. She attracted all sorts of attention for it. Kevin the Stone and Kross the Monk were known for their dedication to training, which attracted admirers as well. His roommate Kane, although not nearly as hardworking, was also a natural who got good marks and was liked by many. Kyle alone seemed to be the oddball in his group; not nearly as talented and not nearly as well-liked.

This was not for lack of trying.

Training kept Kyle busy enough to feel like he was constantly slammed with homework. It required practice and memorization that extended beyond the classroom. And since he had mastered some of the fundamentals, his training was now much more complex.

He had made some progress with AuraBending. He could now see auras with ease. Master Helen had been correct in regards to his own, which like his eyes, was a crimson orange. Garnet's aura also took after her gem blue eyes, making it seem like she was shrouded in water. They had moved on to condensing their aura to protect single parts of the body, such as their hands or legs. This resulted in a stronger shield, but left the rest of the body exposed to attacks. Kyle found this difficult. The only successful part of his body that he'd been able to protect was his back, which for some reason came quite easy to him. During a small test in class, he had even been able block a chair which had been thrown at him. He'd laughed when it happened, having finally learned the reason why the desk and chairs were dented.

Amplifications and PsyBending had not been going as well. Enhancing the body was not as easy as it looked. True, he was already pretty quick on his feet without the enhancement, but it didn't stop the others from making him look like a snail as they flew past him. On top of that, Master Logan had moved them onto enhancing their sense of smell. The master explained that it was like trying to think with your nose. This made little sense to Kyle, which made the task more difficult.

PsyBending was difficult for another reason. Master Ellwood had an increasingly plain interest in the prior development of Kyle's mind. He often made remarks on how much he wished to dissect Kyle's brain, piece by piece, as if exploring it would unlock secrets about Kyle's realm. "Of course," said Ellwood irritably, "you could never survive such an experiment. I suppose I will simply have to cope with your sad attempts at the PsyBending abilities."

Kyle found this quite distracting. It didn't help that Greg the Yeti, a very pale but very brutal-looking tyro, had replaced Garnet as his partner. Garnet had been rightfully placed in the advanced group because of her skills in the subject. All of Kyle's attempts to befriend the Yeti had proved unsuccessful, or so he thought, because Greg only answered him with grunts. An ability to read Greg's mind would please Kyle immensely, but so far he had failed to tell which hand the coin was in behind Greg's back.

MicroDimensions and weaponry were easily his favorite classes. This was mostly because Master Proculus taught both of these classes. On top of that, Kane, Kross, and Kevin were in his weaponry class. Every day, Kyle was becoming better with his Nodachi sword, though he was still one of the worst in the level five class. His friends were among the best, which made him nervous, since he didn't want them to be placed in level six with Garnet while he was stuck in level five. MicroDimensions was going well, but he was only capable of unlocking a dimension that could fit his sword.

It bothered him that no one mentioned when his training in Synchroneity would begin. Neither Grandmaster Dante nor Master Proculus had brought it up since his reading. At the very least, Kyle wanted to learn more about the ability. His friends weren't much help, since they knew very little about it; however, Garnet suggested asking Master Oisin, who seemed to know everything about everything.

One breezy afternoon, Kyle decided that he would finally ask the history teacher what there was to know about Synchroneity. Kyle was never particularly in a good mood after PsyBending, but Garnet always waited for him in the entrance lobby with a smile that lightened his mood.

"Did Master Ellwood want to dissect your brain again?" she asked as they walked to History class together.

"Not today," answered Kyle. "But maybe I should let him since it certainly isn't helping me in that class."

"You'll get it soon enough," Garnet said kindly.

"You got it on the first day." He scowled.

"We can't all be fabulous," she joked. Although Kyle preferred the more relaxed friendship that he and Garnet now had, it was still caught him off guard sometimes. A few months ago, he would have never guessed that the shy girl he sat with on the bus would be joking with him in an attempt to cheer him up. Of course, he hardly would have guessed that he would be living in another realm, either.

They walked into class and sat at the same desk. Moments later, Master Oisin walked in looking particularly happy to be in class today. Kyle wanted to make sure he didn't forget to ask about Synchroneity, so he raised his hand immediately.

"Yes, Kyle," said Oisin in his usual bright tone. "What is it? Need to run to the restroom?"

"Umm, no, Master." Kyle ruffled up his hair as the class snickered. "I just wondered if it would be possible for you to tell me about the

Synchroneity ability. The Reader drew it from me on the day of my reading, but I haven't yet started training to use it."

Some of the class looked at him funny, as if he was making it up.

"Synchroneity," drawled Master Oisin, almost as if the words had taste to them. "Yes, I believe there is some history to that. It has been a long time since we have had anyone capable of learning Synchroneity at Soul Gate Academy. It is a rare ability to have with keys.

"Years ago, before the Reader's Guild had been created to give us readers, our ancestors were left to figure which abilities would best suit their bodies on their own. Imagine the difficulty of that. However, our ancestors had quite the tenacity when it came to using the powers of keys. They developed many of the abilities we have now. I have mentioned all this in class before, I believe." Master Oisin paused in an elegant attempt to capture every student's attention. He had such enthusiasm for history it took very little effort on his part. Every student listened at the edge of their seat, wondering what he was going to say next.

"There was an ability that proved exceptionally different than the rest, and that was Synchroneity. Synchroneity is the ability to unlock the powers of the elements: fire, water, air, earth, and lightning!" He gave a thunderous clap. Some of the class flinched, giving Oisin reason to grin as he continued. "Brilliant, no? This power was highly sought after. Many tried and failed to control the destructive power of the elements. But there were few who mastered Synchroneity and were able to lock elements to their weapons or body. Since then, there have been many attempts to understand why only a few are able to use Synchroneity. All these years later, there still isn't an answer. If you ask me, I believe there is a simple reason: they were not born to do so."

"So who can teach me Synchroneity?" asked Kyle.

"Well," said Master Oisin, "Grandmaster Dante is the only one I know who can. It is a difficult ability, so he must have his reasons for not teaching you yet. My advice is to be patient. Now, enough of that. Let us move on to the real importance of today's class. Today, you will be placed in your mission squads."

The class burst into excited chatter. They'd been briefed about missions and mission squads weeks ago. Master Oisin was responsible for placing tyros in their squads, each of which ranged from two to six people. It was typical for the teams to be a mixture of the newest tyros with a few more seasoned tyros. After formation, squads were sent on missions that were requested by local villages and towns near the Soul Gate Academy. It was a way of paying for the expense of having so many students, while teaching them to work together. Most missions were of historical nature. They ranged from finding information on a lost relative or ancestor, or perhaps hunting down an artifact or bounty. Bounties were strictly for more experienced tyros. Kyle desperately hoped that Garnet would be on his team.

"Follow me outside and we will put you into groups with some other already-formed teams. They will show you the ropes until about next year; then your team is on its own."

The class followed Oisin outside, where a group of tyro squads waited with Master Helen. Most of the groups were made up of three people. Kyle noticed that Owen the Flurry was with a thuggish pair of goons. Owen had left Kyle alone since their first encounter, but Kyle had a feeling that the Flurry was responsible for why many tyros steered clear of him.

"Kyle, Garnet!" yelled Kane from the crowd. "Over here; you're with us."

"Thank you, Kane." Master Oisin's bark was thick with sarcasm. "I hadn't told the class who they were with, but now you have ruined the surprise of it all. Well, get over to them, you two. I still have to tell everyone else."

When Kyle and Garnet made it over to Kane's squad, they were happy to find they were with friends. Kevin and Kane greeted them with warm smiles and even Kross's normally placid face was welcoming.

"We're on this squad?" Kyle grinned as he turned to Garnet.

"Looks like it," she said. "It's a good thing they pay attention to who we hang out with."

"They have to," said Kross. "Imagine being randomly placed with a group of people who hate you." Kyle looked over at Owen and was quite glad for the careful watch of the masters.

"You guys could've told us earlier." Garnet's eyes wandered through the crowd, checking out the new squads.

"We only just found out a few minutes ago," said Kevin's notepad. They could have known a month ago and Kyle wouldn't have minded. He was so thrilled to be on a team with his friends that everything about the day seemed nicer, as though clouds had disappeared to allow the sun's rays through. Garnet being on the team made him especially pleased.

"Every. One. Quiet," yelled Master Logan as he sat down a large treasure chest. He had appeared out of nowhere, which would have surprised everyone, but it was such a normal occurrence at the academy that everyone had grown used to it. He was extremely fast, even for a master. "It is time. For your first. Mission." The crowd of newly established teams instantly silenced. "Master Helen. Will explain the rest." He disappeared.

"Ahem," Master Helen cleared her throat. "Your mission today will be a simple one. Master Logan just dropped these off." She opened the container that held large round gold and silver coins, each with a different animal engraved onto them. Master Helen picked up a few to show the tyros the faces of a snake, eagle, and tiger sparkle across the width of each coin. After everyone had a good look, she threw them back into the chest. "Each squad will get one coin. Send a member from each team to get your coin now." Each of the squads chose someone, sending them to fetch a coin. Kross volunteered to get theirs and came back with a gold tortoise coin. The crowd of students became loud with chatter as they discussed the coin they received.

"Quiet down!" yelled Helen over the crowd. "All gold coin squads come to my left and silver to my right. That's good. This will give you a taste of future missions and how they will work. The gold coin squads are going to search in the forest beyond the wall for a coin that is identical to the one you are holding. Before you think this is impossible, the coin in your hands will help you find the way. It is locked with an aura that will grow colder or hotter depending on how close you get to the other coin. The hotter it is, the closer you are. The coin should be easily visible when you're close, so don't worry too much.

"Once you find the second gold coin, the matching animal silver coin will trail a beam of light directly to the gold coin. The silver team will follow the light toward the other team and then attempt to steal their gold coin. If the gold team is able to get past the silver team and make it to the castle, they will be allowed to skip class tomorrow. If the silver team makes it back here with the stolen gold coin, they will get to skip class."

Everyone cheered at the idea of being able to skip class. It seemed like they never got a break from their training, so a day of relaxation rather than class was a rare treat.

"As you can see, it is quite the prize," Helen said with a nod. "If the gold team for some wild reason does not find their other coin, the silver team automatically gets the day off. Also, you are not allowed to place coins inside of MicroDimensions or BioDimensions. Your coin must be in plain sight at all times. Squads are to act respectively toward each other; keep in mind that there are masters in the forest that will monitor your movements and make sure everyone stays safe. Does everyone understand?"

"What about weapons?" yelled Kane the Ace.

"If you need your weapon, you have fifteen minutes to get them. Don't be late getting back or I'll make you run laps around the castle. Go now! Everyone else, take out your weapons and sit tight."

Those who couldn't use MicroDimensions or BioDimensions sprang into action, running toward the dormitory towers. Kyle, Garnet, and Kross used their keys to take out their weapons. Kyle noticed that rather than using MicroDimensions, Garnet and Kross used BioDimensions, which was noticeably different. As this was the first time Kyle had seen them summoned, he was very curious.

When Kross summoned, a tail made out of scaly looking mud stuck out of the dimensional space handing him his Shaolin spade. It had different razor sharp blades on both ends of the long staff. One end had a curved spade, the other had a blade that looked like a crescent moon. Garnet's creature had a snout that was made out of a green stem with a small sunflower as its nose. Its mouth released Garnet's spear into her hands as Garnet pet its nose affectionately. When she was finished, it returned into the dimension.

"What were those…things?" Kyle wasn't sure what to call them exactly.

"Pan the Lutumdragon," said Kross proudly. "He's a dragon made from clay."

"What about yours Garnet?"

"Umm," said Garnet, "her name is Io the Helianlupus. It's sort of a wolf mixed with a sunflower. She is a very loyal summon, which is the nature of her kind."

"Wow, cool," said Kyle enviously. With less enthusiasm than usual, he turned his key to reach into his dimension to retrieve his Nodachi. Moments later, Kevin and Kane ran toward them with their weapons in hands. They were one of the first ones back, so they joined in waiting for the rest of the tyros to get back with their weapons.

"That looks like everyone," said Master Oisin to Master Helen. "Shall we get them started?"

"Yes. Gold teams, get ready to enter the forest." Twelve teams walked toward the open wall gate. "Ahem, well then. Get going," she said rather anti-climatically. The squads hesitated, but departed in different directions in accordance to how their coin felt. Kross led the way, claiming that the gold tortoise coin was warmest when pointed northwest.

The forest was packed with growth of a variety of different plants that made travel slow. It was clear that area did not get much traffic. Nearly three quarters of an hour passed before their group discovered the second coin. It was lodged in the branches of a small tree. As soon as they dislodged it, the two coins magnetically connected, sending a beam of light that led back to the castle. They knew that this meant the other team was on their way.

"Time for things to get interesting," said Kane. "Let's stick to the plan. Hold on tight to the coin, Garnet. Kross and I will scan ahead. Kevin, you run in front of Garnet; Kyle, hop in behind her. Let's move as fast as we can."

Kross and Kane moved ahead of the group. Blending in with the forest was easy enough, but it did little to comfort them since the same could be said about the silver team that was moving toward them. Nearly a half hour passed, yet they met no other squad. Now they were near enough to the gate that the path was visible. Kross and Kane stepped out onto the path, signaling the other three to join them. There, standing ten paces in front of them was Owen the Flurry and the five other members of his squad. A hundred yards behind them was the gate into Soul Gate Academy. Owen held out his silver tortoise coin with a light shining from it that attached itself to the gold coin in Garnet's hands.

"Oi," sneered Owen. "How 'bout ye just hand over the gol' coin. I don't feel like beatin' the friends of that filthy outsider…today." Owen's team looked daunting. Each of them shot Kyle a disgusted look, agreeing wholeheartedly with Owen.

"Great," muttered Kyle. "Just great."

"Ah," Kevin looked quite serious. "Ah."

"Kyle, stay with Garnet." Kross wiggled his key in his hand. "Both of you try to get to the wall, it's not too far. We'll try to take them head-on to make a path for you."

Kyle frowned. The plan was obviously flawed, seeing as there were six on the silver team and only three of them, but he and Garnet agreed, anyways. Kevin, Kross, and Kane worked well together, like a choreographed dance, as they charged into the team. Kross swept with his Shaolin spade, Kevin came down with his heavy axe, and Kane jabbed with his daggers.

The problem was that Owen's team was skilled, as well. They left no openings. Owen used his spiked knuckles to punch away any attacks. When necessary, the others covered his openings. After a few minutes, Kross fell back to use his key. He turned it forcefully, causing a large scaly lizard made of mud came out of the air. "Soften the ground around those people!" Kross yelled the instruction while pointing toward Kane and Kevin. "And I'll remove the worms from your back later." A closer look and Kyle could see there were a number of wiggling worms on the dragon's back.

"As you wish," said Pan the Lutumdragon. The mud dragon dove into the ground as though it were water, digging a tunnel like a mole in a beeline toward the silver team. When Pan reached them, the ground became soft mud. Owen's squad lost some footing as they sank into muck, but the same was true for Kevin and Kane. The grunts, screams, and clangs of weapons smashing together sounded down the path as though nothing had happened.

"Garnet, Kyle, go now!" yelled Kross as he ran back to help Kane and Kevin. Garnet and Kyle ran around the mud toward the wall.

They made it past the group, but suddenly, a girl with curly black hair swung her spear in an attempt to knock them both off her feet. The mud had not been able to stop all of Owen's team. Kyle jumped over the spear in time, and Garnet reacted with her weapon, defending but dropping the gold coin which began rolling away from them.

"Kyle!" shouted Garnet. "The coin!"

Kyle dove, grabbing the coin just before their attacker could reach it. Garnet moved forward to engage her, rushing in to counter.

"Go ahead," she said. "I'll take her on." The two girls began to fight. Kyle had confidence in Garnet's ability since she was in a higher level of weaponry than him, but a part of him didn't want to just leave her behind. The girls jabbed and swirled their spears with all the skill of well seasoned warriors. Thinking to help Garnet, Kyle pulled out his key, attempting to enhance his calves to run faster. Nothing happened. "Just go, Kyle!" Much against his nature, he left them, sprinting toward the goal at his normal pace.

Suddenly, someone who *could* enhance their calves ran past Kyle and punched him hard in the face. As the world shook inside his skull, he held on dearly to his key, his Nodachi, and the coin. He staggered to the side. Owen the Flurry was now standing in front of him with a sinister smile. Kross, Kane, and Kevin, who were all still behind him, yelled something that was completely unintelligible. He knew his three friends were trying frantically to help him, but they could not get past the other silver teammates.

"Oi," growled Owen. "Hand over the coin."

Kyle stared at him with contempt. The Flurry dashed in, punching Kyle's left leg with the force of a bear. His leg went completely numb with pain. Owen backed off again; he wanted Kyle to hand him the coin in defeat rather than take it away. The thought of giving up simply never came to Kyle.

Thinking on the spot, he turned his key, making aura form around him to create an invisible shield on his back. This was his strongest place of defense now. Energy to keep his shield up sapped his body at an alarming rate, but this only made his determination stronger.

He limped forward in the direction of the gate and Owen. The Flurry looked as if someone had just given him a present. He prepared his fist with sickening cracks. Expecting this, Kyle slashed at him with his Nodachi. The big brute sidestepped the sword, bringing himself around to Kyle's back. He punched with force enough to rival a bull charge, but his fist bounced off Kyle's guard. The blow was still strong enough to cause Kyle pain, but he ignored it the best he could, continuing to limp forward.

Owen was quick to lose his temper and sent flurries of punches at Kyle's back. Luckily, Kyle's defense held against every punch. He limped closer and closer to the gate. He expected Owen to change his approach, but Kyle realized that, strong as he was, the Flurry was simply not bright.

Master Helen and Master Oisin stood just within SoGA's walls, watching Kyle struggle a few feet from the gate. Owen must have realized that Kyle was just moments from reaching the goal because he decided to change his punch to a kick aimed at Kyle's already weakened left leg. It was too little too late. Kane had finally managed to break away from the other group, stopping Owen's attack just in time. The Ace knocked the Flurry back with a powerful slash from his dagger, leaving Kyle free to make it to the gate.

A few steps later, Kyle successfully made it past the gate, where he fell to the ground breathing hard right in front of the masters. He handed Master Oisin his gold coin at which, after a quick glance, the old master burst into laughter.

"Look at this, Master Helen," he said showing the coin to Helen. She looked at it with all the intrigue of having discovered something quite amusing. "Kyle has successfully brought us the gold tortoise coin, all while limping at a tortoise's pace with his back like a protective shell." As Helen smirked, he laughed brightly. "I think this calls for a change to his title. Kyle the Tyro will now be known as Kyle the Tortoise."

Exhausted as he was from keeping the aura shield up so long, he had to agree that the new title was fitting. That didn't mean he was happy with it. *Kyle the Tortoise. That's so...lame.*

The fight between the groups had stopped when he made it into the gate to secure the victory. Owen's group came in disgruntled. Kyle lay on his back trying to catch his breath when his friends surrounded him. They cheered, laughed, and teased him for their victory and for him having become Kyle the Tortoise. He couldn't remember a time he had felt so good, though he could have done without the soreness.

CHAPTER ELEVEN

KEY OF THRONE ARMS

The Tortoise," he muttered to himself unhappily.

It didn't take long for the rest of Soul Gate Academy to find out that the boy from the other realm had become Kyle the Tortoise. Kyle, who was no longer limping after a short visit to Master Yvette in the Nursing Department, was determined to change his new title. How he was going to do this, he wasn't sure. After dinner, they found a large tree with yellowing leaves to sit under as the cool summer breeze began to feel more like autumn. Kyle was enjoying the pleasant weather on his day off, but he still felt frustrated. His friends were happy to continue offering their suggestions, as they had all day.

"How about you try lifting the school up into the air?" asked Kane, trying to lift Kyle's mood. "I think a guy way back did that and they named him—I think they named him the Titan—yeah, that's it! It was Atlas the Titan."

"Atlas the Titan?" Kyle pictured a stone statue of a man holding up a giant globe. "Umm, isn't that a—never mind." Kane was ignoring him, anyhow, in his attempt to think of more suitable titles.

"How about Kyle the Great?" suggested Kevin with his notepad. After the mission, Kevin had been named the Bison. Kyle thought this was a much better title than Tortoise. "Kind of like Alexander the Great. He's a bit of a legend, no?"

"Umm…"

"I know!" Kane pounded his fist into his palm. "Kyle the Hood, like Robin the Hood! Just start wearing a hood all the time, Kyle. It'll be easy."

"Er…"

"I may have a suggestion," said Kross casually, yet a little excitably, which was out of character for him. "How about Kyle the Argonaut? All you'd have to do is search for golden things all the time, like Jason the Argonaut."

"Kross, that's an awesome name!" Kane affirmed. Kross flushed as placidly as he could, but he looked rather pleased with himself. "Kyle the Argonaut. That's perfect!" Kevin nodded as if that settled the matter.

"How do you three even know the names of those heroes—well they're kind of heroes—from my realm?" This wasn't the first time Kyle noticed odd connections between the realms but this seemed too farfetched.

"Your realm?" Kyle and Kross asked in union. Kyle suspected Kevin would have asked the same question, but instead he said, "ah." The three of them did share the same confused look.

Garnet laughed at them. "I swear. Sometimes it's like you three are the same person." The three of them shrugged. Garnet had been given the title the Scarlet Needle. The masters had been impressed with her, and their admiration was well-deserved. She was only a first year and some people were saying that she would have her eternal title by the end of the year. Although Kyle was happy for her, he couldn't help but feel a little envious that she had received a much better title than his own.

"Seriously, though," Kyle continued, "don't you think it's weird that our realms have some of the same heroes?"

"Well," said Kross, "it is possible that they traveled between the realms. Master Oisin has said in class that it is likely that the laws of traveling between realms were not as strict in ancient times."

"I see." Kyle thought about this for a bit, but then he remembered his title. "Ugh, it doesn't change the fact that my name is the Tortoise."

"How about we request our squad for a local mission?" suggested Garnet. "We should be able to now, right? That's how we usually earn titles, isn't it? By doing stuff on missions?"

"That's right," said Kane eagerly. "We should sign up for one today."

It didn't take more than that to convince Kyle. He stood up and ushered the group of them back to the castle. They set off to Master Oisin's room because he was the master in charge of issuing missions to the younger squads. Luckily, they found him sitting at his desk during one of his free periods and asked him immediately for a mission. Before Master Oisin could answer, they were interrupted.

"Oho." The grandmaster stood at the doorway, leaning casually on his cane. "Kyle the Tortoise wants to change his title so quickly, does he?" Kyle nearly twitched at the sound of his title.

"Yes, Grandmaster." He scratched his head. "I don't mean any disrespect by wanting to change it, it's just that it doesn't fit me very well."

"Brilliant," said Master Oisin. "Simply brilliant. A student who wants to change his title, how completely ordinarily brilliant."

Everyone except Kyle laughed at that. Grandmaster Dante was the loudest.

"It's very common for tyros to want to change their titles," supplied Dante. "In my younger years, I was Dante the Gray. " He pointed at his salt and pepper hair. "You see, I've always had a bit of gray up here. Although I take a certain pride in my graying hair, I must admit that my title wasn't exactly what I would have chosen. Luckily, through hard work and perseverance, I made people see that I was much more than just a man with gray hair."

Again, the Grandmaster chortled. He turned to Master Oisin. "I came down here to tell you that I have a mission I need taken care of near Dilu Village."

"I think I have just the group for you. Three of my second years and two first years. All of them show promise."

"Naturally," said the Grandmaster. "However, it's the mission regarding the Kota. I believe I mentioned it to you some time ago. What do you think?"

Kyle looked around at his friends. Everyone's excitement began escalating. Kyle didn't know much at all about what Kotas were, but it sounded exciting. The thrill of finding a legendary weapon made his want to leap with joy. Chances seemed pretty slim, considering nobody even knew if they were real.

"I see," said Master Oisin, now with a look that showed a bit of concern. "How much longer 'til Thullrun delivers the Center Key?"

"At least four months."

Master Oisin closed his eyes as if calculating an answer. "I think this group can handle it in four months. It'll be good experience for them."

"I agree," said Dante. "What do you think, tyros? Will you take on this mission at the request of your Grandmaster?"

Kyle, Kane, Kross, Kevin, and Garnet immediately gave Grandmaster Dante a slight bow, signifying their acceptance of the mission. Kyle was quick to straighten back up, though.

"Can't we go do it now?" He didn't like the idea of being called the Tortoise for another four months.

"Oho," said Dante. "I heard you were a bit impatient, so I must tell you without beating around the bush—no. You will wait. I imagine you don't even know what a Kota is yet, do you?"

"Er…"

"Precisely," said Dante. "I believe Master Oisin is the best person to fill you in on that, so if he has time?"

"Oh, I do," said Master Oisin enthusiastically.

"Oho, there you are!" exclaimed the Grandmaster. "You five are to stay here and listen to Master Oisin's lecture on the Kota."

"Yes, Grandmaster," they shouted in unison. Kyle was a bit disgruntled, but he hardly could argue with Grandmaster Dante. "When the lecture is done, you, Kyle the Tortoise, are to come see me in my office."

"Me?" asked Kyle shocked.

"Yes, you," he said. "You have permission to use the elevator. Well, until then. Master Oisin, I leave them to you." He kicked his cane up and walked briskly out of the room, humming an unfamiliar tune. Kyle thought he might be in trouble, but he pushed the idea from his mind when Master Oisin stood up, eager to tell the tyros about the Kota.

"All of you sit," he said. Everyone except Kane hurriedly obliged.

"Umm, Master," said Kane, a plea in his voice. "I think Kross, Kevin, and I know enough about Kota to be able to skip the lecture, don't you think?"

Master Oisin gave him a speculative look. "Tell me, Kane the Ace. Who created the Kota?"

"I thought they were just legendary."

"I may often mention the Kotas as if they were myths, but, as I have said before, they are very real. Please sit down." After Kane found a seat with a pout, Oisin went on, "Excellent. Now let me get underway. Kota! As you probably know, the word 'Kota' is technically an abbreviation for 'Key of Throne Arm,' often referred to as 'KeyArms' as well. To explain what a Kota is, it would be easiest to show you."

Strangely enough, Master Oisin did not take out a key, yet he still did the motion and unlocked his MicroDimension. He pulled out a short rapier with a fancy hand guard that had many metal twists. The blade was straight and sharp, but at the end there was a squared hook that was very much like the bit of a key. Kyle instantly realized that this was the second Kota he had seen. Although notably different, he remembered that Alexun the Path Guard had also used a rapier Kota.

"As you may have guessed, this is a rapier Kota." The five tyros stared at the Kota in amazement. Kyle noticed a flicker of desire in both Kross's and Kane's eyes. On the other hand, Kevin and Garnet seemed unimpressed as they looked at the weapon. Kyle's eyes locked onto the weapon as awe filled him with the desire to hold it. There was no denying that it looked impressive. "This Kota, like all Kotas, is an extremely beneficial and powerful weapon. Can any of you tell me why?"

Garnet raised her hand and Oisin called on her. "It doubles as a key and weapon," she said. "But Master, how did you open your MicroDimension without it being in your hand?"

"Excellent observation, Garnet. The Kota is a weapon that has been fused with a key, which omits the trouble of holding a key while handling your weapon. When a Kota is obtained, the wielder and Kota become powerfully connected. This connection allows the KeyArm to be used by a single wielder, and because of it, it can be summoned without the use of another key. This is true even if you are not adept with MicroDimensions or BioDimensions. Allow me to demonstrate."

Master Oisin took his sword and threw it powerfully into the back wall of the room. The tyros turned around to see it stuck deeply into the wall like a dart. They turned back to their Master, gazing at him in astonishment. Oisin rotated his hand as if he had a key in it once again. This time, his rapier Kota magically appeared in his hands as though it had never left. Each of them looked back and forth from the wall to Master Oisin making sure that it was the same sword. It was.

"As you can see, this sword is bound to me. Wherever I am, so long as I am alive, it will come to me when I call. These weapons are as rare as they are powerful. Because of that, they are highly sought by those who know of them. That is why I suggest that anyone who ever comes across a Kota should not carry it openly like a fool. If you have MicroDimensions or BioDimensions, then you should use it to conceal the Kota. If you don't have the ability, you should keep it secretly hidden and only summon it when necessary. A connection between the Kota and wielder can only be severed by death. It is important to know what the Kota can do, but it is just as important to know where they came from."

Master Oisin began pacing the front of his room, holding his Kota in his hands behind his back. "Many years ago, long before our oldest ancestors were even born, blacksmith and locksmith were one in the same," he continued. "They were called the King Forgers. The King Forgers eventually died out, taking with them the necessary technique and wisdom that is required to forge a Kota. Some believe it was because the King Forgers used the Kota to start a war to which they were eventually held accountable and put to death. Others think they merely vanished. Regardless of how it happened, with their disappearance, their secrets vanished with them. Since then, there have been smiths who have attempted to recreate the Kota, but none have ever come close. The Kotas are incredible enough to have lasted thousands of years, but look as if they were crafted just yesterday. Truly, they are remarkable weapons."

Kyle quivered at the idea of owning such a weapon. It sounded so limitless and dangerous, like it had the power to make him fly.

"What we know presently about the Kota is that most of them disappeared with the King Forgers. Others were destroyed, hidden, or taken by the Gatekeepers of Librium. And that my young tyros, is, more or less, the tale of the Kota." He twisted his rapier Kota, opening up his MicroDimension again and returning his KeyArm to it. "Any questions?"

This time, Kross raised his hand. "Master Oisin, thank you for explaining the Kota, but you have yet to explain what this has to do with the mission."

"Ah, yes of course. In four month's time, the five of you will be required to leave SoGA and head to Dilu Village. Near the village is a door which leads to a cavern. Hopefully, the cavern offers a number of places still left unexplored. We have been given reason to believe that a book regarding the technique to create Kotas is located somewhere in the cavern. These rumors are likely false, but we can't be sure since the cavern has never been thoroughly searched. This is mainly due to the fact that the town Thullrun holds the Center Key, one of the three keys needed for opening the door. When they deliver us the key—why it is taking them that long is beyond me; that town has always been on the slow side—you five will go exploring the cave and bring back anything you find. A simple mission, but it could turn out fruitful. Once we get the Center Key from Thullrun, you will head to Dilu Village before actually entering the cavern, since the other two keys to enter the cavern are in the possession of Dilu Village's Mayor. Once you have all three keys, you will head for the cavern and give it a good search. Is that clear enough?"

With nothing more to say, they left Master Oisin's classroom with a greater understanding of the Kota. This made Kyle more excited about the mission than he had previously been.

"Wouldn't it be cool if we found a Kota?" he said as an afterthought. "I mean, Master Oisin's weapon seemed incredible." They walked down the stairs to the lobby entrance, each of them separately fantasizing about a Kota that would be theirs.

"Don't you think that this is a pretty big mission for our first one?" Garnet mulled over her own question, her eyes squinting with suspicion.

"Probably a wild goose chase," Kane supplied. "I doubt they'd send *us* if they thought we were gonna find something."

"I agree," said Kross. "It is likely that this mission is just a learning experience."

"But maybe," said Kane hopefully, "they don't want to draw too much attention to the search. Maybe someone's hoping we'll do all the work and get the Kota for them; then they'll snatch it away from us."

"Ah," added Kevin the Bison excitably.

"We're looking for a book," Kross pointed out. He had a knack for responding as though he could read Kevin's thoughts.

"Ah," replied Kevin, his tone now deflated.

"Book or Kota," said Kane. "Who knows what we'll find?"

"Well, I hope we find something." Kyle didn't think it was likely but it sounded thrilling all the same. He would have liked to discuss theories more, but it was getting late and he was supposed to be somewhere. "I guess I should get going to the Grandmaster's office."

Kyle uttered a quick goodbye to them before making his way to through the lobby. It was clear of students now. Most of them had probably made their ways to their bedroom or were outside catching a glimpse of the two crescent moons that glowed in the night sky. He made into the elevator and turned the key labeled "Grandmaster's Office." With a loud click, the doors slid shut.

Seconds later, the doors opened up to a different hallway. It led to a room with a counter desk. Behind it sat what Kyle assumed was the receptionist.

She was pink. All pink. She had a long pink and feathery neck. Her winged arms were crossed as she stared at Kyle with disgust. She had beady eyes and a thin oval head that had two pointy ears sticking from the side of it like antennas. Her hooked beak clicked together while she looked Kyle over. He was strongly reminded of Odin the Tytodwarf, but the pink flamingo lady in front of him now was definitely not a tytodwarf.

"What are you looking at, boy?" she snapped. "Never seen a phoenelf? I swear, all the students who come here look as confused as you. What do they teach down there, I wonder?" Her beak clicked loudly. "My name is Lyn! You best remember it. I don't approve of you coming to see the Grandmaster so late, have you no manners?"

Kyle scratched his head and murmured, "Sorry, I was told to come."

"Speak louder, you spineless prune. At least act like a man."

Kyle gulped, unsure of how to respond. He was glad to see the Grandmaster walk into the room from the door behind Lyn.

"Oho," he said like always. "I thought I heard Lyn getting all fired up. Come on in, Kyle. Pay no mind to Lyn's wicked sense of humor."

Lyn clicked her beak together, but her face looked much kinder. "I do like my jokes."

Kyle smiled clumsily as he passed her. He followed the Grandmaster into a glorious room with a high ceiling. The carpet was a majestic deep blue that matched walls covered with odd trinkets and relics. In a glass display case, there were a number of keys, some of which looked like they were partially melted or broken in many pieces. The Grandmaster's desk looked like it was carved out of the vast stump of a redwood. It was old and deformed, but looked incredibly sturdy. A stone tablet on the desk caught Kyle's attention. On the stone there was a primitive engraving of a man with a large key in his hands.

"This," Dante pointed at the tablet, "is the first picture of a sword Kota, or so I'd like to think. History is mostly guesswork. Though I should add it is often very good guesswork." He chuckled as though it were some small inside joke. "Please sit down." He sat down and waited for Kyle to do the same. "I would like to discuss my plans to teach you Synchroneity."

Kyle felt a jolt of electricity spread through him as though he'd been hit by a lightning bolt.

CHAPTER TWELVE

LIGHTNING

"As I'm sure you already know, Synchroneity is the rare ability to unlock the power of the elements," said Grandmaster Dante. "This ability allows you to lock the elements to your weapons or your body. At a higher level, you can blast the element at your opponent. However, the most important thing to understand is that the elements cannot be truly controlled. It is more like they are being guided. I will personally be showing you how. Do you think you're ready?"

"Yes, Grandmaster," answered Kyle eagerly. "But how? I thought you only knew how to control fire?"

"Oho, right you are. Fire flows through me as I'm sure Lightning does through you." When Kyle thought about this, it was more than right; it seemed to be effortlessly logical. Just as blood flowed through his veins, so did lightning. "I cannot teach you specifically how to wield lightning, but I can show you the fundamentals to using Synchroneity."

"What do you mean, Grandmaster?"

"Let me show you."

Dante sprang to his feet like an energetic youth. With his eyes closed, he waved his cane like a wand, but turned it at the same time. Suddenly, the ground underneath him burst into wild flames, startling Kyle enough to knock over his chair. He stood up to see his Grandmaster smirking kindly. There was a globe of fire in his hands, looking as brilliant as a sunset, but flickering recklessly, as though it struggled to stay in his hands.

"Doesn't it burn?" Kyle stared at the ball of fire, expecting it to scorch his Grandmaster's hand.

"A person who is able to use the Synchroneity ability cannot be hurt by his element," Dante stated. "He or she is immune to it, because it is part of their body." He squeezed the fire globe with his hands, crumbling the flames into a powder that looked like the remains of a crushed red brick. He pointed at the dust. "And as you can see, this is no ordinary fire. I imagine your lightning will also have unique attributes. If you can remember your reading, your lightning was yellow. An unusual color for lightning, don't you think?"

*Yellow lightning...*Kyle forgot how to blink with how amazed and impressed he felt. Excitement combined with respectful fear trembled through his heart so fiercely his pulse could have shook the floor. Even with all the powers of the keys, seeing fire being handled so casually was marvelous. He ached to start with Synchroneity right away. "Grandmaster Dante, when will I start my training?" The Grandmaster rubbed his chin a little as he sat back down. Kyle picked up his chair and then sat back down, raring to go.

"Kyle, you have to understand that lightning, just like fire, is particularly dangerous to others. You cannot feel the pain of the electrical currents, but others definitely can. I need you to promise that you will be extremely careful." Dante gazed at Kyle with a seriousness that chilled his bones.

"I promise, Grandmaster."

"Excellent! Bring out your key immediately. We'll start tonight."

The abruptness of the Grandmaster's change in mood threw Kyle off, but he brought his key out. He could hardly believe he was going to start Synchroneity tonight.

"All key abilities have a lot less to do with the key and a lot more to do with the focus of the person in mind, but the key is still essential. A key's part in unlocking and locking goes much deeper into a person's being than we give it credit for. With Synchroneity, this is no different. You could even say this ability is much more natural to people like us, yet at the same time, it's much harder to manipulate. Just like with all the key abilities, we will start off slow.

"Your lightning is very similar to my fire, so I am assuming that the same principles will work. That being said, we will start your lessons by bringing the lightning to the tip of your fingers. Like this." Dante twisted his cane and let it go. All ten of his fingers now had a small red flame attached to each as if they were wicks of a candle. "You will start with one finger and work your way up to ten, okay?"

In his impatience, Kyle gave a violent nod. Pointing his key at his index finger, he turned it, focusing on lightning, but nothing happened. Grandmaster Dante tilted his head, but said nothing. His intense look was enough to tell Kyle to keep going. He tried again. It felt necessary to figure it out on his own, though he could not explain why. In a way, it was almost like he wanted to impress Grandmaster Dante.

Suddenly, he felt a zappy itch beneath his skin.

Kyle concentrated on his finger harder than ever, while Dante quietly watched. *I can do this.* He closed his eyes to picture a hot flashing volt of electricity stretching out across a dark sky. When he opened his eyes, a slow zigzagging yellow electric current ringed his index finger. Kyle looked at it in wonder. He hadn't really thought that he'd be able to get lightning to come out, but there it was, floating around his finger like a wiggling yellow halo.

"Try the next finger," said the Grandmaster. It was a request, not a demand. Kyle knew he could have stopped if he wanted to.

Directing his attention to his middle finger, Kyle tried as hard as he could to achieve the same result. Minutes passed, but he could not light up the second finger. When the lightning circling the index finger began to dim, the Grandmaster asked him to stop. The little electric halo dispersed immediately, leaving Kyle breathing hard from exhaustion. He felt as if he had just sprinted around the castle with stone weights on each foot.

"Oho, this is quite something," declared Grandmaster Dante as he pondered over Kyle's start with Synchroneity. "I hardly explained enough for you to get that far and yet, you seem to have a natural control of your lightning already. This is good, very good."

"Should I try again?" panted Kyle. "I think I can still keep going."

"No, I think that's quite enough." Dante stroked his chin absentmindedly. "This does change my plans a bit. I had intended to beat the lightning out of you just like my master did to me. Hmm…" Kyle gave a clumsy laugh, but saw that the Grandmaster was entirely serious. "…might still do some good. Hmm…" Grandmaster lost himself in thought while Kyle sat silently, wondering if getting crushed by the Grandmaster would still leave him alive. "No, I suppose there will be no need after all."

Kyle sighed in relief.

"Kyle, you seem to have little need for the initial unlocking, which is impressive as it is lucky. I barely survived when my master 'unlocked' my fire from me. Like I said earlier, you must work your way up to ten fingers. I want you to try and have five electric halos around your fingers by the end of second winter month, Redwood. That will be your individual training. Master Proculus will help you utilize your Synchroneity ability in combat while helping raise your endurance. You will have private lessons with him every Tuesday and Thursday."

Kyle was excited to have another class with Proculus, but he knew it would be difficult. Proculus taught with a ferociousness that was certain to make strong tyros.

"What will Master Proculus and I be doing?"

"Mainly sparring," said Dante. "Fighting with a master will be tough, so you should prepare yourself. But that will be all for tonight. I think I have explained enough for now."

Kyle gulped. Training at the academy was about to become busier than ever. "Grandmaster Dante, you said you would be training me, didn't you?"

"Oho, that I did," he said. "As soon as you can control five fingers, you will meet with me once a week for combat and twice a week for Synchroneity meditation. This of course, will be on top of meeting with Proculus twice a week. Synchroneity takes considerable training and dedication to master, so that you are not electrocuting friend along with foe."

"I will try my best." Kyle tried to omit the impatience in his voice.

"Good," said Dante. "Now you should get going to bed."

They rose from their seats and the Grandmaster Dante ushered him to the exit. Lyn was waiting at the door with her arms crossed. She had been sitting before, so it surprised Kyle to see her towering over them. Her legs were so long that her head nearly touched the top of the doorway. With the way she glared at them disapprovingly, Kyle felt like they had done her some dire wrong.

"You shouldn't keep students up so late, Grandmaster," she snarled. "It keeps me up too long. A secretary needs her beauty sleep. I demand the both of you get to bed at once."

Kyle said a swift goodnight to them before journeying back to his room to find Kane fast asleep. He was happy for this because he was too tired to tell him what the Grandmaster had wanted. Quietly, he climbed into bed and fell asleep fully dressed.

The next day, Kyle woke up to find Kane standing over him. "You came in and didn't wake me up?!"

Kyle wasn't even sure where he was. His eyes were still adjusting to the light. Kane shook him, which succeeded in waking him up faster.

"Sorry," he croaked. "I was tired. Let me get ready and I'll tell you all about it at breakfast."

Kane waited for Kyle to get ready. They went down for breakfast to meet, Kevin, Kross, and Garnet as usual. They helped themselves to some toast and eggs as Kyle told them all about the plans for his Synchroneity training. When he was finished, they were all thoroughly impressed and excited for him.

"You could become Kyle the Thunder God," said Kevin with his notepad. "I read about a guy with a hammer that had the Synchroneity lightning too. Thor the Thunder God always sounded fierce and legendary." Kyle thought of the Norse god and agreed it would be cool to be given a name like that. He came to the conclusion that everyone that sounded amazing in the history of Earth must have somehow been connected to Endera.

"Kyle will get his own title," said Garnet firmly. "No use in trying to pair him up with someone else's name." For a moment, Kyle doubted it, but the way Garnet said it made him feel like it was more than just a possibility. It was certain.

"Thanks, Garnet."

"Hey," came a voice behind them. They turned around to see Nero the Cyclone. Kyle saw him from time to time, and although he seemed haughty, Kyle liked him. "Did you guys hear? Class is canceled today."

"Why would class be canceled?" asked Kross swiftly. "A Grandmaster challenge?"

"Yup, that's it," said Nero. "It's the first one of the year. Supposedly, it's Arnold the Eagle. They're gonna announce it soon; I just thought I'd tell you guys so that you could get a good seat early. See ya." Nero left to join his group of friends that were waiting for him. Standing with them were Annie and James, who waved happily at Kyle as they left the dining room.

"What does he mean 'get a good seat?'" asked Kyle. He had seen a few students fight masters after Jabbar the Cannon's fight with Proculus, but none had needed seating.

"The arena," exclaimed Kane. "The big fights are always done in the arena. It usually floats in the sky with the Master's facilities, but on days like this, the Grandmaster brings it down."

"How exactly do things float in the air?" asked Kyle.

"It's an advanced form of Modifications and AlterDimensions," answered Kross. "He is basically making an area where the same rules of physics don't apply while at the same time modifying the weight of the structure. Kevin knows more about modifying since he's in the advanced class."

"You explained it as well as I could," said Kevin's notepad. "We should get going, though. I would like to see Arnold the Eagle fight Grandmaster Dante up close." He stood up, adding, "Ah" as he stretched. Kane and Kross stood up to follow him. Kyle would have done the same, but something caught his attention enough to make him act like he wanted to eat more.

"Actually guys, can you save me a seat?" he said. "I'm still hungry." All of them but Garnet left, telling him to hurry.

"You've kind of eaten a lot today," teased Garnet.

"I stayed behind because I noticed you haven't eaten a thing today," said Kyle seriously. "Something wrong?"

Garnet's face became pink. She obviously hadn't expected Kyle to notice. "I'm… just not hungry," she said quietly.

Kyle gazed at her, trying to read her. It was moments like this that he wished he could actually do PsyBending correctly. Although in this case, Garnet would be able to fend him off easily.

"You don't have to tell me. I just thought you seemed weird today. Sorry."

"No," she said. "Don't be. I just feel a little under the weather."

"Let's go to Master Yvette," Kyle suggested. "I'm sure she can fix you up quick."

"No, it's fine. I'll be okay."

"Okay." He eyed her carefully. "But tell me if you feel worse. I'll go with you to the Nursing Department, okay?"

"Thanks, Kyle." She stood up, beckoning Kyle to follow her. "We should get going. We want to beat the crowd."

They walked out to the grounds. Far to the right of the castle was a large coliseum that had not been there before. A few small crowds of tyros walked to it, talking loudly as they did so. Over the racket of students, there was completely unfamiliar music playing from the inside of arena. It was so surprisingly odd, that they looked at each other with raised eyebrows.

As they walked on, there was a stifled yelp to their left, behind some bushes. They moved toward the source without thought, creeping behind the bushes to peek for the source of the yell.

What they found was Owen the Flurry and his two thugs, standing over James the First Blade. He was breathing hard and obviously in pain, but that didn't stop Owen from pressing a foot hard on his chest.

"Geroffme!" James's scream was muffled. Owen looked at James in disgust, but removed his foot off. James coughed as he tried crawling away. He barely moved a foot when the Flurry kicked him in the stomach, knocking the wind out of him.

Kyle's anger rose like a bottle building with pressure. Just as he was about to confront them, Garnet grabbed his arm to stop him. He looked back at her in confusion.

"Let's figure out why they're doing this," she whispered.

"Ye brought this on yerself, First Blade," spat Owen. "Derek, Bamid, and me need ta set an example. You and your sister are always greetin' the filthy outsider from another realm like he's welcome here and people need ta see there are consequences for that."

It was true. James and Annie were always happy to greet Kyle. He felt a surge of affection grow for the twins. And a rush of fear now for James.

Derek and Bamid cracked their knuckles. This was the first time

Kyle had paid much attention to those two. They were just as big as Owen and looked just as thickheaded. With every passing second, he grew angrier as he glared at the three bullies. His fists were clenched so hard, he could have crushed a rock in them. Garnet lessened her grip on him, her face covered in complete fury too. They stepped out from hiding.

"Hey, Owen!" shouted Kyle. The three brutes abruptly turned around, trying to look apologetic, until they noticed that it was Kyle and Garnet. "If you have a problem with me, I'm right here."

A sneer crept onto Owen's face. He moved away from James. Derek and Bamid followed suit.

Kyle instinctively whipped his key out. He was so angry he couldn't think. Amplifications had never exactly worked for him, but he pointed the key at his right arm and turned it.

"Send your little girlfriend away," cackled Owen. "Ye don't want her around when your face is 'bout to—"

Kyle's arm began to feel incredibly warm. He ran at Owen as fast as he could with a fist that began pulsing lightning. He hadn't meant to make it happen, but the force seemed paired with his anger. As he drew back his fist, the lightning expanded and zapped wildly. Owen didn't have any time to react. Kyle's fist crashed into his cheek, sending him flying into the Academy's inner wall. His eyes went completely white; he had lost consciousness and his clothes were smoking from the contact with the electricity. It took a moment for everything to register to Derek and Bamid, who were frozen in shock. Then, grunting angrily, they turned to Kyle. It was clear that they meant to make sure he wouldn't get away with what he had just done. He backed up to defend himself, but Master Proculus and Master Helen stepped out of the shadows.

"Ahem." Master Helen looked so infuriated that the air temperature seemed to rise. "You boys can stop now."

Kyle, Derek, and Bamid all halted. Garnet helped James to his feet. He had a bruised eye and was still catching his breath, but other than that he seemed fine. Kyle knew he really would be in trouble now. But when he looked at Owen, he almost smiled. Whatever the punishment, it was well worth it.

"Kyle," said Master Proculus. "That was impressive; I hope you can bring that back out tomorrow when we begin your training with Synchroneity."

Kyle's jaw dropped. He hadn't been expecting that.

"I have to admit too," agreed Helen. "It was an impressive hit."

"We know you did it to help James," explained Proculus. "We wanted to see if James could get out of it, but you had to come and ruin that. James did a good job holding up. Owen, Derek, and Bamid will be expelled. At Soul Gate Academy, we are fine with the friendly fight or duel, but we do not tolerate ganging up on a tyro." Bamid and Derek looked at their feet, ashamed. Proculus and Helen eyed them carefully. "Today, you three have done something irreversibly foolish."

"Hand over your keys." Master Helen held her palm open. "And then fetch me Owen's." The two took out their keys while walking to Owen. They fished his key out and handed them to Master Helen. After taking out her own key, she pressed it into Owen's cheek and turned it. The Flurry woke up howling in pain and outright confused.

"What?" Owen blinked his eyes rapidly. "Master Helen, Master Proculus…"

"We are no longer your masters. From this moment on, Owen the Flurry, Bamid the Catapult, and Derek the Force, you three are hereby expelled from Soul Gate Academy. Master Helen will escort you out. Remember that unwise choices in life will have dire consequences."

Master Helen motioned for them to get a move on. They all shot Kyle looks of deep hatred. "Mark my words," growled Owen, "we'll get ye back for this, Kyle the Tortoise."

"Get on with it," snarled Helen. "Or I'll let him punch you again." The three moved toward the gate with Master Helen following. Kyle sighed in relief.

"You okay, James?" asked Kyle.

"Yeah," said James gratefully. "Thanks, I'm fine."

"What were you doing by yourself?" questioned Garnet. "Weren't you with your sister and your friends?"

"I was, but we were able to find good seats and had plenty of room for you and your squad, so I came back to tell you," he said. "I ran into the Monk, Ace, and Bison and they went ahead. I didn't think I'd get attacked."

"I think we should we take you to Master Yvette?" Garnet advised.

"No," said James at once. "I don't want to miss the fight."

"That's the spirit," said Master Proculus. "You don't look too beat up, but if you are really hurt, I suggest that you do get checked up afterwards, okay?"

"Yes, Master."

"One last thing," said Proculus, looking right at Kyle. "I know you were told not to use your power carelessly. I know I said it was impressive, but you were lucky this time. It very well could have ended badly. This power you have is dangerous and if I catch you losing control of it again, you will be punished. Consider this a warning."

Kyle looked down at his feet in guilt. He had just been proud of using his power, but he had promised the Grandmaster that he would be careful. "I'm sorry."

"Master Proculus," Garnet pleaded. "That's not fair. You heard Owen. Any normal person would have lost control."

James nodded in agreement.

"You're right, Garnet," agreed Proculus. "But imagine if his ability would have gotten away from him. Tell me Kyle, how would you have felt if the ability had hurt your friends or perhaps even killed Owen, because you lost control of your emotions?"

Kyle trembled at the thought. He didn't think he could have lived with himself if that had happened. "You're right, Master Proculus. I'm sorry. I won't let it happen again."

"Do not forget," said Proculus sternly. "Now, let's get going to the match. The Grandmaster said that you might want to pay extra attention today."

Kyle took a deep breath. He still felt guilty, but he tried to think about the Grandmaster's fight. He hardly needed to be told to pay extra attention. Ever since he had seen Proculus fight, he strained his eyes every time a master fought, hoping one day to emulate them. Now that he'd started Synchroneity training, his desire to see the Grandmaster's fire in action eclipsed everything else.

As the four of them got closer to the arena, the shrill music became more distinct. Kyle wasn't sure, but it played like something between a saxophone and violin. Once he got over the surprise of the unique sound, the music was actually quite nice.

"I have duties to attend to," Proculus said as they entered the coliseum. "You three should hurry to your seats." The master left without another word while James led Garnet and Kyle toward their seats. The seating looked more like it belonged in an auditorium. Each chair had plush cushions that were wrapped in seaweed green velvet covers, making them soft as pillows. Students had filled up most of the seats, but it didn't take them long to find Kevin, Kross, and Kane, along with James's group, where three seats were left open for them.

They sat near the front with a good view of the square fighting platform in the center. The ring looked like it was nearly the size of soccer field and made of dozens of stone slabs.

"What happened to your eye, James?" shouted Annie as she stood up to inspect him with a motherly look of concern. The rest of the group jumped to their feet as well, worried for their friend.

James recounted what happened. Unable to help himself, he added an overly enthusiastic amount of detail when it came to Kyle punching Owen. "And then Master Proculus and Master Helen showed up. They expelled the three idiots and that's that. I'm not too beat up, nothing worth missing the Grandmaster's fight for."

When James finished, Annie rushed over to Kyle to kiss him on the cheek. "Thank you so much for helping my brother," she said, gazing at him like a fan would a hero.

Garnet coughed loudly, causing Annie to fall out of her trance. "Um, we should sit. The fight should be starting soon."

Kyle scratched his head. He tried not to feel pleased with himself since he'd just been scolded. After Kyle received a few pats on the back from squad members on James's team, he sat with his group. Kane, Kross, and Kevin congratulated him for sending Owen flying with much gusto. They were especially glad to hear that the Flurry had been expelled. As the crowd grew in size and noise, they resumed with their energized talk about the upcoming fight.

"So," Kane said loudly to no one in particular. "Do you think Arnold will even get a hit on the Grandmaster?"

"Hmm," Garnet answered. "I doubt the Grandmaster will give him a chance, unless he wants to."

"Good point," said Kross. "The Grandmaster is strong."

"More like insanely strong," added Kane.

"Ah." A large smile stretched across the Kevin's face which seemed to annoy Kross, who looked like hadn't completely finished his thought. His thoughts would have to wait because at that moment the music stopped, turning all focus to the center of the stone platform, where Grandmaster Dante stood striking his familiar homerun pose.

"Oho, welcome tyros," boomed Dante. There was no microphone, but instead the Grandmaster's neck looked like it had expanded like a toad's. Garnet, who saw Kyle's puzzled look, whispered in his ear.

"It's Modifications. He modified his voice box and neck." Kyle smiled at her, thankful for having her around.

The Grandmaster continued, "Today I will fight Arnold the Eagle. He wishes to claim his eternal title and has received the approval of Master Primo, Master Haluk, and Master Helen." A thin young man dressed in the tyro uniform with platinum blonde hair jumped up onto the platform. In his hands was a long jousting lance with a deadly looking iron tip. "Well then, let's get right to it." Dante gave his cane a small turn which returned his neck to normal size.

Arnold the Eagle gave Grandmaster Dante a respectful bow, to which Dante replied with a polite bow of his own. When Arnold looked back up, he flipped backwards and the crowd cheered. Staying focused, he brought out his key, turning it while the

Grandmaster just watched him curiously as if they were about to have a serious talk.

Arnold turned the key, rolling his wrist four times. As he did this, roots sprouted out of the ground to engulf him completely. The wood enclosed him in a sphere which made many in the crowd let out a dramatic gasp. Seconds later, the sphere broke apart. The Eagle emerged with wooden vines that wrapped around his body in the form of armor. Kyle was so impressed he let out a loud "cool!" As if the armor wasn't enough, out of Arnold's back grew four lengthy branches. Hundreds of smaller branches then webbed together to create incredible wings. The gaps in the wings filled themselves with olive green leaves. Arnold flapped his wings hard and to the awe of the tyros, he lifted himself easily into the air, readying his lance to charge.

The Grandmaster replied with a couple turns of his cane. Instantly, fire sprang out from the bottom of his cane, wrapping around his arms and shins like guards made of flames. He threw his cane off the platform to Master Logan, who waited to catch it. Dante looked over to the Eagle, prepared in his fighting stance. Arnold took this as an invitation and dived directly at the Grandmaster. The dive was much faster than Kyle had expected it to be with wings made out of wood and leaves, but still the lance missed the Grandmaster, who jumped to the left like a boxer as the Eagle swooped back into the air.

Arnold responded with even faster movements of his wings. He charged at the Grandmaster, leaving baseball-sized holes in the platform with his lance. Dante looked as nonchalant as ever, easily dodging the Eagle's moves, reading him like a book.

All of a sudden, roots sprouted underneath the Grandmaster and began wrapping around him. Some of the roots burned to ashes, but they were too many in number. As the roots entangled him, he was momentarily prevented from moving. Arnold dove in again to strike with his lance, but just before he struck home the Grandmaster broke an arm free and shot out a small ball of fire. The flaming bullet barely missed Arnold, who whooshed back into the air, wariness stamped on his face.

Dante curled up his body as if trying to flex his arms like a body builder. His flaming arm guards and shin guards expanded, burning the wooden roots like dry grass. Now completely freed, he pointed his hands in a dual shooting motion, an ironic take on a child with a make-believe gun. However, unlike a child's fingers, Dante shot more fire bullets at Arnold, who frantically spun and twisted in the sky to avoid them. Some bullets strayed toward the crowd, causing a few of the younger tyros let out screams, even though the bullets were stopped by an invisible wall. After a closer look at the walls around the fighting platform, Kyle saw the unreadable symbols of AuraBending seals surrounding the arena.

Arnold the Eagle was now breathing hard, and looked close to his limit. He brought out his key again while flying around Dante. This time, he pointed it at his lance, making it spiral like a top. When the key stopped, his lance began spinning so rapidly that Arnold had to stop moving in the air. As he did, Grandmaster Dante's fire hit his wings. The wings lit ablaze. Arnold let his lance drop as he flapped his flaming wings. When it dropped just below his foot, he gave it a powerful kick toward the Grandmaster. It shot down at blinding speed. Kyle thought of the javelin that Jabbar the Cannon had thrown at Master Proculus. Compared to this, Jabbar's javelins had moved as though it had been traveling through syrup. Kyle could only make out a shadow before the lance crashed into the platform, making a small crater with its force. At the same time, it began spraying out water like a geyser. The Grandmaster had dodged the lance, but the water was enough to extinguish his flames.

Arnold detached his wings and began falling, but with another twist of his key, he turned his shoes into the wooden talons of an eagle. Though they were wooden, they looked deadly sharp. He descended with full force at the Grandmaster. Just when it looked like he was going to hit, Dante delivered a hard punch to Arnold's stomach. There was an ear-splitting *crack*, undoubtedly from the wooden armor around Arnold's stomach. The punch threw him back with considerable force, but he landed on his talon feet and scraped across the platform. Clenching his stomach he struggled for breath as he fell to the ground face first. The tyros erupted in cheers for the Grandmaster. The fight was over.

A woman with orange-brown hair, dressed in the master's uniform, jumped onto the platform and ran over to Arnold. Garnet pointed out that the woman was her master for Medications class, Master Olivia. A few quick motions from Olivia's key brought Arnold back to his feet. Master Logan also jumped up to the platform to return Dante's cane. The Grandmaster leaned against his cane as he whispered something to Logan, who then disappeared.

Grandmaster Dante walked over to Arnold. A tilt of his head directed Master Olivia to step off for a moment. She swiftly jumped back off the platform. Arnold was left to sway back and forth, but steadied himself and gave the Grandmaster a respectful bow. Dante turned his cane which made his neck swell up in size once again.

"Oho," he said with an amplified voice. "That was a splendid fight, was it not?" The arena boomed with loud cheers. "I am pleased to announce that Arnold the Eagle has indeed impressed me enough to receive his eternal title." Arnold's eyes lit up with surprise. It seemed he had been expecting to fail. "However, it will not be Arnold the Eagle." Arnold's face fell. "With all of you as witnesses, Arnold will now be known as, Arnold the Timber Dragoon! The masters and I think it is a more fitting title." As the applause grew, so did Arnold's smile. "I present the uniform of an eternal title."

Master Logan appeared on the platform again, but this time he had clothing with him. The uniform was the inverted version of the regular tyro. Black replaced the blue vest and pants, while the black shirt was now blue. And just like the master uniforms, there was a unique symbol on the back of the vest. Though Kyle couldn't read it, he knew it meant *Timber Dragoon*. The clothes were handed to Arnold, who again bowed with deep respect.

"Oho, and so we come to the end of this year's first eternal title match." Dante beamed. "Train hard and you might be next. I want to remind everyone that there will be a celebratory feast tonight in honor of the first eternal title this year. I would also like to remind everyone not to get used to class being canceled. The first eternal title match is the only one for which class is canceled. Make sure you congratulate Arnold the Timber Dragoon as you enjoy the rest of the day off."

Shortly after, the Grandmaster dismissed them and the coliseum emptied. Kyle and his friends found themselves enjoying the rest of the day out on the grounds. They saw Arnold the Timber Dragoon walking around, wearing his new eternal title uniform surrounded by a group of friends and perhaps some fans. Kyle wished more than ever that he could change his title from the Tortoise to something else, but knew he'd have to work hard for it.

When they sat underneath their usual tree, Kyle pulled out his key and, against the protest of his friends, attempted to produce electrical halos around his fingers with his Synchroneity lightning. It wasn't until it was time for the feast that he and Garnet could have sworn that they saw a spark show up on his pinky finger. *It's a start, but I still have a long way to go.*

CHAPTER THIRTEEN

THE CONTRACT

With the new addition of Synchroneity training, Kyle found himself extremely busy. His classes, which had been plenty hard already, were becoming increasingly difficult. Fortunately, he felt pretty good when Hickory became Dogwood. Without Owen the Flurry parading about and recruiting tyros to hate him, the school seemed friendlier, though there were still many who whispered as he walked by.

The weather was getting colder, which he didn't mind at all, but it did surprise him. There had barely been a month of fall weather. Kane had explained it to him easily enough. Basically, Endera only had two main seasons a year. This year, they had summer and winter. The next would be spring and fall. Kyle would have wondered how exactly that worked except he was used to not understanding the things that made Endera tick. This realm simply operated differently and though he wanted to know as much as he could, he figured that training would eventually unlock the answers...somehow.

With the cold weather, they were given long moon-gray cloaks. The cloaks didn't look like much except for the emblem of Soul Gate Academy sewn to them. They were specially made by the StitchLockers, infused with key abilities, which meant they were made to keep a tyro exceptionally warm.

What pleased Kyle most about the time speeding by was that he had undeniably become stronger. The first few weeks of Synchroneity with Master Proculus had been brutal. Proculus made him unlock his lightning every Tuesday and Thursday evening. With practically no control of it, the yellow electricity escaped frenziedly out of his body, sapping his strength in the process. In truth, the Synchroneity lessons were similar to his weapons classes, which consisted solely of sparring with fellow tyros while the master shouted advice on how to improve. The difference between this and his Synchroneity class was that he sparred with a master and did so barehanded.

On the first Thursday of Dogwood, Kyle stretched his arms out as he met Master Proculus in one of the empty private classrooms on the fourth floor. Its walls and floors were heavily covered with special mats that had been amplified and modified, giving them extra resilience to prevent dangerous injuries. They also ensured the room wasn't destroyed while they trained. It looked somewhat like a large dojo practice hall.

"You're early," said Master Proculus. "No appetite today?"

"I ate plenty, Master," said Kyle truthfully. He had been eating a lot lately. All his training was draining his body's energy and food helped him regain it. Some muscle had started showing on his thin body as evidence of his hard work. "I just thought I'd get here early to show you this." Kyle smiled as he pulled out his key. He pointed it at his hand and turned it. Shortly after, his right hand had five electric halos wiggling around his fingers.

"Five already!" said Proculus excitedly. "A month ahead of schedule, too. Where is this enthusiasm in your PsyBending class? Master Ellwood tells me you are hardly a step beyond the first day." His voice dropped as Kyle scratched his head. "Do not worry; I was no good at it either."

Kyle smiled appreciatively. He trained hard in all his classes, but PsyBending and Amplifications, much to Kyle's undying annoyance, were going poorly. AuraBending, MicroDimensions, and Weaponry were almost second nature to him now. History class was confusing, but he enjoyed learning facts about Endera. Synchroneity was without a doubt his most difficult class, but it was also his favorite. His ability was smoothly advancing, making his lightning faster, fiercer, and ever more powerful.

"I suppose," said Master Proculus, frowning, "it would be best for us to go visit the Grandmaster now. You will hardly like the next part of this training, but it is necessary."

"Why won't I like this next part?" Kyle was more curious than disenchanted.

"You will see soon enough."

Kyle followed Master Proculus to the Grandmaster's office. When they arrived, they were harshly greeted by Lyn the Phoenelf.

"Here to see the Grandmaster already?" she snapped at them both. "He's barely just in from dinner!"

"Forgive us, Lyn," said Proculus smoothly. "It would be best for Kyle and I to see the Grandmaster as soon as possible."

Lyn seemed to think about this for a bit, but her face was full of boiling annoyance. She stood up, shooting them a look of venom while clicking her beak together disapprovingly. It made Kyle feel warm around the neck.

"I will fetch him," said Lyn coldly. "Wait here!" She strode out of the room with such speed that she might have been gliding.

"Does she always act like that?" asked Kyle. "She seems a bit—"

"Unusual?" suggested Proculus, noticing his discomfort.

"Insane, more like."

"You have to understand, Kyle," said Proculus with a chuckle, "Lyn is a summon that is personally bound to the Grandmaster. Some people may summon a variety of different creatures, which can be random, but suited for many different occasions. Others choose to make a strong pact with a single summon or type of summon. Most people choose the latter and find themselves with extremely loyal and strong summons. Lyn has been with the Grandmaster a long time and she looks out for him. It is as simple as that. Maybe she's a little overprotective and stern."

"Is that the same with Odin the Tytodwarf?" asked Kyle.

"More or less," answered Proculus. "But as you probably have guessed, Master Yvette and Odin have a much different relationship. Nonetheless, Lyn and Odin are both exceptionally strong and wise. Their…eccentric behaviors are only odd to us. I am sure among their kind, they are the norm. Well, maybe not Odin."

Kyle laughed, thinking that it was such an incredible ability and, not for the first time, he wished he had the ability to summon a companion from another dimension. Then again, his classes were hard enough.

Lyn walked back in to usher them into the Grandmaster's office where Grandmaster Dante sat at his desk facing the other direction. "Proculus," said Dante, his voice sounding tired. Kyle's eyebrows jumped. He had never heard him address a master by name only. "I am glad you came. It seems that King Seltios…"

Seltios?

"Ahem." Master Proculus coughed. "I have brought Kyle the Tortoise, Grandmaster."

The Grandmaster whipped his chair around. "Lyn failed to mention that Kyle was also here."

Lyn turned and began walking out the room. "Didn't think he was worth mentioning," she yelled back while slamming the door, making Kyle feel, overall, quite insignificant.

"Cruel as always," muttered Dante. "Don't mind her, Kyle. She's just a bit grouchy. Well, she's always a bit grouchy. Anyhow, what brings you two to my office?"

"Go ahead, Kyle," said Master Proculus proudly. "Show him."

Kyle used his key to bring out his lightning. It hovered around his five fingers, zapping happily before he turned it off again and it all disappeared.

"Oho!" yelled the Grandmaster. "It's hardly been a month. That is something! Well, I am guessing you brought him here to start his next bit of training?"

"I did, Grandmaster," affirmed Proculus. "However, I understand if there are more pressing matters to deal with."

"No, no." Dante waved away the idea. "Let's get right to it. I must warn you, Kyle. This part of training will be extremely painful. Think you can handle it?"

Dante rose from his seat to circle around his desk. There was a deep look on his face as he gazed into Kyle's eyes, as though he was making sure the insides of Kyle's head was suited for the task to come.

"I'm ready, Grandmaster."

"Excellent. Proculus, could you help me with the seals?"

Master Proculus already had his key ready when the Grandmaster turned his cane. Most of the things that were in his room flew to stack themselves neatly against the wall. After that, the two of them performed a variety of different complicated flicks and turns with their keys, activating many different AuraBending abilities. When they were done, there were illegible symbols scribbled randomly on the floor, walls, and ceiling. In the middle of the room, there was a large empty circle with two smaller circles connected to its edge on opposite ends.

"What is all this for?" asked Kyle when they finished.

"This is for your Synchroneity contract," answered Grandmaster Dante.

"Contract?"

"You have to prove that you are worthy of the elemental power."

"How?"

"By enduring the pain of your lightning, just as I did for my fire. It'll be quite excruciating, if I remember correctly." The Grandmaster massaged his right shoulder absentmindedly. "You'll have to concentrate and allow yourself to be vulnerable to blasts of lightning for some time. I am not sure how it'll go for you, but when I did this, my fire attacked me. I endured the pain, thus proving myself worthy of wielding fire. Your experience will be your own, but I'm certain it'll be similar. It's best just to get these kinds of things over with. I'm sure you'll be fine. You have your key around your neck, correct?"

Kyle pulled out the necklace that had his key attached to it.

"Good. Now I want you to keep your key out like that and go lay down right in the middle of the big circle. Stay there 'til I tell you to do anything else."

Kyle did as he was told and laid himself down. The floor was bare and hard as stone, but he was not uncomfortable. He looked up and felt that the ceiling was much higher than was possible. He heard Master Proculus and Grandmaster Dante sit down, one in each of the smaller circles. It made him feel anxious to know that they were staring at him. He waited silently, wondering if he should do anything in particular. His hands found his way to his key and he squeezed it hard.

"I, Proculus the Master, vouch for Kyle the Tortoise."

"I, Dante the Grandmaster, vouch for Kyle the Tortoise. Kyle, make your lightning halos around your five fingers again—and good luck."

Silently, Kyle pointed his key at his hand, turning it with a slow drag of breath. The five halos zigzagged around his fingers like normal. He let his key drop back onto his chest and reached for the ceiling with both hands without really thinking. Suddenly, the halos of electricity stretched to the size of dinner plates while sporadically branching out around him. Kyle kept completely calm as the lightning expanded rapidly from his hands, enclosing him in a zapping yellow lightning coffin. The lightning was acting on its own. He knew his masters were watching him cautiously, but the lightning emitted such a sinister aura, acting like a chilling warning. It was clear that getting near the electric coffin was more dangerous to them than it was to him. Just as the lightning completely encased him, his vision faded into darkness.

When he opened his eyes again, he found himself floating in space. The cosmic blackness and stars spread around him. His key, still attached to his necklace, floated carelessly in the zero gravity. With his left hand, he gripped his Nodachi sword, which had appeared out of nowhere, so he reached for the key with his right. Everything moved as if he had sunk into water. He felt his hair wave slowly as he fell backwards into nothing in particular. When he tilted his neck back, a shining amethyst star emerged in front of him. It changed colors to gold then to blue, white, orange, dark red, and finally fading into black before starting over again. He had never seen it before, yet it looked remarkably familiar. A closer look and he knew what it was: A keyhole discharging violent, color-changing electricity. Then…

"You are," shrieked a voice directly in his mind, "Kyle Demore, also known as Kyle the Tortoise?"

"Yes," answered Kyle with his own mind. "Who are you?"

"I am no one." The voice was much calmer now. It sounded like an ancient man, weary and prudent. "I am only what you would have me become."

"I don't understand."

"I am power, in theory and reality. I am the storm, but not the wind nor the rain. I am the flash, with force and heat. But I am no one without you, Kyle."

"You are Lightning?"

"I suppose if you must name me something then yes, I am Lightning. You humans always need your names. We do not."

"We?"

"The elements."

"I see. But how can you talk?"

"Have you ever tried talking to an element before?"

"Er, no."

"Perhaps you should have tried."

Kyle didn't respond. He wasn't entirely sure what to make of the situation. It seemed farfetched that he could be talking to an element. When he thought about it, the only logical answer was that he was dreaming and he would be waking up soon to resume his contract. "You are not dreaming, Kyle."

"Then what is this?" he asked incredulously.

"This is your inner eyes at work. This is the infinity of your mind and I am attached here as I have always been and always will be. Did you not come to prove your worthiness to wield me?"

"I—yes." Kyle had not expected the contract to be like this, though when he thought about it, he wasn't sure what he had been expecting.

"I wonder if you are ready to wield me." Lightning's voice now contained a hint of concern.

"But I can already use you," said Kyle. "I practice all the time."

"No," said Lightning firmly. "You have not fulfilled the contract. You have not suffered the strike of my blade. The control you have over me is like an untrained dog on a leash. You release me and our energy flows out, running from you. Elements are not so keen to give command of our powers to those who do not prove their worth."

"How can I do that?" Kyle was annoyed to be talked down to in such a manner. They were in *his* mind.

"You must suffer the strike of my blade."

"I don't understand."

"To understand the pain that lightning causes to others, you must first suffer that pain. If you do not, then I will not answer your calls when you attempt to use Synchroneity. That is the term of our contract."

"So I have to be struck by lightning?"

"Yes."

"Now?"

"When you enter your key into the keyhole, I will be unlocked and then yes, you will feel my strike."

"Will we ever talk like this again?" asked Kyle.

"I wonder," said Lightning. "Indeed, I do wonder."

After that, there was silence. Kyle knew Lightning would not answer again. He floated in the space of his mind for a small time, curiously looking around. He stared at the flashing keyhole, wanting to reach it but unsure how.

Unexpectedly, the keyhole moved toward him, becoming smaller as it did. It zapped and crackled as electricity escaped from it. Kyle could almost feel the pain as he placed his key in. Electricity began coiling around him like hundreds of slithering yellow snakes. Without hesitation, he turned the key, instantly waking up in the office—screaming in pain.

It felt like a thousand daggers trying to stab their way out of his skin. The electric coffin expanded outward, becoming a dome of violent lightning that struck down at him again and again. He started to spasm as darts of lightning fell like bullets from a machine gun. The pain was blinding and intense, so hot that his shirt disintegrated.

It all stopped a heartbeat later. Kyle was sweating and panting, but was relieved it was over. The dome that had formed around him was now massing into a condensed sphere the size of a basketball. Where the lightning had been yellow and white, it was now sangria and black, looking almost as if blood had mixed with the night sky. A sinister aura surrounded it, stinking like anger and death.

Thunder boomed and the orb suddenly fired a single lightning bolt at his chest. Rather than disappearing, the jolt stood on the center of his chest wiggling like a giant electric pencil. The force of it crushed Kyle to the floor, smashing against his chest. The lightning's heat became so fierce that he thought it had become lava. He screamed in agony as the zigzagging bolt of lightning split into four, charring his skin as it worked its way toward his shoulders and hips. It engraved a burn into him, marking its signature. The pain was so intense, so beyond his imagination, that he knew he was dead. It was unbearable. Nothing could ever feel more agonizing, more excruciating.

As if the lightning had been waiting for this, it abruptly stopped.

It disappeared, leaving his skin raw and scarred. A fresh red *X* was carved into his chest. He touched it in a sad attempt to stop the pain, but yelped as it caused him to arch his back and shake as if having a seizure. He tried to calm himself, but the pain would not leave. Tears streamed down his face to join with the snot and sweat draining on to his scar like acid. Pounding the floor with his fist, he tried to remember a time without pain, but every part of him screamed. Everything was on fire. Everything.

Except his key, which now cooled the center of his new scar. As though a gentle wind had blown into the room, the cold metal did what he could not on his own. It brought calm. This did not extinguish the pain in the slightest, but he at least remembered where he was. Master Proculus and Grandmaster Dante stood over him, both looking quite pleased.

"Oho," said Dante. "You survived!"

"That he did," said Proculus happily. "He does, however, look a bit under the weather."

They looked at each other and like the ending of a prayer they said, "We acknowledge that Kyle has met the terms of the contract with Lightning. May he use Synchroneity with wisdom."

Kyle, no longer able to stay awake, closed his eyes and fell asleep, hoping that Lightning would not come to visit him again anytime soon.

CHAPTER FOURTEEN

X MARKS THE SPOT

Kyle woke up not knowing where he was at first. It didn't take long to realize he was in the same bed he had been in when first arriving at SoGA. Clouds cluttered a starless midnight sky, telling him it was nighttime. He was alone in the large room, but there was dim light coming in through the white curtain draped over the doorway. Quietly and stiffly, he sat up, causing his blanket to slip off. On the center of his bare chest, there was now a large jagged scar in the shape of an *X*. It looked raw and dark red.

He knew now why he was in the Nursing Department. *I must have passed out after completing the contract.* He followed the scar with his fingers, tickling his skin, but the pain was gone. He fell back with a sigh of relief; it was pain he'd rather not relive. Then as he lay there, he heard people who were obviously trying but failing to hush their voices.

"Are you two barkin' mad?" The growl belonged to Master

Yvette. "He's only been here a few months and ya had him complete a contract with an element. He could've died!"

"Now, now," murmured the Grandmaster. "Yvette, I did my contract at thirteen and he's fourteen."

"You've known the power of keys all your life," snapped Yvette. "And if I remember correctly, you were a prodigy. A year ago, Kyle thought keys did nothin' more than open doors."

"The world grows darker," said Proculus. "He needs to be ready. We thought it best to teach Kyle as soon as possible." His voice quavered; it was very unlike Proculus.

"Darker?" Master Yvette's retort could have cut stone. "I don't care if the moons are fallin' outta the sky. There's absolutely no reason to rush these things. He could've died!"

"We made sure it was safe," said Proculus.

"He's not Kyros," said Yvette sadly.

"Kyle's father has nothing to do with this," interjected the Grandmaster. There was an uncomfortable change in the next room. Kyle could barely believe what he was hearing. He had trained himself to never really think about his parents; he thought it was better to just live life happily without them. He'd grown used to them not being around, why should he change that? However, he could not help but be curious. Proculus had only ever mentioned that he knew Kyle's mother. "I am the one that thought Kyle was ready, which I'll remind you, he was. Proculus just aided me in doing so; it had nothing to do with Kyros *or* Melissa."

"I see," said Yvette. "And do ya ever plan on tellin' him what happened? The boy has to be curious about his parents."

Kyle's heart began to beat incredibly fast.

"When he's older," answered Dante. "There are too many

questions to which we don't know the answers. Right now, it would just confuse him. He seems happy the way he is. In a few years we will know more and we will tell him, okay?"

Kyle relaxed. He was content with this as he laid there listening to them. He hardly felt like tackling the parent issue. Training was plenty enough to be worried about for now. But Kyros and Melissa, his parents had names now. It was an odd thing for them to have names, but no face or voice.

"Fine," Yvette sighed. "Forgive me, Proculus. I should not have said that."

"Nothing to forgive." Proculus's voice became tender. "I have to admit that Kyle does remind me of Kyros. Has the same intense eyes. It is uncanny."

"Oho, he does indeed." Dante laughed loudly, trying to lift the mood. Yvette had to hush him. "Let us go check on him. I'd like to wake him up, if that's okay?"

"I guess, it should be," said Master Yvette. "He shouldn't be in pain anymore, but that scar'll be with him forever."

"I expect it will," agreed Grandmaster Dante. There was movement of chairs and Kyle knew they were about to come in to the room. He closed his eyes to imitate sleeping. The next thing he knew, he was being gently shaken awake by Master Yvette. He had plenty of practice pretending to wake up to Nana's shakes back in his old realm, but that seemed like years ago. He wasn't sure he could pull it off now.

"Oh," Kyle rubbed his eyes. "Where am I?" As he opened his eyes clearly, Yvette gave Kyle a harsh smack to his chest making him yelp in pain.

"He's awake already," said Yvette as tears formed in Kyle's eyes. "Don't try and fake us out like that again, or you'll get much more than a smack." A sad smile stretched across her face as she turned to leave. "I'll leave him to you two. He looks good enough, but I'd like to keep him here for the weekend. I'm off to bed." She strode away.

"I'll be with you in a moment, dearest," said the Grandmaster, trying to get Kyle to crack a smile, which he did. "Oho, how are you feeling, Kyle?"

Kyle sat up. He was glad they ignored the fact that he had eavesdropped on their conversation. "I'm good, Grandmaster. I don't think I have to stay here all weekend."

"Master Yvette is not giving you the option to leave," said Master Proculus. "So you will stay put until she releases you, understood?"

"Yes, Master," he muttered bitterly. Three days in the Nursing Department would be incredibly boring. "When can I start training with Synchroneity again?"

"Oho," said Dante. "Not even fazed by your new scar, are you?"

"It's proof I endured the pain of my lightning. You have a scar too, don't you Grandmaster?" Somehow he knew that the Grandmaster did.

"I do." Dante unbuttoned his vest and then his shirt. He took them off to reveal quite a few scars. The largest was on his right shoulder, running down to his bicep and some down his rib cage as well. It looked as if it had been scorched. "Fire left his mark on me, as well." He put on his shirt and vest again. "We'll start your training again next week. Just as planned, you'll continue two days with Master Proculus and then three days with me. Two meditation days, one sparring."

"That sounds good," said Kyle. "Do I have to light up all ten of my fingers now?"

"I suppose you do," answered Dante. "But I'd be surprised if you get your sixth finger by the end of this year. It won't be like the first five. Each finger from now on will signify a level of mastery that will be much more difficult than anything you have done up to this point. You've done well to get this far already so don't worry, you have time."

"I see." Kyle could feel himself growing impatient already.

"I should be off," said Master Proculus. "I just wanted to make sure you were okay. Goodnight." He walked out the room, throwing a casual wave back at them.

"Kyle the Tortoise," said Grandmaster Dante. "I expect your experience was quite thrilling. Would you like to tell me about it?"

Kyle nodded and Dante pulled up a chair next to the young tyro's bed. Kyle told him about how he had floated in space and talked to the element Lightning. He turned red after his description of the pain he had endured. The Grandmaster listened with all the understanding of someone who had made a contract, as well.

"Was your contract like mine?" asked Kyle when he finished with his recollection.

"It was very similar." Dante smiled. "But Fire tried scaring me into not wanting his power. Rather than floating in space, I was trapped in a burning house. Lightning seemed like more of an enjoyable fellow. I think that should be enough for tonight. You should get some rest; I'll see you Monday in the same classroom that you meet Master Proculus for sparring." He stood up to leave.

"Grandmaster Dante," said Kyle as something suddenly came to mind. "Something unrelated to Synchroneity has been bothering me."

"What would that be?"

"Who is King Seltios?"

Dante's eyes widened. Kyle couldn't tell if it was from fear or surprise.

"It's just that you said something to Master Proculus earlier about it when we came into your office, and I don't know, the name seems familiar to me. I know I didn't hear it in History class."

The Grandmaster threw a hand into the air, signaling Kyle to stop talking. "I'll be honest with you, Kyle," he said. "I'd rather not tell you, but—Seltios—is an enemy. He is the Western King. His goal is to combine the realms into one."

"Combine the realms? Why is that a bad thing?" It would mean that he could see Nana and Paps anytime. The very thought filled him with joy.

"Combining the realms would bring chaos. Imagine how your old realm would treat Enderians. Would they understand that using keys is as natural to us as breathing? The realms operate differently and humans do not react well to differences. Thousands would suffer all for the selfishness of one man. He believes combining the realms will somehow give him immortality or make him a god." Dante rubbed his temples, looking as though he regretted saying anything.

"Are you trying to stop him?" Kyle asked.

"I am. Not alone, though."

"But why? SoGA is just a school, isn't it?"

"True. We are just a school."

"Then why would you try to stop a guy who is trying to combine the realms? It doesn't seem like something a school should be worried about." Kyle knew he was pushing his luck, but he was tired of not knowing anything.

"Seltios looks to wage war," said Dante. "When war ignites, it affects the schools just as well as everything else."

"Isn't there an army full of adults to fight a war?" Shocked as he was to learn that a war might be imminent, Kyle didn't understand why the Grandmaster sounded like he was directly involved.

"There is." Dante looked at him wearily. "I don't mean to sound arrogant by saying this, but I am strong and knowledgeable. I have the means to make a difference and it is my responsibility to do so. I think you would agree that with power comes duty. You have just earned the right to utilize a significant amount of power. Did I make a mistake in aiding you to do so?"

"You didn't." Kyle gulped, fearing he had pressed for too many answers. "I—you're right, Grandmaster. I'm sorry I've been questioning you so much."

"It's not a crime to be curious," said Dante. "I know things must be overly confusing for you still. Switching realms has to be mystifying business. Tell me, though. What do you honestly think about combining the realms?"

Kyle hesitated and thought hard before speaking. The idea of combining realms really didn't sound so bad to him. Would people really suffer? Did it matter? He just wanted to see his foster parents again. "I don't know. It sounds bad, I guess."

For a moment, Grandmaster Dante glared at him so coldly that Kyle thought he was about to be attacked. But when he spoke, the calm in his voice diminished Kyle's fear.

"Kyle, there are great choices every person must make. Things won't always be clear, but you'll see it as you get older. Evil will always do what it can to seduce and control you, but it is nothing more than delusion. Don't let yourself be swayed by selfish thoughts."

Kyle looked away, his face burning with shame.

"I trust you will not say a word of this to anyone. Seltios' endeavors and goals are not common knowledge here at SoGA and I'd like to keep it that way."

"I understand, Grandmaster."

"Good." He patted Kyle affectionately on the head. "Get some rest. Goodnight." He walked out of the room, leaving Kyle alone.

Kyle stared at the ceiling for some time, thinking as he drifted off to sleep. *King Seltios must be incredibly powerful to give the Grandmaster a serious look like that.*

Kyle woke up, surprised to find Garnet bringing him a tray of food. He could tell that it was nearly noon by where the sun stood in the clear, beautiful sky.

"Garnet, What are you doing here?"

"Hello to you too." She set the food down next to his bed. "I volunteered to work at the Nursing Department this weekend. You want to tell me what happened to you?"

Kyle sat up and again the blanket slipped off, revealing his scar. Garnet gasped.

"Can I eat while I tell you?" The food was making his mouth water.

Garnet nodded and he began shoveling down toast and eggs while telling her about his contract with Lightning.

"How can they make you do something so dangerous?" she said her voice full of heat. "And why are you so eager to hurt yourself?" She looked at him half with concern and half with fury. It made Kyle feel guilty.

"I'll be more careful," said Kyle. "Sorry." Garnet frowned but seemed pleased by this response.

Much of the weekend went by with them talking about nothing

in particular, making for a nice break from Kyle's usual routine. Garnet gave up much of her free time to spend with him and he was grateful, since most of the time they were normally accompanied by Kane, Kross, and Kevin or surrounded by other tyros. It was nice to have Garnet on her own as she fussed over his wellbeing. The Ace, Monk, and Bison came to visit him Saturday afternoon and, again, he explained what had happened. Though Kyle could tell they were shocked and awed, they gave him approving nods and compliments like 'manly' and 'tough-guy.' Kane even suggested that Kyle's new title should be the Invincible, but Kross gave reasons for why that would not fit; the first being the large scar across Kyle's chest which "obviously shows that Kyle is not invincible!"

Odin the Tytodwarf came in to visit a few times, which gave Garnet and Kyle a good share of laughs. And just like that, the weekend flew by. At the end of it, Kyle longed to really stretch out his legs and get back to training, but it had not been as bad as he would have guessed.

On Monday, Kyle's new training with the Grandmaster started. He wasn't sure what to expect with meditation, but he was sure it was more or less self-explanatory. When he entered the dojo-looking classroom, Grandmaster Dante was sitting on the floor. He sat cross-legged, arms on his lap, and still as the air. Without looking, he waved Kyle over to sit ten paces in front of him. Kyle sat down, doing his best to mirror the Grandmaster.

"Oho," said the Grandmaster in his normal tone. "From now on, you will sit exactly like this as you meditate. As you might have guessed, this is not your conventional meditating. Watch." He turned his cane like a key, set it on the floor, then rested his hands on his knees and closed his eyes. A moment later, the Grandmaster became surrounded by warm, red flames. They were unlike any Kyle had ever seen. They were well-controlled, forming a thin layer of fire that looked like a bubble around Grandmaster Dante. Kyle expected the flames to go out of control, but the orb stayed in place as though fire always acted this way. Such transparent fire had a certain beauty to it that nearly made Kyle forget the heat that radiated from it like an oven.

As quickly as Dante started the demonstration, he stopped it. "You must concentrate on making an orb around you like the one I just showed you," he said. "It will be hard and it'll take time, but this will help with controlling your element. Any questions?"

"Eh…er," stuttered Kyle. "How exactly did you do that?"

"Just imagine making a bubble around you, Kyle. You will find it similar to Aura bending, but unlike your aura, your lightning has its own movements. Don't worry. The lightning will be a guide. It will know what to do."

He turned his key while resting his hands on his knees just as Grandmaster Dante had done. With closed eyes, he imagined a bubble of lightning around him.

He was nervous. This was the first time he was using Synchroneity since his contract with Lightning. He could feel the scar on his chest tingle, though there was no pain. Through deep concentration, he could feel the lightning zap softly along his skin. In many ways, it felt like insects crawling on him, though not nearly as unpleasant. He envisioned a bubble with all his might, allowing the lightning to leave his skin. He opened his eyes, still concentrating on the bubble. Rather than an orb, a lone bolt of lightning zapped around him, much like an oversized hula hoop. It zapped and popped with a certain air of uncontrolled clumsiness that Dante's fire had not had.

"That's a start." The Grandmaster grinned. "Keep at it; you still have a ways to go. Close your eyes and really focus."

For the next hour and a half, Kyle concentrated on creating the lightning orb, but it developed no further. In fact, the hula hoop of lightning had become feebler as it exhausted him. This did not stop the Grandmaster from looking most pleased when Kyle left. "See you Wednesday for sparring; same time, same place."

Wednesday came and he found himself again in the dojo room. He was beginning to feel that he was in that room more than anywhere else. Again, Grandmaster Dante waited for him, this time holding his cane like a sword. Dante commanded Kyle to bring out his own sword, which he did while the Grandmaster jumped right to the demonstration.

"As you know," said Dante, "your sparring with Master Proculus is basically the use of your lightning as an extra internal force that helps stun and zap, and overall delivers a much harder punch or kick. This sparring will help you mold the lightning into different forms that will help you during a fight. You saw my fight with the Timber Dragoon?" After Kyle nodded, he went on, "Good. Then you will remember that I used my flame as guards for my arms and shins. This training will be the foundation for using Synchroneity in similar ways. We will start by molding our element around our weapons. This itself is not difficult, but the real test is to keep it up while fighting." He twisted his cane, making fire shoot out of his arm to envelop his cane. "Go ahead, give it a shot."

Kyle turned his key, concentrated, and easily enough, lightning coiled around the long blade of his Nodachi. The sword, which looked pretty fierce on its own, looked significantly more intimidating with lightning attached to it.

"Oho," said the Grandmaster holding his burning cane. "Let's get right to it, then. Try attacking me. Focus on keeping the lightning on your blade."

Kyle hesitated, but then attacked Grandmaster Dante. The lightning on his sword instantly disappeared like a candle that had been blown out. Dante swatted Kyle's sword away with ease. "Again."

CHAPTER FIFTEEN

DILU VILLAGE

The next few months of Dogwood, Redwood, Spruce and Ash flew by so quickly that Kyle could hardly keep track. He grew stronger, which pleased him, but he was happy to have some time off from training halfway through the frosty month of Willow when Thullrun finally delivered the Center Key necessary for their first official mission.

"Kross will be the squad leader for this mission," said Master Oisin to the five friends who were lined up shoulder to shoulder in his room. "I expect you five down at the gate, ready to leave in twenty minutes. I'm sure I don't need to tell you, but I will anyway. It's cold, so wear your cloaks."

Kross, Kane, Kevin, Garnet, and Kyle, who had prepared themselves earlier, went straight to the gate. They exited the castle, walking across the grounds in the bitter cold wind with a sense of purpose. Snow had fallen heavily the night before, but this did nothing to cool Kyle's anticipation. His excitement boiled fiercely, causing him to pace back and forth. He couldn't wait for the chance to see a part of Endera outside of Soul Gate Academy.

"You think we'll get any free time in Dilu Village?" Kyle asked Kane, who was closest to him.

"I doubt it," mumbled Kane. "Not with Kross lording over this mission."

"What's the village like?"

"Lots of shops," he answered. "I went there with my sisters a few times. They always dragged me along." He laughed in a bittersweet way that made Kyle wonder what his sisters were like. Kane had mentioned before that he had sisters, but he never liked to go into detail. "No chance of shopping today, but maybe we'll catch a glimpse of a cute girl or two. They make them nice in Dilu Village, but they're always hiding behind those—"

"You'll probably be bored in two seconds," cut in Garnet, who had been listening to the conversation.

"Are you kidding me?" Kyle looked beyond the academy's walls as he had done many times before. He could hardly contain himself. "It'll be an adventure. Plus it'll just be cool to finally see something besides SoGA."

"If you say so." Kane shrugged. "But I doubt this will be much of an adventure. We're still a pretty young team to be getting anything exciting. It does sound better than what we got last year, though."

"What'd you get last year?" asked Garnet.

"We delivered someone a letter," said Kane.

"What else?"

"We had to find someone's pet cat."

"Ah," added Kevin. His notepad was tucked away under his cloak.

"I was going to tell them," said Kane, sulking.

"Tell us what?" asked Garnet.

"We had to find the cat twice."

"Twice?" Kyle and Garnet looked at each other. "Why twice?"

"We sort of got the wrong cat the first time," muttered Kane. "The first one ended up wreaking havoc in the owner's house."

Garnet and Kyle broke out in laughter while Kane scowled and Kevin smiled, as always. Kross, who had been waiting with crossed arms, frowned at them all.

Soon after, they saw Master Proculus trudging through the snow with Master Oisin close behind him. Oisin carried something the size of a baseball bat wrapped in an emerald silk cloth.

Once they arrived, Oisin removed the silk to reveal a large key. "This is the Center Key," he said while handing it to Kross. "It will be one of three keys that will open the door into the cavern. I would let your summon handle this until you reach the cavern."

"Thank you, Master." Kross immediately pulled out his key and placed the Center Key into his summons's dimension.

Since Kevin is the only one who knows how to open a ShiftDoor, I suggest you make use of it," continued Oisin. "It is not far, but better to shift to Dilu Village rather than walk in this cold. I, personally, am freezing. Good luck hunting for the book, and be careful." He gave them one last serious look and then left. As he did, they all turned to Master Proculus.

Proculus smirked at the unspoken questions surely written across their faces. "Don't worry; I won't be spoiling your first mission together by coming with you." After Kane and Kross let out a noticeable sigh of relief, he continued, "I am just here for a quick word with Kyle."

As Kyle followed Proculus away from the group, a sense of dread set in.

"This isn't to tell me I can't go is it, Master Proculus?" He tried not to sound hostile.

"Of course not. I just wanted to tell you that you are not to use Synchroneity on this mission. I doubt you'll need to on a mission like this, but it would be unwise for me not to advise you against doing such a thing. You still need more training."

"But what if I have to?"

"Kyle, this is an order from the Grandmaster, and I'll add that I agree with him. Do. Not. Use it. You are not ready and you could hurt the others. Is that understood or should I pull you from this mission?"

"I won't use it, Master," said Kyle reluctantly.

"Thank you, Kyle. Let us not make your team wait any longer. Good luck. If the book is there, it'll probably be in a very old black leather binding."

Proculus turned and made his way back to the castle while Kyle returned to his squad. Perhaps it was to be expected, but he could not help feeling a little disgruntled at being told not to use the power he trained so hard to control. But after some thinking, he absentmindedly grabbed his chest, almost feeling his scar split open again as he remembered the pain of his meeting with Lightning. The element should never be taken so lightly.

After leaving the front gate of SoGA, they turned right and walked down a path covered with snow. Trees lined each side, blocking some of the wind, but were hardly enough to keep them warm. They followed the lane until it brought them to a small hill. They climbed it and it gave them a view of a long path leading into a snow covered meadow parallel to the ocean. At the end of the path was a large harbor town.

"Ah," said Kevin into the wind as he pointed at the town. His axe, which was strapped around him, bounced against his back.

"That's Dilu Village," said Kross.

"How is that a village?" asked Kyle in disbelief. "It's huge." The others grinned as they gazed at the town still a couple miles into the distance. Dilu Village started at the beach and extended for miles inland. There were tall buildings in the center, while on the outskirts of the town there were sturdy looking huts. In the harbor there were a handful of ships, all docked.

"I'd hate to walk that path," said Kane, shivering. "There're no trees. The wind would freeze us to death."

"It's not a problem," said Kross. "We're far enough from the school; we should be able to use a ShiftDoor now. Wish I could do it myself. I'll try to get it this year. Whenever you're ready, Kevin"

"Ah," said Kevin, pulling out his key.

Kyle wanted to ask them what it took to be able to open a ShiftDoor, but the wind kept him from talking. He, like the rest of them, just wanted Kevin to shift as soon as possible.

Kevin jabbed his key into the cold air. He turned it, making plumes of frosty wind as he did, and a wooden door painted baby blue appeared ahead of them. He returned his key to his pocket, opened the door, and walked in. Garnet, Kyle, Kross and Kane followed.

Kyle was taken aback for a moment. He had expected the shift to be similar to the one he took when shifting to Endera with Proculus, but it simply felt like walking through a doorway. With just a few strides, they had traveled a couple miles, landing in front of the gate into Dilu Village. The huts that he had seen from afar were not used for shelter. Instead, the structures had been locked together to make a tough wall that surrounded that village. It had taken someone with powerful knowledge of the Modifications ability to pack the huts together in such a fashion.

"Let's get inside," said Garnet between trembling teeth. "My face is going to freeze."

"Yes, I agree. Let's try and get in." Kross knocked on a small door that was a part of the gate. A moment later, a narrow hatch slid open with a pair of papery yellow eyes staring out of it.

"What brings young tyros from Soul Gate?" grumbled the doorman. "Cold enough to freeze a grown man down to his bones, isn't it?"

"Yes, sir—"

"I mean, you lot don't really seem like you got much meat on you, do you? You'll be ice in no time, won't you? I imagine the StitchLockers have a hard time making clothing warm enough for this weather, ya' think?"

"Yes, sir," snapped Kross impatiently. "You can imagine our desire to enter Dilu Village?"

"Oh ya need to come in?" he asked. "Of course you do, don't you? Not a problem; helping young tyros from Soul Gate Academy is a job of mine, isn't it?"

Kyle almost laughed, but thought better of it. He didn't want the doorman to be offended and lock him out in the cold.

"I'm unlocking it, aren't I?" The doorman snapped the hatch closed and the group heard a loud click on the other side before the door slid open. "You'll want to come in now, won't you?"

They hurried inside and instantly felt warmer as the bitter wind became significantly blocked. As the gate slammed shut, they heard another loud click that locked the gate again. The doorman hopped back to his post, causing Garnet to give a squeal of surprise. They had been expecting a man, but instead there was a wooden kangaroo towering over them like a giant puppet. Around the yellow slits that were his eyes, were two vibrant blue iris flowers.

"An Irismacrufus," said Kross under his breath. "Extraordinary."

"The name is Joey," said the Irismacrufus. "And I'm one of the village's doormen, aren't I? Well technically, I'm not a man, am I? Well, not a problem, is it? Be on your way, shouldn't you? It's still a bit cold inside the village walls, isn't it?"

Joey trailed off, muttering questions to himself as Kyle and Kane stifled laughs at his expense.

As they walked into the village, Kross took out a small notebook from underneath his cloak along with a pen. He opened it up and scribbled with ferocious speed.

"What are you doing?" asked Kyle.

"He's writing in his diary about that creature," answered Kane. "He does it all the time. He wants to summon them all or something. Right, Kross?"

Kross ignored him as he continued to scribble on his notebook.

"Isn't it better to only have one summon?" BioDimensions always intrigued Kyle.

"Not necessarily." Kross returned his notebook to his pocket. "It just depends. And it's not a diary."

Kane rolled his eyes.

"What'd you write down about him, anyway?" asked Kyle.

"Just some notes to help me remember what he was like. And of course, his grade."

"Did you write down that he's a bit insane?" said Kane. "Also, he asks lots of questions and wanted to let us freeze to death."

"Something like that," answered Kross distractedly. "But it's neither here nor there. We shouldn't waste time; we need to find the mayor."

"Where exactly do we find her?" asked Garnet.

"Her office or her home, I would guess. She should be expecting us." Kross led the way through Dilu Village. They walked down the main street, which ran straight through the large town. It was full of people hustling from store to store. The locals were dressed in an array of cloaks and trench coats that were not so different from what the squad wore, but most looked more fashionable rather than practical. What struck Kyle as oddest was that most of the people wore masks, each of them unique. Some only covered a single eye or half the mouth; some were stylishly tilted on their heads like a hat; others were more typical masks that covered whole faces. There were also a few villagers who decided not to wear masks on their heads at all. Instead they had them attached to their shoulders or hanging from a belt. Though among all the locals moving about, there were also foreigners who were easy to spot since they did not wear masks.

"Why are most of these people wearing masks?" wondered Kyle as they passed masked and unmasked people alike.

"I think it's just Dilu Village tradition or something," said Kane. "I like the masks though, reminds me of the Reader."

Garnet let out a slight cough.

Many of the people twisted their necks to catch a glimpse of the Soul Gate Academy emblem on their cloaks and then scurried off in a happy gossipy way. Kyle felt impressive for some reason.

"Why are people staring at us like that?" Kyle ruffled his hair, feeling overly aware of his body as a group of cute girls scurried by them with excited whispers.

"It's obvious isn't it?" Kane raised his voice. "I'm quite good looking, aren't I ladies?" The girls giggled, but raced off into the crowd.

"Ah," said Kevin softly as he watched the girls trail away. Kyle guessed that his big friend would have very much liked to follow.

"Oh sure," teased Garnet. "Kane the Handsome, with looks so good, women sprint away."

Kane scowled as the group, even Kross, let out a small laugh. Kyle looked to Kross for a more serious answer, but it was Garnet who answered instead. "Soul Gate Academy is a prestigious academy. It's well respected and so are the tyros who come from there."

"Why is that?"

"Well mainly," said Kross, "because new SoGA tyros must be recruited by a master or an eternal title. They cannot apply or buy their way in. Because of that, it is different from other academies around Endera."

"Why do they recruit—" Kyle interrupted himself as a realization hit, making him feel reasonably stupid. "Wait a second! There are other academies?" Some people on the street heard him and looked at him oddly.

"Yes." Kevin had taken out his notepad, and it issued the answer but didn't elaborate. He just looked around, notepad ready. Kyle presumed that he was hoping the girls might come back.

"Did you think we were the only tyros in this realm?" asked Kross. "The realm is huge; there are many academies. But Soul Gate Academy is the best."

"I see." Kyle was still surprised, but silently scolded himself. *Of course there are other academies. Look at all these people.* He changed the subject. "Why exactly do we need to go see the mayor?"

"Because." Kross frowned. "The Mayor will tell us where the cavern is and also give us the other two keys needed to enter it."

"Three keys to enter a cavern." Kyle messed up his hair again. "I hope we find something."

"Quit doing that," Garnet fussed. "We're in public."

"Yeah, yeah." Kyle shrugged but he stopped.

As they walked farther into the town, they passed a hefty blacksmith sweating as he worked over a blazing fire, hammering away at an unfinished blade. The blacksmith stopped shaping the weapon for just a moment to turn a large key that stuck out the side of the oven. As the group walked by, they could feel the heat of the fire become greater. Further on, there were two enormous StitchLocker stores. One had a big decorated sign reading *A Key and Stitch.* On the side of the large sign, there was a rotating key that made the sign flash on and off. Directly across the street from them, with a smaller sign, were their competitors, *The Stitch Department.* Instead of a flashing sign, there was a key with a long piece of violet silk floating behind it, like a lengthy cylinder kite.

As they continued, Kyle peered through a window displaying a range of odd trinkets and antiques. Another store, called *Keyspheres,* sold orbs the size of baseballs and golf balls that looked like keyholes had been painted on them. The place captivated Kyle. Through the windows, he watched people searching the aisles of what seemed like endless little keyspheres. He had a strong desire to join them. Something about the little orbs drew him away from his group unnoticed. Just as he was about to enter the store, Kane placed a hand on his shoulder.

"Those are banned at Soul Gate Academy." Kane's tone was very serious.

Kyle eyed the store in longing. "Why?"

"Keyspheres have Keyhole Disruptors on them. The Grandmaster is particularly against it. In his eyes, using a keysphere is cheating."

"Keyhole Disruptors." Kyle was almost infatuated. "What's so bad about them?"

"It is destructive yet powerful, damaging the key and the user," said Kane quietly. "Still, I wonder if it could be of use to learn."

Kyle now saw that Kane had a ravenous longing in his eyes. The observation made him break from the spell—and notice that Kevin, Kross, and Garnet were getting farther away from them.

"Well, let's not get left behind, huh, Kyle?"

Kyle nodded and followed him. "So shouldn't the Disruptors be against the law or something?"

Kane shrugged. "It's prohibited to put the Keyhole Disruptors on your body, but somehow it's okay to put them on orbs. Either way, it's all illegal for us."

"It's not like I have money, anyhow." Kyle saw the group a little ways ahead of them. "What is money in Endera made of, like gold or something?" Kyle had never thought of this since he had been in the realm. It made him feel notably out of place. However, money had never been one of his main concerns. Even in his old realm, he had seldom handled money. Since Soul Gate Academy took care of all his needs, there was no need for him to use it here, either.

"Gold, silver, and bronze, of course. What else could it be?"

"Paper." Kyle laughed. "In my old realm, we have mostly paper money. We have a few coins, as well, that stand for different values."

"Really?" said Kane. "That doesn't seem very…smart."

"Maybe." Kyle scratched his head. They reached the rest of the group, who were huddled up near a long line of people. They had noticed that Kyle and Kane were not with them. Kross scowled as the two of them walked up to them.

"We have to stick together," demanded Kross. "I will not have my first mission this year be a failure! I'll make sure you're both titled the Tortoise permanently if you keep moving so slow."

Kyle's face reddened while Kane ground his teeth. Kyle doubted that Kross had the authority to permanently title the two of them, but Kross's stern face was enough to suggest otherwise.

"Sorry," they muttered together.

Kross shot them both a look of fury, but he was soon distracted by the line of people nearby, who started to chatter loudly.

"Hey, don't you dare try cutting in line!" A person yelled.

"Yeah, we don't care if you're from Soul Gate, get to the back," agreed someone. There were plenty of people who muttered in agreement.

Kross motioned for the group to move away from the line so as to make sure they would not cause any trouble. The squad promptly listened and heeded. Now away from the line, Kyle could see the sign above a large keyhole-shaped doorway that led into the store. It read *The KeyMakers.*

"They make keys here?" asked Kyle.

"Nothing gets past you," teased Garnet.

"I just thought that most people would already own keys. Why's there such a long line?"

"Most keys wear out after use," said Kevin with his notepad. "But some good keys can last forever. The KeyMakers here work as keysmiths and collectors. They buy and sell old keys, as well as make new keys from scratch. These guys are the most popular in the New World. People come far for their keys."

"Keys go bad?" Kyle was surprised. He pulled his key out to examine. "Mine always feels good as new to me."

No one had a chance to respond to this because a dreadfully angry man came out of the KeyMakers store. "Ridiculous!" he shouted to no one in particular as he walked briskly toward the group. The line of people paid no attention to him as they tried frantically to get into the store. He was a tall man with brown hair and a hooked nose. A tiny white mask only covered his right eye and clashed with his bronze colored cloak. "The best in the New World, ha! I've seen more keys in a kitchen drawer. I need a drink." He stopped dead in his tracks when he saw Kyle standing in front of him, with key still in hand. "You, boy; let me see that key!" He walked directly over, but Kyle shoved his key back into his cloak.

"Er…"

"I will pay you for that key," implored the man. He rubbed his hands anxiously, which made Kyle and his friends all take a step back. "One hundred gold coins, if it's the key I think it is."

"Sorry," muttered Kyle. "It's not for sale." Kyle looked to his friends, who seemed to share his perplexity.

"Come on, young man." He took a step forward. "There must be something you want. Name it and I'm sure that I could do something for you."

"Sorry," Kyle repeated. "There's nothing."

Veins began to bulge on the man's face. "Listen here, boy! I work for a certain somebody."

All of sudden, Kross, Kane, and Kevin stepped in front of Kyle. "I believe he said it's not for sale," said Kross calmly. "Please be on your way."

"Oh, I see. I thought I saw the emblem. SoGA brats, huh?" sneered the man. He spit on the ground. "Don't get cocky."

"Is there a problem?" asked a lady of about forty, now standing behind the rowdy man. She wore her light blonde hair in a tight bun, where she had a small mask hairpin fashionably placed. She had a round pleasant face that stuck out of her ruby-colored silk robe, which looked expensive. She stood with an air of importance. Kyle had no doubt that if anyone could get rid of the man, it was her. The man looked at her with contempt, grudgingly changing his face into a wicked smile.

"None, Mayor Nova." The man almost twitched from his fake smile. "I was just telling these young tyros how unfortunate it is to make mistakes when they're stubborn."

"Wise words, Sergio the Hollow Eye," she said with a stern gaze. "I suggest you take them back to your master. I also think it would be wise for you to leave town soon." It wasn't a threat, but it might as well have been. The man looked angry, but with great difficulty held his retort. His bronze robe swished as he sped down a dark alley and disappeared. Mayor Nova, who had until now looked lethal, looked at Kyle and his squad with kindness.

"Mayor Nova," said Kross formally. "We are from Soul Gate Academy."

Mayor Nova held up her hand to stop him there. "Follow me to my home. We'll talk there. It should be a good deal warmer." Without waiting for a reply, she set off at a fast pace for her house. All along the main road, people greeted her. Kyle and his friends kept silent as they followed.

As they passed a street that was full of bars and inns, a pretty girl hardly older than Kyle wearing a pointy witch's hat and a clean yellow dress robe, stumbled out of a bar and onto the street. She swayed back and forth as she walked toward them, clearly drunk. The Mayor stopped with such force, she could have left a dent in the ground. She looked more deadly than she had when she confronted Sergio the Hollow Eye.

"'Ello Mother," said the drunk girl. Her long hair was light blonde, exactly like the Mayor's. "Funny seein' you here, in'it? And look it, you 'ave all dese cuties here. I suppose I can show 'em a thing or two about drinkin' if you'd like."

Kyle thought Mayor Nova might explode, but she said nothing, as if words were temporarily failing her. She attempted to grab her drunken daughter, but the girl dodged and flung herself onto Kyle. Kyle shot everyone a look for help, unsure what to do, but Kane snickered silently as the Mayor's daughter wrapped her arms around Kyle. Kross diverted his eyes in an attempt to keep his composure, though he looked like he was trying his hardest not to smirk. Kevin beamed before just saying, "ah." And Garnet? She looked almost as furious as Mayor Nova.

"Have you no shame, Rayne?" hissed Nova. "You're only sixteen. Your father would turn over in his grave if he knew. How dare they serve you!"

"Legal drinkin' age is sixteen," slurred Rayne. "Ya' can't change da laws of da king." She latched onto Kyle tighter. That was when he noticed that her eyes were a pastel pink, and she looked rather cute. "Don't get your panties in a bunch. I'll come home now. I'm just lettin' this guy escort me home, okay?" She let out a hiccup.

"Fine!" snapped Mayor Nova. "Please continue following me, tyros." The group tailed Nova as she picked up the pace to her house. Rayne pressed up against Kyle so tightly, they could have been attached at the hip. It made his whole body feel hot. So hot in fact, he thought the bitter wind outside the walls of Dilu Village would be a haven.

They turned down a few other streets, finally making it to the Mayor's house, which was surrounded by a tall fence. The house was definitely the largest in the area, standing three stories high and stretching wide enough for ten windows to fit on each floor. A man in a butler tuxedo paced back and forth in front of the gate. He stopped when he saw Mayor Nova.

"Lady Nova." The butler bowed low with the upmost respect, but he didn't look very butler-ish as they came closer. He had long scruffy black hair and wore a turquoise mask that covered only his mouth. "It appears that Lady Rayne—ah, she is with this young man. A marriage candidate?"

"What?" Kyle's face could have heated an oven. "Marriage? No! Er, not to say she's not umm—guys could you help me?"

Kane burst out in laughter while Garnet looked like she 'd burst in a much different way.

"This lot is from Soul Gate Academy, Baldwin," explained Mayor Nova. "Please inform Dean to bring out tea. Then I want Yumi to take Rayne and give her an icy bath. I'll deal with her later."

"Of course, Lady Nova."

"And Baldwin," added Nova. "Please fetch the keys."

Baldwin nodded as he opened the gate. The mansion didn't have much of a yard, but it was well kept, even in the winter. Baldwin escorted them into the estate before disappearing so fast he could have shifted. Mayor Nova led them to the living room, where they all sat down on cushiony couches surrounding a coffee table. Rayne was still attached to Kyle's arm until a maid came and pried her off. Kyle squirmed in embarrassment as Rayne gazed at him one more time before she left. Her eyes sparkled and her lips, just a shade darker than them, were tilted in a tiny smile. She was pretty, there was no denying that.

"I apologize for my daughter." Mayor Nova's eyes were on Kyle, but she was addressing all of them. "She's been a bit troubled since her father passed away."

"It's nothing to apologize for, Mayor," said Kross at once.

"Thank you," she said as Dean the butler walked in. Dean was a short man who wore a tiny mask over each of his ears, which made them look like headphones. He had a tray full of tea and little yellow cakes with a chocolate covered strawberry on top. He placed a dessert and drink in front of everyone in the room and left without saying a word. "Please help yourselves." Each of them did. The cake was delicious and the tea warmed them up nicely. After they were finished, the Mayor spoke again.

"Well I obviously know why you are here. And I'm certain you'd like to be sent on your way as soon as possible, but please at least tell me your names."

"Of course, Mayor Nova. I am Kross the Monk."

Kevin dashed across his notepad. "Kevin the Bison."

"Kane the Ace."

"I am Garnet the Scarlet Needle."

"Kyle the... Tortoise."

"Excellent." A smile found its way to Mayor Nova's face for the first time since they'd met her. "I am pleased to meet you all."

"The pleasure is ours," said Kross.

"Ah, right on cue," said Nova as Baldwin walked in holding a wooden case the length of a golf club. He handed it to Mayor Nova, cleared the coffee table, and left the room. As he left, Nova opened the case to show them the two long grey keys. Kyle thought they looked remarkably similar to lead pipes. "These are the two other keys: The Right and the Left. I am assuming you have the Center already and I am guessing you are the squad leader, since you are doing most of the talking." She closed it and handed the case to Kross. "The cavern is located outside Dilu Village, on the beach. It'll be about fifty strides from the wall where a large boulder is laying in the middle of the beach. It is locked so that it is unable to be seen unless you have the three keys. When you reach the boulder, it should be obvious what you need to do to get in. After you're done with that, I'm not sure what you'll find, but if there is anything else I can help with, please don't hesitate to ask. I am forever in Soul Gate Academy's debt."

Kross stood up and the squad followed suit. "Thank you, you have been most helpful," he said. Each of them bowed respectfully. "I will make sure the keys are returned safely."

"If you find something, report back to SoGA first. I can get the keys back later."

"Thank you," Kross said again. "If that is all, we should be on our way. We still have the most difficult part of the mission to carry out."

"Of course." Mayor Nova rose, too. "I will see you out."

The five tyros shuffled after the Mayor. Each of them muttered a soft good-bye before leaving the house. Just outside the Mayor's gate, Kross asked Kyle to place the keys into his MicroDimension. "My BioDimension will not take any more objects," he said. After Kyle finished, Kross led the way, not allowing anyone to be distracted by the crowds of villagers moving about the streets. In no time at all, they reached the front gate.

Joey the Irismacrufus opened the gate for them without hesitation. With the wind still howling, they hugged their cloaks close as they stepped out of Dilu Village to follow the wall to the beach. With every step they took toward the ocean, Kyle's face felt colder, making him glad when they reached the sandy shore. Turning away from the wall, they saw the lone large boulder that sat about fifty strides away from them. Hurriedly, they jogged to it. When they reached the great stone, Kyle and Kross lost no time in using their keys to retrieve the Left, Center, and Right keys.

Once they'd taken out the three large keys, the boulder began to glow sunlight yellow. They walked around it, looking for clues. As they circled it, they found three large keyholes facing the ocean. Light was brightly emitting from the keyholes and curving to encase the enormous rock. Kross took each key, placing them in the correct keyholes. Each fit as easily as pieces of a puzzle. When they were snugly placed, he turned them, but nothing happened.

A slight frowned etched onto Kross's face. He turned all three of the keys again and still nothing happened.

"What are we doing wrong?" asked Kyle impatiently.

"I don't know."Kross stared at the boulder intently, arms crossed.

Kevin moved forward to have a closer look at the keyholes. "Ah." Without saying anything else, he took one of the keys out which instantly provoked a reaction. The boulder began to split, leaving it with narrow crack before stopping.

"At least tell us before you're going to do something," said Kross, sighing heavily. "Well, pull out the other two."

Kevin pulled the other two keys out. The boulder split in half, making it look like an oversized open book that led down to the cavern. Dazzling sunlight gleamed from the bottom of the stone steps, which was quite the opposite of what they had been expecting from a cavern. Kyle jumped down to the first step eagerly. It was impossible to see the bottom of the staircase from where they stood.

"No point in staying in the cold," Kyle said to an annoyed looking Kross. The others followed, anxious to get out of the cold and search the cavern.

CHAPTER SIXTEEN

THE FORGER'S CAVERN

When they reached the bottom of the stairs, it landed them in a corridor that led to the source of the light. They walked toward it, unsure of what to expect. Since learning about the mission, Kyle had anticipated the setting to be teeming with chilly fog, sunless as an abyss, and drenched in slimy water that soaked many of the cavern's moist rocks. Instead, he walked into one of the most beautiful places he had ever laid eyes on. The area was so large, he suspected that the SoGA castle could easily fit inside. To the left of the entrance was a pleasant waterfall spilling its river into a jade-colored pond. The splashes left a mist in the air that made the place heavy with humidity. The sound of gushing water bounced off the cavern walls, creating a constant hiss. The pond broke off into several streams that disappeared under the walls of the cavern. Most of the cavern was green paradise: lush trees, bushes, and wild grass surrounded the pond; however, the most supernatural aspect about the place was the sunlight. Hanging high and dead in the center was a large orb of fire, burning bright. Not only did it keep the place lit, but paired with the thick humidity, it made the place downright hot. They lost no time in taking off their heavy winter cloaks.

"There must be powerful Modifications unlocking done here," said Kross as he studied the large source of light. "Maybe some Amplifications also, because that fire looks like it's burning brighter than normal. To burn indefinitely though; it's acting like a miniature sun…how is that possible?"

They all stared at the light, mesmerized by its glow.

"Kross," said Kane, sounding troubled. "It looks like we've been closed in."

The group turned around and could not see the doorway from which they had just walked through. There was only the mossy stone wall. However, there were three keyholes similar to the ones that had been on the boulder on the wall.

"It probably automatically locks to make sure that people without the keys cannot follow us," guessed Kross. The three large keys clinked in his hands. "I am sure we'll be able to unlock it again with our keys. First, we should search for the book." Kross frowned, looking unsure of where the book could possibly be.

"Where exactly do we look?" Garnet looked confused. "This isn't what we were expecting." She bent down to touch a beautiful white lotus with pink airbrushed tips that floated near her down one of the streams.

"I doubt they would put a book in here," said Kane as sweat trickled down his brow. "It's too humid."

"Ah," agreed Kevin. He scribbled something down on his notepad. "I think there is something more to this cavern."

"Me, too." Kyle scanned the area. He wasn't sure why he thought this, but something about the cavern seemed oddly similar to the Soul Gate Academy. "I don't see any other openings to any other part, but I think this is just the entrance. Like a lobby area or something."

"A lobby area?" repeated Kane. "Why would you think that?"

"Look at that sun closely." Kyle pointed at the fire overhead. "It kind of reminds me of a chandelier." Everyone except Kyle stared into the blinding mini-sun in an attempt to see the chandelier. By the looks on their faces, it was easy to see that none of them saw it in the slightest. They shot him looks filled half with worry and half with amusement.

"Kyle, are you okay?" asked Garnet. Kyle moved away from the group. He felt drawn to the pond, like something wasn't quite right about it. "Kyle, where are you going?"

When he reached the water's edge, he looked into the water. Even though it was jade green, he could see the floor of the pond. There on the floor were symbols, much like the ones he would see during use of AuraBending.

"There are symbols here." He grinned. "I have no idea what they say, but they're definitely there."

Kross, Kane, Kevin, and Garnet came to his side to look at the symbols while Kyle backed away, pleased with himself.

"Ha," he joked as he stuck his thumb to his chest proudly. "Maybe they should call me Kyle the Detective."

"It's too easy," said Kross. "There's no way that this means anything. This cavern has been searched in the past, there's no way they didn't see this."

"Ah, come on Kross," said Kane. "It obviously means something. No need to be jealous."

"Jealous?" snapped Kross, his face reddening. "Why would I be jealous?"

"No reason." Kane rolled his eyes.

Kross turned around abruptly to seemingly defend himself to Kane, but before he could get to it, he accidently dropped the Left, Center, and Right keys into the pond. They landed with a splash, sinking to the shallow floor of the pond's edge. "Ah, look what you've made me do." He dropped to his knees to fish the keys out of the water when something emerged from the bottom of the pond. All of them instinctively jumped back. Three smooth stone blocks ascended from the pond, stopping when they stood like a set of Olympic podiums covered in ancient symbols.

"Looks like I did something," whispered Kross, as if speaking too loudly might trigger something else.

Suddenly, the symbols on the podiums began glowing gold and swirling sluggishly. Each of the stone blocks had the same wriggling symbols, but they could not decipher the meaning. There was little need of translation, anyhow. There were unique engravings on the podiums that looked like they would fit the Left, Center, and Right keys perfectly.

"Well I think we're supposed to put the keys there," said Kane needlessly. As though agreeing with him, the pond spit out the three keys which landed at the group's feet.

"It could be a trap," Kross ventured, though he looked like he agreed with Kane. He picked up the keys and stared at the podiums hesitantly.

"It does seem too straightforward," said Kevin with his notepad. "Should we look around more before making a move?"

"If only we could read what it said…"

Kane, Kross, and Kevin crept forward, trying to get a better look at the podiums. As they did, they discussed possible solutions to the problem that Kyle couldn't hear. That was when Garnet leaned closer to his ear.

"I don't think it's a trap," she whispered. "The symbols say 'Welcome to the Forger's Cavern.'"

Kyle looked at her with raised eyebrows. "Can you always read symbols like this?"

"No," answered Garnet. "It's weird; I haven't been able to since—"

"What are you two whispering about?" Kross asked irritably. "This is not really the time."

"I think we should place the keys on the podium," said Kyle. "We'll just prepare for the worst if it's a trap, but I really don't think it is." The stones began to make a sucking noise as the podiums sank gradually back into the pond. Kross considered Kyle for a moment, pondering over what to do. Kyle stared at him confidently, wishing that he could simply tell them that Garnet used to be a reader.

"I think he's right," said Kane abruptly.

Kross tore his gaze from Kyle to look at Kane. Kevin stood beside him, nodding. At last his eyes found Garnet.

"Me too."

"Fair enough." Kross let out a long sigh. "I'll do it, so stand back."

The podiums were close enough that Kross did not have to enter the water. He carefully placed the keys on the sinking podiums, one at a time. They fit snug into the engravings and instantly prevented the blocks from sinking any further. Kross backed up to stand with his squad, all of them looking nervous.

All was silent except for the hissing splashes from the water falling into the pond. Then, there was a loud crack as the waterfall began splitting in two. The walls of the cavern made loud rumbling pops as they moved from each other like a sliding door. Water continued to fall into the pond, now from the two smaller waterfalls that had been formed. Between the waterfalls was a large entrance leading into a long hallway that stretched to another part of the cavern. From where they stood, it was too far to see anything at the end of the new pathway other than darkness. Everyone's jaws could have hit the floor had they been any shorter.

"Looks like we have to swim," said Kane as he stared in awe. But just as he said this, a number of stone blocks popped out of the water behind the podium, extending over the length of the pond. The bridge connected to the other side perfectly.

When the initial shock wore off, everyone looked at each other with wide grins. Kyle was willing to bet that Master Oisin and Grandmaster Dante never planned for them to discover a new part of the cavern. It made him feel elated and he was certain that his friends felt the same way. Of course, it helped that they had an ex-reader in their mix that had given them a nudge in the right direction.

"Shall we?" said Kyle eagerly. He jumped up onto the podium, careful not to touch the keys laying on them.

"Wait!" yelled Kross with some authority that shocked them all. "I want us to go in there a little more prepared, at least with weapons ready."

"Fair enough," said Kane as he unsheathed his daggers. Kevin unstrapped his axe while Kyle, Kross, and Garnet used their keys to retrieve their weapons. Kyle swung his Nodachi, Kross gripped his Shaolin spade, and Garnet twirled her spear with some skill.

Kyle, who was already on the stone bridge, led the way into the next part of the cavern. The path was moist and slippery. It had obviously not been used in years, but the smoothness of the stone path proved that it had once seen heavy traffic. After they walked for a few minutes, the hallway opened up into a dark space. They each spread out, barely able to see ahead. A powerful and unpleasant odor lingered in the dark cavern, like vinegar and sweat mixed together.

"I can't see a thing," said Kyle, thinking of his Synchroneity lightning. He could give everyone a bit of light if he hadn't been forbidden from using it. "What should we do?"

"Hold on." They all heard Kross move around. A moment later there was light, coming from a lamp Kross held. A key stuck out of the collar of the lamp. It glowed dimly, but it illuminated the room well enough for them to see each other. The ground had changed from stone to wood, and there were a few broken bottles scattered on the floor.

Kevin, who was standing next to the pathway entrance, noticed a key sticking out of the cavern wall. It looked like a light switch key similar to the ones they had at SoGA. Without much thought, he turned it.

A large overhead lamp erupted with fire shining much brighter than their lamp. The room it revealed could be nothing other than an empty tavern. There was a long counter with many stools lined up next to it. Behind the counter was an array of bottles. Some were broken, others still intact and full of amber liquid. The room spread out into a small dining area full of decaying wooden tables and chairs. There was a small stage covered in mold that had caved in. In the center of the stage was a rusty instrument that looked almost like a tuba that had been hammered into the shape of a star.

"Well." Garnet scrunched up her nose. "I'm guessing that there wasn't much reading going on here."

"Still," said Kross, "we have to check. Wish we had more hints about the book, though."

"Master Proculus mentioned that it would probably be a book with a black leather binding," Kyle told him.

"Good enough for me. Everyone spread out and look for a black book, and be careful. This place looks like it is about to fall apart."

As they spread out, the wooden floors creaked loudly beneath their feet. Kyle found his way behind the bar. He set his sword down on the counter, knocking over a few bottles. They shattered into brown crystals. "Sorry!" He searched the drawers and shelves but the only things he found were a large number of spider webs, grimy glasses, and more bottles.

Kevin knocked over a few tables simply by walking near them. Being the largest of all of them, he took every step with great caution, clearly fearing that at any moment the floor would collapse. Kross found an old magazine lying on one of the tables. It crumbled in his hands as he picked it up. Garnet walked straight to the far end of the bar near the only other doorway. She blew dust off an old sign that had been stuck next to the door, but it was still too dirty to read, so she had to wipe it clean with her hands. Kane searched around the stage with his daggers. He ventured off to the side of the stage, where it looked like there had once been an entrance to another room, but the ceiling had fallen to ruin long ago.

BOOM!

Kane jumped back so far that he slammed into a table, causing it to fall over. Kevin reacted similarly, which resulted in him landing so hard that his foot broke through the floor. Kyle instinctively grabbed his sword, causing him to knock over some more bottles.

"What happened?" cried Kross. Dust filled the air like a heavy brown smoke.

"I don't know," coughed Kane. "Something slammed into the wall."

"Quiet," hissed Garnet. Her advice was unnecessary. Each of them kept still and silent, hardly drawing a breath. After a few moments, nothing happened and the dust cleared.

"Must have just been something collapsing," said Kross, breaking the silence.

"Yeah, probably," agreed Kane.

"Would someone mind helping me?" said Kevin with his notepad. "My foot is stuck."

Kane and Kyle hurried to help Kevin. With a few great tugs, they freed him. Kross and Garnet were now standing over the sign she had been cleaning. "Hey guys." Garnet waved them over. "I think I found something."

Kyle, Kane, and Kevin joined them, excited at the idea of something more than webs and rotten wood. The sign was actually a map directory with the title *The Forger's Cavern* at the top. Kyle shot Garnet a sudden look, which she returned, but they diverted their attention back to the map directory. It looked similar to one that would be found in a mall. A small golden key symbolized they were there. It also indicated that there were five other main sections of the cavern. Next over from the Bar, there was an area called the *Forge*. Behind the Forge was the largest block, labeled the *Inn and Dorms* where there were many numbered boxes that marked each room. On the other side of the Forge, the directory labeled a place called *Unlocked Eats*, which they guessed to be a cafeteria. Connected to

Unlocked Eats was the *Library*.

The whole group stared at the map with hope in their eyes. The mission was looking optimistic now. It didn't seem like they would be going back without a book. Where else would the book be but the library? The last block on the map was the smallest with a label they could barely read. The *King Forger's Office* was right next to the library.

"King Forger's Office?" said Kane. "There could be a Kota there!"

"Our mission is to retrieve the *book*," Kross declared. "Nothing else. If we find something other than that, we report back to our Masters before taking it."

"All right, all right," muttered Kane. "Murder me for getting excited, why don't ya?"

Kross ignored him. "I think it's obvious we have to search the library. I'd like to give the King Forger's Office a good look too. Of course, they just happen to be at the end of this cavern. If we can't find anything in those places, we'll search the Inn and Dorm rooms."

"That could take forever." Garnet gripped her spear. "I don't really think this is the best place for us to stay overnight."

"You're right," agreed Kross. "Let's hope we find the book quickly."

"Did you guys see something?" asked Kyle as he looked cautiously through the doorway leading to the Forge. "I thought I saw something move just now." A man's silhouette vanished into the darkness like a wisp of smoke in the wind, but no one other than Kyle had seen it.

"That's just your eyes playing tricks on you." Kane pointed at the broken stage. "Look at this place. It's been hundreds of years since anybody has been here. Nothing down here is alive enough to be moving around." Kyle relaxed a little, but he still felt certain that he had seen something move.

"I think we should get moving," said Kross.

"Wait!" Garnet's gaze was still glued to the map, examining it carefully. "Look here." She pointed at one of the room squares.

"I don't really think you should be picking out a room," Kane jested.

"Oh ha ha," she said mockingly. "I'm more interested in these little skull things that look like they were scratched onto some of the rooms. And look it's not only the rooms; the skulls are spread throughout the cavern, too." The rest of the team looked over the map directory again. It was an easy thing to miss if you weren't looking closely, but Garnet was right. Little skulls were engraved onto a number of places. "What do you think it means?"

"Probably nothing," said Kross. "Let's not get distracted. We have a job to do so let's get to it."

Everyone nodded in agreement. Although Kyle did not say it, he wanted to find the book and leave the Forger's Cavern as soon as possible. Something was making him feel strangely uncomfortable.

They left the bar through the only available doorway. A short walk down a wide corridor led them to the Forge. Light shined from the Forge's ceiling when they walked in. It felt bizarre to Kyle that he was finally seeing a part of the cavern that looked most like what he imagined a cave would look like. Pointy rocks hung from the ceiling and the rest of the large room was mostly stone. There were at least two dozen ovens, some of them built into the wall while others stood like small stone houses. Next to them were anvils that were paired with large stone tables and the remains of large wooden tubs that had nearly decomposed to nothing.

"I'm guessing a lot of blacksmithing happened down here," said Kane needlessly.

Bits of rusty metals and half-finished weapons littered the place, all worthless. They made their way across the Forge without trouble; however, as they reached the opposite end, an oven erupted with fire. Before they could whip around, more ovens began to do the same. It didn't last long, though. The fires all went out, leaving bits of smoke lingering around each oven.

"Are there ghosts in Endera?" Kyle scanned the Forge for any movement. He felt stupid for asking, but he figured that it didn't seem that unlikely.

"Ghost?" said Kane with a higher voice than usual. "That's ridiculous."

"We must have hit a switch or something," said Kross.

"Yeah, quit being all paranoid." Kane let out an uncomfortable laugh. "'Ghost' he says."

Kyle shrugged. Was he being paranoid?

Three paths led to the next part of the cavern, but two paths had collapsed. The third path looked perfectly fine, but they walked cautiously. When they arrived to the Inn and Dorms area, the place could best be described as a disaster. Several large crystals had fallen, destroying most of the area and leaving rubble of rotten wood, broken furniture, and crumbled rocks. They counted themselves lucky when they found just enough room in the mess to make it through to the next part of the cavern.

"So much for being able to search this place if we don't find it in the library," said Kyle. He felt less hopeful of finding anything and he could tell that the feeling was shared among his friends. Still they continued forward, stepping carefully over the debris as they worked their way toward the door that led into Unlocked Eats.

Once they made it through, it took a few tugs to pry the door open to enter the next part of the cavern. The next room was dimly lit and extremely dry. Kyle expected to see Unlocked Eats in ruin like the rest of the cavern, but the room was completely empty except for the overwhelming feeling that something lingered in its shadows.

"Ah," said Kevin. Kyle wasn't sure but he thought there was fear in his voice.

Garnet edged herself closer to Kyle as they all cautiously moved forward. He gripped his Nodachi the point of pain. The dim light gave him a limited view of the room, sending a ghostly feeling through him, like he had just been doused in cold water.

"Let's get to the library quick," muttered Kross. "I think it's up those stairs."

There was a stone staircase to the right that led to a brightly lit room that was the source of light for Unlocked Eats. As they moved closer, they could see a bookcase. Kross lost no time in leading them up the stairs.

If Kyle had not known he was still in a cavern, he would have guessed they had just shifted to a library far away. The Library's high ceiling was made from sleek whitewood. All the walls were completely covered with bookshelves, and loaded with books. A large spiral staircase led to the second floor, which had more books and a door. Couches and tables, looking brand new, clean, and quite different from everything they had previously seen in the cavern, gave the place a comfy atmosphere. If the previous sections of the cavern had been weird, this was weirder still.

"Is this stuff new?" asked Kyle. He touched one of the couches as if it would turn alive. "How is that possible?"

"I don't know." Kross looked thoroughly frustrated. "Just spread out and look for the book. Master Oisin told me it should be painfully obvious, but I suppose he didn't know the cavern would have a library."

"I think this is it," said Garnet before they could even really search. There was a large black book in a glass cube case about the size of a watermelon. Through the glass, they could see that the book cover had a simple gold key imprinted on it. "Should I try opening it?"

They surrounded the case and all frowned at it. Once again, they had come across something that seemed entirely too easy.

"This has to be a trap," declared Kyle. "We move it and it'll be all Indiana Jones in here!"

"Indiana Jones?" asked Kane.

"Er, sorry. Earth thing."

Garnet giggled, but noticed the looks on the other three who were hardly amused.

"We have to take it," said Kross. "It's our mission."

With a deep breath he stepped forward to lift the glass gently. When it didn't move, he gave the case a hard pull. Still, the glass case stayed in place.

"Need some help there?" Kane chuckled.

"It won't move." Kross backed away, looking at the case with annoyance. "Give it a try if you're so confident."

Kane stepped forward, gripping the glass case. He lifted till his face was beet red and his veins looked ready to burst, but the case did not move.

"Allow me," said Kevin with the robotic voice of his notepad. Kevin attempted, but ended with the same result. He and Kane then worked together, but still the case would not move. Kyle wanted to try himself, but he knew that if Kevin had failed, there was little chance that he would be successful. Kevin was physically the strongest amongst them.

"Are you Enderians or what?" said Garnet. "It's obviously been locked. We need to unlock it." She stepped forward with her key in hand and pointed it at the glass case. She turned her key to the left, but nothing happened. She looked crestfallen. "Looks like we're going to need a specific key."

"Ah," said Kevin holding up his hand. He then wrote on his notepad. "I have wanted to try out a Modifications ability. Please allow me to try one more time." He set his axe down and took out his key. He pointed it at his right arm, turned it, and then did the same for his left arm. His arms began to grow, doubling their size. The growth resulted in two arms that were bulging with muscles, making him look a bit like a gorilla. Kyle knew that it must have been a difficult Modifications ability because Kevin was breathing hard already. "Ah," he added before gripping the glass case tightly with his hands. He heaved with all his might, but nothing changed.

"I don't think we're going to be able to pull it off," said Garnet.

"Ah," said Kevin, looking defeated. His arms were returning to their normal size. It didn't look like he was able to hold the ability for a long time.

"This isn't good," said Kross. "I guess we'll have to find the right key."

"The chances of that are pretty slim," said Kane. Most of this place is a mess. And I doubt someone just left the key lying around."

"We have to at least try," muttered Kross.

"Let's check the King Forger's Office first," said Garnet. "That should be it right there."

"If we can't find it, then we'll head back and report this to the Grandmaster," decided Kross. "With all these ruins, we can't search this whole place for a key."

Kyle, Kane, Kevin, and Garnet nodded in agreement, leaving the glass case alone for the moment. The spiral staircase took them to a massive oak door. Kross barely pushed on the door, but it swung open with unnatural force. They entered the room warily. It was an expansive office with a ceiling lamp that illuminated the room as clear as day. A large desk sat straight across from the door. There was another bookcase that covered the entire wall to the right of the door. Papers and tattered books littered the room. The chairs were tipped over and the desk was incredibly dusty. They searched through the desk and around the office, but the office was scarce; everything of any worth looked like it had been taken, and in a hurry too.

"Guys!" said Kane excitedly as he examined an old sword with grooves resting on a wall mount. "I think this is a Kota!" He wrenched it down from its place.

"No it isn't," said Kross. "This place has been ransacked. Whoever did this wouldn't just leave a Kota. It's probably just a replica."

"Ha, don't be jealous." Kane swung the sword, showing off his newfound treasure.

"Ah." Kevin held his hand open, signaling his desire to see the weapon.

"No way," said Kane.

"Ah," insisted Kevin.

Kane hesitated, but then handed it to the Bison. Kevin slid a finger along the sword as he inspected it. Without warning, he swung the blade against the wall, causing it to snap in half easier than a twig.

Kane's jaw dropped. "What'd you do that for?"

Kevin handed him the destroyed replica and then wrote on his notepad, "A real Kota wouldn't have broken." He smiled as a disgruntled Kane tossed down the worthless weapon.

"Will you two quiet down?" hissed Garnet. "Something about this place just doesn't feel right."

"Don't be scared," Kyle reasoned. "We haven't run into anything yet; we'll be fine."

"That's my point! We *haven't* encountered anything. Things have gone too smoothly. Who just enters into an ancient cavern and doesn't come across a single problem?"

"Who knows?" Kyle shrugged. "I don't know too many people who have been running through ancient caverns, do you?"

Garnet glared at him with disapproving eyes. She turned away toward Kross and asked him, "Did you find something?"

Kross was looking at a paper he had grabbed from the desk. "It says *For Emergencies.* Kane, there should be a lever near you—oh wait no, Kevin that blue book right in front of your left shoulder. Pull it."

Kevin tilted the book back like a lever and then the bookcase split into two. He jumped back. fearing that he would fall down what looked like a slide.

"An emergency slide all the way back to the pond." Kross smirked. "Could be pretty useful."

"It's probably not the safest," said Garnet, pointing out the obvious. "You saw all those cave-ins. For all we know, this escape is blocked."

"True," said Kross. "Well, it doesn't matter. We'll just go out the same way we came in. It doesn't look like there's anything of use in this office. Let's give the library another look. Maybe the key to unlock the book is somewhere…"

Kyle became distracted as Kross kept talking. He picked up a paper that had landed on his foot when the bookcase slid open. On it was a hand-sketched picture of a human skeleton. It looked like a normal skeleton, except for a key floating where the heart should have been. Under the drawing, someone had scribbled a note.

> THEY SLEEP IN UNLOCKED EATS. THE PICTURE ABOVE SHOWS THE SIDE EFFECTS OF CREATING A SKELETON KEY. WE WERE FOOLS, ALL OF US. THE KING FORGER WARNED US BEFORE HE LEFT. THE SKELETON KEY HAS MADE US ITS SLAVES. THEY SLEEP IN UNLOCKED EATS. I HAVE DESTROYED THE ORIGINAL SKELETON KEY, BUT IT WAS TOO LATE. ALL MY FRIENDS, ALL THOSE WHO HAVE FORGED WITH ME FOR YEARS...SKELETONS. DAMN IT, I'M CHANGING NOW. IF YOU READ THIS, THE ONLY WAY TO STOP A SKELETON IS TO DESTROY THE HEART KEY. DAMN IT...I'M THE LAST ONE...THEY SLEEP...WE SLEEP IN UNLOCKED EATS...

It sent a chill down Kyle's spine.

"Kyle!" shouted Kross from downstairs, making Kyle jump. "Get down here!" Kyle rushed with the paper in his hand, gripping his sword tight in the other. He was relieved to see them waiting for him around the glass book case. He sprinted down the stairs. "What were you doing?"

"I was just—" Kyle was interrupted by a low groan from the doorway. The squad spun to face the silhouette of a very skinny man. A skeleton of yellow stained bones stepped into the light, moving as if it had muscles. It stared at them with hollow eye sockets. A jet black key floated right where its heart should have been.

The skeleton tramped forward, dragging a large battle axe on the ground similar to the one Kevin wielded. The weapon only added to its grim appearance. A second later, another skeleton showed up. This one held a long broadsword against its shoulder. They groaned loudly in unison and were anything but welcoming.

"Kyle," ordered Kross, "try to figure out a way to grab the book and put it in your MicroDimension. After that, everyone run upstairs. Kane, Garnet, Kevin, weapons ready. We'll hold them off."

The two skeletons let out another groan and staggered toward Kyle's friends.

"I'm on it," yelled Kyle as he moved to the glass case. He struggled with the urge to ignore Kross's order and join the fight with them. It was the Monk's way of keeping Kyle out of danger since he was the weakest. He hated the idea of being treated like this, but he knew it was the truth. Kyle also knew that Kross was not likely to leave without doing his very best to get the book, so if he could figure out how to get it, they could flee immediately. And after reading the note, he suspected their survival depended on leaving as fast as possible. "Aim for the heart key! That's the only thing that will stop them." The group didn't question how Kyle knew this, but they took his advice and aimed for the skeleton's key. This, however, turned out to be more difficult than they could have anticipated. The skeleton men were strong and skilled and putting up a fight.

Kevin and the skeleton with the axe exchanged heavy blows while Kane tried to get in close for a jab with his daggers. Garnet and Kross were busy keeping the skeleton with the broadsword at bay. Both skeletons moved their bony arms without wasted movements, defending their attacks well.

Suddenly, there was a loud crack of bones. Kevin managed to hit the skeleton's femur. The skeleton dropped to the ground but did not let up with its attack. It swung the axe, just missing Kevin's stomach. Luckily, Kane took the opportunity to jab his dagger between the skeleton's ribs. He struck the black heart key, making it shatter like a broken vase. The skeleton fell still and dead—the group's preferred way of enjoying its hospitality.

"Got one!" shouted Kane. "Now we just need to finish—"

Two more skeletons stumbled into the room, groaning just like the others. The only difference: one cracked its whip while the other jabbed a spear.

Desperately, Kyle turned back to the book and its protective case. He tried to pry it open with his own strength, but it still did not budge. Then he did something without thinking. A pretty stupid something.

After tightly squeezing his sword in both hands, he gave it a mighty swing. The blade smashed into the glass, causing it to shatter with the subtlety of a gunshot. Seconds later, an earsplitting siren set off, sounding like a high-pitched fog horn as it echoed through the cavern. He thought he heard his friends yell, but could not tell for sure with all the noises jumbled together. Trying not to panic, he took out his key to open up his MicroDimension.

The air became distorted, and he stuffed the paper he had taken from the upstairs office into his dimension. As he reached for the book, he saw a spear thrust coming in the corner of his eye. He dodged just in time—though in doing so, didn't grab his key, which still floated in the air with his chain dangling from it. As he circled the skeleton, he thought the skeleton would try to grab it. Instead, the skeleton ignored the key, focusing on stabbing Kyle through with his spear. Kyle deflected the lunge with his sword.

I have to end this now.

He spared a quick look to see his friends still fighting. Another skeleton had come in, swinging two sickles around wildly. Where were they all coming from?

He waited for another attack of the spear, which the skeleton sent a moment later. He dodged to the left and lunged at the skeleton's chest, his long blade aimed directly for the heart key. He half expected the spear to crash into his side, but it did not. Finally, Kyle smashed his blade through a rib bone and stabbed the heart key, causing it to shatter. And then the skeleton was still.

Kyle moved to grab the book, jamming it into his MicroDimension.

"I got it!" He yelled before placing his key necklace on his neck again. But his friends were too busy in their fights to move back to the stairs. Each of them now fought separate skeletons. Garnet sidestepped an attack, dashing in and slashing the skeleton's heart key clean in two.

Turning to Kyle, she gasped, "Help me push this bookcase!"

Without another word, Kyle moved to help her. He could hear the grinding shuffle of bones moving across the stone floor of Unlocked Eats. They rammed the bookcase, trying to ignore the fifty skeleton men staggering toward them. The presence of Kyle and his friends, along with the alarm still going off madly, was drawing the monsters to the library.

The bookcase was too much for only the two of them. Luckily, Kevin finished off his skeleton and rushed over to help them. With one final shove from the three of them, the bookcase crashed down, smashing two skeletons to bits as they had attempted to run in through the doorway. At the same time, two other skeletons crumble down into a heap of bones as Kane and Kross finished their fights.

The library was in shambles. One of the couches had a big axe stuck in the cushions. A spear that had skewered a stack of books was stuck into a wall. Other weapons littered the floor, and loose book pages shuffled about like tumbleweed.

And there were bones, plenty of bones.

"How'd you know destroying their key would stop them?" asked Kross, breathing hard.

"It said so on a note I found in the King Forger's Office," answered Kyle. "That's what I was doing when—"

BOOM!

They all lunged back as the skeletons pounded on the bookcase, trying to claw their way through.

"We have to get out of here now," said Kyle. "Fifty more of those things are down there. When they break through, we won't have a chance."

"Looks like we're using that emergency slide" There was a bit of panic in Kross's voice. "First let's put another bookcase down and then get to the King Forger's office."

The pounding became louder, and then an axe head bit through the wooden bookcase. They hurried to set the second one down, which took little effort between the five of them. Kane and Kross took out their keys, jabbing them into the second bookcase. They turned their keys together, amplifying the wood to make it stronger. As soon as they were done, they rushed upstairs.

Kevin came in last, slamming the door shut behind him as Kyle and Kane began pushing the desk in front of the door.

"Kyle, did you get the book?" Kross joined them, tugging the desk from its other side.

"Yeah," gasped Kyle as they gave the desk one final nudge against the door. "I smashed the glass with my sword and that set off the alarm." The five of them were breathing hard, looking disheveled and wild like they had run through a cage of lions.

"Good." Kross eyed the escape slide hesitantly. "I want us to store our weapons. Can you handle taking Kane's and Kevin's?"

"Yeah."

"Good," he said again. "I don't want anyone stabbing themselves on the ride down, which I imagine is going to be bumpy. Garnet, are you okay? Garnet?"

She was white as a ghost and barely holding on to her spear. "I'm fine— just a bit shocked and tired is all."

Kross gave her an understanding look as he turned his key and pressed his Shaolin spade into his BioDimensions. "Are you able to put your spear away?"

"I can handle it," said Kyle. "Give it here; my dimension is big enough." Kyle took hold of the spear which Garnet reluctantly let go. Kyle was worried, she looked like she was about to become sick. "Are you sure you're okay?"

She nodded weakly, leaving Kyle with little else to say. This was not the place to press the issue. Kyle placed their weapons into his MicroDimension. The groans from the skeletons seemed to be getting louder.

"Everyone ready?" They nodded without hesitation. "Kevin, I want you to go last, pull the book again and slip in before the bookcase slides shut. Got it?—I'll go first, and if I don't yell back—"

"Just get on with it," interrupted Kane. "We haven't got all day."

Kross stood at the edge of the emergency exit slide, looking skeptical. "Who in their right mind would create such—"

Kane pushed him in and followed. Garnet went in next, looking pale and fragile. Kyle, worried, went after her immediately. He knew Kevin would not hesitate in the slightest, and heard his friend pulling the book then jumping in as the bookcase shut behind him.

The five of them slid rapidly down the smooth slide. It reminded Kyle of a bobsledding race; as the slide turned, their bodies followed as though they were connected to it. They could not see a thing as they sped onwards. Kyle had no idea how far Garnet was ahead of him, nor how far Kevin was behind him. He couldn't remember a time his heart had beat faster.

Suddenly, there was a steep drop. Kyle slid faster toward some light shining ahead. That could only mean they were near the end of the ride.

Before he could react, the slide was no longer under him. He shot out and fell, hanging in the air for a moment before plummeting into the pond at the entrance of the cavern with a great splash. He swam up to the surface only to be splashed heavily by Kevin who nearly landed on him. When Kevin came up, they burst out in laughter while treading water. Everything seemed a hundred times funnier as their heads bobbed up and down in the water. Everyone was okay, and they had successfully retrieved the book.

Their laughter stopped abruptly when they heard a groan echo through the pathway between the waterfalls.

"We have to move the keys!" shouted Kross as they all rapidly swam to shore.

Kane was the fastest swimmer, making it to shore before the rest. He removed the keys which made the waterfalls move to become one again. The skeleton couldn't walk fast enough; it waved its sword defiantly as the rocks crushed its bones to dust.

They rested on the shore, breathing heavily. Kyle felt his clothes drying which, not for the first time, made him appreciate the powers of the StitchLockers. They'd freeze to death if they had to go back into the cold with soaked clothing. When his clothes were dry, Kyle sat up to see Kross with his hands covering his eyes and Kevin looking hungry. Kane looked tired and Garnet looked like she had gotten back a little bit of color, but still looked ill.

"Ah," said Kevin.

"You're right," said Kross, somehow understanding. "We should get going. Can you handle opening a ShiftDoor? I'd like to get back to SoGA."

Kevin nodded.

The team stood up and Kyle returned Kane and Kevin's weapons to them. Garnet opted for Kyle to continue holding her spear, which he was glad to do. *She doesn't look like she has energy to spare on opening a BioDimension anyhow.*

"Garnet—"

"I'm fine," she snapped.

He dropped it.

They walked to the entrance where they had left their cloaks and put them back on. None of them liked the idea of going back into the cold, but they were eager to leave the cavern. Kross used the three keys to open up the stairway. However, it did not open the path. Instead, sliding doors opened up into an elevator much like the one at Soul Gate Academy. They were confused, but decided that it must be the proper exit. As soon as the five of them entered, the doors slid shut.

When the elevator opened again, icy wind flew in. They exited, knowing they had made it back to the surface. Kyle stomped onto the snow, looking around to see the elevator had dropped them off in the middle of the field between Dilu Village and Soul Gate Academy. He let out a huge sigh of relief. The elevator disappeared, but Kevin replaced it with a ShiftDoor for them to teleport as close as they could to SoGA.

Not wanting to speak with the cold wind again biting at their skin, they followed Kevin silently into the ShiftDoor, anxious to get home.

CHAPTER SEVENTEEN

OUT OF OPTIONS

Kyle stepped out of the doorway on the hill, staring over the large field of snow where they had just been standing. The wind whistled softly as he turned around to make sure Garnet had come through, as well.

A feeling of relief washed over him. He and his friends had gone through a trial that had been both terrifying and exhilarating. He tried not to feel too satisfied with himself, but he had to admit, it felt good to successfully complete their first mission together. It had been a thrilling adventure. He gave Garnet a grin. She looked like she was just about to smile back when something behind Kyle made her eyes open wide in fear. Before Kyle could do anything, he felt something hammer into his back, shoving him directly into Garnet. Both of them were thrown back through the ShiftDoor as they heard the shouts of Kane, Kross, and Kevin.

They tumbled and skidded onto the powdery snow before finally coming to a stop twenty feet from the door. Kyle laid with the wind knocked from his lungs, struggling to take in the situation.

"Garnet!" He gasped for breath. "What happened?"

"The Hollow Eye." She stumbled to her feet with her key shaking in her hand.

"The Hollow Eye?" Kyle was bewildered. "The man who wanted my key?"

Garnet nodded feebly.

"What about Kane?" He ground his teeth. "And Kross and Kevin?"

"I don't know." She seemed flustered to the point of tears. With some difficulty, Kyle got to his knees. He attempted to massage his back, speculating that a large bruise was beginning to form. "I think they separated us on purpose."

"We have to get back," said Kyle. "We have to help them."

She twisted her key and from the distorted air came out a wolf made from sunflowers and green stems. The Helianlupus.

"Master," the sunflower wolf growled, "Why have you called me? You are not well."

"We've been ambushed, Eva," panted Garnet. "Focus on the door. An enemy may come through it at any moment." Eva the Helianlupus obeyed, baring its sharp thorny fangs at the ShiftDoor.

"Ugh," muttered Kyle as he stood up. He pulled out his key and turned it to bring out their weapons. He handed the spear to Garnet who took it in her wobbly hands. He shot a glance toward the hill looking over the snowy meadow to see if he could see the rest of his friends, but he saw nothing. "Hurry. Let's go before the ShiftDoor closes."

Eva began to growl.

"You won't be goin' anywhere," spat a coarse voice from the doorway. Kyle pivoted to face the familiar voice. Sergio the Hollow Eye stood in front of the door, his one-eyed white mask looking grimmer than it had in town. The spear in his hands looked different than a normal spear. It appeared as though the shaft and head of a metal arrow had been stuck onto the staff of a spear: a roman pilum. "Not until I get that key."

"Garnet, get back!" Kyle hollered as he eyed Sergio.

He could tell there was something serious wrong with his friend now. Her face had lost most of its color and she barely had the strength to hold up her spear. He twisted his key twice more, slipping it back underneath his shirt as his aura extended out, shrouding Garnet, leaving a circle of AuraBending symbols around her. He left some to surround himself as well, but it was hardly better protection than his own skin. "I'll handle him on my own."

Sergio let out a sickening cackle that made Garnet wince.

"You'll handle me on your own?" he sneered. "Don't be a fool, boy." The man brought out a key of his own, pointed at nothing in particular, and turned it. The air didn't distort nor did AuraBending symbols show, leaving Kyle clueless as to what the Hollow Eye had done. He raised his sword in defense, his hands trembling as fear sat in his stomach.

A moment later, Sergio launched his pilum high into the air, much too high to have been aiming at Kyle or Garnet. In the second Kyle's eyes followed the spear, Sergio disappeared. Kyle couldn't sense his presence at all, as if the Hollow Eye had decided to retreat. But then Sergio reappeared directly in front of Kyle, close enough to pat the young man on the shoulder. Before Kyle could think or react, the Hollow Eye's fist drilled straight into his stomach, sending Kyle rolling in the snow.

He coughed up blood as he came to a complete stop. Kyle's small amount of aura had completely been shattered. As he lay on his back and stared up at the sky struggling to breathe, he saw a dark grey dot closing in on him.

The spear!

He rolled to his left just in time as the pilum sank into the ground where his head had been. By the sinister smile on Sergio's face, Kyle knew that the man had planned it that way.

"Oh, it missed you just barely," Sergio jeered. "Although I'm sure you're as bigheaded as most SoGA students, you must know the large gap in our skills by now. I won't hesitate to kill you."

Kyle seethed as he struggled back to his feet. He had managed to hold onto his sword, so again he put it up defensively. He wasn't going to let Sergio win that easily. He charged at the Hollow Eye as fast as he could. Sergio disappeared yet again, making Kyle slide to a stop. He spun around madly, looking for where Sergio might appear again. A rough hand palmed his face, slamming it to the ground. If the snow was not so thick, Kyle's nose would have broken. Still, hot dizzy pain shot through his head, jumbling his senses. He couldn't tell what was up or down. The world was just a blur.

"Kyle!" screamed Garnet. She turned to her sunflower wolf. "Eva, attack the Hollow Eye!"

Like Garnet, Eva seemed to be moving sluggishly. This did little to deter the wolf from obeying her master. She pounced at the man's neck, ready to sink her fangs in, but at the last moment, Sergio delivered a hard kick to the wolf's side. With a loud yelp, she disappeared, returning to her dimension.

Kyle was finally regaining his senses. He could see Sergio standing over him. Kyle swung his sword at him, but the man stomped on his wrist. Kyle screamed, trying to punch out with his free arm. Sergio stepped back to easily dodge it before delivering a swift kick to Kyle's stomach, lifting him up into the air like a ball. He landed with a hard thump, barely able to hold onto his sword.

"Hand over the key, boy."

I'm no match. Kyle hated that it was true. He forced himself to stand up, pain making him cringe.

"I won't!" said Kyle defiantly.

"Is that right?"

Garnet, who had been ignored, snuck up to Sergio. She lunged at him to take off his head with her spear, but Sergio deflected her with a slight swat of his hand and jabbed her in the stomach. The spear flew from her hands and she fell to the ground, coughing. The Hollow Eye placed a foot on her back, pressing her hard into the ground. She struggled to free herself but could not move.

"You sure you don't want to reconsider?" asked Sergio coldly. "Maybe I should pop your girlfriend's head off and that'll change your mind?"

"Leave her alone!" shouted Kyle. He ran at them, his legs feeling like they had tripled in weight.

"Not another step!" barked the Hollow Eye, making Kyle halt only ten paces away. "I'll kill her if you take another step." Kyle knew he wasn't bluffing. Sergio balled his hand into an iron fist. "It's simple. Give me the key and I'll let her go."

Kyle stood still, unsure what to do. Garnet was in trouble, but all of his being screamed at him not to give up his key. Losing his key would be like losing part of himself. Sergio stomped down hard on Garnet and she let out a heart piercing scream.

"STOP!" Kyle began to shake with fury. Time slowed as he stared helplessly into Sergio's one eye. Kyle no longer felt the cold or the pain of his injuries, just loathing. Hatred for the Hollow Eye raged through him, consuming him like an inferno. Sergio seemed capable of sensing Kyle's feelings and only grinned as he pressed his foot harder into Garnet's back. Her scream brought Kyle back to reality.

"The key, boy!"

"Fine!" he roared. "I'll give you the key! Get off her first!"

Sergio stepped off Garnet and glowered at Kyle. "You make any funny movements and her blood will decorate this snow like rose petals. Understand?"

Kyle nodded. Without taking his eyes off of Sergio, he thought of a plan as he reached in his shirt to get his key. Doubts circulated through his mind. He knew his strategy might get him and Garnet killed, but there was no guarantee that Sergio would let them live once he had Kyle's key, anyway. He had to try something.

Carefully, he reached for his key, turning it as he dragged it out. With his eyes dead set on Sergio, he concentrated with all his might on *Synchroneity*.

In a flash, lightning bolts shot from Kyle's sword hand. They shot wildly at Sergio, surprising him. The zigzagging lightning bolts hit the man square in the chest with the force of a wrecking ball, then enclosed him in an intense electric web. Suddenly, the Hollow Eye flew backwards. Sergio was now sprawled out facing the sky, his eye mask cracked and his other eye rolled up inside of his skull. It would be some time before the man could move again.

In his in impatience, Kyle sprinted to Garnet before the lightning completely died out. Some of it hit her for a brief moment. She let out a short scream of pain, but then was silenced.

"No!" he cried, fearing the worst as he stopped to lock his lightning. He kneeled, putting his ear near her lips. She was breathing, but shallowly. He turned her over gently and tried to shake her awake, but she did not budge. He needed to find a way to get Garnet out of the cold. His first instinct was to return to the ShiftDoor, but it had disappeared.

He tried frantically to open his own ShiftDoor. Nothing happened. He looked toward the hill, hoping to catch a glimpse of Kevin, Kross, or Kane on their way to help him, but they were nowhere in sight. Again, he tried shaking her awake, but she reacted to nothing. He was nearly out of options. Panic began to sit in.

"I have to get her to Dilu Village," he said in an attempt to make himself think clearly. Forming an instant idea, he removed his cloak and wrapped Garnet to keep her warm. The cold showed no mercy, attacking his skin with its icy breeze, but he did his best to ignore it.

Pointing his key at his calves, he focused on Amplifications harder than ever in his life. For the first time since he had begun practicing Amplifications, he felt something. As he picked up Garnet in his arms, he noticed lightning emitting from the bottom of his feet, wrapping around his calves. It hadn't been what he was expecting, but now was not the time to be picky. With his desperation fueling his ability, he began running toward the Dilu Village gate.

He was running so fast, it felt like he was gliding across the snow wearing roller blades made of lightning. He left a trail of melting snow as he moved. The speed was becoming so dangerously fast, he thought he'd crash into something. Everything became a blur.

It seemed like only seconds had passed when he skidded to a stop near the gate. He pounded on the door for entrance.

"Joey!" he yelled. "Please let me in. I'm a tyro from Soul Gate Academy." The narrow hatch slid open with the same yellow-slit eyes peering through.

"Oh, back so soon?" asked Joey. "You look—"

"Please, hurry," Kyle cut him off. "My friend is hurt."

"I suppose I should let you in then, shouldn't I?" Joey closed the hatch and opened the door. Kyle stormed past the wooden kangaroo without a glance back. His lightning left static residue zapping on the ground as he glided by on his way to the only place he could think of to get help.

Moments later, he pounded on the Mayor's front door, breathing hard and silently thankful he had not slammed into anybody. Baldwin, the scruffy-haired butler, opened the door and looked at Kyle with wide eyes.

"Please help!" wheezed Kyle. "Mayor Nova…earlier…SoGA… I'm Kyle…My other friends…ambushed on the way to SoGA… need help." He swayed left and right. Behind the butler, he found a pair of pink eyes staring into his.

"Baldwin, help them!"

With this, Kyle staggered forward pressing Garnet into the arms of the confused butler as he fell to the ground and lost consciousness.

CHAPTER EIGHTEEN

THE TIMEKEEPER'S KEY

Kyle woke up shirtless in a dark room on an incredibly soft bed. For a moment, he thought he was back in his room at Soul Gate Academy, but he knew that could not be true when he saw that there was only one bed in the room.

His mind began to race. There was no time to lose; he had to find out what had happened to his friends. He jumped out of bed, wincing as he stiffly stepped away. His entire body was sore and rigid.

While he felt his way around the dark, foreign room, he noticed that he had been stripped down to his boxers. "Where are my clothes?"

The door suddenly swung open, bringing in bright light. A girl holding what appeared to be a tray peered into the room.

"Oh, you're awake," said the silhouette with a tone of slight embarrassment. "Umm, maybe you should put on some clothes, then." She turned the light switch key that ignited the overhead light. Rayne stood there, looking away from him with pink cheeks. She was dressed casually in jeans and a red sweatshirt. "Your uniform is over there." She pointed to Kyle's clothes folded nicely on a foot bench. "I'll leave the food here. Your Masters and friends are downstairs talking to my Mother. Eat up and come down." And with that, she set the tray down, closed the door and left him standing there speechless and embarrassed.

With the light on, he could see that the bedroom looked like it may have belonged to Rayne. The bed was twice the size of his at SoGA, covered in pink blankets and pillows. There were books stacked on a big desk along with a small box that looked similar to a radio. Girls clothing scattered throughout the room. On the walls, there were posters of people Kyle did not know. A couple of odd plants in vases were positioned next to the windows, which showed the night sky.

Kyle speedily dressed himself and made for the door. His stomach grumbled for food as he exited the room. He wished he had time to eat the tasty-looking biscuits and gravy that Rayne had brought him, but there was no time to sit through eating a meal right now. He needed to know if his friends were okay.

He walked into the hallway to find Rayne waiting for him.

"You really should eat," suggested Rayne kindly. "At least drink something."

"I don't need it," Kyle lied. "Where is everyone?"

Rayne shrugged, "Follow me." Kyle followed her down the hallway, still moving clumsily, but keeping up. "My name is Rayne."

"Er, yeah, I know," said Kyle awkwardly. "I'm Kyle." The walk to the stairwell was short, making Kyle think it was pointless for her to have to escort him downstairs, yet he was pleased all the same.

Kyle walked into the living room after Rayne. It was the same room in which they had been seated before the mission. Master Proculus, Master Logan, Kane, Kross, and Kevin were seated facing the Mayor, unable to see that Kyle had walked in. Kyle felt his heart beginning to panic at the thought of his worst fears coming to light.

"...the Oracle is—" said Mayor Nova, but she stopped when Rayne and Kyle entered. "Rayne, there was no need to wake him."

The Masters and his friends turned around, surprised to see him.

"I didn't." Rayne plopped herself on the chair nearest her mother. "He was already awake."

"Kyle!" said Kane and Kross together.

"Ah!" said Kevin at the same time. The three of them stood up, surrounding Kyle and bombarding him with questions.

"What happened?"

"Are you okay?"

"How did you beat the Hollow Eye?"

"Ah?"

"W-where's Garnet?" asked Kyle, ignoring their questions.

The room fell silent.

"All of you, sit down," said Master Proculus, who along with Master Logan looked relieved to see Kyle. The students returned to their seats, with Kyle taking up the chair at the end of the coffee table. "Kyle, the situation with Garnet is a bit complicated."

"What's wrong with her?" Kyle felt guilty, ashamed, and worried all at the same time.

"She is in a locked state," answered Proculus. "What you might know as a coma."

"A coma?" Kyle's eyes watered. He couldn't believe it.

"It's not your fault," said Mayor Nova in a motherly voice that reminded Kyle strongly of Nana, which made him feel all the more ashamed. "You were—"

"I was there! I was there and I should have protected her and then I—I used lightning and I…" He sank his head into his hands. "…and it hit her. It's my fault."

"Lightning?" asked Rayne. She looked confused but interested. Her mother shot her a look that could have made the strongest of men turn silent as stone. "Sorry," she whispered.

"Not. Your fault." Master Logan suddenly waved his hands as if the idea of Kyle hurting Garnet was ludicrous. It was. "Tell us. Exactly. What happened."

Kyle's shoulders drooped as he told them what had happened, starting at the beginning of the mission. He told them about the cavern, the skeletons, Garnet looking ill, and then Sergio the Hollow Eye. They listened without once interrupting him. "…and the last thing I remember was seeing Baldwin." This last part was not technically true. The last things he had seen prior to passing out were Rayne's eyes, but even with all that had happened, all that seemed so much more important, he was too embarrassed to say so.

Master Proculus hummed before questioning, "Sergio the Hollow Eye? Are you sure?"

"We told you it was him!" said Kross. He looked strained, making Kyle feel even guiltier. "This is my fault. I was the leader. We're sorry we didn't follow in time, Kyle. There were five others that attacked us. We—"

"Kross." Proculus stopped him from continuing. "Kyle, are you sure?"

"Yes," responded Kyle. "That is what Mayor Nova called him in town."

"You allowed him into town?" Proculus turned to Nova with fury that surprised Kyle. "What possessed you to do allow such a thing?"

"I had no choice," snapped the Mayor. "Refusal to let him in would have sided us against King Seltios. The Hollow Eye himself made that very clear. I believe it was the Grandmaster's request that Dilu Village should appear neutral until it is deemed necessary to do otherwise. He wanted to come in to look at keys, which left me with little reason to deny him entry. He did nothing while he was here; when he left I thought it was the end of it."

"That man!" Proculus rubbed his temples, his anger clearly still boiling. "I know you would never do anything to put your people or the tyros in harm's way, but tyros have been hurt on what was supposed to be an easy first mission and it leaves me frustrated to say in the least."

"Of course," she said, sighing.

"It seems the mission itself was much more than it had been intended to be," said Master Proculus. "To think that you first encountered the Forger's Cavern and skeleton keys…then to meet Sergio the Hollow Eye. It is a miracle all five of you survived. The Hollow Eye could have killed all of you easily; however, his overconfidence is what gave you an opening. You did well to unlock your lightning when you did, Kyle."

"I hurt Garnet and put her into a coma," snapped Kyle. "I should have just given him my stupid key."

"It is not your lightning that put her into a locked state," said Proculus.

"It isn't?"

"No. Her reader powers," said Master Logan. "Have left. A

strain. In her body. That's why. She was ill. Nothing to do. With your electric. Current."

"Reader powers?" said Kane, who along with Kross and Kevin wore the same confused expressions. "What do you mean 'reader powers'?"

Master Proculus sighed. "The three of you must never speak of this to anyone else, but Garnet was SoGA's reader. Due to certain circumstances, she lost her powers, but stayed at SoGA as a student. We thought her health was not an issue, but it seems we were wrong."

Kross, Kane, and Kevin all looked shocked to receive this information.

"Wait a second." Kane noticed that Kyle was not stunned like they were. "Kyle, you knew?"

"Yeah," said Kyle. "It's my fault she lost her powers, since I knew her name."

"We will have time to discuss this later," said Proculus before Kane could respond. "Right now, we have more pressing matters to deal with."

"Where is Garnet?" Kyle asked.

"She is resting in my bedroom," supplied Mayor Nova. "Yumi the Maiden is looking after her. She is a servant to the household and skilled with Medications. That is how we know about her condition."

"I see." Kyle wanted to go see her now, but there was still more he wanted to know. "Thank you, Mayor Nova." He tilted his head respectfully. Nova said nothing, but gave him an acknowledging nod. Kyle turned to his masters again. "How did you know we were here, Master?"

"Master Proculus. Was worr—" started Master Logan.

"—Master Logan and I were in the middle of a run," said

Master Proculus cutting him off. "We found Kane, Kross, and Kevin fighting against men and rushed to help them. When they saw us, the cowards shifted away almost immediately. We followed them to the field where you had fought. They picked up Sergio and opened another ShiftDoor. We wanted to find you and Garnet so we didn't follow them again. We hurried here to Dilu Village, following the trail of melted snow. No one other than the doorman saw you, but many pointed out that a trail of zapping, yellow electricity led to the Mayor's home. We came directly here to find you and Garnet unconscious and the Mayor doing everything in her power to help you two."

"I see," said Kyle quietly. "So how can we get Garnet out of the coma?"

"That's the problem," Proculus said sadly. "We don't know if we can. From the looks of it, the condition might be irreversible."

Kyle couldn't believe what he was hearing. "But we have keys," he pleaded. "They can do anything, can't they?"

"It's not that simple, Kyle."

"We have to do something!" Kyle's chest was feeling tighter and tighter by second. "We have to. We can't just let her die!"

"There might be something that can save her." Nova didn't sound like she was making any promises. "As I was saying before you came in Kyle, the Oracle himself is coming and he may be able to help Garnet."

"The Oracle?" asked Kyle.

"The very first Reader," said Proculus. "He is also one of the twelve Gatekeepers, just like Alexun the Path Guard." Kyle nodded as if this explained everything, but he still hardly understood what had happened with Alexun. He imagined that like Alexun, the

Oracle would be a man in a white tuxedo. "When is he coming?"

"I'm not sure," answered Nova. "He vaguely said 'soon.'"

"Typical," said Logan, smirking.

"At any rate," said Nova, "we have to give it some time."

"But Nova my dear, time is, how you say, of the essence," said an old raspy voice. Under the doorway stood an ancient man with his back hunched and long old stick as a cane. He wore a cinnamon brown fur cape that touched the ground. His hair was gray and combed neatly to the left, and his skin was the color of milk chocolate. He smiled with bright white teeth. Kyle thought that he looked half majestic yet half barbaric. As soon as the group saw the old man, all of them, except for Kyle, fell from their seats to kneel as though he were a king. "And I hope you weren't belittling a Gatekeeper, Logan the Supersonic."

"Never, Gatekeeper October." Logan's voice resonated with the upmost respect. "Just. A joke."

"Of course." The old man snorted loudly. "And please, I'm not even a gatekeeper at the moment. Just call me Decimus. Oracle is fine, too." Logan gave a respectful nod, but kept on his knee. "So the boy from the other realm finds that I am not worth the respect of a king?" He glared at Kyle with old eyes, making Kyle fumble to his knee. Decimus cackled. "I kid, of course. The gesture is kind, but please, all of you, back to your seats."

"We are honored to have you here, Oracle," said Mayor Nova.

"You should be," joked Decimus. "No, no. Now get up all of you. I cannot speak to the top of your heads."

The group sat back down in their seats. Decimus strolled over and settled in the chair next to Kyle. He massaged his right knee, working out an ache. Everyone watched him silently, as if talking would be some great offense.

"So we have a full house here," grunted the Oracle. "Nova, dear, if it's not too much trouble, could you ask Dean to add in some extra sugar when he brings out the tea?"

"Yes, of course." The Mayor stood up. "I'll have him do that right away."

"And Kyle the Static's stomach will be grumbling, so if some food could be prepared, it would save him some embarrassment." The Mayor Nova nodded and walked out briskly. Kyle raised his eyebrows, impressed yet confused.

"Um, Oracle, sir," said Kyle, unsure why he was correcting him, "actually, I am Kyle the Tortoise."

"I know who and what you are," said Decimus theatrically. "You are Kyle Demore, the boy from another realm. You impressed Gatekeeper December, but you know him as Alexun the Path Guard. You have been known as Kyle the Tortoise 'till now. Your Masters should have given you your new title, but by the sounds of it, they have failed to tell it to you. So I shall take the honor and bestow upon you your new title: The Static."

"How do you—"

"I am not called the Oracle for nothing."

"You always impress me, Oracle." Master Proculus cracked a tiny grin. "Your knowledge is as accurate as ever. It is true, Kyle. It was Master Logan's decision; you have been titled the Static. I believe you've earned it."

"I..." started Kyle, but instantly stopped himself. He wanted to tell them that he didn't deserve the new name. He wanted to scream at them for even suggesting it, but he sat there knowing they'd already made the decision final. "Thanks."

A frown fell over his face. He thought when he had earned a new title, his friends would be there helping him celebrate. Instead, one was in a coma, while the other three might have been happier at a funeral. The moment felt lonely and bittersweet at best.

Mayor Nova returned to the room. Dean followed her, pushing a cart full of tea and some food. Kyle's stomach grumbled happily when Dean placed biscuits and gravy in front of him. He began shoveling food into his mouth and Rayne let a small giggle escape. Kyle looked up from his food, having completely forgotten that she sat at his side. He scratched his head and dived back into his plate.

"Ah, this is splendid tea, nice and sweet. Thank you, Dean." The Oracle smacked his lips.

Dean nodded, turning to leave the room.

"Is there anything else I can get for you?" asked Mayor Nova as she seated herself.

"No, no. This will do. Thank you." Decimus rubbed his hands together. "Now, let us get to business. I suppose I should begin with explaining why I'm here." He sipped on his tea before setting his cup down. "As the first Reader, it is my job to oversee all Readers. A few months ago, Garnet the Scarlet Needle, who should have been a Reader for many years to come, heard her name."

Kyle coughed as he finished his last bite. With an uneasy gulp, he faced Decimus, who eyed him down suspiciously. Kyle felt as if this conversation was solely for him.

"You helped with that, didn't you?" the Oracle asked.

"Yes, but I didn't mean to," said Kyle nervously.

"As the Oracle, I should have seen it coming," he said. "I did not. Just goes to show you how impossible it is to truly know the future in its entirety, but that is neither here nor there." Again, he took a sip of tea, smacking his lips as he placed the cup back down. "It turns out that this is much more of a problem than I thought it would be. As Yumi has guessed, losing the Reader's ability so quickly has caused a significant strain to Garnet's body, mind, and soul. It is as if each of the three are trying to pull away from each other.

"Our bodies all consist of a certain lock that binds our body, mind, and soul together. You all know this lock to be called Balance. Balance is essential to everybody and without it we would, in a sense, fall apart. Garnet's Balance has been nearly destroyed."

"So she's really a reader?" said Kane, still in disbelief.

"Of course, boy," said the Oracle with annoyance. "Did you think that it was all a joke being played on you?"

Kane shook his head before sinking in his seat, joining Kross and Kevin in continued silence.

"Where was I? Ah, I remember. To put things in simple terms, Garnet the Scarlet Needle is falling apart. Think of her reader powers as a thread holding together a cloth. At first, it is strong and firm. After many years, this thread begins to bend, becoming looser and easier to maneuver. Eventually, by the time a reader learns their name, it has becomes so loose that it falls out of the cloth, leaving little damage. Garnet had her thread ripped from her, leaving a huge tear in her Balance. This problem is, in all honesty, a death sentence."

A grim silence fell over the room. Kyle's throat became painfully dry. He thought someone might say something, anything, to tell him that everything would be all right. Instead, everyone looked deep in thought. Decimus began massaging his knee again, as if he had just said something much less morbid. Proculus rubbed his chin while Logan rapped his foot softly. Kross tapped his temple with his index finger. Kane folded his arms, and Kevin drummed his fingers against his knee. Mayor Nova sat like a statue, keeping her eyes respectfully on the Oracle. Rayne's eyes shot back and forth from her mother to Decimus.

Kyle, meanwhile, leaned back in his chair. Exhausted from his frustration, he looked up at the ceiling in a sad attempt to think. Just the thought of Garnet dying made him want to cry.

But then the old man yawned, which drew back Kyle's attention. "Fortunately, I am known as the Gatekeeper October. This entitles me to know a few secrets here and there, so we're not out of options yet. I am here to tell *you* how to save her."

In that instant, Kyle was certain that Decimus was speaking directly to him. The rest of the room seemed to feel that the Oracle was indicating the same thing.

"Surely," said Proculus almost apprehensively, "you don't mean for Kyle to save her?"

"But I do." The Oracles eyes became cold and serious. "I mean that exactly."

Kyle was unsure if he should say something. He would do anything to help Garnet, but it seemed odd that the Oracle was actually expecting him to save her.

"Forgive me for saying this," Master Proculus's voice was on edge, "but I have to object—"

The old man held up a palm and the master stopped talking immediately. "Aren't you the one that wants to save her the most?" he asked Kyle, as though this were the only reason needed.

"Yes," answered Kyle swiftly. "I mean, she's my friend. I'll do anything I can to save her."

"We all want to save her," said Proculus. "What are you

proposing, Oracle?"

"Hmm." He stood up and walked to the large window in the center of the room. He stared out at the changing horizon. Sunlight was beginning to melt away the night sky. "I should mention that there is little time for Garnet. She's not likely to survive the rest of the day."

"What?" Kyle stood immediately. "What are we waiting for? What do we have to do to save her?"

"Kyle," Proculus gave him a stern gaze, "sit down and calm yourself."

Kyle returned to his seat with a hard thump. "Well?"

"The Timekeeper's Key," said Decimus, now making his way around the room. "If there is any chance to save her, it lies in that key. And that key is located in the King's Temple."

"The King's Temple!" blurted out Proculus.

"Is there an echo in here, Nova?"

Mayor Nova tried looking less confused, but it was obvious that she, like the rest of them, had no idea what Proculus and Decimus were talking about. "Yes, Storm. I know that you are one of the few living that have been to the King's Temple, but keep your thoughts to yourself for the moment and allow me to explain." Proculus silently gritted his teeth, looking either panicky or angry. Kyle wasn't sure which. He had never seen his Master look so agitated. Something about the King's Temple affected Proculus badly, that was certain.

"Locked inside the King's Temple is the Timekeeper's Key," said Decimus. "It is an old relic once belonging to a man named Elias the Timekeeper. He was a very intelligent man. Often, he knew when something was going to happen long before it actually did. It was not so different from being an oracle, but

Elias became obsessed with time. He related it to all things. To him, nothing ever happened by accident. Every instance was always meant to happen at a precise time. This obsession led to his disappearance, but prior to that, he did spectacular things with time. One of these things was the creation of TimeBent Dimensions. These dimensions have long been used to train readers, and Garnet was no different. Two years of her life passed while in one of those dimensions while barely a day passed here. When she learned her name, the memories of these two years were ripped to pieces, throwing off her body's rhythm, so to speak. Being the extraordinary key that it is, the Timekeeper's Key can fix this by speeding up or slowing down the body's rhythm, allowing for her heal. Easy enough, no?"

"Er," stuttered Kyle. He didn't really understand any of it, but he did understand that finding the key was the only way to save Garnet.

"This doesn't make sense." Kross finally broke his silence. He looked uncomfortable to be speaking, but his frown indicated something was on his mind. "How can a key do any of that?"

"Much of what the Timekeeper did hardly made sense," said Decimus diligently. "But for reasons beyond me, they worked. Regardless, it is the only chance of saving your friend, so I suggest you stop questioning the advice of the Oracle."

"Sorry," muttered Kross.

"Oracle," said Proculus, "you did not explain how we can retrieve the key."

"That is something I don't know." The old man rubbed his chin. "As an oracle, I know where you're supposed to go, but how you get there and whether or not you succeed, well, that's up to you."

"So we just have to get to the Temple and get the key?" reaffirmed

Kyle. "We should go now."

"Excellent," said Decimus. "I'm afraid I cannot partake in your mission, but I can lend a hand in getting you there." The Oracle tapped his stick on the ground then turned it twice. A grey door began sprouting out of the living room floor. When it stopped, it nearly touched the ceiling. "This ShiftDoor will stay put for thirty minutes. If you should so choose not to take it to the King's Temple, Garnet will most certainly not be saved. There's just not enough time. Well, I believe I've said all that I needed to say. Nova my dear, could I have a word with you in private?"

The Mayor seemed to wake from a daze when she heard that she was being talked to. "O-of course." Nova stood up to lead the way out of the living room.

"Good luck, Kyle the Static. Proculus, Logan, good luck training this one." He pointed at Kyle with a bright smile, but Kyle thought he looked more worried than happy. "Don't think I've forgotten about you, Rayne the Floret." That earned him a confused look from Rayne. "Your time will come Rayne; I suggest that you wait for it. And you should stop giving your mother trouble, too. Kevin the Bison, Kross the Monk, and Kane the…Ace, she's your friend too, no? Well, farewell to all of you." Laughing softly, he followed Mayor Nova outside, walking unhurried, his ancient stick tapping the floor with every step.

Nova softly closed the door behind them as she and Decimus the Oracle left the group.

"We should go now," Kyle insisted. Kane, Kross, and Kevin stood up, nodding in agreement. It seemed they had taken the Oracle's last farewell to heart. "He said we didn't have time."

Master Proculus rubbed his chin and Master Logan stood up

to pace around the room with his hands behind him, looking livid.

"This is. Not good," said Master Logan, breaking the silence. "I should report. To the Grandmaster."

"I agree," answered Proculus. "Make your report. In the meantime, I will try to retrieve the Timekeeper's Key. The boys should stay here."

The four young men immediately began to raise objections, but Proculus spoke first.

"The King's Temple is not the kind of place to send inexperienced tyros!" said Proculus fiercely. "To be honest, it is not the kind of place to send anybody."

"But I have to go," roared Kyle. "I have to save Garnet. You heard the Oracle. It has to be me!"

"The Oracle is a wise man. One that I respect, but I still cannot allow you to go," said Proculus heavily. Kane was about to say something, but Proculus cut him off. "The same goes for you three. The King's Temple is a dangerous place, located in the heart of Dawn, the Western Kingdom. And the last I heard, Dawn was a step away from declaring war on us here in Dusk."

"The war. Is coming," Logan said it with frozen simplicity.

"Who cares about the war?" Kyle protested. "Garnet will die if we don't go. I'll worry about the war after we save her." As soon as the words left him, he knew he shouldn't have said something so inconsiderate, but it was the truth. At the moment, he could care less about a war. The only thing that mattered was making sure Garnet lived. Not to his surprise, both of his masters frowned.

"I used to not care about the war, either," said Rayne suddenly. Her eyes were deep in thought as she twisted her long blonde hair with her fingers. "But I guess when your father is killed in front of you, it's a real eye-opener."

Kyle's mouth became dry. He looked at Rayne, regretting he had opened his mouth. "I didn't mean anything by it, I'm sorry about your dad."

"So am I," she said sadly. "I think that I've listened in enough today. I should get ready for school. Master Proculus, Master Logan, Kane, Kross, Kevin, it was a pleasure to meet you. Bye, Kyle the Static." She stood up and walked out the door. There were soft thumps that indicated her ascent up the stairs and Kyle felt thoroughly worthless, but he couldn't let that get him off track.

"I am going." Kyle decided. He'd fight if he had to. "You can't stop me."

"I can and I will," said Proculus. "I won't allow you to find death so easily."

Kyle's retort would have to wait. Mayor Nova walked back into the room. She looked troubled when she sat back into her chair with a long sigh. "Where did Rayne go?"

"She excused herself a moment ago," answered Proculus.

"I see," said Nova.

"I must leave," said Master Logan. "It is important. That we let. The Grandmaster know. What has happened."

"Wait a moment," said the Mayor. "Keeping Garnet here isn't a problem, but Yumi has to sleep sometime. If you are going back, I would like you to inform the Grandmaster that I am requesting the help of an eternal title student or perhaps Master Yvette herself to help watch over Garnet. I know this may be farfetched, but it would be very helpful."

"I will. Let him know." Master Logan left the room without another word.

"Master, what would you do if you were in my situation?" Kyle reasoned. "If you had a friend that was about to die, would you just sit here and wait? Even after someone told you how to save her?"

"I agree with Kyle," said Kross. "You cannot expect us to just sit here and wait."

"We are not so weak, Master Proculus," added Kevin with his notepad.

"You have to let us try," said Kane.

Proculus opened his mouth, but no sound escaped. He looked at all four tyros, his eyes eventually meeting Kyle's. Kyle glared at his Master, standing his ground. He was going to King's Temple to save Garnet and nothing was going to stop him.

Master Proculus sighed deeply, admitting defeat. "Very well. The four of you may come, but you are to do exactly as I say. We don't know what the area is like, so we'll have to tread carefully. It could be guarded by King Seltios' men. If that is the case, it would be best for us to avoid any confrontation. If we do run into someone—well, let's just try not to. If for some reason we are separated, we are to meet at the same place we arrive. If for any reason, the four of you need to abandon me, you are to open a ShiftDoor to Dilu Village and come here without hesitation. Is that clear?"

The four of them nodded together.

"Weapons ready," commanded Proculus.

Kross opened his BioDimension to retrieve his weapon while Kevin and Kane grabbed theirs, which sat near the entrance to the room. Kyle opened his own MicroDimension, only to realize his sword was not there.

"My sword's not here," said Kyle, panicking. He doubted Master Proculus would let him go without his sword. "I must have left it in the field."

"It is in my room with Garnet," said Mayor Nova. "When you arrived, we put you both in the same room. We left it there after prying it from your hands. Come with me if you'd like to get it."

"I'll be right back." Kyle followed Mayor Nova.

They passed the stairway and ventured further down a hallway. Opening a door to her right, Mayor Nova showed him into a large bedroom with a grand bed in the middle of it. It seemed fit for royalty; its walls were a pleasant gold and of spectacular design. The carpet was a brilliant scarlet that meshed well with the walls. A fireplace glowed, making the room comfortably warm. Kyle rushed forward to stand beside the woman he presumed to be Yumi the Maiden tending to Garnet, who lay almost motionless on the bed.

Yumi was a short, slender woman with long black hair. Her maid uniform was paired with dress pants, making her look more like a business woman than a servant of the household.

"Lady Nova." Yumi turned around and bowed to the mayor. Her mouth was covered by a half-mask, leaving her emotionless eyes to peer at them as they stepped closer to the bed.

"I hope Garnet is still doing fine?" asked the Mayor. "And we need the sword that Kyle had with him. Did you put it somewhere?"

"She is well, Lady Nova," the maid said almost robotically. "As well as someone who is locked can be. The sword is here." Yumi picked up Kyle's Nodachi. It had been leaning against a closet drawer. But he'd temporarily forgotten about his sword. He walked up to the side of the bed, on the opposite side of Yumi. Only Garnet's head stuck out of the blankets that rhythmically lifted and fell with her every breath. Her red hair and pale skin looked less vibrant than he'd ever seen it, making him feel like he was already too late. It wasn't like him to be so scared. He wanted to reach out, touch her, somehow help her, but he stopped himself.

"She'll be okay, right?" Kyle asked more to himself than to anyone, but the Maiden's eyes shot to Kyle, ready to answer.

"No, she will not. Her Balance is irreparable. I can watch over her, but I know of nothing that can fix her."

It seemed surreal to Kyle for an adult to answer him so bluntly, so coldly, so hopelessly, but somehow it was exactly what he needed. He felt a surge of purpose warm his chest, a destiny that only he could fulfill. Yumi could not save Garnet. Master Proculus couldn't, either. Not even the Grandmaster could help her. It was up to him. He grabbed the sword from Yumi, staring directly into her emotionless eyes.

"Please just watch her then," he said. He added one last thing before he left. "I will find a way to save her."

CHAPTER NINETEEN

THE FOUR KEYS

"Whoa," mouthed Kyle when he walked out of the ShiftDoor door behind Master Proculus. He expected things to look different on the eastern side of Endera, but he hardly expected it to be this. The trees had been glazed in ice, making them look they'd been encased in diamonds. Just looking at the dense forest made Kyle shudder.

Master Proculus led them away from the ShiftDoor, which soon disappeared. Their feet pressed into the snow with every step. Kyle scanned the new setting from left to right. All around them, branches weighed down heavily by hundreds of icicles shimmered in the sun's morning beams, reflecting through the forest like mirrors.

"The locals call this place Mirror Forest," whispered Proculus as he stopped. "Although when the weather warms, this is just a forest like any other. Keep quiet; we'll be getting close now."

They edged forward, each of their steps in the snow hardly

audible. When the trees became less dense, Proculus stopped to look around. Kyle, Kross, Kane, and Kevin followed his example. Just ahead was a clearing that seemed undisturbed.

"Keep low," Proculus hissed, a steely look on his face. He stealthily moved forward with the most massive sword Kyle had ever seen, though in the master's grip, it seemed light as a feather. It was a great, two-handed, long broadsword with a wide black blade.

They crouched as they neared the clearing. Kyle kept expecting a bear or dragon to come running out at them, but things were unusually calm. Part of him wished something would happen already.

A little ways ahead, he noticed footprints in the snow that could only belong to humans. "Master," he whispered.

"Shhhh," hushed Proculus. "I know."

They continued to where the trees cleared, parting to reveal the King's Temple. It looked like a pyramid that, just like the trees, was covered in ice. A massive golden crown sat at the top of the temple emitting its own light as the sun reflected off of its icicles. Below the ice, Kyle could see the ancient and worn grey stone that made the body of the pyramid. Still, the crown was enough to mark it as impressive. If the ones who made the footprints in the snow were around, they would surely now spot the five of them as they moved closer. Kyle went to step forward, but Proculus tugged his shirt gently.

"You four wait here." Without another word, Master Proculus pointed his key at the middle of his chest then turned it. Snow engulfed him entirely so that he looked like a skillfully detailed snowman. Another turn with his snow-covered key, and his sword looked like it was made entirely of ice. Kyle didn't think that the snow and ice would successfully camouflage his master, but as Proculus moved away, Kyle completely lost track of him. They hid themselves behind a tree waiting noiselessly, waiting for the return of their master.

"AHHHH!" screamed someone in the direction that Proculus had gone. Kyle's stomach tightened. The sound echoed around them like a cannon had just gone off. The four of them poked their heads around the tree that they were hiding behind, but saw nothing.

"What should we do?" asked Kyle. "Do you think that was Master Proculus?"

"Ah," answered Kevin, shaking his head.

"Kevin's right," assured Kane. "He's too strong. That can't be him."

"Shouldn't we make sure?" said Kyle.

"He told us to wait here." Kross reasoned.

"AHHHH!" someone screamed again.

"We have to help!" Kyle rushed out of hiding behind the tree, into the opening.

"Wait, Kyle," hissed Kross. Still, he and the others followed Kyle into the opening. They ran in the direction they had seen their master go, but found nothing. Leaving the trees left them feeling vulnerable as they closed the gap to the temple. They slowed to a walk as they edged toward the corner of the large pyramid, unable to see what was around it.

"Hello?" Kyle called it softly as he walked forward, his long sword held up. "Is that you, Master?"

"Master?" responded a voice that sent chills down Kyle's back. He knew this sneering, disgusting voice. "So, we have young tyro here. I cannot tell you how anno—"

"The Hollow Eye," Kyle said breathlessly. And suddenly standing in front of Kyle was Sergio once more. He looked at Kyle vehemently with his one eye. The other was now covered by a black patch.

"You," snarled Sergio the Hollow Eye, but then his expression changed to a smile. Kyle felt more disturbed by this. "The scream works every time for you wanna-be-hero-types, I suppose. AHHHH!" It was the same scream that had lured them out into the open.

Kyle's head fell. *I'm so stupid.* They had been tricked.

An evil leer was stretched across Sergio's face, as if someone had just given him a very amusing gift. "I knew someone was sneaking about, but to find you! Like finding a gold coin on a rainy day, don't you think?" He laughed viciously.

"What are you doing here?" Kyle tried to build up his courage, but the sad fact was that he was out-classed here. Last time he had been lucky and that was the simple truth.

"What am I doing here? This is the property of Seltios the Western King. You SoGA brats are trespassing. I'll do him a favor by getting you off his land and I'm sure he won't mind if I pay you back for yesterday." Sergio took out a key and turned it. The air became distorted and he removed two axes with short handles but large jagged heads. They looked as cruel as Sergio himself.

"He wants me, guys," muttered Kyle. "Make a run for it while I hold him off."

"Fat chance." Kane took out his daggers. "We'll take him on together." The four of them instinctively spread out to surround Sergio, but the man dashed toward Kyle, ignoring the other three.

Sergio smiled mercilessly as he delivered a heavy blow that smacked against Kyle's sword, pushing him back. The power of it made Kyle's arms numb, and he didn't know if he could take another one.

Without having time to think, a downward slice aimed for his shoulder came in at blinding speed. Kyle was a second from losing his life when Kevin parried the attack with his battle axe. Coming out of nowhere, a thick brown rope whipped at Sergio with such force that the ground shook. Kane and Kross had grabbed the back of Kyle's and Kevin's cloaks, pulling them out of the way just in time. As Kyle stared at where he had been a moment before, he could see that the rope that slammed into the ground was actually the large tail of Kross's summon, Roko the Lutumdragon. For a moment, Kyle thought that Sergio had been crushed by Roko's clay tail, but a loud cackle told them otherwise.

"Lucky you have your friends here, aren't you?" said Sergio, standing unharmed and out of Roko's reach. "It doesn't seem like you'll be able to use that summon much longer, so I hope that's not your only trick."

He was right about Roko. The dragon's moist clay scales were already beginning to become icy and hard. The cold was just too much for him. Kross told Roko to return to his dimension immediately. The Lutumdragon obeyed, roaring ferociously as he disappeared.

As soon as he disappeared, Sergio charged at them again. Kyle raised his sword to defend, but as the blades nearly made contact, a shadow slipped in between them stopping Sergio's axe. The Hollow Eye's one eye looked full of surprise as he jumped back defensively. Proculus stood in front of Kyle, Kane, Kross, and Kevin with his big blade.

"Proculus the Storm," croaked Sergio. "Babysitting as usual?"

"A much better job than the one they've given you." Proculus eyed him carefully. "Tell me, does King Seltios always have you pick fights with kids?"

"How about I pick a fight with you?" barked Sergio. "My men

can have fun with your little tyros." Sergio banged his axes together three times. They rang louder than a police siren, signaling to his comrades to come to his aid.

"They won't be coming," said Proculus calmly. "I have paid them a visit already."

Sergio looked at him in disbelief but then shrugged. "I'm enough to take you on." Sergio threw his axes down in the ground, where they stuck easily. With one hand, he ripped off his eye patch to reveal an unnaturally black keyhole where his eye should have been. Looking into the socket made Kyle quiver, while the other boys backed away in fear. Master Proculus sighed heavily.

"So that is why they call you the Hollow Eye," said Master Proculus almost sadly.

"Figured it out, huh? They sure make 'em bright at SoGA." Sergio laughed as he shoved his key in to the keyhole on his face. After he turned it, the key sank into his face, deteriorating into darkness. The effect was immediate. Sergio's body began to emit a blood-red mist, surrounding him like some grim-looking aura.

"Boys," whispered Master Proculus, "when I attack, the four of you run around to the other side of the temple and wait for me. You should be safe there."

The four of them readied themselves to run. A moment later, Proculus launched himself at Sergio with his big blade. Sergio picked up his axes and jumped out of the way. Proculus's sword hit the ground, shaking the earth, while the Hollow Eye ran toward the forest, leaving a trail of red mist behind him. Proculus followed him without hesitation.

"Let's go!" Kyle cried as he ran. The other three were right behind him. As they ran to the other side of the King's Temple, trees and ice cracked thunderously as if they were being torn from the ground. They stopped when they reached the entrance into the temple. An idea came to him as he stared at the entrance regain his breath. *What if things get worse out here? We have to get the Timekeeper's Key for Garnet before it's too late.* Waiting for Proculus wasn't going to be an option. The only problem now was that they needed to find a way in. The entrance was blocked by a sturdy-looking stone door. "We have to get in."

"Shouldn't we wait for Master Proculus?" said Kross. He looked at the door apprehensively, tapping it with the tip of his Shaolin spade.

"He sounds pretty busy at the moment," said Kane as another tree snapping in half echoed through the sky. The sound of the ice crashing into the ground was like glass was raining down from the sky. "We should do this on our own."

"What do you think, Kevin?" asked Kross with hopeful eyes.

"We can do this," Kevin said with his notepad. "Things might get more dangerous out here. I think we should do this before anybody else shows up. Once we have the Timekeeper's Key, we can find Master Proculus and then return to SoGA."

Kross thought about this for a moment, but then seemed to agree that it was an acceptable course of action. "Fine. Any idea on how to get it?"

"Here," said Kyle, indicating something small in front of him. His friends hovered behind him to get a look at what he was pointing at. Four keyholes were lined up on the door. Kyle placed his key into the one furthest to the left. "There. You three put your keys in now."

"What?" said Kross with a touch of irritation. "Why would you do that? We have no idea what that will do."

"How else are we supposed to get in?" It seemed obvious to Kyle to put the key in. "If you don't think it'll work, I guess I'll take it out." Kyle reached for his key to remove it from the keyhole. It would not budge. He tried to pull it out with all his might, but it proved impossible. "It's stuck."

"Great," snapped Kross. "What should we do now?"

"It probably needs all four keys to be in." Kane shoved his key into the second keyhole. The massive stone door still did nothing. "Well don't just stand there. Come on, you two." Kross looked like he was about to explode when Kevin put his key into the third keyhole. Each of them except Kross had placed their key in. "Now it's your turn, Kross," Kane prompted.

"Are you three crazy?" Kross tried not to raise his voice. "What happens if we can't get our keys back out?"

"Kross, Garnet is counting on us. This will work," Kyle commanded with an unfaltering gaze. He knew that mentioning Garnet would change his mind.

"Right," said Kross after a minute. "You're right." He looked more confident about the whole situation.

Another loud crack rang out through the sky. Kross let out a deep breath as he placed his key into the last keyhole. The door did not open, but golden light began to emit from each of the keyholes.

"Now we turn the keys," said Kyle boldly. As they did, the door effortlessly swung open as if on well-oiled hinges. The door had been so quick to move that the keys slid out of their keyholes, back into the hands of their rightful owners. "Er." He stared in disbelief at his key. "It worked."

Inside, torches lit a long corridor, but Kyle could not see where it led. With loud gulps, the four of them nervously entered the King's

Temple. The corridor was curved and climbed up at a small angle. It wasn't long before they could no longer see the light shining from the entrance. After a while, it finally opened up into a large open chamber.

The temple chamber seemed larger than was physically possible to fit inside of the temple. In fact, the ceiling itself made no sense. Rather than angling in toward the center, it was as level as the floor. It appeared as though the ceiling extended higher than the crown on top of the pyramid. It was beautifully decorated with marble floors and walls full of murals that depicted men and women of royalty, mythical creatures, and several clocks. Most of the paintings included weapons of many different varieties; some even looked like Kotas. Six enormous stones, carved in the shape of keys, served as pillars that supported the ceiling. Hundreds of torches lit the whole room brightly as though the sun was shining through the walls.

The most spectacular thing in the room was a magnificent floating stream of water that glistened with speckles of gold as hundreds of clock gears swam through it. It curved and twisted through the air, flowing throughout the entire chamber. Parts of the stream glided upward toward the ceiling, wrapping itself around the pillars like a wild vine made of water. As Kyle walked by the pillars, he was full of awe, but also felt incredibly small.

All the streams flowed to the center of the ceiling, where a clock the size of an elephant hovered. Kyle had no idea if the clock's purpose was to tell time, since there was only a single large symbol painted black in the center of the clock while the gold speckled water swirled around it like a slow moving whirlpool.

"I wonder what that symbol means," Kyle mumbled to himself.

"You say something?" asked Kane.

"I was just wondering what that symbol meant." He pointed at the large clock.

"Who knows? Could be anything."

"This place is colossal." Kross stuck the end of his Shaolin spade into the stream. "The power of keys is definitely at work here."

There were also stairs leading to the top of a large altar in the middle of the room. It stood much too high for them to see the top. Unsure of what else to do, they decided to climb the altar's stairs. As they came to the top of it, they found nothing but a thick layer of dust.

"Ah," said Kevin, disappointed.

"There has to be something here." Kyle's voice echoed. He could see nothing else of significance in the entire chamber. "We'll have to look harder, that's all."

"Master Oisin says things tend be obvious if you know where to look," said Kevin's notepad. He walked around the altar, inspecting it like a detective. He dropped to his knees, moving dust with his hands slowly at first then rapidly like he was a child who had found a buried treasure in the sandbox. "Ah!" he said pointing at keyholes.

"STAY AWAY FROM THOSE!"

From nowhere, something flew at Kevin. Kane reacted first, diving at Kevin to shove him out of the way. Hardly a second later, something smashed where Kevin's head had been. Kyle and Kross raised their weapons in defense as Kane and Kevin rolled down the steps of the altar. Dust blurred their vision and they could scarcely see in front of them. Kyle waited for whatever had attacked to come rushing at him, but nothing happened. Kyle listened intently and strangely heard the soft *cling-clang* sound of metal hitting metal like pocket change. Moments later, the dust dispersed and a woman stood in front of them. Kane and Kevin hustled back onto the altar to stand next to Kyle and Kross.

She was the most bizarrely dressed woman Kyle had ever seen. She wore an eggplant purple sleeveless blouse that had hundreds of different keys hanging from it. Her plain white witch's hat and short white skirt held significantly less keys, but still sported many dangling ones. After the initial shock of what she was wearing, Kyle noticed she looked hardly ten years older than him, and quite nice-looking. Her long, bushy brown hair fell down to her shoulder blades in pretty waves. She didn't seem dangerous to Kyle, but he knew better than to let his defense down after she had just attacked Kevin.

"Who are you?" asked Kyle. She stared at him with curious eyes and tilted her head, seeming confused by his question.

"Blimey, you don't know?" The woman's voice was smooth as silk. She waited patiently for an answer and when she didn't receive one, she sighed. "I'm Elleneya the Guardian, Ellen for short, Protector of the King's Temple for as long as I see fit. You are my first visitors in a long time. I have answered you, and it is only fair that I ask who the four of you are?"

"I am Kyle the Static," said Kyle with a touch of annoyance. "This is Kross the Monk, Kane the Ace, and the one whose head you almost took off is Kevin the Bison."

"The Static?" She tapped her index finger against her lips. "Never heard of you. I knew a few Aces, Monks, and Bisons, in my time, but they're long dead. Funny how names come and go."

Kyle could hardly believe that she was the guardian of anything. Her mannerism seemed so flaky and childish. He wished that the Oracle or Master Proculus had warned them that someone would be waiting in the temple. "Why are you here?"

"We're looking for the Timekeeper's Key," answered Kyle. "We need it to save a friend and we were told by Gatekeeper October that it was located in the King's Temple."

"October," Elleneya said with a chuckle. "I haven't seen that grumpy old bloke in such a long time. He could visit, but no, he sends me strangers."

"Umm, you know Gatekeeper October?"

"Sure. Us Gatekeepers have to know each other, don't we?" It took a moment for Kyle to catch on. He suddenly felt as small as he had when he walked by the key pillar.

"Yo-you're a gatekeeper?"

"Yup. I'm Gatekeeper July." She smiled brightly, but Kyle was lost for words.

"Then you know where the Timekeeper's Key is?" asked Kane when he realized Kyle wasn't going to say anything. Kevin and Kross shifted uncomfortably, but kept their weapons ready.

"Oh yes, of course I know where it is."

"Then can you give it to us?" asked Kyle hopefully.

"Oh no, definitely not. You'll have to throw me off this altar if you'd like to get to it. I doubt you'll be able to do it with those, though." She was indicating the weapons they held. "You'll need ones like this."

She ripped one of the keys off her blouse and let it drop to the floor. With a soft 'clunk' it bounced up and began to transform. The key grew and extended. When it was finished, it was a Kota. It looked like a long double-ended hammer, reminding Kyle of Kross's Shaolin spade. On one end, it had a boxy-looking bow of a key that looked heavy and more flat than the head of a sledgehammer. The second hammer was one-sided and looked like the bit of a single-bit key with grooves in it. If Kyle hadn't been close to Elleneya as she held the double hammer Kota, he would have thought she was just holding a large key.

"I'll have to ask you to leave," said the Guardian tediously. "Or I'll have to kill you."

"We need the Timekeeper's Key," said Kyle, readying to charge. "And we're not leaving until we get it." With the idea of throwing her off guard, he attacked her with a downward swing of his Nodachi. She avoided it easily by backing up.

"Jeez, hold your horses. Ya' know, impatience leads to regrettable choices." Elleneya stuck her Kota into the floor, turning it. The stairs rose to become level with the altar itself. Now, it looked like a wide ten foot high platform. Kyle and his friends edged closer, readying to give her a fight. She sighed. "I can see that you're determined, so how about this: if you can destroy this altar, I'll let you take the key. If you can't, you die. Or you can simply walk away now."

"Kyle," whispered Kross, "I can destroy this with Roko easily."

"I have to warn you," she said as if she knew exactly what Kross was thinking, "this is not a normal altar." She jumped high into the air then crashed into the corner of the altar with her double hammer Kota. The edge of the platform shook violently before breaking off. It instantly began regenerating the part, making it look like it had never been damaged.

Elleneya's keys were still jingling as Kyle wondered if it was even possible to destroy the altar, but what choice did they have now? They had to save Garnet. He glanced at his friends, who looked as unsure as he felt. However, they each nodded to him with confidence that could not be shaken.

"We'll do it," said Kyle. "Just sit back and watch."

The Guardian nodded.

Kross took out his key, turned it, and for the second time that day, summoned Roko from his dimension. The clay lizard looked at Kross with happy affection.

"You called again?" he asked in a gargled voice.

"Wow," said Ellen. "That thing looks a bit like a bogey, doesn't it?"

"I'd like you to eat the stone of this altar," said Kross, ignoring her.

"As you wish." Roko dove into the altar with ease and began chomping on the stone as if it were rice. At first, bits of the altar disappeared but as time went on, the altar, like earlier, reappeared as if nothing had happened. Roko saw this and began eating with more frenzy but after a quarter of an hour, he grew tired and full. "Forgive me, I can eat no more."

"Don't be." Kross petted the great lizard's snout, making his hand dirty. "Return and let the stone digest." Roko disappeared.

"Is that all?" asked Ellen.

"No," Kyle insisted firmly. He turned to his friends. "Let's all attack it at once. Go all out and we can bring this thing down."

"Ah," said Kevin stopping them and signaling for them to huddle close together. He scribbled as fast as he could on his notepad. "Guys, I think it is supposed to be a trick. She wants us to waste our energy attacking the altar, but I think what we are really supposed to do is place our keys into the four keyholes in the middle, just as we did at the entrance." Kyle looked over his shoulder. The four keyholes were positioned at four points perfectly around the center. Kyle thought it was a good idea, but doubted that Elleneya would allow them to do so. "What say you three?"

"I think Kevin's on to something." Kane had his key ready in hand.

"I don't think she'll let us." Kyle suspected that the moment they tried, she would attack.

"Don't know unless we try," said Kane. Kyle shrugged, but Kross and Kevin nodded. "Let's go for it."

They broke up from their huddle and walked to the center where the keyholes were, trying to be discreet. Elleneya didn't seem to care since she just watched them from her corner nonchalantly. As fast as they could, they rammed their keys into the keyholes, and turned them, bracing themselves for what was to come.

The only thing that happened was Elleneya's deep sigh as they turned to face her.

"Each of these keys," she said, pointing at them with pride, "are from twits like you who had the same bright idea. Well without your keys, you're definitely goners. I suppose I should just do what I need to."

The four of them shot panicked looks at each other. They tried yanking their keys from the keyholes but it was as if they had been cemented down to the altar. It was exactly the same as Kyle's had been at the entrance.

Kross, Kevin, and Kane stood up, readying their weapons as she crept toward them. Kyle stabbed his sword at the keyhole in hopes of loosening his key. It bounced off helplessly, but still he worked at it harder. The sound of her keys gently banging against each other as she edged forward was eerie, making Kyle panic even more. He wished they had waited for Proculus; he wished he had been more patient. Elleneya had been correct when she told him "impatience leads to regrettable choices." His impatience had led them all to their graves.

In his panic, his blade slipped to the right of the keyhole and slid abnormally easily into the hard stone altar.

He tried to pull it out, but now that too would not budge. Losing hope, he let go of it. His Nodachi slid in easier than Roko had when he dove into the stone. When the blade had completely sunk in, he felt a small rumble beneath the altar, but then it stopped. He had an idea.

"Wait!" cried Kyle. His shout stopped Elleneya the Guardian just short of coming within their reach. "Guys, come here."

"Take your time." She yawned, looking completely unfazed.

"Where's your sword?" Kross scanned the platform for Kyle's weapon.

"It sank into the altar," explained Kyle. "I was trying to stab the keyhole to loosen my key, but it slipped and slid right into the floor. Then I let go, and it sort of just melted into the altar. That's when I felt a small rumble underneath us. I think we're all supposed to let our weapons fall."

They looked at Kyle, clearly thinking he was insane.

"We can't risk that." Kross gripped his weapon tightly. "We lose our weapons and we really are done for."

"I wonder if you boys can help me with a riddle?" said Elleneya suddenly.

"What?" The four of them turned to face her in disbelief. They had no idea what she meant by giving them a riddle.

"If we do, will you take us to the Timekeeper's Key?" said Kross hopefully.

"Of course not," she said. "I told you. You have to destroy the altar for that."

"Then why should we help you with a riddle?" snapped Kane.

"Because I'm bored, I suppose. I've never been able to figure this riddle out–I know! How about I give you a clue if you help me solve it?"

Kyle could hardly believe her. She really was like a big child.

"Fine," said Kross. "If you give us a clue, we'll help with the riddle."

"Excellent." She beamed. "You only get one chance, though. Let's see if I can remember it correctly. Two bodies have I, though both joined in one. The stiller I am, the faster I run. What am I?"

"An hourglass," answered Kross immediately. Kyle, Kevin, and Kane's jaws nearly hit the floor. It was their only chance for a clue and Kross had blurted out an answer. They never even had the chance to discuss it.

"An hourglass, huh?" muttered Ellen. "That makes sense."

"How did you know that?" Kyle couldn't believe it. They might be able to get out of this mess after all.

"I heard the answer long ago. The monk who taught me loved riddles."

"Well I suppose I owe you a clue," said the Guardian. "Let's see. I got it. Your weapons are useless against me."

"What?" Kross protested. "That's hardly a clue. You said nearly the same thing earlier when you took out your Kota."

"Well jeez, Mr. Riddle Man," she said grumpily. "You figured out the riddle in half a second. So how about you figure out the clue, too."

Kross looked deeply offended by the injustice. Kevin and Kane shuffled uneasily, losing hope with every second. Kyle, on the other hand, was reassured that he was right. It really seemed that getting rid of their weapons was their only way out of this mess.

"Guys, I think I'm right. The clue, I think she wants us to get rid of our weapons."

"You're just forcing her idiotic clue to fit with your theory, Kyle," said Kross. "There's no guarantee that it'll work."

"I'm not forcing anything. Don't you see, it all just fits. It'll work. Trust me."

"What do we have to lose?" Kane tapped his blades against each other. "She's a Gatekeeper. We try and fight her with just our weapons and we're dead anyways." He dropped his daggers and they melted into the altar just like Kyle's Nodachi. Again there was a small rumble underneath them.

"There!" Excitement began coursing through Kyle. "Did you guys feel that?"

"That could have been anything." Kross threw his arms up in exasperation. "What if it's just one of the trees from outside like earlier? There's still no guarantee that we're not just throwing away our weapons."

"Ah," said Kevin, who without his key could say nothing else for the time being. "Ah." He dropped his battle axe and the mighty weapon fell straight through. The ground shook stronger this time.

Kross smacked his head, letting out a groan. "The three of you are going to be the death of me." He dropped his Shaolin spade and the altar ate it up.

For a moment, nothing happened, but then a soft tremble began to grow louder until it shook the floor violently. As it happened, Kyle turned to the Guardian, who gave him a sly smile. With the ground quaking even harder, Kyle lost his footing and fell down. When he looked up again, she was gone.

"We have to get down from here!" yelled Kross over what sounded like an explosion beneath the altar. Without warning, the altar began to crumble around them. Each of them tried jumping to safety, but it was too late. They came down with the debris, falling deeper than the floor of the chamber had been. Much deeper.

When everything finally stopped moving, Kyle choked on the powdery stone cloud surrounding him in all directions. He moved his fingers and toes to test that all of his limbs were still intact. He sighed in relief as he swatted the dust away from his face. He felt bruises all over but was able to stand up on the uneven rubble.

"Kross!" he yelled. "Kane! Kevin!"

"Ugh," croaked the sore voice of Kane. "I'm all right over here."

"Me too," coughed Kross. "How about you, Kevin?" They waited for a response from Kevin, but nothing came. Kyle's heart leapt.

"KEVIN!"

Close to Kyle's left, there was the loud movement of rubble being shifted.

"Ah," said the tired voice of Kevin. Instantly, Kyle felt relieved.

"Don't scare us like that, ya' big oaf," said Kane with some coughs. "Honestly—I know you can't hear, but you almost gave us a heart attack." Kyle was sure that if he could see Kane, he would be smiling despite his best effort to frown, but he still couldn't see a thing. They moved around, trying to straighten themselves in the rubble. When they all got back to their feet, the light of a torch shined dimly through the dust. More torches ignited, giving them a view to a passageway.

"Everyone, work your way to the light," said Kross who, by the sound of it, seemed closest to the newly lit torches. Kyle heard the others trudge over the crumbled remains of the altar. He tried to move toward it as fast as he could, but it still took some time. After a little while, Kyle was the last to reach the light. When he saw the other three, it looked like he had fared best in the fall.

Kane had smeared blood just above his eye and an unfocused look on his face. Kross hugged his right rib cage and surely had a couple broken ribs by the pained expression on his face. Kevin's left arm looked torn to shreds, but he still was able to move his fingers. According to Kane, that was a good sign.

"If only we had our keys," said Kyle needlessly. Kevin was the only one of them who could do Medications, but it was his weakest subject so it probably wouldn't have helped as much as they needed it.

"We won't be able to find our keys in this mess," said Kane. "Not now, anyhow. Let's keep moving and get out of here. Master Proculus will have an idea."

"I agree." Kross was breathing with difficulty.

"Okay, listen," proposed Kyle. "You three are more beat up than me, so I'll scout ahead. If there are any problems at all, I'll run back. Sound good?" The three of them, who were in no state to argue, nodded in agreement.

Kyle walked briskly down the new stone passageway that in many ways mirrored the one they had entered into the King's Temple, however, he discovered that there was no need to scout ahead. The hall was considerably shorter than the last one, and where it led was much less grand. When he entered the room, his friends were only moments behind him.

"This looks like a tomb," said Kyle as they caught up to him.

"I don't think so." Kane leaned against a wall. "That looks too big for a coffin." In the middle of the room there was a large silver crate. Dim orange light began to shine through the cracks of the oversized coffin, making the room feel warmer as they moved closer.

"Ah?" Kevin pointed at marks on top of the coffin.

"What is it?" Kross's voice seemed to be getting weaker.

They edged close enough to see the marks. At first glance they didn't look like much, but Kyle noticed that the one farthest to the left looked familiar.

"They're not marks," Kyle rushed forward. "Those are our keys—look!" He impatiently tried to pry his key from the crate. The others tried to do the same, but with less energy. Moments after touching their keys, they disintegrated into nothing, leaving only their engraving on top of the casket. "NO!"

"They disappeared," said Kross hopelessly. He whimpered softly as he walked to the nearest wall and slid to the ground to catch his breath. Not long after, Kevin joined him. They both looked tired and defeated. "How can we get the Timekeeper's Key if we don't even have keys ourselves?"

No one answered him.

In his frustration, Kane slammed his fist against the top of the crate. Kyle had never seen him so angry. He slammed his fist again on the silver top again and was about to do it a third time, but he suddenly stopped and decided against it.

"Any ideas?" Kane asked Kyle with uncharacteristically cold eyes.

"I don't know." Kyle felt utterly useless.

As if on cue, a clock the size of a dinner plate emerged from the silver coffin. A single clock hand moved so fast inside of it that Kyle got dizzy. When it stopped, he noticed that the clock was only labeled from zero to ten. The hand had stopped exactly at the number ten.

"Is that a clock?" Kross struggled to stand up.

"Yeah," Kane was inspecting it closely. "It's weird. It only has ten numbers."

Pop!

"Ah?" said Kevin, helping Kross up.

"Look!" said Kyle. The hand had moved from ten to nine counter clockwise. "It's moving." It moved from nine to eight.

"It's counting down," said Kane.

"To what?"

Seven…six…

A bomb?

They backed away, not sure what to expect. Kyle held his breath. He was so completely taken off guard that all he could do was watch the timer count down.

Five…four…three…

Two…one…

Zero.

With a loud hiss, a section of the crate slid open like a morgue drawer. Kyle, relieved that something had not exploded, moved forward to investigate. As he did so, three other sections of the crate opened in the exact same way. He peered into the first drawer.

Inside, there was a glowing weapon. Or was it a key? Kyle could hardly believe it when the truth hit him.

A Kota.

In many ways, it resembled his Nodachi that had sunk into the altar earlier, but it was shorter. The sharp side was still close to the same, except near the hilt of the sword, it now had the bumpy teeth of a key. On the dull edge, right at the tip of the blade was the single bit that now separated in to jagged edges. The entire blade was a brilliant onyx black, like his key would have been if not been rusty.

The sword's hilt contrasted the blade by being platinum silver. A chain of the same color wrapped around the blade near the hilt. The handle went straight through the middle of the key's circular bow which looked similar to a hand guard. Kyle bent down to pick it up and instantly felt comfort, like an old friend was giving him a hug. This Kota was his and his alone.

"This is my sword and key," he said quietly. Kane's eyes widened as Kyle straightened up and brought it into view. "This crate; it somehow made them into a Kota."

"How…" Kane couldn't even finish his statement. He was looking into the second drawer.

Kross and Kevin struggled to move, but they were soon at the crate looking into the other two drawers. Kyle was still in awe over his new weapon. He moved away from the crate to give the Kota a few practice swings. He had never felt so pleased with anything in his life. When he tore his eyes from his own, he saw the others sharing similar reactions to their new Kota.

Kyle expected to see Kane with two dagger Kotas, but instead he only held one. His Kota's blade was about as long as his forearm, but twice as wide. One half of it was ivy green, the other brilliant gold. Both the gold and green side had a key bit, sharpened to its point. Also, similar to Kyle's Kota, the hilt ran down the middle of the bow, but it was edged at every corner with sharp points that looked as deadly as the blade itself. As Kane fiddled with it, there was a soft click, splitting it in two. It left the inner edges with jagged key teeth that correlated with each other like puzzle pieces. Kane held one half of his Kota in each hand, cracking a satisfied grin.

Kevin held his battle axe Kota in his good arm, beaming with pleasure. At first glance, it hardly looked much different from his original weapon. The handle had changed into a blade, making the whole weapon look like a sword had been added into the combination of key and axe. It was iron grey with a long golden streak that ran through the middle up in to the head of the Kota, which look remarkably like a double-bit key. The rectangular bow and long hilt was glossy as ivory and dyed brown, making it the most bizarre axe Kyle had ever seen. It was also seemed like the deadliest.

Kross's Shaolin spade Kota also looked close to his original weapon. The difference in the spade end was most profound. Instead of a curved spade, it was now a pentagon shaped bow with three gaps in it like that of a house key. The crescent moon end was now burgundy, looking more or less the same, except for a new sharp point in the middle of it that had the small bits of a key.

As Kross finished inspecting his new weapon, Kevin pointed his Kota at him and turned it. It didn't take long for some color to return to Kross's face as his breathing eased.

"Thanks, Kevin," said Kross, rubbing his ribs sorely. "But you should have healed yourself."

Unable to write on his notepad with his Battle Axe Kota, he only said "Ah." He was breathing harder now, due to the large amount of energy it had taken to heal Kross. He turned his weapons before setting it down. It looked awkward since he could only use one hand, but he managed to start writing on the notepad by using his finger, "A slight turn and I can write on my notepad with a finger. It seems that with this Kota I can do more than I am used to. When I regain some energy, I should be able to help this arm a little. This is quite amazing, is it not?"

"It is," agreed Kross. "But how did this happen?"

"I don't know," said Kyle. "Maybe we're special?"

"Doubtful." Kross shook his head. "It doesn't make sense, Kota are only supposed to be made by a King Forger. Maybe these are fakes."

"I don't think so." Kyle tried to find the right words. "I've never felt anything like this." He looked at his Kota with admiration. "It feels so…"

"Perfect," Kane finished for him. Kyle nodded.

"Maybe." Kross still looked doubtful. "Well Kota or not, so long as we can still use the power of keys, it should be fine."

"It has worked for me, has it not?" said Kevin with his notepad.

"True." Kross massaged his ribs. "So what do we do now?"

"We still have to find the Timekeeper's Key," said Kyle. "Four new keys doesn't change that."

"Do you think it's in the crate?" Kane pointed at it with his one of his daggers. "It's still glowing."

The crate still had light leaking through the cracks in it. The morgue drawers retracted back in, making it appear as though they had never been there. Kane sheathed his Kota and tried to push the top in an attempt to slide it off, but it did not budge.

"I don't think that will work." Kross grinned. "I think we have to use our Kota. This place seems to like making us use our keys." He pointed his Kota at the coffin-like crate and turned it. It moved just a hair, but it was not enough to open it. Kevin did the same and the lid moved smoothly to its right, creating a larger gap. Kane and Kyle pointed their new KeyArms at it to finish the job. The crate's lid fell off to the side with a loud smash into to the ground.

As the sound of the crash died down, Kyle was left with the feeling that these new Kotas were going to be capable of doing extraordinary things.

CHAPTER TWENTY

The Basilisk

The four of them peeked into the dimly glowing crate. That proved to be unnecessary since the sides of the crate started to crumble, making them hop back.

"How come everything we unlock destroys itself?" moaned Kane. Kyle and the other two ignored him. Now standing in front of them were three small pedestals. The one on the left was empty. The one on the right had a thick book with a black leather binding sitting on top of it. It looked similar to the book they had taken from the Forger's Cavern. On top of the middle pedestal, there was what looked like a large golden pocket watch.

Without thinking, Kross picked up the book to inspect it.

The other three were far more interested in the pocket watch. It was nearly the same size as the book. The gold cover was smooth and looked like it had just been polished. It made Kyle nervous. He kept checking over his shoulder to make sure that Elleneya wasn't waiting for them to touch it so that she could attack. Since he was sure that her noisy jingling keys would warn them if she were to approach, he strained his ears. Kane, on the other hand, did not hesitate to open the pocket watch.

It opened easily, revealing a typical watch that had roman numerals running from I to XII. The large and small hands moved abnormally fast. It didn't take long for the small hand, which had been pointing at the number XI, to move past the number XII as the large hand made an entire rotation. For the most part, except for the speed at which the hands moved, it appeared to act much like a normal clock.

"I thought this big pocket watch would give us some clue to find the Timekeeper's Key," said Kevin's notepad. "It seems we will have to search more."

"Yeah, this is just an oversized pocket watch," said Kane. "Think we should take it with us?"

"This book might be the biggest find of the century!" Kross did not pay attention to the clock in the slightest. "It displays maps that lead to hidden armories full of lost Kotas. This information could—"

"That's the Timekeeper's Key!" Kyle pointed at a small blurry metal ring with two tiny metal rods sticking out of it. At first he thought it looked like someone had stuck together two gender symbols. But as he continued to stare at it, he knew it was the key. "We don't have to take the whole thing, just the key."

"Is it really?" Kane squinted, trying to look at it more closely. Without warning, he smashed through the glass with his KeyArm and grabbed the rotating key. He held it up, displaying for the others to see. It was a distinctive looking key which looked like two keys had been attached to the same bow. "You're right,

Kyle. It has the name 'Elias' engraved on it. It was Elias the Timekeeper, right?"

"This book could change the face of the world." Kross flipped through the pages with concentrated interest. It was like he was trying to memorize every page in half a glance. "We have to get it to Master Proculus right away."

"Well, we have the key and the book is a bonus," said Kyle with relief. "Let's find Master Proculus and get back to Garnet."

"No," said Kane oddly. "I don't think so."

"What?" Kyle was unsure if he had heard him correctly. Kevin and Kross glanced at each other with raised eyebrows, surprised and uncertain.

"I said no." Kane's eyes were shifting back and forth, starving to consume everything in front of him.

"Are you feeling okay?" asked Kevin with his notepad.

"I am better than ever. I will finally be free."

Kyle, Kevin, and Kross looked at Kane worriedly. There was something off about him.

"Kane," said Kyle, thinking of Garnet. "How about you give me the key?"

Kane responded by laughing manically. "Not a chance. *My* Master will be pleased to have this."

"Your master?" asked Kyle. "What are you talking about?"

"This is not the time for a stupid joke, Kane." Kross slammed the book shut. "Give Kyle the key. He can use MicroDimensions to put it away."

"My Master—"

"*Your* masters are at Soul Gate Academy!" shouted Kross. "What is the matter with you?"

"Nothing," said Kane, turning his Kota in his hand. With the other hand, he threw the Timekeeper's key up in the air. It flipped like a quarter; each turn seeming to take forever. "There has just been a change in plans."

"Who is your Master?" roared Kross.

Kyle had been scared earlier; scared that they were about to die, scared that they wouldn't succeed in saving Garnet, but nothing scared him more than the way Kane smiled at them. It was more than mocking and menacing; it was dangerous.

"King Seltios." The words slid from Kane's lips like a happy song. "I think you've heard of him."

"That's a stupid lie," spat Kross. "You're from Dusk, just like the rest of us."

"I don't need to explain anything to you," he said tiredly. "Just give me the book."

"Over my dead—"

Kane suddenly disappeared then reappeared right behind Kross. He had moved just like Master Logan. Kross tried to move away, but he was too injured. Kane tore the book from his grip, drilling a punch straight into his injured ribs. Kross screamed in pain as he flew back into the wall. He collapsed into unconsciousness a moment later. Kyle stood frozen in shock. This was not how it was supposed to happen. They had the Timekeeper's Key. Why couldn't they just leave together?

"AH!" bellowed Kevin. Kyle had never seen him look so infuriated, either. Kane simply chuckled before releasing an annoyed sigh. Kevin turned his KeyArm which caused his right arm to grow double in size while AuraBending symbols formed a circle around him. "Ah!" Kevin was trying to avoid fighting Kane by threatening him, but Kane scoffed at the very idea.

"You've just seen me smash your friend into a wall," said Kane. "And you think I'm not prepared to fight you? How thick can you be?"

Kane turned his dagger Kota and disappeared again. He broke through Kevin's aura much like he had broken through the glass of the pocket watch. He landed a powerful kick into Kevin's stomach, knocking the wind out of him. The Bison slammed into the wall violently then joined Kross in unconsciousness.

There was silence. Kane looked at Kyle as if they were just meeting each other for the first time.

"W-why a-re you doi-ing this?" Kyle wanted to rush to help Kross and Kevin, but he felt powerless. He backed away with small steps, tightening his grip on the only thing that could possibly help him, his Nodachi Kota. With the book tucked under his armpit, Kane was still flipping the Timekeeper's key as though he didn't have a care in the world. "You're our friend. We've trained together. It doesn't make any sense; how are you so strong?"

"It was my mission to do this," said Kane. "Master Seltios commanded me to do this, so I did it. It's as simple as that. And this, Kyle, this is not strength. Master Seltios can show you true strength. He can give you real power. Join us. I know he would be pleased. You have great potential. Soul Gate Academy will only slow you down." He caught the key again, but then started spinning it around his index finger carelessly like a pinwheel.

"What have you done with my friend, Kane the Ace?" Kyle asked foolishly.

"The Ace?" Kane scoffed. "The Ace is the name I earned from that ridiculous academy, but that is not my true name."

"The Ace is who you are," said Kyle in denial.

"I AM," he screamed with a menacing glare, "THE BASILISK!"

"Basilisk?" repeated Kyle. Kane's gaze petrified him.

Suddenly, Kane turned into an enormous snake, looming over him, hissing and baring its fangs. Keys couldn't make someone turn into animals, could they? He shook his head. When he looked up again, the snake disappeared but now Kane was right next to him. Kane twisted his Kota once before taking a stab at Kyle. He jumped back to dodge it, allowing only the tip of the weapon to sink into his left arm, leaving only a small scratch.

The attack woke up Kyle. He knew that Kane was no longer his friend. *The Kane I knew was a lie. I have to get that key for Garnet. I have to beat him.*

He went to place both hands on his sword, but then noticed that his left arm would not move.

"Your arm's been petrified," laughed Kane. "My skill with ThoughtBending is unparalleled. Join me, Kyle the Static. You're outclassed here."

"Outclassed?" Kyle looked at his useless arm. He hated being weak and just for one fleeting instance, he considered joining Kane. The idea seemed ludicrous, but he couldn't deny that since his arrival to Endera, he had done whatever he could to become stronger. And now Kane offered him the opportunity. Was it really so terrible? Wasn't that what he wanted? He had known Kane just as long as he had known Kross and Kevin. They were best friends, like brothers almost. He found the idea alluring in more than one way. But despite all that, he shook his head. "Garnet needs that key, Basilisk. I won't join you or your master."

"That's too bad." Kane set down the book and key on one of the empty pedestals. "Don't get any crazy ideas. There's no chance of you taking these from me. I'm just setting them down because I have to finish you off."

Kyle's training with the Grandmaster and Master Proculus hadn't been for nothing. He turned his sword Kota three times as fast as he could. This caused lightning to engulf his calves. It worked its way down to his feet just like it had when he had carried Garnet to Dilu Village, but something was different. The unique yellow lightning he'd grown accustom to seeing was blue now. Not only that, it felt stronger. Kyle wished he knew what was going on, but he didn't have the chance to think about it. Kane watched him with widened eyes, doing nothing and staying a safe distance away. Kyle continued, controlling his new lightning to wrap around his KeyArm.

The lightning was draining his energy fast, telling him a drawn out fight was not an option. The last turn had gone unnoticed. It had been used to set up his aura around Kross and Kevin, shielding them safe from the fight.

Kane looked positively amused, and turned his Kota casually. Though he was slowed by his useless arm, Kyle charged at him with alarming speed. His lightning sword, zapping dangerously, slammed into both of Kane's daggers. Kane was forced to fall back momentarily before moving so fast that he was behind Kyle. Luckily, Kyle anticipated this and swept his blade behind him, almost catching Kane in the arm. Or so he thought.

Kane leaped to the left, bringing his right leg into Kyle's side, knocking him down to the ground. Kyle rolled over, wasting no time to stand back up. He wanted to grab his side, which was throbbing with pain, but his only working arm held his weapon. The blue electricity attached to him became weaker.

Kane stood up and laughed. "You really do have potential. King Seltios—"

Kyle charged at him once again, but this time, he disappeared which seemed to surprise Kane. A zap of lightning appeared to the right of Kane, luring his attention. Meanwhile, Kyle reappeared on his left. He was moving so fast that he almost overshot his destination. Thinking fast, he stabbed his Kota into the ground, using it to slow himself down by dragging it along the temple's floor. Kane was too slow to react; Kyle swung himself around to kick the Basilisk hard in the face.

Kane lost his footing and fell hard to the ground, rolling backwards. Without faltering, Kyle turned his Kota, which was still stuck in the ground. This opened up his MicroDimension. He grabbed the Timekeeper's Key from the pedestal then jabbed his hand toward the distorted air leading into his MicroDimension.

But Kane recovered immediately. He lunged at Kyle in an attempt to prevent him from placing the key in the dimension. Everything seemed to happen in slow motion. Kane sliced one of his daggers down at Kyle's hand as it moved toward the opening to the other dimension. Kyle released the key with a little push toward the distorted air before pulling his hand back to avoid the blade. The dagger Kota just missed Kyle's hand, but he heard the blade make contact with the Timekeeper's Key just before it entered his MicroDimension. The well-being of the Timekeeper's Key flashed in his mind, but Kane slashed his other dagger, forcing him to leap away from his own Kota.

"I stand corrected." Kane tried forcing his hand into the distorted air. That proved impossible; his hand continued on as if the opening to Kyle's MicroDimension was not there. "I shouldn't have gone easy on you."

Kyle was breathing hard now. All his energy was depleting and his only weapon was now standing next to the person who was trying to kill him. The Kota continued to zap like an electric rod, which gave him an idea.

"I want you to take the key back out for me, Kyle. I'll even let you live if you do that."

"Not a chance," growled Kyle. Against his body's wishes, he struggled to summon his remaining strength. "I'm taking it to Garnet."

"Garnet?" Kane rolled his eyes. "Is that all you care about? You can barely stand at the moment and you still talk about saving someone. Please, Kyle the world doesn't need any more useless heroes."

"I'm no hero." *Almost there.* "I'm just trying to save a friend."

"Hah," spat Kane. "Typical hero nonsense. Then let's see. You have two friends lying right over there. I wonder if Garnet is more important than them. Give me back the Timekeeper's Key or I'll kill them." Kyle could tell that he wasn't bluffing, but he was finally ready. This move would be all or nothing. "Well?"

"Wait!" Kyle let the lightning energy around his legs disperse.

"Finally coming to your sens—"

Then with the loud clap of thunder, Kyle concentrated all his energy on the AuraBending that protected his friends as well as the electricity on his sword Kota. The Kota began to emit a scary amount of lightning. It shot out in every direction. Kane jumped out of the way just in time.

"You fool!" screamed Kane, but it was drowned out by the crackles of the lightning, now thrashing out of control. It hit the walls with such a force that it was causing the whole room to shake.

BOOM!

The lightning burst a hole through the temple's side, allowing sunlight to shine in. Kane did not hesitate. He dodged the lightning as expertly as a swordsman avoiding his opponent, but his face showed signs of panic. He dove for the book that was still on the pedestal and grabbed it while running at the opening in the wall. He crashed through it like a football player, making the rest of the wall crumble as he disappeared from sight.

Moments later, Kyle focused on calming the lightning. It took him some time, but soon it fizzled away. Yet it did nothing to stop the thunderous noise that surrounded him. The King's Temple sounded like it was falling apart. The lightning had shot many holes into the walls, and all around him things were collapsing due to the excessive shaking.

Kyle stepped forward only to fall to one knee. He was exhausted. He strained to stand but collapsed to the same knee again. Panic began to sink in. He thought about his friends, lying unconscious as the temple came down. *I have to save them.*

He rose to his feet to stagger toward them, but it was too late. There was a loud crash and Kyle knew that the whole temple was about to come down. He reached out for his friends.

"We're going to die," he whispered.

But right before his eyes, both Kevin and Kross disappeared. A glimmering blur had taken them both. He looked around in search of their savior, but saw nothing through the dust that surrounded him. A moment later, he was lifted off his feet and heard the *cling-clang* sound of metal hitting metal.

CHAPTER TWENTY-ONE
HEALING

The next thing Kyle knew, he was being dropped carelessly to the ground. He laid there for a moment trying to look toward the sky, but his eyes needed a moment to adjust to the bright sunlight. He turned his head to see Kross and Kevin lying beside him, both tattered and bruised, but still breathing.

It took him a moment to notice that Kane was not there. It was hard to comprehend. Then the reality of the betrayal sent a shock through Kyle's heart like a needle poking at a fresh wound. They had almost died and Kane was responsible. He balled his working hand into a fist to the point of pain until he felt a thunderous shaking once more, causing him to sit up. The King's Temple was crashing down. In front of him, watching every stone of it fall, was Elleneya the Guardian with her keys dangling as freely as ever.

"Not every day you get to see your house turn to rubble," she said absentmindedly. She had brought them all to a safe distance from the crumbling temple. "Although I suppose it's what I would have wanted in the end, anyways." She laughed at her own joke as the crown on top of the pyramid temple fell from the top. It rolled dangerously into the forest, causing the icy trees to bend and break. It sounded like a mixture of gunshots and dishes breaking. A little while later, the destroyed King's Temple finally came to rest. Bits and pieces of the ruins still broke periodically, but the true danger had passed.

"You saved us?" croaked Kyle.

"You figure that out yourself, champ?" Elleneya grinned as she faced him. She let herself down to the ground with a soft *thump*. As unladylike as could be, she sat cross-legged, exposing her underwear to Kyle. Kyle looked away with a reddened face.

"Er, your…"

"Oh how embarrassing," she said without the slightest hint of embarrassment. "Let me fix that." She turned a random key on her skirt that caused it to 'grow' into pants. "You can look now." Kyle looked back more at ease now that she had modified her skirt.

"Why did you save us?"

"Because you would have died if I hadn't."

Kyle could hardly argue against that, but she had threatened to kill them not too long ago. "That's the only reason?" asked Kyle.

"Well." She tapped her finger gently on her mouth, apparently in an attempt to look cute. "I wanted to see which one of you used the Synchroneity lightning. It exploded straight through two of the pillars. I tried to fix it, but the damage was too severe. It made me curious, I guess. You've got potential, you know that?"

"So I hear," Kyle said miserably.

"Kyle!"

It was the voice of Proculus. The master suddenly ran up to Kyle. He looked tired, with fresh cuts around his arms and torso, but otherwise in good health. His giant sword had been replaced by a normal broadsword. He looked relieved to see Kyle, but his face fell when he saw Kross and Kevin in their states. "What hap—Who are you?" He raised his weapon to the back of Elleneya's head, while the Guardian kept completely calm. In Kyle's opinion, she looked bored—until Proculus moved into her view.

She wolf-whistled happily. "Tell me your name handsome, and I'll tell you mine."

"I am Proculus the Storm," he said with a weak frown. He looked a little less tense, but did not lower his guard. "A master of Soul Gate Academy."

"I am Elleneya the Guardian," she purred. "Also known as July the Gatekeeper."

At that, Kyle expected Proculus to drop to his knees or at least lower his sword, but he did not. In fact, he sharpened his eyes to look deadlier than blades. "Were you the same guardian that was here about fifteen years ago?"

"Nope. I've been a guardian of many things, but I've only been here about ten years. I don't know who was here before me, you could check at the Guardian Headquarter. I can take you there if you'd like." She blinked, obviously hoping that he would take her up on the offer.

"That won't be necessary." Proculus said it through gritted teeth. There was a strange look in his eyes. It did not look as simple as anger; it was something more like an unquenchable rage ready to be released through a rampage. It scared Kyle. A lot. Kyle wondered what the Guardian Headquarter was, but felt it might be pointless to find out now. There were more important things going on. For instance, at that moment, Proculus gripped his weapon a little tighter.

"She saved us." Kyle hoped that this might stop his Master from attacking her. Proculus certainly looked like he was about to, and Kyle didn't fancy the idea of another fight breaking out. It seemed to work. Proculus' rage disappeared, but was replaced by vigilance.

"I see." Proculus looked over Elleneya inquiringly, as though trying to figure out if she was truly a Gatekeeper. With a restrained nod, he seemed to decide that she was who she said she was. Finally, he lowered his sword and titled his head respectfully. "It is an honor to meet you, Gatekeeper July." He said this with considerably less respect than he had shown Gatekeeper October, but all the same it lessened the tension in the air. Turning away from Elleneya, he looked to Kyle. "Where is Kane?"

"He's gone," said Kyle sadly. Proculus gave him a puzzled look that required answers. Kyle began explaining everything that had happened, starting with the threats from Elleneya, to the Kotas, to Kane's betrayal. He left out no detail. "…Then he got away with the book and Guardian Elleneya saved us as it all started to come down."

Proculus scratched his chin, thinking deeply before responding. "How did all of that happen in the fifteen minutes that have passed since I instructed you to wait for me on the other side of the King's Temple?"

"Fifteen minutes?" Kyle could hardly believe that. He felt as if days had gone by, which he knew couldn't be true, but it had at least been a good hour.

"I can partly explain that." The Guardian's keys jingled with how excited she was to be part of the conversation. "The Timekeeper's Key has some way of locking time. If it is spins clockwise, time in the temple goes by faster than it does outside. So if it was only fifteen minutes out here, then it could be a lot more time inside the temple. If it spins counter clockwise, time goes slower inside than it happens outside. That means two days can pass out here, even if only fifteen minutes have passed inside."

"I see," said Proculus as if this explained everything. "That would make sense. You should have waited, Kyle. I could have stopped Kane." Kyle was about to apologize, but Elleneya cut him off.

"If five of you had entered," she said blankly. "I would have had to kill you all." Kyle looked at her to see if this was some sort of sick joke, but she was completely serious. Proculus frowned at her. "I'm glad you didn't. I think it would have ate me up inside to kill a handsome man like you. And the kids too, I guess."

Master Proculus ignored her. "Well in any case, our priority is to get these two healed up so we can get this key to Garnet."

"I can help with that." The Guardian clapped her hands with glee. "I'm quite good in Medications."

Kyle could hardly believe someone could act like this in the given environment. Her home lay in ruins behind her. Men she would have killed had they done the slightest thing different sat in front of her, and half of them weren't even conscious. Yet she acted as though there were all drinking sweet summer wine and enjoying radiant sunshine.

"Can we trust you?" asked Master Proculus with a heated gaze.

Surprisingly, she didn't answer right away, but instead returned his gaze. "You can." Her simple answer seemed enough to please Master Proculus.

"Then please heal them," said Proculus sincerely.

Without another word, she obliged. She removed another

random key and directed it at Kross and Kevin. She turned it slowly at first then she followed it with numerous rapid turns. Proculus scanned the perimeter, making sure the area was still clear. Eventually, he turned to Kyle, who lay back down in the snow. "So you were able to retrieve the Timekeeper's Key?"

"Yes, Master," said Kyle tiredly. "But I have to get a new key to use my MicroDimension. I wasn't able to grab my Kota when she saved us."

Proculus shook his head. "I know Master Oisin did not forget to tell you that Kotas bound to their users until death. Summon it to your hand and it will come."

Kyle could hardly believe that he had forgotten. He focused his thoughts on the Kota. Instinctively, he turned his hand in the motion that he would have, had a key been it. Instantly, the platinum hilt solidified in his hand. The black blade gleamed in the sunlight, looking as new as it had been when he pulled it out of the oversized crate. It was hard to believe that a temple had just fallen on top of it.

"Impressive," said Master Proculus in an approving tone.

"Did you kill the Hollow Eye?" asked Kyle. He had been wondering what had happened to him.

"I am sorry to say that I did not. The Hollow Eye escaped as the temple began collapsing. I was too worried about the four of you to chase him." Kyle was sure that Proculus could have crushed a boulder to dust with how tightly he was squeezing his fist.

As for Kyle, the idea that Sergio was still out there haunted him a little. He didn't like the idea of running into him again.

Proculus patted Kyle's shoulder, somehow reading his mind. "You have enough on your mind right now. Do not worry about the Hollow Eye; one day he will face justice."

"I hope so," said Kyle. "Should I take the Timekeeper's Key out now?"

"I think so. I'd like to make sure we got the right key, wouldn't you?"

Kyle nodded then turned his Kota. Just above his hand, the air began to distort as it always did. He reached in to take out the Timekeeper's Key, pulling it out carefully. His heart stopped when he saw only half of it come out of the distorted air. Having never seen the whole Timekeeper's Key, Master Proculus was perplexed to Kyle's look of horror.

"What's wrong?" he asked. "Is that not the key?" Kyle didn't answer, but reached frantically back into his MicroDimension to grab the second half of the Timekeeper's Key.

It had been cleanly sliced in two.

"It must have been—when Kane and I were fighting." Kyle held the pieces up to give to Master Proculus. "Will it still work? Can we put it back together?"

"Maybe." But the Master's face looked uncertain. He took the two halves and inspected them. "It definitely would seem that this is the true Timekeeper's Key. Only a Kota could have sliced through it." He took out his key and whispered something incoherent as he pointed his key at the Timekeeper's Key. The key jerked mildly but then remained motionless. Proculus scratched his chin. "We can only hope that it will still work. Here—place this back in your MicroDimension." With a sullen face, Kyle placed the two halves of the Timekeeper's Key back into his MicroDimension. "Good. No use in getting upset about it. We got what we came for, even if it is in two pieces." He offered no hope or comfort. Instead, he turned to Guardian Elleneya, who was still healing Kevin and Kross. "How is it going?"

"Just—about—done." She smacked Kevin and Kross each hard in the face and both of them woke up with zombie-like groans. "You two nitwits feeling better?"

They wore the same look of confusion and fear, but after some explaining they both relaxed. They summoned their Kota a little while afterwards, with as much ease as Kyle had. They, like Kyle, wore expressions of deep thought, which was surely due to Kane's betrayal. Although the four of them had been like brothers, Kross and Kevin had been together with Kane much longer than Kyle.

"We should get going," said Proculus. "The sooner we get back, the sooner we can figure out what needs to be done for Garnet."

Kyle almost looked at his Master in contempt. It seemed absurd to be thinking about leaving yet. Weren't they going to find Kane and drag him back? Weren't they going to do something?

Anything?

Without a word, Kevin and Kross both stood up, readying themselves to leave. It was an unspoken answer; Kane was gone. Kyle, with his left arm dangling, struggled to do the same.

"Why haven't you mentioned that arm?" said Elleneya. "I should be able to heal it up."

"Oh, do you know ThoughtBending, as well?" asked Proculus. She shook her head. "His arm has been locked by someone very skilled. Only another person who can use ThoughtBending will be able to unlock it. I am curious to what you intend to do, Gatekeeper July?"

"Oh, please." She faked a blush. "Just call me Ellen. And I was thinking I'd go with you. I can help with whatever."

She winked at Proculus, but he ignored the flirtation. "I suppose that is fine," he said. "I'm sure the Grandmaster will have an idea." Elleneya looked ecstatic.

Kyle tried discarding the dread running through him. The Oracle had made it clear that the Timekeeper's Key was the only thing that could make Garnet better. Now with the key split in half and Kane gone, the idea that he might lose Garnet made him shiver in fear.

"Ready, Kyle?" Proculus asked.

Kyle nodded despite the fact that Proculus hadn't really been looking for an answer. The Master opened up a ShiftDoor that would lead them away. Kyle looked over it to see the fallen ruins of the King's Temple. As he walked into the ShiftDoor with the rest of his group, he silently wished he would never see the place again.

They arrived at the doorsteps of Mayor Nova's mansion a little while later. Kyle's left arm still dangled uselessly when the butler Baldwin answered the door. His turquoise mask covered the lower half of his face, but his eyes smiled when he saw the group. Kyle thought they must have looked odd. Most of the townspeople who had seen them did their best to steer clear from them. It hadn't helped that Guardian Elleneya was covered in keys and acting like an overgrown child.

"Lady Nova has been worried about you all," said Baldwin as he showed them in. He eyed Elleneya carefully. He, like most of the world, thought she looked odd. "Master Yvette arrived shortly after you left. I hope your mission proved successful?"

Kyle's heart sank. He didn't know if it had.

"We will see soon enough," said Master Proculus. Baldwin led them into the living room where Kyle had met the Oracle, but nobody sat down.

"Don't worry about making the place dirty," said the butler. "Please sit."

"We would like to see Garnet and Master Yvette," said Proculus. "Are they available?"

"Of course," said Mayor Nova, who came striding into the living room. She finally looked like she had gotten some rest. "I'll take them to my room, Baldwin. Could you have Dean prepare some food for everyone? This lot seems like they've had a rough morning." Baldwin nodded and left the room immediately. "Everyone, please follow me."

The Mayor knocked politely on the door, which was answered by Lyn the Phoenelf, looking as pink and annoyed as ever. She clicked her beak in agitation before opening the door.

"Mayor Nova and Master Proculus are here, Master Yvette," said Lyn. She looked over Kyle, Kross, and Kevin in distaste. Their clothes still carried the grime from their mission; it added to their battered and broken look as they filed into the room. Where her eyes found Elleneya, she looked downright offended by the outfit with dangling keys. "Along with some questionable looking ones as well."

"Oh good," said Master Yvette, who was setting a spear against the wall next to Garnet's bed. Garnet looked completely unchanged since Kyle had last seen her. Master Yvette looked at them with surprise. "Where's Kane the Ace?"

Kyle, Kross, and Kevin all looked down at the floor. None of them could bear to answer her.

Proculus spoke for them. "In a moment, I will do my best to explain to you what happened. But first, I think it would be best for us to attempt to heal Garnet with the Timekeeper's Key."

"All right," said Yvette, clearly trying to control her distress. She eyed Ellen with particular interest, but she turned her gaze toward Garnet. "Let's try it."

Without being told, Kyle summoned his Kota sword to his hand.

"A Kota?"

Doing his best to ignore Yvette, Kyle twisted his KeyArm to open his MicroDimension. He placed his Kota into it, then grabbed the two halves of the Timekeeper's Key and handed them to Master Yvette who took them with uncertainty. Meanwhile, Kyle turned his empty hand as if a key were still in it to lock the opening to his MicroDimension with the Kota safe inside. Without much effort, the distorted air turned back to normal. If the situation had been less grim, he would have surely wondered how far his new weapon would extend his power.

"Those are the two pieces of the Timekeeper's Keys," said Kyle. "It was accidently split in two. Do you think it'll still work?"

"I don't know," said Master Yvette. "My honest answer is no. But seeing as we received no instructions on how the Timekeeper's Key could be used to help Garnet, I really have no idea. We won't know 'til we try. But first, what's wrong with yer arm?"

"It's nothing," murmured Kyle. "I'll be fine to wait. Can we please just try to get Garnet up and moving?" Kane was Garnet's friend too. What would they tell Garnet when she woke up?

If she woke up.

"Fine," Yvette said, nodding kindly. "Everyone please stand back."

Kyle and the rest of the group moved away from the bed. Kross and Kevin looked like all the happiness had been sucked out of them. Seeing them that way stung as much as thinking about Kane. Elleneya looked uninterested, as if the whole situation was beneath her. The Mayor and Proculus shared the same serious face of concern.

Master Yvette exhaled deeply, taking half of the Timekeeper's Key in each hand. She directed them at Garnet, her eyes closed to concentrate. Kyle held his breath, silently hoping for it to work. A moment later, Yvette the Harmony turned both hands simultaneously. A small wisp of grey smoke escaped the tip of each key with a weak hiss. Garnet remained still as ever. Yvette frowned, but said nothing. She repeated the process once more, but it yielded the same results.

Refusing to admit defeat, she placed the pieces of the broken key into the hands of Garnet's motionless hands. Yvette gently closed Garnet's hands over the halves of the keys. Master Yvette gripped Garnet's hands tightly, focusing so strongly the whole room seemed to fall still. This time, a rosy pink light shined through the cracks between Garnet's fingers. Hope spread through all of them, but Garnet remained still and serenely asleep.

Without warning, Master Yvette fell to her knees, breathing hard. Master Proculus rushed to her aid without missing a beat. He helped her up, supporting her weight. She looked older than she had a moment ago. Her face was pale, more wrinkled, and less confident than Kyle had ever seen it. It made him lose all hope.

"I've done all I can," she said weakly. "I'm sorry." Kyle looked at her, almost wanting to yell, but a tear slid down Master Yvette's cheek and he knew she was in pain, too.

Kevin and Kross stared blankly, tears building in their frustrated eyes. They were suffering at the thought of losing Garnet, as well.

"Perhaps," said Master Proculus, "it would be best for us to get some rest. We can discuss other options later." He finished, trying to add a bit of hope to what certainly seemed like a hopeless situation, but there was a disturbance in the normal assurance of his voice.

"Yes," the Mayor agreed with a tone was full of her unwavering professionalism. "Let's get you all well rested then we will figure out what else is to be done."

Kross and Kevin agreed with feeble grunts. With the help of Proculus, Master Yvette began walking toward the door.

"Wait!" cried Kyle. Everyone turned back. "Elleneya, you're the Gatekeeper July! Isn't there anything you could do?" Everyone stared at Kyle with deep sadness. Elleneya looked at him peculiarly.

"I'm sorry," she said. "There is nothing I can do. The Timekeeper's Key is not for me to wield. It has rejected me before and if I tried to help her now, especially with it broken, it may do more harm than good. It may be best to think of other options."

Kyle nearly choked on her words. It felt like a huge weight was being pressed against his chest.

"Come on," said the Mayor, placing her hand on his shoulder. "You need your rest."

"No," Kyle pleaded. "Let me stay here. I'd like to be with Garnet. Please."

They all nodded before filing out.

When they had left, he walked to sit in the chair next to Garnet's bed. He thought he would cry, but instead he just sat, staring at her as devastating helplessness loomed. Guilt consumed him, making him enraged with himself. *I should have moved faster…I should have known about Kane…I should have…*

He buried his face in his hands. "I'm sorry, Garnet." His voice was just above a whisper. "I'm so sorry."

The bedroom door then swung open and was shut. Rayne walked in dressed in a pumpkin orange and grey uniform. Two little mask earrings dangled from her ears, and she carried a spear that looked similar to Garnet's. As she leaned her spear against the wall, she sat on a chair opposite of Kyle so that Garnet was between them.

"Hi," she said suddenly.

"Hey," said Kyle softly. He didn't really feel like talking to anyone, but he stopped himself from saying so.

"I home early from Dilu Academy. Probably not as good as Soul Gate, but I think we do all right." She tried smiling at him, but he stared at Garnet's hands. She still clutched the Timekeeper's Key halves. "My mom just told me about what happened and I thought I'd come check up on you." After Kyle's shrug, she went on, "there's no reason to lose hope. Garnet's still right here. There's still a chance."

Kyle's mood didn't raise any, but at the very least he could look at Rayne now. She had a strong gaze fixed on him.

"What do you want?" croaked Kyle.

"They say that sometimes, when people are in locked states, these comas, that it's good to place things that were familiar to them while they were awake in their hands. Maybe someone close holding her hands is all she'll need and the Oracle was wrong about this key thing. He's been wrong a few times." She reached toward Garnet to remove the key that was in her hands. Unhurriedly, she took the first one out and looked at it. "These famous keys always have a way of looking disappointing, ya know? So maybe you should just hold her hands?"

Kyle didn't have a chance to respond because as soon as she reached to unclasp the second part of the Timekeeper's Key from Garnet's hand the same rosy pink light from before began shining much more brightly. It formed into an expanding pink bubble, engulfing Garnet and Rayne. Kyle thought he was about to be enveloped also, but the pink bubble acted like a giant hand, shoving him back and knocking him and his chair over. He stood up, totally bewildered. The bubble continued to grow until it swallowed everything within five paces from the bed.

Then it just stopped.

At first, the bubble was transparent enough for Kyle to see Garnet and Rayne, but the rosy pink light intensified to the point of becoming completely blinding. He thought to yell for help, but his mouth would not move. He stared, unsure of what to do.

With a loud buzz, the bubble began pulsating. It was as if the wind inside was spinning uncontrollably, like a hurricane. The door flew open and in came Master Proculus and Mayor Nova, looking lost for words. They turned to Kyle, but knew by the look on his face they would get no answers.

Without warning, the bubble popped, erasing all evidence that a bubble or light had ever existed. Rayne stood up, looking completely disheveled and confused. For some reason, she was holding her spear in her hands, but something was different about it. The head of it looked a bit longer, and it had gaps in the blade now teething in it. One small neon pink wing that pointed at the ground was directly underneath the spearhead and a small hour hand of a clock pointed away from the spear. A small bow fashioned at the bottom completed its similarity to a large key. It had become a Kota.

From underneath the large blanket on the bed, a small groan escaped. Kyle's eyes widened as he edged closer. Garnet peeked above it, exposing her red hair and face. She searched the room, her gem blue eyes darting around in confusion. She was adjusting to the light and brought her hands up to rub her eyes, only to stop when she noticed that she had something in her hand. It was in fact a Kota like Rayne's, though there were two major differences. Garnet's spear

Kota had a metallic blue wing that pointed up. And second, rather than a short hour hand, it had the long minute hand of a clock that was sharply pointing as the tip of Garnet's Kota.

"Kyle?" said Garnet, disoriented. "Kyle! Wh—Where am I?"

CHAPTER TWENTY-TWO

THE VISITOR

"Stop messing up your hair and tell me what happened properly," said Garnet rather irritably at Kyle's bedside. He stopped scratching his head and grinned. She was the same old Garnet and he had missed her. "Or how about one of you two; tell me what happened again with, Kane!"

"We were out cold," said Kevin with his notepad. He was in another bed, sitting up and looking quite bored. "As we have told you already."

"Kyle's already told you everything," Kross reminded Garnet as he flatly lay in the bed nearest to the door.

"But how did he get so strong? Why did he just betray SoGA like that? Why did he betray us? Ugh. This is what I get for dozing off. If I ever see him again, I'd like to give him a good punch in the face..." Garnet began hissing angry little comments under her breath. She had done this the past few days to vent her frustration.

It had been three days since Garnet woke up. Other than her initial confusion, she was as healthy as she had ever been. In fact, she seemed more energetic and expressive than Kyle remembered. This, of course, was a good thing, but Kyle had to admit that he had relived the ordeal that had taken place at the King's Temple too many times already, so he hardly felt like explaining it to Garnet once again. They were still enjoying relative peace and quiet at the Mayor's house, since Mayor Nova insisted that they stay for a few days. Master Yvette had happily agreed. Master Proculus, however, wanted to inform Grandmaster Dante of all that had passed and immediately returned to SoGA. The Guardian Elleneya and Lyn the Phoenelf decided to accompany him.

Rayne had been spending a lot of time with them over the past few days. Kyle, Kross, Kevin, and Garnet welcomed a peer who seemed to fill the void that Kane had left.

"You four still talking about it?" asked Rayne casually as she entered the room that Mayor had prepared for the boys upstairs. They were under strict orders from Master Yvette to stay in their beds. Everyone's injuries seemed to be healing well except for Kyle's arm, which was now in a sling. Though Kyle feared that his arm would never be usable again, Master Yvette assured him that Master Olivia, known as Olivia the Key Surgeon, would be able to heal him as soon as they returned to Soul Gate Academy.

"Yeah," said Garnet politely, answering Rayne. "I guess I just can't wrap my mind around it."

"That's understandable," said Rayne as she fell into a chair. "It is still a pretty fresh wound. Speaking of wounds, your arm any better?" She turned to Kyle.

"I'm able to move my fingers," Kyle answered. "But I don't think I should be able to. Master Yvette told me it should be completely useless until I see Master Olivia."

"Maybe you're super human," joked Garnet.

"He could be." Rayne smirked. The girls had often agreed like this throughout the past few days, which Kyle thought was strange. It started with them trying to prod Kyle with a harmless joke that they alone thought was funny. They were all getting along well, but Kyle thought at times they seemed overly stiff with each other. He assumed that girls were just hard to understand.

"Ha ha ha," said Kyle sarcastically as he wiggled the fingers of his left hand. "Really super human, this is."They snickered together a little oddly at first, but that made them burst out with more chuckles. It felt good for them to laugh since it felt like ages since any of them had. Kyle could tell that this was especially true for Rayne.

"Ya know," said Rayne seriously, "I wanted to ask all of you something that's been bugging me, but I didn't know if I should say it. Don't you think it's odd how we all have a Kota? I mean, these weapons are extraordinarily rare. Some people spend their whole lives looking for one and then the five of us—well, six including Kane—just happen to, I don't know, get them. That's crazy, right?"

"What's more odd," added Kross, "is that these Kotas were created before our eyes, with our old keys and weapons. Well, the Timekeeper's Key for you two."

"But that's the thing," said Rayne. "Kotas were supposedly only created by King Forgers, those who are blacksmith and locksmith combined into one. All of these were created without one."

"Maybe the King Forgers were nothing more than a myth," Garnet suggested. "Maybe they never existed and this is how all the

KeyArms were created. I mean, nobody has ever seen a King Forger."

"That could be right," agreed Kevin, scribbling across his notepad. "Ours seem perfectly genuine, so maybe that is true."

They discussed other theories, but Kyle kept himself from commenting. He listened, but his mind was elsewhere. Rayne brought forth the theory that perhaps the King Forger's were spirits who created the Kota in front of them, but they were simply invisible. Kevin liked this idea, also. Kross thought perhaps they'd created the weapons themselves. How exactly that was possible, he did not know. As optimistically as ever, Kevin approved of this idea, too.

"Are you okay?" Garnet asked Kyle when she finally noticed that he hadn't said a thing.

"Yeah," responded Kyle. "Just, I don't know. I was just thinking that it was magic."

"Magic," scoffed Kross. "Oh come on, Kyle. That's hardly an explanation at all. Plus, what exactly do you consider magic? We don't run off of magic, we run off the power of keys."

Kyle shrugged. "Where I come from, keys and all the things we do with them would be considered magic. There's no explanation, there's no reason as to why we can do all these amazing things with the keys, and it just is what it is. Magic."

"So what are you saying?" asked Rayne.

"I don't know. Are the Kotas weirder than anything else that goes on here? I mean, when we dream, there's not really an explanation as to *why* we dream. Maybe there is no real reason. Maybe it's just some sort of magic." He laughed, which seemed to make Kross, Kevin, and Rayne a little nervous. Garnet, who came from the same realm as Kyle, looked at him with understanding. "Sorry, I guess I just don't know how to explain myself."

"I think I understand," said Rayne unconvincingly. Kross and Kevin looked just as skeptical, but gave nods to Kyle. "I guess it doesn't really matter. I'm sure the Kotas will help us with whatever we decide to do with them."

Shortly after, Master Yvette walked into the room followed by none other than Grandmaster Dante.

"Oho," he said theatrically. "You all seem well. That is good, very good."

"They're all strong," said Master Yvette in an approving tone. "They all heal fast on their own. Kevin especially seems to heal unnaturally fast." She frowned at Kevin the Bison. Master Yvette had originally thought that even with Medications treating Kevin's arm, which had been battered and bruised, it would still take a good month or two for him to regain his strength. Much to Kyle's amusement however, he had awoken this morning to find Master Yvette scolding Kevin for doing pushups.

"Well, they've been trained by some of the best masters this realm has to offer," said Dante.

"Are they ready?" asked Master Proculus as he walked through the door. "We really should return as soon as possible."

"We cannot leave just yet," said the Grandmaster. "Mayor Nova has insisted that we stay for dinner. It would be rude of me to deny her after she has taken care of our tyros so well. We can afford to stay a while longer."

"Of course, Grandmaster."

"But before that." A hard line formed just above Dante's eyes. "I'd like to tell you all that I'm sorry about Kane." It seemed like everyone in the room had stopped breathing. Kyle, Kevin, and Kross, who had been caught off guard, stared at the Grandmaster. "If beating around the bush about this were a better option, I would do that, but it is better for me to be straightforward. He tried to kill you three, and if he had succeeded, it would have resulted in Garnet's death, as well. It goes without saying that he has been expelled from Soul Gate Academy. In fact, I'll be blunt with telling you that there is now a bounty on his head. A few eternal title tyros will be trying their hardest to capture him."

Kyle, Kross, Kevin, and Garnet all shared the same lost expression. They had discussed what had happened over that past few days, but the reality seemed much harsher after hearing the Grandmaster sentence Kane.

"It'd be wise for you four to cut your bonds with Kane," said Dante, "if you have not done so already. Especially if he is working with King Seltios. But let's forget about that for now, unless you have any questions for me?"

"I have one." Kyle was surprised at the steadiness of his voice. "When can I start training again?"

Kyle could feel everyone's stares of disbelief, but Grandmaster Dante had a grin on his face. "Soon enough," he said. "But I imagine you'll want to enjoy the dinner Mayor Nova has prepared for us. Let's not make her wait much longer; she does so well at showing us her unwavering hospitality. We are in her debt."

Nearly an hour later, they were seated in the Mayor's dining room waiting for dinner, which looked like an exquisite feast. They had eaten dinner in here the past few days, but Mayor Nova had gone the extra mile to make things more extravagant than usual. There were ribbons, candles, and even a couple of silk banners sprucing up the room nicely. All sorts of foods were spread on the long table that easily accommodated all of them. There was even a large cake decorated with frosted keys.

At first, the dinner felt gloomy, but as the food and the Grandmaster's high spirits relaxed their nerves, the feast became quite lively. Kyle helped himself to three large servings of everything within reach. Mayor Nova became more cheerful with every glass of wine. Master Yvette joined her after a little while. Garnet bickered happily with Rayne, Kross, and Kevin about which was the best key power. ("Synchroneity has to be the strongest," said Garnet as she shot a quick glance toward Kyle, who ruffled his hair with a satisfied grin.) Even Proculus, who had been so rigid and serious as of late, had become much more like his usual self and was laughing heartedly as the meal came to an end.

"We should get going," said the Grandmaster as he stood up. "It is not wise for me to be away from the academy for so long."

"If you must," said Mayor Nova as she stood up. "I hope you all will call on my house if you ever need anything again."

"You can count on it." Dante smirked. "And as always, Soul Gate Academy is at your service."

Everyone filed into the yard. It had only been a few days since Kyle had been outside, but the chill of winter cold felt less distinct. The wind tickled his skin pleasantly. The SoGA inhabitants began exchanging goodbyes with the Mayor, Rayne, and their servants, but it was only when Garnet and Rayne were exchanging overly polite farewells that Kyle remembered Rayne would not be coming with them to Soul Gate Academy. He had become used to her presence. As her light blonde hair whirled in the wind, he knew he would miss her. It was an odd feeling, and he was unsure what it meant, though when noticing that Garnet's scarlet hair danced with the breeze just as enjoyably, he scoffed at himself. The feeling must have been one of a typical friendship with a girl and nothing more.

"Farewell, Kyle the Static," said Nova, looking at him with a strong gaze. "Stay safe."

Kyle chuckled then nodded. "I'll try." He uttered a gracious goodbye to Nova and Rayne before the group heading to Soul Gate Academy left. Rayne, Nova, Baldwin, Dean, and Yumi waved until they could see them no more.

They exited Dilu Village while still in a merry mood. The snow covering the meadow showed signs of early thawing, which left small specks of yellow-green to decorate the field. Kyle shuddered when he looked at the spot where the Hollow Eye had attacked him and Garnet. As they walked away from the gate, Dante, who had been behind everyone, hurried pass them all and stopped abruptly. Kyle would have walked into him if Proculus hadn't stopped him. Kyle thought the Grandmaster might be opening a ShiftDoor, but up ahead a man was walking toward them casually.

"Grandmaster Dante!" The stranger had a deep voice and wore a bronze colored hooded cloak, which hid his face. Kyle noticed Proculus, and Yvette shift into positions in front of Kyle and his friends. "Peace, Dante. I do not wish to fight." He lifted his hood and Kyle saw a bald black man who had a thick charcoal beard and uniquely light grey eyes that were only a shade darker than the white of his eyes. His face was expressionless and cold. He stroked his beard while staring at the group.

"You risk much by coming here, Seltios," said Grandmaster Dante.

At that moment, Proculus's hands moved so quickly that Kyle could hardly believe it when he took a sword and a javelin out of his MicroDimension. If King Seltios was fazed by this, he did not show it.

"Do nothing, Proculus!" commanded Dante.

"I risk nothing," said the King still stroking his beard absentmindedly. It was almost as if it were an annoyance to have to speak. "I come in peace, to offer peace."

Garnet pressed against Kyle. Normally this would have made him hot with embarrassment, but his body erupted with goose bumps as his instincts screamed that this man was dangerous.

"Peace, is it?" said Dante carefully. "What you are pursuing can hardly be called peace."

"I wish to avoid war, so I came to visit you hoping to speak of alternatives."

"Alternatives?"

"Yes. As a show of goodwill, I thought it would be best to discuss with you an idea I had to bring together the East and the West rather than wage war. It's simple, really. Will you hear me out?"

"Let's hear it," said the Grandmaster losing his patience.

"I would have gone directly to the East King Zephyr," said Seltios. "But he is feeling hostile towards me at the moment."

"Get on with it," growled Dante.

"Patience, Dante," he said with a menacing smile. For some unknown reason, the smile triggered Kyle's mind to think properly. This was King Seltios; Kane's master. Kyle clenched his fist to the point of pain. "It wasn't so long ago that Dawn and Dusk were friends. I would like to restore that friendship. Of course we have a murky history at best. Both sides have done wrong; I know *I* have done wrong. But there was once a time when the two kingdoms rose above their petty differences for peace and prosperity. I wish to reignite that peace. I wish to spread the prosperity. My plan is simple, old friend."

Old friend?

"What better way to do this than to reinstate the Lunar Tournament?" Seltios concluded.

In Kyle's opinion, the speech was well done. Perfectly timed and said with a warm enough voice that even the most skeptical might have believed him. But there was something about the king's eyes that left him with a resentful feeling.

"You expect me to believe that you would turn away from your selfish goals now to host an abandoned tradition?" spat Dante. "It is a tournament long forgotten and, if my memory serves correctly, you have teetered on the edge of war for years now. All of a sudden, you expect us to believe you offer peace? We would be fools to leave the East for some tournament in the West!"

"You misunderstand me, Dante." Seltios shook his head. "I do not intend to host this tournament in the West. I ask that *you* host it here in the East. I think you will find my offer hard to resist. Either way, I am sure Zephyr will love to hear my offer. It's hardly the decision for the Grandmaster of Soul Gate Academy to make. You must obey the old laws and take my offer to your King, no?"

"Do not mock the old laws," growled Dante.

"No mocking intended. I just do not understand your obsession with them. You are the only one who still follows that outdated sense of justice."

"I can hardly take advice from someone with no sense of justice."

"Perhaps. Well then, I've said what I needed to say." He removed a key from his pocket and turned it unceremoniously. A great midnight blue ShiftDoor appeared to his left. "I believe it would be rather unwise for any of you to follow me." He opened the door, but Kyle ran to the Grandmaster Dante's side before Seltios moved.

"Wait!" yelled Kyle. Master Yvette's and the Grandmaster put their hands on Kyle's shoulders, but it felt empowering rather than an attempt to pull him back. King Seltios turned to face him and looked surprised as Kyle stared daringly into his.

Garnet, Kross, and Kevin shifted uncomfortably behind Kyle, as though they were trying to avoid the King's gaze.

"You have good eyes, young one," he said in a voice that was almost impressed. "They remind me of another's who I came across some time ago." Veins on Proculus' face looked ready to burst and Kyle knew he was seconds from throwing himself forward, but he stayed put. "I suppose a king must sometimes listen to the cries of ants; speak if you wish."

Kyle took one step forward, almost leaning into his words. "Tell Kane the Basilisk that Garnet is fine and I'll be here to beat him if he ever tries to hurt my friends again."

"Hah!" Seltios clapped his hands. "A boy who likes to play hero expects a king to be his messenger? I'm sure Kane will love to hear it. What's your name?"

"Kyle the Static."

"I look forward to seeing you again." He stopped for a moment to study Kyle who glared back heatedly. "Till then." King Seltios entered the ShiftDoor, leaving in an anticlimactic manner.

Master Proculus walked forward carefully like he was going to follow Seltios, but instead he chanted, "the world grows darker," softly under his breath, turned his key, and threw his javelin into the doorway.

Kyle thought he would be reprimanded for his slight outburst with the king, but everyone looked like they were deep in thought. "Is life in Endera always so intense?" he said to no one in particular, though his answer seemed to come from nature itself as the sun began to set, making the sky and ocean glow in extreme violet-red. *I suppose it's neither here nor there.* His eyes searched the horizon. *Because this is just the beginning.*

While he soaked in the beauty of the scene, Master Proculus used his key to open a ShiftDoor. Together they walked through the door back to Soul Gate Academy.

Acknowledgement

A special thanks to my brothers, Isaac and Paul. You two are my best friends and without you two this book would not exist. Thanks for always being there for me.

To my sister, mother, father, I couldn't be more different than the three of you, but each of you can still stand to love me. That's something I cherish every day.

To my Readers, Stef, Sam, Amanda, Erica, Martha, Travis, and Nate who gave me some much needed feedback and helped little by little make this story better than I ever could have hoped. You were the first to visit my mind as Readers and that'll be special to me forever, I promise.

To one of my best dudes, Schu, for helping my brothers and I make an office space more work friendly. It would have taken even longer to get this book to where it is today without that place. You never had to help us, but you did. Thanks man.

To my editor, from Seraph Editing Services, for seeing something in my story from the very beginning and making my words mean more and my world feel real.

To Fer and Dave, for lending me your artistic talent and making my imagination come to life.

To my friends who continuously listened to my talks about a book that seemed like it would never come out.

And a final thank you to all the writers, creators, ninjas, and wizards out there who have helped me see so many fantastical worlds from so many brilliantly different perspectives.

Samuel J. Vega never knew he wanted to be a writer until he got to university where he used his expertise of watching anime and reading books to make himself into a horrible college student all the while learning that he had a passion for storytelling. His love for the geek world is quite immense and always increasing. Nowadays, he spends his days formulating stories with his brothers in the small town of Gibsonburg, OH. *Kyle Demore and the Timekeeper's Key* is his first novel.

For more information visit samueljvega.com

Made in the USA
Charleston, SC
13 January 2014